White Knight

The hardest part is losing the person someone else loves...

Staci Stallings

Spirit Light Publishing

White Knight
Copyright © 2012 by Staci Stallings
All Rights Reserved

Cover Design: Allan Kristopher Palor
Contact info: allan.palor@yahoo.com
Interior Formatting: Ellen C. Maze, The Author's Mentor,
        www.theauthorsmentor.com
Author Website: http://www.stacistallings.com

Spirit Light Publishing
ISBN-13:
978-0615671604
ISBN-10: 0615671608

Also available in eBook publication

Spirit Light Publishing

PRINTED IN THE UNITED STATES OF AMERICA

~*~

For the first responders -- the heroes who show up,
pick up the pieces,
salvage what they can,
and return to pick up more the next day.

We owe you more than we could ever repay for how you put
your hearts on the line
to help others--those of us you serve whom you will never even
know.

Thank you for all you do from the bottom of my heart!

~*~

One

"This place makes the best potato skins in the world," Dante Ramirez said from his position next to Eve Knox in the overcrowded booth. Six were stuffed into room for five, but Eve wasn't complaining. It had been months since she'd laughed this much, and laughing felt good for a change.

"Well, for as long as they made us wait, they'd better be," Gabe Teague said in annoyance from the other side of Eve. His deep bass shook the air around him. "I just want you to know, if Ashley kills me, I'm sending you the bill."

"And it'll be stamped NSF just like all the rest of the bills I pay," Dante said.

"NSF? I thought you had some secret trust fund," Jeff Taylor said from beside his wife Lisa.

"Yeah, it's so secret I don't even know about it," Dante said with a shake of his head, and the gel-slicked, black hair caught the light like a reflector.

"Darn," Gabe said. "You mean we can't off you for your millions?"

"Millions of bills or millions of creditors?"

Jeff looked at Gabe skeptically. "Maybe offing him wasn't such a good idea."

"Uh, you think?" Gabe asked.

"You forget, he's a fireman," Lisa said, punching her husband in the ribs. "He makes what you make."

Jeff shook his head. "Ugh. Definitely not worth it."

"Definitely," Gabe said and then looked around the restaurant. "So is anybody going to take our order or is that going to take another two hours?"

"Friday night," Dante said. "It's always like this. Oh, I'm sorry. I forget you're out of commission."

"Married," Gabe said. "They call it married."

Even as she laughed, Eve's gaze fell to the table. She remembered married.

"So, A.J.," Lisa said, addressing one of the two non-conversational occupants at the table, "were you less nervous this year?"

A.J., the one person at the table that Eve hadn't been around at every excuse Jeff and Lisa could come up with—Thanksgiving, Christmas, New Years, every major holiday and three or four non-major ones they had managed to include her in as well. If she hadn't been so tired of looking at her apartment walls, she might have come up with a few more excuses to get out of their well-meaning excursions. However, the reality was she hated that apartment and all the memories that went with it.

"At least I didn't throw up this year." A.J. ducked so that the light bounced off his light brown hair streaked with soft blond tones. Soft. It was a good word to describe A.J. Knight. Features, light brown eyes, manner, tone—they all fell right into the soft category.

"That's a definite improvement," Jeff said, laughing. "We almost had to call the other paramedics to come stitch up that gash you got when you fainted off the stage last year."

"He did not," Eve said with instant concern.

"No." A.J. glanced at her defensively, but instantly his gaze dropped back to the table. "I just missed a step."

"Yeah. Ca-thung. Ca-thung. Ca-thung," Jeff said, spinning his hands over and over themselves teasingly.

"You're one to talk." Lisa punched Jeff again as she came to A.J.'s defense. "Who was it that needed a paper bag this morning before he went on?"

Jeff shrugged. "For my lunch."

"Yeah, those ham sandwiches can just take your breath right away."

Eve laughed at them. Jeff and Lisa. Such a sweet couple, now looking forward to their first child. It wasn't hard to see how much Jeff worshiped Lisa, nor was it difficult to see the love in Lisa's eyes when she looked at her husband. As she put her head down, Eve remembered feeling that look in her own heart. That time seemed so long ago as to have been another lifetime.

"So, Eve," Dante, the one guy she always seemed to get paired up with at every social function she was trapped into attending, said as he laid an arm the color of brown sugar over the booth behind her, "how'd Lisa con you into this speaking thing anyway?"

With a smile Eve looked across the table at the woman who had become her best friend over the last year. "She asked."

Lisa smiled back. Together. Two women in a sea of men, and because of the other, they were holding their own.

"No arm twisting or hair pulling?" Dante asked far too into the whole cat fight scenario for her.

"Nope. None of that."

"Darn," Dante said. "I would've paid to see that."

"Hey," Jeff said, leveling an index finger and a warning gaze at Dante. "That's my wife you're talking about there."

"Oh, sorry. I'm just saying she's hot."

"That's not any better," Jeff said darkly.

Lisa patted his leg. "It's okay. I'm five months pregnant, and I feel like a blimp already. If the man wants to say I'm hot, don't complain."

Jeff's gaze went to his wife's face and frame, and it was clear he had no complaints.

"Is somebody going to take our order or not?" Gabe asked in frustration.

"I think they forgot about us," A.J. said quietly.

"Well, get somebody's attention, Jeff," Gabe commanded.

"Me? Why me?"

"Because you're on the end, and because this was your idea, and because as your commanding officer, I told you to," Gabe said.

"Oh," Jeff said, nodding. "Well, since you put it that way." He looked around, put a hand in the air, and snagged the first waitress's attention who happened by. "Umm, could we get some menus over here?"

Amazing, Eve thought as she watched the scene. When she had met him two years before, she would never have believed that Jeff could get so many words in a row out, in public nonetheless. However, it was abundantly clear that he had grown—in confidence and in stature since the night Dustin had first brought home his newest friend from the academy. Part of it was the job.

Leading others in to fight fires had to inspire a certain amount of poise and confidence, but it was more than that. He had a woman by his side now who believed in him, who trusted him implicitly, who looked to him for guidance, and it showed in every movement he made.

In seconds the waitress was back with the menus. Each took one, and Gabe looked at his watch. "Order something that doesn't take long to cook."

"Like what? Kid's grilled cheese?" Dante asked.

"You should've invited Ashley," Lisa said.

"Yeah," Jeff said. "Why didn't you?"

"She had to work. Besides she's heard me speak, and she wasn't impressed."

"I, Gabe, take you, Ashley," Dante said serious and teasing all at the same time. "I can see why."

Eve socked Dante's arm. "Hey, that wasn't funny."

In surprise Dante looked over to Jeff who was trying not to laugh. "It was too. Wasn't it, Taylor?"

"Like I'm stupid enough to get in the middle of that one," Jeff said as he buried his gaze into the menu.

The waitress walked up at that moment to take their order, and when she was gone, Dante turned back to Eve. "You know that Van Gogh Exhibit is coming to the Museum of Fine Arts the first of November. Didn't you say you wanted to go to that?"

"Is it that time already?" She sighed. "I was hoping I'd be through the spring buying by then."

"Well, I'm free," Dante said, hinting in his tone, "if you wanted me to get us some tickets, I could."

He was being nice. Dante had been nothing but nice since the first time Jeff and Lisa had dragged them out on what no one dared to call a double date. Still every time Eve thought about going out with him, her heart jerked in the other direction. Slowly she shook her head. "I'm not sure I can get off."

"It's a Saturday," he said as though the others weren't sitting there listening to them. "Even firefighters don't work all the time, you know." He tapped her on the shoulder playfully, trying to get her to look up. However, her heart just couldn't look at him.

Wishing it wouldn't, Eve's gaze traveled down the table and caught Lisa's. The pity in Lisa's eyes told her too much. Her friends felt sorry for her. They wanted her to find someone. What

4

they didn't know was that there would never be another someone in her life. She'd had a someone once. Now he was gone, and she had no desire to find another one.

"A museum exhibit?" Gabe asked incredulously. "Ugh. Ashley roped me into one of those once. Can you say, 'Torture City'?"

Across from Eve, A.J. laughed although none of the other occupants seemed to think it was all that funny. She ducked to keep the laugh in her own chest from finding her own throat.

"I just thought it might be fun," Dante said softly, and suddenly he didn't look nearly so confident or so sure of the offer.

Knowing there was really no good reason to turn him down, Eve smiled over at him although to be honest, she didn't see him at all. "It sounds like fun."

On the other side of the table, A.J. felt the annoyed gazes of his hosts find his face, and his eyes widened as if to say, "What did I say?" Neither Jeff nor Lisa looked happy with him. He hadn't been around them all that much, but Eve didn't seem like someone who would be hanging out in museums all day—the mall looked more her style. But as much as she didn't, Dante seemed even less the type. Strong, take charge, get it done so you can go have fun—that was Dante. Someone more likely to make fun of people who went to museums than someone lining up for tickets.

However, it was perfectly clear from where A.J. sat that getting in the way of Dante and Eve invited a fate worse than death. He understood that, of course. He had been there at the graveyard the day she had buried her husband. He had sat in the church and listened to Jeff's heartfelt words about the friend he had lost, but more than that, he had been there that awful night when her husband had taken that final ambulance ride.

Yes, she had lost more than he would probably ever have, so he was smart enough to back off even when Gabe continued.

"Doesn't make any sense to me," Gabe said. "You meet someone, you go out with them, you try to make yourself be someone else the whole time, then you get married and boom. Who are you again?"

"I'm sure Ashley was thrilled when she figured out who you were," Jeff said, and A.J. could tell he was trying to steer the conversation in a different direction.

"Ashley?" Gabe asked incredulously. "What about me? The first time I saw her with that awful green mask thing on, I thought I'd pass out."

"She was trying to be beautiful for you," Lisa said.

Gabe scrunched up his face. "She didn't have to try that hard."

The waitress arrived with their drinks and a dish of potato skins. A plate at a time Lisa passed them around the table. "I am starving."

"Here," Jeff said, dishing one potato skin onto a plate for her.

"Hey!" Dante said. "Who ordered these?"

"If you're pregnant, you argue." Jeff leveled the fork in Dante's direction. "If not, get out of the way." He put some sauce on the plate and handed it to Lisa. "There you go."

"Thanks," she said, ducking in embarrassment.

A.J. watched as the others dished up their own appetizers. Jeff was always taking care of Lisa, always making sure she was all right before he worried about himself. That was how love should be, A.J. thought. Not that he'd ever been around that many people who had found it. No, finding that kind of love took a heap of luck, and to this point he hadn't had much in that department.

"So, A.J.," Gabe said, skewering him with a glance. "Who are you taking to museums these days?"

Slowly A.J. shrugged, and the potato skin on his fork nearly slid right off into his lap. "No museums for me." Then he looked across and caught the displeasure in Lisa's gaze. "Not that there's anything wrong with museums of course. I just..." He was drowning, fighting for the surface. "Well, there's Melody, but she's more of just a friend really."

"A friend? Oh, boy. You've got to watch those friends," Gabe said with a serious shake of his head. "That's what I told everybody about Ash for a year."

"Until she knocked you over the head with a frying pan?" Jeff asked.

"Something like that. I swear, I think you ladies have something figured out that you should really clue us guys in about," Gabe said.

"We try to be subtle," Lisa said. "Not our fault it takes a brick."

"I'm telling you," Gabe said, leaning over to A.J. although his volume was loud enough for the whole table to hear. "Watch out for those friends. They're trouble waiting to happen."

"I'll keep that in mind."

By eight o'clock the gathering was breaking up. Jeff said he had to get Lisa home. Gabe slipped out as soon as the checks arrived, saying Ashley might never let him out of her sight again. A.J. had offered to walk Gabe to his car although Eve thought that if trouble happened, Gabe looked far more likely to be the defender than A.J. did. And so, when everyone else was gone, she and Dante were left to walk to the parking lot together.

Subtle, she thought. So terribly, terribly subtle. As they pushed out into the cool October, Houston city night, her hand brushed Dante's, and in the next breath his hand slipped around hers. Not once in all the time they had spent together had he taken her hand, and the instant hers was in his, Eve wanted to run the other direction.

"If you don't want to do the museum thing, that's cool," Dante said. "It was just an idea."

Backing out, getting away from him, running as fast as her heart was racing all sounded like very good ideas, and yet what was she running from? The fact that he wasn't Dustin. He wasn't. He never would be, and neither would anyone else. Her heart fell even further at the thought. "Are you sure you want to go? I kind of thought the clubs would be more of your style."

"Can't a guy broaden his horizons once in awhile?"

"No crime there. I just don't want you to be bored."

Dante turned intense deep brown eyes on her. "If you're there, I could never be bored."

Her chest hurt. She hated the look in his eyes—that don't-kill-me-by-turning-me-down look. For as long as she could remember, she had been a sucker for that look. True, the guys had always turned out to be nice enough, but they always had earth-shattering soul mates in mind. It never quite made it that far for Eve. "If you're sure you won't be bored…"

"I'm sure," he said as they got to her car. "I'll call you the Friday before… just to make sure."

"Okay."

"And I can pick you up if you want."

"Oh, that's okay. There's never any telling what I'll be doing. It'll probably be better if we just meet there."

"Okay, but you do want to go, right?"

She nodded. "I'll be there." Trying not to be obvious, she let go of his hand and climbed in her car even as fear that he might in fact kiss her flooded through her consciousness. "See you then."

"Yeah."

As she pulled out of the parking lot, the act she had been corralling around her since she had met Lisa early that morning as they headed for the second annual Cordell Youth Conference dropped away. Everything was so hard. Every moment was about holding it together, watching, noticing, making sure that no one saw beneath the mask. That was how life was now that Dustin was gone. It was called getting on with life. They all wanted to help, but the truth was no one ever could. It was like being dead without being in a grave.

Twenty-nine and living a hollow, empty, shell of a life. If it didn't hurt so bad, she might have laughed at the irony. For it was she who had told so many people that life was not to be taken for granted, that the point was to live every single moment as if you might never have another. Yet that was exactly what she now wanted—to never have another. The moments lining up, staring her in the face collapsed her spirit. Crying didn't help. She had come to that conclusion long ago.

Pushing the thoughts back, she hit the radio button. Not even the music helped much. There were just too many thoughts, and Eve thought at that moment that there would be forever.

"Melody came by," A.J.'s mom said when he walked into the little kitchen around nine. "She was looking for you."

"Oh?" He grabbed a couple Oreos out of the cabinet.

"She said something about playing a game she got."

He poured a glass of milk. "Was she going home?"

"She didn't say."

"I'll call her."

His mother nodded and left the room. Picking up the phone he dialed the number without really looking at the keypad. He'd had it memorized since he was twelve. Melody Todd, tomboy extraordinaire. They had been friends so long, he'd forgotten when they weren't. "Mel? Hey, it's A.J."

"Well, it's about time. Where've you been? I was going to show you the new Rodent's Revenge Game I got, but now Kendra's coming over and we're going out."

"Oh, that's cool." He bit into the cookie. "Have fun."

"You could come with us," Melody said.

"I've got work tomorrow."

"Likely excuse. You just don't want me to set you up with Kendra."

"Like I said I've got to work tomorrow."

"Okay, okay, I know. Shadonna was a mistake. I admit that."

"A mistake?" A.J. asked in shock. "She read me my star charts before we got in the car, Mel."

"I said I was sorry."

"Yeah, and then you turned around and set me up with Monica. How's she doing anyway? Has she found herself yet?"

"Not unless herself was hiding in the Australian outback," Melody said hesitantly.

"Australia? Huh, well, she'll be right at home with all those kangaroos. Oh, and let's not forget about Teresa. Shall we?"

"What? You don't like table dancers?"

"Not when they're my *date*." He shook his head at the mere memory of that night. "Let's get real, here, shall we, Mel. You haven't exactly had a stellar track record with this matchmaking thing."

"Oh, come on, A.J. Kendra's different."

"Already this is not good."

"No, I don't mean different, different. I just mean… well, different."

"You're trying too hard, Mel." He ate the last bite of cookie and chased it with the milk.

"Well, you're not trying hard enough. It's one night, A.J. Just one. Come on. It'll be fun."

"Nope. I'm thinking thirty minutes in the garage, and then I'm going to give up and hit the sack."

Melody sighed. "So you're really not going then?"

"No, I'm really not going."

"Fine. See if I ever try to set you up again."

"Finally," he said, breathing an audible sigh of relief.

Her side went silent for a moment. "How about tomorrow

night? This game will explode your head."

"Head explosions? Cool. Here or there?"

"Better make it there. Mom's on a no-popcorn-in-the-living-room kick again."

"No problem. I'll see you then. Oh, and Mel. Have fun tonight."

"Yeah, yeah, yeah. And hey, don't ruin your hearing. Okay?"

He laughed and signed off. Melody, the next door neighbor who actually lived five houses down had been his best friend forever. Well, since sixth grade anyway, but that was as close to forever as he got. With a push he stood from the cabinet and stepped into the living room. "I'm going to the garage."

Off-handedly his mother waved. Funny even at 25, ever since moving back home a year and a half before, he had felt the need to keep his mother informed about his whereabouts. She didn't ask anymore, but he always told her just in case. When he opened the garage door, one hand went in front of him and snapped the dim light on. Over the concrete he walked until in the opposite corner, he stepped up to the royal blue plastic tarp. Carefully he pulled it up and wrapped it around his arm so that the blue pearl trap set underneath came into view.

From the wall he pulled the headphones on, hit the power button, and sat down on the little stool. With one drumstick he hit the play button and twirled the stick around his fingers twice as the other picked up the first beats of the song. In seconds he was immersed in the music—so deep, air seemed hardly necessary. He didn't sing much, but the words and the beat drifted over him like soft rain on a cool summer day. His hands traveled effortlessly to a beat he had committed to memory years before. When he hit the break, every part of his body hit a drum and stopped. Hit again and stopped. Five consecutive hits, and he was flying on the music again. It was the one place that always felt like home to him, and he knew it always would.

"Good news," Lisa said ten minutes into their phone conversation the next Tuesday evening as Eve put the finishing touches on a dish of microwaved ravioli. She licked her finger off and picked up the plate to take it to the table.

"Oh, yeah? What's that?"

"Gabe and Ash are having a party."

"Cool." Eve turned the plate a quarter turn as she sat by herself at the table. "I'm sure Gabe's thrilled."

"Oh, no. Him and Jeff already have it all figured out. Pool. All night in the basement."

"Nice, and what are you and Ash going to do? Sit around and stare at the walls?"

"Keep the chips and dip going I guess. No, they're having like people from her work and his work come. He said you're welcome to come too if you want."

Eve corralled her long, black hair in her fingers, flipped it over one shoulder, and picked up her fork. "Me? I'm not from his work."

"Well, it's not just people from work. Besides I think Dante's going to be there," Lisa said.

"And this pertains to me how?"

"Come on, Eve. I know he likes you, and I think if you'd just let yourself, you could like him too."

"He's okay, but I'm not really interested in anything serious right now."

"I'm not saying you are, but it doesn't hurt to go out with some friends once in awhile either. Sitting there all by yourself all the time isn't getting you anywhere."

"You know, you sound just like..." A knife went through her heart, and she sighed. "When's the party?"

"Friday at eight."

"You can bring a date if you want," Jeff said as A.J. sat in the dark living room, watching the little mouse careen one way and then the other over the crazy multi-colored screen.

"Why are you inviting people to Gabe's party?" A.J. asked, leaning into the turn that Melody threatened to take too wide.

"He just mentioned you, and since he didn't have your number... But if you're busy, that's cool."

As the mouse burst through the final door, A.J. laughed when Melody threw the controller to the floor and collapsed over it. "It sounds cool, but I can bring a friend?"

"Yeah."

"What time?"

Two

A.J. thought about just not going. Melody had come down with a bad case of "I have to work the late shift," and he really didn't want to go alone. However, sitting at home all night on a Friday night didn't sound like much fun either. So he found himself pulling up next to a curb two houses down from the house that was streaming light from every window.

October would soon fade to November, and the chill was already in the air. The light orange jersey he was wearing although just right for a party was a little cold for walking the streets, and he crossed his arms in front of him. At the door he didn't even have to knock as two people came out the other way and pushed the door open for him to enter. Carefully he stepped in, looking around for someone he recognized. Music poured out of the speakers in one corner, and the television babbled away in the other.

"Hey! Hey! Look who made it!" Dante said, stepping from the hallway a drink in one hand and Eve's hand in the other. "A.J., my man." He dropped Eve's hand and shook A.J.'s. "Good to see you."

"Hey, how's it going?"

"You're just in time. Jeff and Gabe broke out the pool sticks downstairs."

"Cool."

Next to Dante in his black sport jacket and white shirt and Eve in a soft flowing silver outfit that looked like it had been made exclusively for her graceful frame, A.J. felt horribly underdressed. His hand went nervously to his backward black cap.

"Come on," Dante said, either not noticing or not caring.

"They've got a spread that you won't believe!"

A.J. followed the two of them through the crowd, and for a moment he wondered how Eve wasn't absolutely freezing. From behind he realized the blouse of her outfit had very little back to it, and it was held together only by a complex network of string. He relocated his gaze to the other partygoers—there were enough of them to hold his attention until they got to the dining room.

"These brownies are out of this world," Dante said, reaching for one and handing it to A.J. "Here, you've got to try this."

Never one to be self-conscious, A.J. suddenly found himself swimming there as both gazes turned on him for his reaction. However, that thought evaporated when he put the creamy rich pastry in his mouth. "Brownie" was a poor substitute of a word.

Dante nodded at the look on A.J.'s face. "See. What'd I tell you?"

A.J.'s hand went up under his mouth as a piece of the brownie broke off without warning. "Man, that's good."

Dante's arm swung around Eve's bare shoulder possessively. "She's a good cook. Isn't she?"

Surprise jumped through the enjoyment. "You made these?"

Eve shrugged. "I had some time."

"Hey! The troops have arrived!" Jeff said, walking up behind them and clapping Dante and A.J. on the shoulders. "Anybody up for a friendly game of cutthroat?"

"Never played," A.J. said as he downed the last bite.

"Oh, it's easy," Dante said.

"Simple," Jeff agreed. "Come on. Gabe's racking them up downstairs."

"Lead on, my friend," Dante said as he grabbed Eve's hand. "Lead on."

Jeff turned first, followed by Dante and Eve; however, just before he followed, A.J. reached down and grabbed another brownie. He'd hate for them all to be gone by the time he got back.

Since Dante had met her at her car out front two hours earlier, Eve had felt like a dog on a leash. He didn't let her go no matter where they went. It wasn't until she met up with Ashley in the basement that Dante had the good sense to let her hand go—either that or he knew she couldn't escape by way of the stairs without going by him first.

He was playing pool with the others, and although they had invited her to join them, it had taken very little to convince them she wanted nothing more than to sit at the bar and watch.

"Fun party, Ash," Eve said, turning to the bar where Gabe's wife worked restocking chips.

"You think?" Ashley pushed a wedge of wavy blonde hair from her face. "I think Gabe went a little overboard on the guest list."

"Well, you invite this one, and this one invites that one who just has to bring the other one…"

"And pretty soon my house is trashed."

Eve reached for a Cheeto. "Just be glad we're not still in high school."

"Ugh. Ain't that the truth."

The noise level at the pool table crescendoed suddenly, yanking Eve's attention to across the room. On one side Gabe stood, taunting Dante who stood on the other side. "Na-na-na-na-na-na."

"Lucky, lucky, lucky. That was so lucky," Dante said dismissively.

"Lucky? That was good."

"Good? Ha. You want to see good? I'll show you good."

Eve laughed and turned back to Ashley who raised her eyebrows.

"Well, at least some of us are older than high school," Ashley said, shaking her head in mock exasperation.

"So, have you seen Lisa lately?" Eve asked as Ashley ripped into another bag of Doritos.

"She was up making veggie dip in the kitchen last I saw her."

"Yea!" a cheer erupted at the pool table.

"Figures," Eve said, looking over as Gabe and Jeff high-fived each other over their apparent win. "The men play while the women work."

"Without us, they'd starve."

"Without us, they probably wouldn't even notice," Eve said, nodding toward the raucous celebration still going on behind them.

"That's scarily true," Ashley said. Then she looked at the bar. "Well, I'd better go back up and make sure the others don't starve. You want to come?"

For one half-second Eve considered saying, "Yes," but when she looked over at Dante, he smiled and closed one eye as a silent sign he was happy she was there. "No, I'll stay."

"Bravery," Ashley said sarcastically. "I like that."

"Bravery or insanity?" Eve asked.

Ashley raised both hands to indicate she had no intention of choosing. "You said it." With a laugh she started for the stairs, but just before she got there, Gabe stopped her with an arm. She allowed herself to be folded into his embrace.

Eve's heart turned over at the sight. "Yeah, I said it all right."

Just then A.J. walked up and pulled a handful of Doritos from the bowl. "So are you the official chip guard tonight?"

"Chip guard?" Eve asked, her hand falling from where it had been combing through her hair absently.

A.J. motioned to the bowls. "Well, you're not eating, and I know you're not watching, so I figured you must be guarding."

"Oh." The melancholy melted away from her as she bought into the joke. "Yeah. That's right. I'm the chip guard, and if you go over your limit, I'm authorized to karate chop you in half." Her tone was so serious that A.J.'s face fell, and he stopped eating. After a moment she laughed. "I'm kidding. I don't even know karate."

His eyes were saucer-like. "I'm glad because you had me worried there for a minute." Gingerly he reached into the bowl to snag another chip—keeping his gaze on her lest she really karate chop him.

"So, where's your friend?" Eve asked A.J. as Dante racked up the pool balls noisily.

A.J. sat down on a stool by the wall. "My...? Oh, Melody?"
Eve nodded.

"No could come. Midnight Madness at Galaxy Shoes."

"Out on Edgebrook?"

He nodded, clearly surprised that she knew it.

"I love that place. They've got really nice stuff. Real affordable, too. In fact, I think I got these there." She lifted her foot to reveal a silver strapped heel and five perfectly painted toenails. Letting her foot drop, she reached for a Cheeto. "So what does your friend... uh, Melody do there?"

A.J. shrugged. "She works the floor whatever that means."

"Ugh. The floor. Fun. Give me a rack of clothes and a

backroom any day."

"Hey, A.J.," Jeff called. "You in or out?"

"Oh, I'm in." He stood, took one step away, then stopped, and grabbed another chip. Eve laughed at the taking-my-life-in-my-hands look he shot at her. Quickly he wiped the excess cheese on the leg of his black cargo pants.

"You going to play or eat?" Dante asked.

"If I'm real lucky… both," A.J. said. He slid his stick back and forth through his fingers, sizing up the table. "What are we anyway?"

"Stripes," Gabe offered cannily from the other side.

"Solids," Dante quickly corrected. A.J. nodded and carefully lined up his shot, taking aim at the two ball. One crack and the two skittered into the side pocket.

"Way to go, partner!" Dante said happily as he stepped over to where Eve sat and wrapped a casual arm around the back of her chair. "Nothing like Friday night with friends."

"Nope," Eve agreed, and this time the word almost made it to her heart.

At 12:15 Dante sidled up to her again. His arm had a way of finding itself a place around her. "You ready?"

"For what?" Eve asked in genuine surprise.

"I'm on shift tomorrow at 6:30." He looked at his watch. "I'm looking at four hours of sleep max the way it is."

"Oh," Eve said, suddenly seeing where this conversation was headed, and frantically she looked around for a way out. Her gaze landed on the near-empty chip bowls. "Umm, I thought I'd stay and help clean up a little."

"Oh," he said, taken aback for a moment. "Well, then at least walk me to my car?"

She tried to think of a logical excuse but came up with nothing. Slowly she slid off the stool. "Okay."

Dante's arm rested across her waist as they started for the steps.

"You're not bailing on us, are you?" Gabe asked when he noticed.

"Early shift tomorrow," Dante said, slapping Gabe's outstretched hand.

"Well, don't be a stranger."

"Don't worry." Together they went to the stairs where Dante turned and waved at the others. "'Night, guys."

"Night," Jeff said, smiling happily at Eve even as he said it.

"Night," A.J. said without really looking up. He was too busy lining up his break shot. With that, they left the basement. Upstairs was much less crowded than it had been earlier. Apparently Dante wasn't the only one who had an early shift the next morning.

"Thanks, Ash," Dante said when they came upon Ashley picking up cups in the living room.

"Oh, you're welcome. You guys leaving?"

"Gonna have to, but it was fun," Dante said before Eve could get a word out.

"Well, thanks for coming."

"Thanks for having us," he said with an easy smile.

Us. Eve hated that word. It made her feel as though she had no identity of her own. It was ironic how wonderful that word had felt during another part of her lifetime, and how horrible it felt now. They crossed through the dwindling crowd and out into the cold night air. Slowly they strolled down the sidewalk to his shiny black Mustang. When they got to the car, he leaned against it and draped both forearms over her shoulders.

"So, we still on for next Saturday?" he asked.

"The museum?" She looked at him, and another face drifted through the air where he stood. Its appearance sent her heart and gaze fleeing. "Yeah, I guess so."

"You sure you want to go?"

"Yeah," she said, forcing the sadness down in her heart. "It sounds like fun."

Dante's eyes softened as he gazed at her. "It's always fun when I'm with you."

She tried to smile, but the mere motion hurt the center of her heart. Slowly he leaned into her space, and in the next second his lips were on hers. Tears sprang to her heart and to her eyes. Nothing about this felt right. Nothing. Her hand went up and landed on his chest—more to push him away if need be than from affection. When he broke the kiss, his gaze drilled right through her skull.

"You take care of yourself," he said softly.

Her head nodded as her gaze found the concrete at her feet.

The chill around her suddenly invaded her spirit as well, and she put her hands on her arms to ward it off. Instantly he wrapped her into the scratchiness of his sport coat. "You better get back in before you freeze."

"Yeah," she said, willing the tears not to find her voice.

After a moment he released her and reached for his door handle. "Night, Eve."

"Night." She backed up and stood there on the curb, watching him get into the car. The headlights sprang to life, and then the car sliced its way onto the night. Her gaze dropped from the departing taillights to the darkness of the asphalt as her spirit took a nosedive for the ground. She wanted to cry. She wanted to scream, what she did instead was sigh and turn back for the house.

It made no sense to go back in. They thought she had left. But if only for a few more minutes she needed to be with friends. So, she treaded her way up the walk and to the door. Alone in the darkness was no fun. Even together in the darkness wasn't fun anymore. Light did nothing to exonerate the pitch blackness in her soul, but at least, she thought opening the door and stepping back inside, the shell that was left of her felt better in the light.

Three

However, once in the house, Eve wondered why she had come back. Nobody she knew seemed to be anywhere around. Suddenly exhaustion invaded her being, and all she wanted to do was sit down and disappear for a few minutes. She slipped around the room to the far end where the couch stood in front of the babbling television. With one hand she grabbed some popcorn from the bowl as she collapsed into the off-green leather, not really paying attention to who was sitting on the other end.

One piece of popcorn was already in her mouth when the other occupant looked over at her and sat up.

"Hey, I thought you left," A.J. said, and when Eve looked over at him, she couldn't quite believe she hadn't noticed him. The orange of his jersey should've been hard to miss.

"Dante left. I thought I ought to stay and help clean up," she said, settling back into the couch. "What're you watching?"

"Oh, I think it's MTV or something. I don't know. I just sat down."

She watched for a minute but quickly bored of the images. "You're not playing pool anymore?"

In exasperation he shook his head, and the soft brown hair beneath his baseball cap moved with it. "I gave up on that one. Jeff and Gabe started playing cutthroat. I think I was out in five shots."

"Friends. They're such a pain."

He flashed a bright, toothy smile at her. "Tell me about it." Carelessly he wiped the bottom of his nose once and reached for more popcorn; however, three kernels didn't make the whole trip and landed in various places across the floor and on his knee. As if it was easy, he picked one up, flipped it into the air and caught it in his mouth. Slowly he chewed that piece before munching on more of the ones in his hand as his gaze took in the television images.

Despite herself, Eve was fascinated. "How do you do that?"

"Do what?" he asked in genuine surprise.

"That… that throwing the popcorn in the air and catching it thing. I always get popcorn everywhere when I try it."

Disbelief crossed his face. "It's not hard. You just have to gauge your trajectory."

Skepticism rained over her. "Oh, yeah. Sure. Sounds easy."

"No, here, I'll show you." He scooted a little closer to her and flipped a piece in the air. At the last second his mouth moved under it, and munching, he looked at her. "See, easy." He laughed at her uncertainty. "Here, try it."

Eve looked at the popcorn in her hand doubtfully.

"Just throw one up and catch it," he instructed, and as he said it, he demonstrated the technique again.

She considered arguing but decided against it. Carefully she took one piece of popcorn in her other hand and threw it into the air. However, her strength was too much for the piece, and it flew backward over the couch. A laugh escaped from her instantly, but she squelched it when she looked at him. "Oops."

He sat for a second, trying not to laugh, but he was helpless to stop it. When he finally regained his composure, he said, "Come on. Try again. Think straighter this time."

"Straighter." Concentrating on the piece in her hand, Eve threw it into the air; however, this one landed squarely on the coffee table. Although she tried to dive for it, she didn't even come close. "I don't think I'm getting this."

"I noticed," he said. "Here." He backed up on the couch a little, picked a piece out of his hand, and aimed it at her. "Open your mouth."

"What?"

"You heard me. Open your mouth."

Trying not to choke laughing, she did as instructed. The first piece hit her in the nose and bounced off. She was laughing too hard to keep her mouth open.

"No. No. No. Try it again," he said excitedly grabbing another piece.

Forcing herself to, she squelched the laughter and opened her mouth. From the corner of her eye, she saw the three practice throws he did before he actually let go of the popcorn. This one landed right on her tongue, and jubilation surged through her. "Yes!" Not really thinking she threw her hands in the air and found one of his coming the other direction.

"I told you," he said as he casually flipped another into the air and caught it himself, "it's easy."

She munched her piece. "And how long did this easy thing take you to learn?"

"Oh." He threw one in the air, but it sailed past the arm of the couch. His gaze followed it all the way to the floor. For a second he looked at where it landed, then he shrugged. "Three or four years."

"Three or four years?"

"Hey, I was only four at the time. What do you expect?" He reached for some more from the bowl. "You're a natural though."

Another laugh engulfed her. "Yeah, I could tell." She grabbed some Doritos and collapsed back into the cushions to watch the screen.

For a moment they just sat enjoying, then A.J. pushed himself up and turned to her. "Here's something."

"What's that?" she asked not even thinking she should be nervous.

He leveled a serious gaze at her as if he was about to ask the meaning of life. "Doritos or popcorn?"

"Doritos or popcorn... what?"

Casually he spun and flopped back on the couch. "Which one do you like better?"

"Hmm." She considered as if she actually was trying to determine the meaning of life. "Doritos."

"Me, too." He sat forward and fished the last couple Doritos pieces out of the bottom of the bowl. "Except the Ranch kind. I hate those."

"They're not so bad."

His nose wrinkled at the thought, and he shivered all over. "I can taste them for days afterward."

She laughed. After another moment, he shivered again.

"Okay, here's one," she said without really looking at him, "Cheetos or potato chips?"

21

"Lays or Pringles?"

"Lays."

"Ugh. Cheetos definitely."

"Okay. Pringles."

"Oooo, that's a tough one. I'd have to go with Pringles."

"Hmm." Her mind traced through all the things she liked about both, but she couldn't really come up with her own decision.

"How about popcorn or kettle corn?" he asked before she had decided.

"Ugh. Not kettle corn. That's sick."

His eyes narrowed in concentration and then brightened. "Popcorn or Cracker Jacks?"

"Definitely Cracker Jacks."

That toothy smile was back. "Me, too."

"And now for the moment we've all been waiting for," Ashley said, walking into the room behind them and obviously not seeing them as she picked up trash from the floor.

Eve sat up and realized that there were precious few partiers left. Instantly she sat forward and grabbed for the empty chip bowls. She looked back at A.J. and held one bowl that still had some chips in it out to him. "You want some more?"

He dusted the salt off of his hands and shook his head. "That's enough for me." Without prompting, he stood, picked up two of the bowls and three cups with liquid in them.

"Oh!" Ashley said when she saw them. "I didn't mean you had to help."

"Well, we helped make the mess," A.J. said. "Surely we can help clean it up."

When Eve wound her way into the kitchen, she found Lisa at the sink doing dishes. "So, is this where you've been hiding out all night?" Eve asked, cozying up to her friend as she set the chip bowls on the counter.

Lisa looked at her and smiled. "I was afraid Ash might drown in all these dishes."

A.J. set the things he was carrying on the counter next to Eve's offerings and slipped back out of the room. Lisa's gaze followed him out questioningly. "Where's Dante?"

"Oh, he left a little while ago. Early shift."

"Ah," Lisa said with a nod as she went back to the dishes.

Eve surveyed Lisa disapprovingly. "You know you really

shouldn't be on your feet doing dishes."

"Why not?"

"Well, aren't you supposed to take it easy in your condition?"

A pained look spread across Lisa's face. "My condition? It sounds like I have malaria or something."

"Here let me have that." Eve reached out and grabbed the scratcher before Lisa could really protest. "You go sit down. Let me do these."

A.J. returned with another armload of cups. "What do I do with these?"

"Dump them in the sink and you can probably just trash them," Eve said as she started washing bowls. At her elbow, A.J. dumped them out one at a time and then stacked them together and threw them in the trash.

"Are Jeff and Gabe still in the basement?" Lisa asked.

"Think so. I just heard the balls break," A.J. said as he wound his frame around the island and headed for the dining room.

"Those guys." In frustration Lisa stood and walked toward the stairs. At the top she yelled down, "Hey! Are you guys going to play all night?" Her words faded as she descended the stairs.

"Okay, who brought the silly string?" Ashley asked, pushing a handful of trash into the can.

"Silly string?" Eve asked, glancing behind her. "You're kidding, right?"

"I wish," Ashley said as she held up three multi-colored strands. "See, silly string."

"Now, that's just sad."

Ashley went back to the living room as Eve stacked another bowl in the rinse sink on top of the three that were already there.

"I thought the dip was supposed to go *on* the chips," A.J. said in exasperation. He held the bowl smeared with French onion dip out for Eve's inspection.

She shook her head. "You give these people way too much credit." Her other hand transferred a sudsy bowl to the rinse sink as she took the smeared bowl from him.

"Need me to rinse?" he asked, crossing behind her.

"That would help."

He took up position at the rinse sink and turned on the water. For three dishes he was quiet. "Okay, here's one. Dishes or laundry?"

"Ugh. Neither."

"No, no fair. You have to pick." He set a bowl in the drainer.

"Do I get a dishwasher?"

"And a washer and dryer too if you're real nice." The smile on his lips shone through his eyes.

She considered the choices as she handed him the bowl that was no longer smeared. "Umm, dishes I guess."

He rinsed that bowl and set it with the others. "Here, hand me that," he said, pointing across her to the cabinet beyond.

"What?" she asked, seeing only more stacked dishes to wash.

"That... here." Without pretense, he reached across her to retrieve the towel.

"Kitchen towel?" she asked teasingly. "Would that be the word you were looking for?"

He picked up a rinsed dish and ran the cloth over it. "Yep, that would be the one."

"Okay, remind me again why I thought this was a good idea," Ashley said as she lugged a table through the kitchen.

"Oh, here," A.J. said, setting the dish down and throwing the towel over the drying bowls. Three steps and he took the table from Ashley. "Where do you want it?"

"Garage," Ashley said. "I'll go get the chairs."

The upstairs was back in semi-order by the time Gabe, Jeff, and Lisa emerged from the basement thirty minutes later. Even most of the dishes had been put away. Lisa put the basement bowls where the others had already been cleared, and Eve sighed. "More?"

"'fraid so," Lisa said.

"Here, Eve, I can get the rest of these," Ashley said as she gently pushed Eve.

However, Eve reached past her and grabbed one of the bowls. "Four more bowls and I'm finished."

Ashley shrugged. "Suit yourself."

"So, who lost?" A.J. asked, sitting down on one of the bar stools around the island.

"I cleaned his clock," Gabe said, straightening his shoulders so that he stood a full head taller than Jeff.

"And which clock would that be?" Jeff asked. "The one before or after you sank the eight ball three times in a row without

24

bothering to clear the rest of your trash off the table?"

Gabe took a playful swing at Jeff, who easily deflected it.

"Glad I got out when I did," A.J. said, taking a sip from his glass.

"Yeah, we noticed you bailed," Jeff said. "What's up with that?"

"What's up? I got smart. That's what's up."

Eve set the last dish in the drainer and looked around. "Is that everything?"

"Think so," Ashley said, coming in from the dining room. "No thanks to *somebody*." As she passed by him, she rammed a hip into Gabe who, unaware of her intentions, spilled his drink down the front of himself with the hit.

Annoyed, he wiped his chin off. "And would you be referring to anyone in particular with that statement?"

"I wouldn't know," she said in exasperation.

Gabe looked at the other two guys with a what-did-I-do look. Then he shrugged and pulled up a stool. "Well, I thought the party was a great success."

"Uh-huh," Eve said as she leaned against the sink, "and next time you're going to come do dishes all night while us girls go down and play pool."

"No problem. When are you coming?" Gabe asked gamely.

However, Jeff punched him. "She said dishes, man. You've really got to know when to shut up."

"He's got a point," A.J. said, pointing at Jeff.

"Well, thanks, Eve," Ashley said as she laid the towel over the oven bar. "I hate to think how long it would've taken me to clean this up."

"No problem," Eve said. Then she looked down at the thin silver watch she'd just put back on her wrist. "Well, I hate to say it, guys, but I'm going to have to get going too. Our shipments are supposed to start coming in on Monday. That means no sleep next week."

"Me, too," A.J. said, sliding off the stool. "I'm supposed to help my sister move tomorrow. Oh, joy."

"We'd better get home too," Lisa said as she rubbed a hand over Jeff's back. "I think my feet could use a nice long bath."

"Umm, mine too," Jeff said as he turned to her smiling.

Eve smiled at them in spite of the memories. "Gabe, Ash,

thanks for a really nice night."

"It was fun," Ashley said as they all started toward the door.

"Oh, and if you find popcorn over by the couch," A.J. said as Eve retrieved her small jacket from the closet and slipped into it, "That was Eve's fault."

"Ah," she said as if she had been wounded. "That wasn't very nice." She took a swing and caught his shoulder with her fist. He shrugged away from the punch even as he laughed.

"Well, I didn't want her to blame me!"

Ashley and Gabe laughed.

"Well, come back and we'll make some more popcorn just for you," Gabe said as he laid a hand on Ashley's shoulder.

"Just tell me when," A.J. said. "I never pass up free food."

Eve leveled an exasperated gaze at Ashley. "He's such a guy."

"You act like that's a bad thing," A.J. said, looking at her with a smile in his eyes that rounded down into his apple-curved cheekbones.

One look at Ashley and she and Eve said, "It is!"

Good-byes flew in all directions as the last four partygoers stepped out into the cold night. At last the door closed behind them, and the light of the streetlamps guided their journey down the sidewalk.

"Drive careful, you two," A.J. said, waving to Jeff and Lisa when they got to the end of the sidewalk and he and Eve started to turn the other direction.

"You too," Jeff said, and then he stopped. When he looked at Eve, all playfulness was gone. "Do you want us to follow you home?"

Eve's face scrunched in annoyance. "I'm a big girl, Jeff. I think I can get home by myself."

"Are you sure? Because it's really no trouble."

Eve smiled softly. "It's an hour out of your way. Just get your wife home and into a bathtub. I'll be fine."

"Okay," Jeff said uncertainly after a long moment. He stared at them, sizing up the situation and her. "Do you want to call us when you get there?"

"I'll be fine," Eve said in exasperation. "It's not like I haven't driven by myself before."

"Well, which direction are you headed?" A.J. asked, breaking into the conversation.

"South," Eve said shortly.

"I'm headed South. I'm going as far as Elgin. I can follow you that far if you want."

Eve looked at Jeff for his blessing. "Happy now?"

Jeff took a moment to assess A.J. and another to decide. "Yeah, I guess that'll work."

"Good," Eve said, crossing her arms over herself, "because it's freezing out here. See you, Lis."

"Call me," Lisa said as Eve turned and started for the cars, but ten steps down the sidewalk she realized that A.J. wasn't with her. In annoyance she turned just in time to see him shake Jeff's hand and nod. On her heel she turned and stomped to her car. She wasn't a baby. She had managed to make it through 29 whole years without Jeff's constant protective gaze following her every move. How she had ever managed, she was sure he couldn't quite tell.

Just then she heard the tennis shoes on the concrete behind her, and in the next heartbeat A.J. jogged up beside her.

"I've got ten cents that says you drive better than he does," A.J. said.

"Ten cents? Boy, you have a lot of confidence in me."

"Okay, make it 20, but that's my final offer."

She glanced at him skeptically.

"Hey," he said, his tone serious, "I have to eat this week you know."

Eve shook her head and laughed, and as mad as she was at the whole situation, for some reason she just couldn't be mad with him at her side. "Okay, twenty cents it is." Without question he followed her across the street and to her car, and then it was time to say good-bye. Gratefulness poured through her as she glanced at him. "I had fun tonight."

He shrugged. "It was a party. You were supposed to have fun."

"Well, it was extra fun."

That apple rounded across the top of his cheek. "I thought so too."

For a moment she stood, not really wanting to leave.

"Take care driving home," he said and backed away from her. At the door to the little brown Honda Civic across the street he stopped. "And don't lose me either."

"Try to keep up," she retorted teasingly.

He laughed as they both climbed in their cars. For all the darkness Eve should've found when she crawled into her car, there was a lightness in her heart that she hadn't remembered being there when she went to the party. Yes, it was good to be with friends.

Keeping an eye on her little silver Celica wasn't all that much of a problem. It, like her, shone like a brilliant supernova under every light it flashed through. A.J. retraced his mind through the night. They were fun—all of them. He liked hanging out with them. Even though he hadn't been a charter member of their little group, it seemed like he had been accepted with no questions. A smile broke onto his face as Gabe and Dante's jabs at each other floated through his mind. And even Ashley and Lisa, who had initially seemed so intimidating, actually turned out to be nice.

Then there was Eve. He was glad for how her life seemed to be going, glad she had found Dante after the horrible year she had been through. Dante was perfect for her—classy, cultured. He could blend right into her life without so much as a misstep. They were perfect for each other, and A.J. was happy for them—for Dante, but more for Eve. She was one special person, and she deserved to be treated with the respect that Dante obviously held her in.

As his exit neared, A.J. considered simply hanging back and following her to her turn. Jeff's admonition to make sure she was okay as they stood on the sidewalk flashed through A.J.'s mind, but then he remembered her obvious annoyance with Jeff's concern. No, she would know if he didn't turn off. So, he pushed the pedal to the floor and raced to catch up with her.

When his car was even with hers, he glanced over into her window. The light of her smile was shining as brightly as ever. With a slight wave and a smile, he told her goodnight through two car windows going 70 on the freeway and then backed off and crossed the lanes to take his turn off. "God, I guess you're going to have to keep an eye on her the rest of the way."

A.J. smiled at the thought. God, it seemed, had done a pretty good job of that to this point.

Somehow Eve had thought that A.J. would find a way to follow her all the way home. Not that she wanted him to of course, but somehow she figured Jeff had told him to. When the little brown car disappeared into the darkness off the ramp, Eve couldn't help but feel more alone than she had all night. She ran a hand through her hair and reached over to turn up the radio. She was a big girl, just like she had told Jeff. Fun or no fun, she was a big girl who was now on her own. The problem was it felt far more like no fun than anything.

Four

"Have you nailed down the plus-size selection yet?" Mary Jo Brockmeyer, Eve's boss asked as she strode through the room to her drawing table.

"I'm working on swimsuits," Eve said as she worked her way through the buyers' catalog on her desk.

"And then you're finished?"

"Yeah."

"Good, we need to get this summer line finalized before Thanksgiving." Mary Jo pulled her white pant-suited frame onto the stool across the way and set her shimmering gold reading glasses on her nose. At one time Mary Jo had been the height of fashion, but three kids and forty extra pounds hadn't helped in that department. Still she knew her stuff, and she was consistently on target with what to buy, how much to buy, and when to buy.

As she went back to her work, Eve thought how glad she was that Dustin had pushed her to take this job in the first place. Despite the sometimes long hours and out-of-town trips, he had said it was an opportunity she just couldn't pass up. He had always had the uncanny ability to know what was the right opportunity when. She missed that about him. Unconsciously she splayed one set of fingers under her hair and dropped it onto her shoulder. She had learned a lot in the last two years, and only part of that was about the fashion industry.

"What do you think about this one?" Eve asked, holding up a drawing of a frilly black and turquoise number.

"What do you think?" Mary Jo asked, gazing over the top rim of her glasses.

Slowly Eve set the catalog on her desk and bit the inside of her cheek lost in thought. "It's cute, but the cut of the bodice looks binding to me. It seems like it's too high up under the arm to really be very comfortable."

"And your gut says…?"

"There's something better," Eve said as she flipped that page over.

Mary Jo smiled, and the light freckles on her nose danced under the shimmering of her glasses. "Good girl."

"I'll spot you 14 points," A.J. said.

"14 points?" Lerone Barnes asked next to him as they sat in the ambulance eating lunch in the grocery store parking lot. "You've got to be kidding me."

A.J. took a bite of his sandwich and grabbed for his root beer. "It's charity, man. I'm being generous here."

"Generous? Ha. Generous would be giving me a real chance. There ain't no way Jacksonville will score more than seven, and that's if they're real lucky."

"So, then you're betting that the Titans can't make more than 21."

"The Titans can make 21 in their sleep!"

"I said, 'More than 21,'" A.J. said, emphasizing the difference with his root beer can.

"And I said there ain't no way I'm taking that bet. I ain't no fool."

"Really?" A.J. asked, looking over at the young man who had been his partner for six months. "'Cause you look an awful lot like one to me."

"Man, you are so funny, they ought to put you on the Tonight Show."

"Well, they called last week, but I had to turn them down." A.J. took another bite. "So, you're really not going to take my bet?"

"No, I'm really not going to take your bet."

A.J. shrugged. "Your loss."

"No," Lerone said slowly. "It would be my loss if I took that bet. I could just say, 'Bye-bye little twenty.'"

The radio between them squawked to life. "High rise heart attack, Buckner and Robin."

In a flurry of wrappers and cans, they threw the rest of lunch in the bags as A.J. started the ambulance.

"Dispatch," Lerone said, grabbing the relay. "This is Unit 5. We're on it."

"10-4," the response came.

"Well, so much for a relaxing lunch," A.J. said, angling the ambulance into traffic as he flipped the emergency lights and siren on.

"And I thought this job might be boring."

A.J. glanced over at his partner. "Ain't nothing boring about it."

By the time Eve made it home, it was after eight. That was okay. The less time she had to spend in the apartment, the better. She went into the little office off the kitchen and dropped her work things next to the drawing table. With a yank she shrugged out of her black jacket and hung it on the chair. Heels were the next thing off, and by the time she made her way back to the kitchen, the only parts of her outfit left were her hose, her straight black mini skirt and the white button-down shirt. For good measure she unbuttoned another button of the shirt and pulled the tail of it out. She would change eventually, but for now just being in the apartment and not falling apart were enough.

She always hated this time of day. On his days off, this was the time that she had always enjoyed most with Dustin. Either there would be a glass of wine waiting for her or dinner would be on the table or even just the fact that she could be with him again was enough to make it the best time of day. Now there was just emptiness filling the air around her to the point that sometimes it was hard to breathe.

Off-handedly she flipped the dark hair back over her shoulder and reached into the refrigerator for the shrimp sauté she had managed to make three nights before. Even cooking, which was normally something she loved to do, had lost its mystique. Without someone to share it with, what was the point? She pushed the plate into the microwave and hit the number two button.

Depressing, she thought as she opened the mostly empty refrigerator and looked inside for something to go with the shrimp, everything was depressing. Not really paying attention to her own actions, she reached in and grabbed a bottle of water, twisted off the lid, and pitched it into the trash. Another meal for one. Another night all alone in a place that felt utterly devoid of life.

When the microwave dinged, she pulled her plate out, grabbed a fork and made her way to the living room. The couch bed which she hadn't bothered to push back in from the night before took up most of the room, so she slipped past it to the chair. With one hand she picked up the remote and hit power. Noise, blessed, wonderful noise filled the room, and she laid the remote down. It didn't matter what it was: news, sports, movie, music. As long as it filled some piece of the deafening silence, it was welcome. Pushing all of the thoughts from her, she sat back and forked a small amount of rice into her mouth. This was called getting on with your life, and as much as she hated it, she knew it was the space she was doomed to live out her days.

"How was work?" A.J.'s mom asked when the two of them were seated at the little table over chili macaroni.

"Fine," he said. They could have tape-recorded the conversation and just played it over each night. The parts never changed, and after almost two years, he had the whole thing memorized. "You?"

"Fine." She ate a piece of macaroni. "We got magnolias in. Ugliest things you've ever seen. The flowers were the size of quarters and the leaves were pitiful yellow. Did you get that box taken over to Chelsea's?"

"No, I didn't have time."

"How long does it take to drop a box off?"

"I figured she'd find six other things she forgot so I might as well wait."

"She should've let me help her move," his mother said.

"We got it done," he said. "It wasn't that hard."

"Yeah, but she already forgot a box of clothes. Who knows what else she forgot?"

"Chelsea could forget six boxes of clothes, and she wouldn't exactly freeze to death," he said, shaking his head.

"Just because you wear the same pair of jeans for three weeks…"

"You should be happy, less laundry that way," A.J. said. "Less laundry, less water. Less water, less money to the city. See, it's a good thing."

Slowly her dark-tinged red hair shook side to side. "When did you start worrying about water bills?"

"The first time my water got cut off because I hadn't paid it."

"Well, at least L.A. was good for something."

Every extended conversation eventually wound back around to L.A.—no matter how far away it seemed at first. "Imagine that. You thought I'd ruin my life, and I actually learned something useful."

"Yeah," his mother said. "Imagine that."

His interest in the chili mac waned, and he stood. "I'm going out to the garage."

He heard the sigh even though it wasn't audible. "Don't play too loud. I don't want Mrs. O'Malley to call the cops again."

"I'll try to keep it down," he said as he bent to kiss her cheek before he made a hasty exit.

The ten o'clock anchors were busy reporting the day's events before Eve finally talked herself out of the chair so she could shower and get ready for bed. She ran water over her dish and put it in the dishwasher just as a small smile crossed her face.

"Which do you like better? Dishes or laundry?" he asked again, and she laughed softly.

Dishes or laundry? What a question. Grateful for something else to focus on, she closed the door and thought back to the party. Her mind skipped right over the depressing points to those moments that held some kind of levity. Almost every one of those involved one person in particular, and her heart smiled at the thought of him. He seemed so utterly free of any and all encumbrances like propriety and respectability. Not that he was an oaf, but he just didn't seem to really care what anyone else thought. It must be nice to live that way.

In the bathroom she snapped on the light. She started the shower and gazed at the woman gazing back at her from the mirror. With the practice of a hundred thousand times, she reached up and clipped her hair up. Thoughts of their few moments together slipped through her mind, and she shook her head so that the tendrils of hair that had escaped the clip danced. It had been more than a year since she had laughed that hard. He was such a nut. It would've been impossible not to laugh.

"Here, open your mouth." She laughed outright at that thought as she slid out of the skirt. Never in her imagination could she have pictured doing something so childish and yet nowhere in her being could she even care at this very moment what anyone else had thought. With a soft sigh she stepped under the gentle cascade and closed her eyes.

Dustin would have liked A.J. Eve could see them together, playing pool and trading jokes. Then again there weren't too many people that Dustin didn't like. That was how he was—he'd never met a stranger, and she doubted now whether the term "stranger" was even in his vocabulary. Her mind slipped back to her first company party, and the sixteen pairs of shoes they went through trying to find just the right ones. She knew he didn't really care, but because it made so much difference to her, he had. He knew nothing about fashion, but it was her passion, and he had learned.

Tears stung her eyes when her mind fell over the memory of him sprawled at the bottom of the steps that now rose just above her, shoes in every color of the rainbow scattered on the steps above him. She wanted to laugh, but that hurt too much. The details of why he was hurrying to get the box to the top escaped her memory now, but the sight of him dazed at the bottom of those stairs still hadn't.

Stairs. It was strange how easy it was to stay away from them, and yet how they kept pulling her, body and soul, to them. One simple set of stairs, up to a bedroom that she still remembered him carrying her into the first time. It wasn't their first home, but it was the first one they had found, planned, and bought together. Water combined with the tears streaming from her heart as their happiness at entering that bedroom the first time melted into the first time she had entered it without him.

Never could she have imagined how horrible that ache could be. She hadn't even had the heart to sleep in the bed that first night. Instead, the cold floor had held her as she cried. The three nights since that first one she had actually spent there without him were so miserable she had finally given up. Now her bed was the couch, her living space anything that had nothing to do with those stairs. She didn't even turn the light on to them anymore. They were much better off swathed in darkness and forgotten.

Hitting the faucet to cut the water off, Eve put her head down and crushed her eyes closed in a futile attempt to get the memories to stop, but still they scratched across her heart like a serrated knife-edge. Her face crumpled into the soft towel she pulled from the wall. She would never understand why God had looked at their love and thought it not worthy of intervening to spare Dustin's life. It had to have been God's choice because she knew it wasn't Dustin's. He would have moved Heaven and earth to get back to her, so the fact that he was no longer here, put that choice clearly in God's corner.

Avoiding eye contact with herself, she pulled her nightshirt over her still damp body, grabbed a hairbrush, and walked out of the bathroom. As she walked through the apartment, she ran a hand over each and every light switch, plunging the area behind her into spirit crushing darkness. In the living room, she folded herself onto the couch bed and crossed her legs.

The late night comedians were bantering back and forth, and slowly she ran the brush through her hair. One day down, one night to live through, and tomorrow she would be that much closer to seeing Dustin again, to feeling his arms around her, to hearing the sound of his "I love you" ringing in her ears. One day, and one night...

She flipped her hair to the side and collapsed onto the pillow, watching the images flit across the screen. They were her only refuge, the only way her brain could have something else to focus on. Slowly her eyelids drooped forward, and fatigue caught her on its undercurrent. The yawn sank through her, and she pulled a blanket over her bare legs. They were joking about the president. She didn't get it, but she laughed anyway—a hollow, uncaring laugh as sleep dragged her down with it into its unknowing abyss.

The rhythm flowed easily beneath A.J.'s drumsticks. Lost in the middle of the music, he always had the luxury of forgetting about how hollow his life really felt. Even in high school when his latest crush broke up with him or when he was cut from the soccer team, the music could always make the whole world disappear. True, most things seemed to be working out at the moment, but there was still that deep, intense need to just forget that everything else existed for a few hours.

It was probably why the whole band dream had taken such hold of him. He remembered that first gig he and the guys had performed for the little nightclub nobody had ever heard of. That was the experience of a lifetime. To be swathed in darkness punctuated by neon blue and fuchsia light, playing like he had nothing to lose and living like he never had before. He had been chasing that feeling ever since.

The little garage was hardly a substitute, but he had no better choice. Working, honing something he wished was a natural talent into something a group might consider using had all seemed so worth it until dirt broke the electricity had been cut to the rat hole he was living in. The landlord generously called it an apartment. It wasn't. By that point it was a simple choice between chasing a dream and starving to death. Amazingly he had even managed to make himself believe it wasn't so bad for three days, but then they had laid off half the staff at the playground equipment store he grudgingly called his job. He was number three to get the news.

Both drumsticks pounded their way into the crescendo. Reality. That's what his mom and Chelsea called it when he got back to Houston. From where A.J. sat, reality was the prize at the end of playing the sucker's game of chasing a dream. When that song ended, he reluctantly looked at his watch and reached over with the drumstick to hit the off button. Tomorrow would be another day he didn't want to face.

Carefully he pulled the tarp over the drum set and sighed. If somehow he could just wake up tomorrow and be someone who actually enjoyed life, he would've given almost anything to make that happen. But life was life, and in A.J.'s world that meant that enjoyment had nothing to do with it.

Five

"'Starry Night' is one of Van Gogh's premier works," Dante said as he stood at Eve's side on Saturday afternoon in the museum.

"How do you know that?" she asked, wondering how he would know such a thing.

"That's what it says in this little brochure thingy." He held out the off-white paper as if reluctant to show her he was cheating.

"Oh." She smiled at his attempt to sound like he knew something about art. "What else does it say?"

"Let's see… He painted 2,200 works including several that he copied from previous artists. And he cut off his own ear."

"Now that one I knew."

Dante looked at her with disgust. "Why would somebody cut off their own ear? Ouch."

Eve shrugged. "Maybe he was tired of listening to Mrs. Van Gogh."

He started to laugh but seriousness crossed his face first. "I think he was just crazy."

"Yeah," she said, the joke gone. "Probably."

"So, who's your favorite artist?" he asked as they drifted over to the next painting. Tall and dark from hair to features, Dante was plenty nice looking. But he always seemed to be tiptoeing around her, and after months of that, it was getting old.

"Artist? I don't really have one. My favorite designer is Nicole Miller."

"Designer of what?"

"Clothes," she said as though that should be obvious. "I love the lines she's done. Sleek but fun."

Slowly Dante shook his head and a forced smile came to his face. "I don't really know much about designers. I'm just lucky to not clash when I get dressed."

She laughed. "You sound like Dustin." As soon as the name was out of her mouth, she wished she could take it back. Dante's reaction coupled with hers said saying that name was the wrong thing to do. However, it was too late, so she plunged ahead in a futile attempt to salvage the mistake. "He didn't know satin from rayon. Give him cotton and he was happy."

Dante's side of the conversation evaporated as they walked slowly to the next painting. He looked down at the brochure and then up at the painting. "This is one of Van Gogh's early works."

"Presumably before he cut his ear off," Eve said, fighting desperately to turn back time and do the last few minutes over again.

"Yeah," he said uncertainly. "Presumably."

He was trying so hard, Eve thought when she looked at him. He wanted this to work so badly, but as much as he wanted it to, it just wasn't.

"Do you really want to see the rest of the exhibits?" she asked, hoping he would take the gentle hint and agree to stop the charade.

When he looked at her, it was with a mix of confusion and sincere effort. "Yeah. I think we should... since we're here."

Since we're here... it was the worst reason for doing anything she'd ever heard. Pulling determination to her, she smiled. "Well, then let's see what they say about this next one."

"Okay, that's it," Melody said, ripping the headphones off of A.J.'s ears before he even knew she was in the garage.

For a single moment the drumbeat continued to transfer from his ears to his hand before he realized the beat in his ears was gone. "Mel...? Where'd...? What...?" He reached over in dazed confusion and hit the stop button with his stick. "I didn't know you were coming."

"Sneak attack." Melody corkscrewed her mouth and narrowed her gaze at him.

"I can see that," he said as she reached around him and hit the power button.

"You're going to turn into a drum if you're not careful. Now come on." She grabbed his hand and yanked with all of her blonde might.

Grudgingly he allowed himself to be pulled up. "Can I ask where we're going?"

"Farin is meeting us in an hour."

"Farin?" he asked as she pulled the tarp out of the storage bin. "Who's Farin?"

"A girl from work. I met her last week, and she's perfect for you."

He exhaled in frustration. "Mel."

"No. This one isn't like the others. She's really cool, and she's really cute, and I told her I would bring you."

This was getting worse, and he closed his eyes. "Haven't we had this conversation already?"

"Yes, we have, and if you would just be a little more cooperative, maybe we could stop having it." Melody threw half of the tarp to him. "Now cover that thing up, and let's go."

"But I'm not even dressed."

"That's why we're going to have to hurry."

As slowly as possible A.J. helped her cover the drum set. "Would it matter if I said I didn't want to go?"

"No."

"I didn't think so."

"Come on. I know what you can wear so Farin will fall head over heels for you." Melody grabbed his hand and pulled his reluctant body from the garage. "You know that nice shirt I gave you for your birthday last year?"

"The one that feels like a wool sack?"

They trekked through the living room and to the stairs.

"Going out?" his mother asked from her perch on the recliner.

"Yes," Melody said just as he said, "No."

Melody yanked him in front of her and pushed him up the steps to his room. Once there, he sat down on the bed and watched her scour through his closet.

"See, this shirt," she said, pulling the light purple pressed button-down shirt out. "And these pants…" Black Dockers. "And this belt." Thin black with a gold buckle. "And, oh yeah, here it is."

His world spun when she pulled the next item out. "A tie? Mel."

"Yes, a tie. Farin likes ties."

"Just my luck."

"Here." Melody thrust the clothes at him and pulled him up from the bed. "Now get in there and get beautiful."

His feet dragged across the floor.

"Oh," she said just as he got to the door, "and do something with your hair. Moose it or gel it or something. And no baseball cap."

"No baseball cap? Ugh." With no energy whatsoever A.J. closed the door on her instructions. Why couldn't he just have a peaceful night at home with the rock music blowing his brains out? Why was that so much to ask?

Some type of fast food would have been fine with Eve. At least then they wouldn't have had to endure hours of forced conversation. However, Dante had no intention of taking somebody like her to anything but the best, which meant they ended up at a French restaurant staring at menus listing things she couldn't pronounce and prices she knew he couldn't afford.

"Really, we could go somewhere else," she whispered, using her menu as a screen from the rest of the restaurant.

"Don't be silly," Dante said although the tinge of white circling his face told her he was lying with each word. "Go ahead, order whatever you want."

She wanted to argue, but that did no good with Dante. She had learned that much. He was being nice, and she couldn't be mean to someone who was trying so hard. With no other options, she ordered the cheapest salad on the menu when the waiter arrived.

"You don't want an entrée?" Dante asked in puzzled concern.

"I'm not all that hungry," Eve said, smiling as she handed the menu to the waiter.

"Oh." Dante ordered quickly, and the waiter left. An incessant, gloomy silence settled over their table as they both fought to come up with something to say. "So,...?"

"What...?"

He smiled uncertainly as their words collided awkwardly. "Sorry, you first."

"Oh, I was just going to ask what else you do for fun," she said.

"For fun?" Bit-by-bit awkward dropped away from him, and

41

he slid an arm over the back of his chair casually. "Umm. Well, I like to watch racing."

"Like what kind?"

"Drag racing mostly, but stock car is cool too."

"Oh," she said, trying to get interested into that sound. "That's cool. You ever been to a race?"

"A couple. They were pretty cool. All the crashes and stuff."

She nodded, searching the files of her brain for any information she had on stock car racing. The more she searched, the less she found.

"I like movies too," he offered.

"Oh really? What kind?" she asked, pouncing on that topic. Finally they had hit on something they could talk about.

"Action," Dante said, nodding, "but I really like the sci-fi stuff. *Star Trek*, Aliens…"

"*Star Wars*," Eve added because that was the only one she knew.

His face scrunched incredulously. "*Star Wars*? No, I mean real science fiction."

She wanted to ask why *Star Wars* didn't qualify as science fiction or what made the others better, but from his tone she knew he didn't think *Star Wars* was even worthy of discussion.

"So, how about you?" he asked, leaning onto the table and staring at her with that intent look that scattered her nerves. "What kind of movies do you like?"

"Chick flicks mostly," she said, fighting like mad to squelch the sigh. "Action's okay. Sci-fi, is all right if that's the only thing available, but no horror. No way. I hate horror movies."

Fire lit into his eyes. "Ooo, Texas Chainsaw Massacre. The all time great movie."

Eve pushed her revulsion under her need to appear interested. "I've never seen it."

"Oh, man, then we're going to have to rent it some night. It's unbelievable."

Good word, Eve thought. For the date as much as for the movie.

"You're going to have to come over some night," he continued, getting more excited about the idea the longer he talked. "We can rent movies and order in. It'll be great."

Thankfully the waiter picked that moment to arrive with

dinner—agreeing would have been the biggest lie of her life.

"Your tie's crooked," Melody said as they stood in the line to get into the Bar Houston.

"It's too tight," A.J. said, yanking at it.

"It's crooked." Exasperated, Melody reached over, straightened it, and then cinched it tighter for good measure. When he reached for it, she glared at him. "Don't touch it. It's perfect."

No. Perfect would've been being at home in front of a television or banging on his drums. This was not perfect. At the door they showed their IDs and entered the smoke and lights.

"I told her to be by the dance floor," Melody said as she grabbed his hand, presumably so he couldn't get away. Ten deep into the crowd, Melody spotted Farin, and without warning, he was suddenly being dragged past, over, and right through people.

"Sorry. Sorry. Excuse me," he said, fighting to keep his balance. In the next heartbeat Melody stopped, and A.J.'s momentum just about carried him right into her.

"Farin!" Melody squealed as the small girl in the tight leather pants squealed in the same pitch when she saw them. A.J. narrowed his eyes to ward off the sound.

"I thought you were never going to get here," Farin gushed, hugging Melody as though they hadn't seen each other in years. Then Farin glanced at A.J. and stopped cold. "This isn't...?"

Melody stepped back. "Farin Jerell, this is A.J. Knight."

His manners were the only thing that pulled his hand up to meet hers. "Hi." Wide-eyed Farin took his hand as she stared at him until he thought more than his tie must be crooked. "What?"

"Oh, Melody, you said he was hot, but wow!" Farin said, arching her eyebrows for emphasis.

Wow. A.J. retrieved his hand and slipped back an inch at the passion in that statement. "It must be the tie," he said. hoping that would throw her off and wishing his brain could think in a logical pattern.

"And funny, too," Farin said although she didn't laugh. "Melody, you are some matchmaker."

When A.J. looked at Melody, her smile said she already knew that.

"Come on, A.J. Let's go see if you dance as good as you look,"

Farin said. Without waiting for him to accept, she grabbed his hand and headed for the dance floor. There was no getting out of this nightmare, so with a sigh he allowed himself to be led like a prisoner to the guillotine.

●

"I had such a great time today," Dante said softly as they stood at her car next to the museum, which had been closed for hours by that point.

Eve couldn't quite believe how serious he sounded, nor could she quite fathom the look in his eyes. How could he not see how extraordinarily bad they fit together?

"So, what do you say? Next week, my place?" Dante asked, gazing at her as if she held all the secrets of the universe.

"Next... Umm..." She ducked her head and fumbled for anything to keep her from having to say yes. Finally she tossed her hair back from her face. "Lisa and I are supposed to go shopping on Saturday. Baby stuff." True, she hadn't called Lisa, but as long as Lisa didn't know the whole story, she would agree without question.

"Friday then," he said.

"Umm, Friday I'm helping my mom... hang curtains in her living room." Again not the whole truth, but her mother had asked for her help a month ago, and if she showed up and said she was ready, they could hang curtains.

"Oh," Dante said, and his gaze dropped from her face. Gently he reached over and took her hand. "I'd really like to see you again, Eve. I really like being with you."

The pleading of his gaze tore her heart out. "Well, maybe the next weekend," she finally said, hating herself for not just telling him no and being done with it. As much as she wanted to, her heart just wouldn't let her.

"Okay," he said, brightening instantly. "The next weekend then." His one hand slipped up to her shoulder, and he bent forward. She couldn't explain it, but every time his lips touched hers, her heart fell into her shoes. Why was she kissing him? Why was he kissing her? Why were they standing there together with nothing between them except his pity for her and her need to not reject his kindness?

When he pulled back, that look was back in his eyes. "I can't wait."

"Yeah," she said softly as he pulled her into his chest, and the 'neither can I' got lost.

"Watch this," Farin said as she set the full shot glass on her forehead. Its balance wavered precariously, and A.J. fought not to rescue it before it splattered everywhere. Finally she broke the pose, took the shot glass off her forehead, downed the shot in one gulp, and looked at A.J. "Your turn."

"Oh, no," he said instantly backing away from the challenge. "I don't have that great of balance."

"All the better," Farin said, grabbing for one of the full glasses on the table. She held it out to him. "Come on."

"No, I don't think so," A.J. said. "I'm driving."

"Melody can drive," Farin said as she looked at Melody. "Can't you, Mel?"

"Yeah," Melody said softly from where she sat on the other side of the table. "Sure, I can drive. Go ahead, A.J."

One look at Melody's vanished smile told A.J. that the evening was going as badly as he thought it was.

"Come on, A.J.-way-jay. Show me what you've got," Farin said, sliding closer to him and wrapping her vine-thin arm through his.

Repulsion coiled around him. "I think it's about time for us to make tracks."

"Make tracks?" Farin asked, backing up only slightly. "But it's early."

"I've got work in the morning," he said, standing. Melody looked at him with wide-eyed shock as he pulled her to her feet. He looked back at the anaconda still slithering in her chair. "Take care, Farin."

"Yeah," she said sullenly. "You, too."

Melody's eyes were the size of small tires as he pushed her ahead of him to the door. It wasn't until they were in the parking lot that she actually got words to connect with her tongue. "I cannot believe you just did that."

"Me? Okay, let's talk disbelief here, Mel." They crossed the parking lot, waiting only for one passing car as it sped by them. "You set me up without even asking me, and then my date turns out to be Glen Close's character from *Fatal Attraction*!"

"Farin's nice," Melody protested.

At his car, he crawled into the driver's seat, hit the unlock button for her, and slammed his door. "I guess I'm going to have to take your word for that one because I certainly didn't see it." He started the car and backed out. They were in traffic before he looked at her again. "She's not my type, Mel."

A pout crossed Melody's features. "Well, I'm beginning to think I don't know what your type is at all."

"Yeah," he said, nodding seriously. "There's a good start."

Bugs Bunny was racing across the screen when Eve pushed her eyelids open the next Saturday. She took one look at the television and closed her eyes in exhaustion. Vaguely she remembered two a.m. Three a.m. was clearer, and four o'clock was as clear as this moment. It was points after five that she faded out on again, and now here she was awake at seven a.m. with no desire to ever wake up like this again.

There were still mornings sparsely sprinkled across her life when she woke up that for a single moment she thought he was there with her. In some perverse way she liked those mornings. She went to sleep hoping for them every night because as bad as figuring out it was a dream was; those single moments were almost worth it. However, most mornings were like this—just misery. Hating Bugs' chipper voice, she reached over and punched the remote, but she hit the channel button instead of power.

"…only $100 down can get you in your new apartment. Furnished and unfurnished units are available. You can use your table or ours, but come on down and see us. We're conveniently located just minutes from the Galleria…"

Eve's eyes flipped open.

"…That's right. $100 can make the dream of having your own space or just a new place a reality…"

A new place. In a way it sounded wonderful. In another it sounded like death itself. A new place meant moving on, leaving the past behind—leaving Dustin behind. Her heart dropped at the thought. As long as she was in this place, there was that absurd thought that still said he might come home. That one morning he would just walk back through that door again like nothing had ever happened. It seemed stupid, but her heart refused to see that. All it saw was that if she left, if she moved, he would have no way to find her if it all been some horrible mistake on the part of the universe.

She rolled over and fanned her hair out on the white pillow behind her. Without really thinking, her gaze traveled across the room to the off-white wall beyond. Prominently displayed in the center of that wall was the gold-framed picture of her in her wedding dress. Strange, she thought as she looked at it, there was no Dustin in that photo just her and a black background. It was almost like a premonition of how her life would turn out—just her alone, standing in a sea of blackness, smiling for all the world to see.

What they couldn't see, what they could never even guess was the number of tears behind that smile. Her mind drifted back to that awful week after she had picked up that phone and gotten that summons. Most of the ensuing week was a fog, but the bits and pieces she remembered stung her heart. Those around her probably thought she had been the Rock of Gibraltar. The truth was it was all she could do to hold it together. It was as if she was but one small tremor away from total collapse from that moment to this.

When she cried, she made sure no one was around. When she didn't, she wanted to. It wasn't that a piece of her had died. It was more that she herself had died in that fire. Heart and soul she had died so that the only thing left was this body that had somehow not gotten the message.

Slowly her gaze slipped from the photo down the wall to the fragile pink crystal rose sitting on the table, and the fog broke. Pain seeped through her as her mind traced back to the moment she had first seen it. Her first birthday present from him. She could still see his eyes shining in the knowledge that she was as in love with the present as she was with him. Her arms went around the pillow she held, and she crushed it to her chest, wishing it was him but knowing it never would be again.

"...Don't miss out," the television announcer broke into her thoughts again. "Spaces are limited, and once they're gone, they're gone..."

Before sanity or something like it could retake control, Eve grabbed for the phone, wiped her eyes, and dialed the number on the screen.

Six

"A.J., this box is still sitting here," his mother called from the other side of his door the next Saturday afternoon as Metallica blared through his speakers. With a sigh he turned the stereo down and went to the door. His mother stood there, hands on hips, and an angry face to match. "I thought you were going to take this to Chelsea."

"I was going to get to it."

"When?"

"Eventually."

"Well, let's just call now eventually." His mother kicked the box closer to his door.

"I'm busy."

"I'm sure. Look, I'm tired of tripping over this thing. Besides it's not going to kill you to do one nice thing for your sister."

As though he had never done a single nice thing for her in the past. He started back into the room. "Fine. I'll do it in a little while."

"No, do it now so I can watch you and make sure you take it."

"Mom," he whined like a teenager.

"A.J.," she whined back, drawing out each letter so that each was at least four syllables long. "I'm not arguing about this. Now hop to it."

In exasperation he bent and reached for the box. It was heavier than it looked, but the trips to work out for paramedic training had served him well. Clumsily he hoisted the box to his shoulder and looked at his mother. "Anything else?"

"Yeah, I have a few dishes downstairs you can take too."

He had to ask.

Somehow Eve had never noticed how many things she actually owned until she started putting them into boxes. The movers had already taken most of the stuff the day before although for some unknown reason they couldn't make the trip across town until Monday. Her plan, meager as it was, was to take her carload of stuff to the new apartment and then come back here for one more night's sleep on the floor. It wasn't a great plan, but at the moment, she couldn't really see how any plan could get close to great.

Carefully she picked up the last box and set it on her hip. When she got to the door, her gaze betrayed her and took one more trip across the now-empty space. It looked so sad. Dustin would understand. She knew that, but as she looked at the barren room, she wondered if she ever would.

She didn't really watch as her hand reached for the knob. With the smallest of snaps, the door swung open, and she stepped out. Softly she closed the door behind her and slipped out through the cold drizzly day to her car. Not the best of days to move—if there was indeed a good day to move. She shoved the last box on top of all the others in the passenger's seat and ran around to squeeze herself under the steering wheel. Tomorrow she would call Lisa and tell her. But somehow even when Eve had talked to her friend earlier in the week, she hadn't had the courage to tell her.

Twice the words had been right there to say, but they disappeared before they found the airwaves. They would understand, and yet Eve couldn't bear the sight of their reluctant faces helping her move. No, it was better like this—alone, by herself. Once it was done, she could put on that mask that said it was just time, and no one would have to see how the doing of it yanked the tears from her eyes at every turn.

There was the coffee pot. Should she take it or should she not? He was the only one who drank coffee, and yet it hadn't moved from the countertop in all the time he had been gone. There was the bedspread that they had picked out together, settling not on the one he liked or on the one she liked, but on the one they both didn't just hate. And then there was the closet full of his clothes—the one she had slowly but surely moved all of her clothes out of and relocated downstairs to the office closet.

Somehow it wasn't until she had swung the door open to unload the shelves that she remembered them. Slowly she shook her head as she drove down the street to the freeway, but the vision of her sitting in the middle of the closet floor, holding his one pair of good brown shoes and sobbing was going nowhere. They were just shoes, and his least favorite ones at that. Nonetheless, her tears hadn't really seen the need to get technical about it. All they saw was another piece of him that had been discarded along with everything else.

When the people from Goodwill had come to pick up the items she had laid out for them, Eve couldn't watch. She had sat in her office, telling herself that the summer clothing line needed finalizing while the two men trekked up and down the stairs. Then one of them had come to tell her they had everything and would she like a receipt. A receipt. As though Dustin's whole life could be reduced to some writing on an insignificant piece of paper.

"No, that's okay," she managed to say to the man, who nodded and tried to smile at her.

She hated that smile. She saw it everywhere. As she pulled onto the freeway and picked up speed, Eve wished she never had to stop. Then maybe she could out run those smiles and those sad, pity-filled looks that seemed to follow her every step. They said they understood, and yet they didn't. They couldn't. No one could.

Hoisting the box to his shoulder again, A.J. crossed the little parking lot of the La Paloma Apartments. They were nice enough. Certainly nothing fancy, but nice. He pulled open the front door and crossed over to the stairs. At least today it was only one box. The last time it had been a couple hundred. How one person could accumulate so much junk in 26 years was beyond him.

Even when he left for California, a suitcase and a few pillows was all he needed. But, as his mother was fond of pointing out, Chelsea was not A.J. No, Chelsea was a woman now, and she needed to present herself in a certain way to the world. Apparently that included having lots of her own things. A.J. had little use for things. They tended to tie his life down too much. Freedom was much more important than having the right kind of DVD player. On the third floor, he turned the corner to the left of the stairs, walked down the hallway, and reached for the door. Three knocks and he stepped back waiting for the inevitable, "Who is it?"

A moment. Two, and he knocked again. After three knocks,

he realized that somehow he hadn't bothered to ask if Chelsea would in fact be home. He knocked again. "Chels, it's me, A.J. Open up." But his entreaty was met only with silence. Frustration poured over him as he reached up and knocked for the fifth time.

It was at that moment that he first heard the noise on the stairs.

"Oh, no!" the soft voice murmured. "No. No. No. No. No. Oh…help!"

With no thought to the decision A.J. dropped the box from his shoulder to the floor and ran for the stairs. There, midway up, behind three unstable and sliding boxes, stood a figure half on one step, half on the next, fighting to keep control of the boxes lest they cascade right over the railing but losing the battle badly.

"Here." A.J. descended the steps quickly and reached out for the top two boxes just before they had the chance to slide off into the abyss below. He didn't bother to ask. The soft plea was enough to tell him that his help was both needed and wanted. When the two boxes slipped from their precarious base into his hands, A.J. smiled at the face they revealed. Long, slender nose, almond-shaped eyes, small, squared forehead under a mass of near-black hair that was secured to the top of her head but falling down all around her face at the same time. A moment passed, and then recognition hit him like a punch. "Eve?"

"A…J.?" she asked, and her face dropped in shock. "What're you doing here?"

The smile came easily. "Waiting for you I guess." When her face fell in confusion, he laughed. "Trying to drop off a box of stuff for my dumb sister who doesn't seem to be home." He jerked his head back to Chelsea's door. "But I thought the other sounded better."

The sadness and fear etched in her eyes dissipated. "Huh. Well, I'm glad. For a minute there, I thought my stuff was a goner."

He looked over the side of the railing dubiously. "Yeah, three flights down airborne? That might not have been a real good idea." Gently he shook the boxes in his hands. "'Specially if there's something breakable in here."

"Hey, careful with that," she said, jumping.

"See, not such a good idea to just toss it over the side." His smile slid onto his face as he made the slight motion of throwing the boxes overboard. "So, where are these going anyway?"

"End of the hall, right," Eve said, nodding in that direction. "But you can just set them at the top. I can get them."

A.J. pursed his lips together. "Seems to me it's only right since I rescued them from certain destruction that I carry them the rest of the way."

She put her head down as if she might actually decline his offer. "Okay," she finally said softly.

He swung the boxes up the steps in front of him. "Lead the way."

Carefully she stepped past him, and it wasn't until they were midway to her door that A.J.'s senses picked up on why she looked so different today. In gray warm-ups under a mud-brown cable-knit sweater that draped over her like a tent, she looked like a starving college student more than a fashion mogul. At her door, Eve fumbled with her keys for a moment and then released the lock and stepped inside.

The space beyond resembled Chelsea's digs except it had an airier feel to it. Two huge windows spanned the wall to the right where the dining room was—or would be. Save for the three boxes they carried, the whole place was empty.

"Nice," A.J. said as he walked to the windows and looked out without bothering to put the boxes down.

"Not much of a view, but I thought it would be good light for my drawing table," Eve said from behind him as she set her box on the floor. Then she straightened and watched him for a second.

He turned, and the vulnerability evident in her stance and features touched his heart. "It's great." Then he remembered the boxes. Carefully he lifted them as if to ask where to put them, and she jumped to life.

"Oh, you can put those anywhere. Kitchen. Living room. Dining room. It doesn't matter."

Nodding, he stepped by her into the living room. At one end stood a stone fireplace with bookshelves on either side of it.

"Just over there is fine," Eve said, waving at the expanse of room.

He slid the boxes onto the fireplace hearth and turned to her. "You just getting started?"

One slender hand traced its way up her neck tensely. "Trying to. The movers are supposed to bring the big stuff on Monday, but

I wanted to move some of the little things myself."

"Oh." Until that moment it hadn't sunk in that she was the one moving, and suddenly he didn't know where to go from there. "So, do you have more downstairs or what?"

"Some," she hedged. "But I'm sure I can get it."

Off-handedly he shrugged. "What's a white knight for if they can't help carry a few boxes?"

A small smile cracked through the melancholy of her features. "A white knight, huh?"

"It sounded good, didn't it?"

Her smile became a laugh. "Must be nice."

"What's that?"

"Having so much confidence in someone so insufferable."

"Insufferable?" he asked, splaying his fingers across his chest. "Ugh. That hurt."

"Are you going to deny it?" she asked, and he liked the teasing in her tone.

"I might."

She crossed her arms in front of her. "Oh, boy, this could take awhile."

He swung the door open for her to exit. "Then while I'm denying it, maybe we could go get something done."

"Okay," she said, slipping past him and through the door.

As they walked down the hall, Eve noticed how A.J. mirrored the very cadence of her steps. With one finger she pushed a stray strand of hair over her ear. "So, shouldn't you get your sister's box or something?"

He shrugged. "I'm sure it'll be there when we get back."

Eve leveled an unconvinced gaze on him. "Well, I'm not so sure about that." She spotted the little door off to the side of the stairs. "Hey, there's a mop closet. You could put the box in there until we get back."

"Ah, it'll be fine."

"Yeah, it will," she agreed, "in the closet. Now, come on. I'd feel terrible if her stuff got stolen because you were helping me."

Slowly he sighed when it became apparent that she wasn't going to go down the stairs without first taking care of that box. "Okay." He walked to Chelsea's door, and with one jerk he picked the box up. "Where's the closet?"

"Right here." Eve opened the little door to a space that was empty. "The landlord said there used to be stuff in it, but they had to take it all out. Too many things conveniently disappeared."

A.J. vanished into the closet's darkness, and when he reemerged, he looked at her skeptically. "And this is a good place to put something so it won't get stolen?"

Seeing the speed bump in that logic, she wrinkled her nose and then laughed. "Well, we'll get it out as soon as we get back. Then we can put it in my apartment."

Slowly he closed the door. "And this is better than just leaving it in the hallway..."

She started for the stairs. "Oh, hush. It's better, and you know it."

"I know no such thing," he protested. "And what I want to know is who's going to explain this to Chels when her clothes are gone."

Eve shrugged as step-for-step they descended in rhythm. "You are."

"Me?"

"Well, she's your sister."

"Well, it was your brilliant idea."

"Yeah, and yours was a whole lot better. Sure, just leave it in the hallway. Nobody would *ever* think of taking anything from there."

"I hardly think grand theft would occur in the span of the three minutes it's going to take us to get back up here," he said.

"Three minutes?" She landed a skeptical glance on him. "You sure don't underestimate yourself now do you?"

"Nothing to underestimate," he said with a teasing grin.

"Ugh! You're awful." At the bottom, she pushed through the door and out into the parking lot.

"If I'm so awful, then why don't you just tell me to leave?"

"I did, and look how much good it did me."

Side-by-side they strode to her car.

"You did not tell me to leave," he said as she unlocked the little silver door.

"I did too," she protested as she pulled a box from the car and put it in his outstretched hands. "I told you that you could put those boxes at the top of the stairs, and I'd get them." She handed him another box.

"That's not telling me to leave."

"Sure it is."

"No, it's not."

"Oh, yeah? Then what is it?" she asked, stacking one more box on top of the others and then reaching for the stack of pillows and blankets in the backseat.

"It's…It's…okay, it kind of is, but you didn't say, 'A.J., you're in the way. I wish you would leave me alone.'"

"Oh, so that's the magic words?" Eve asked as she kicked the door closed with the heel of her tennis shoe. "I'm going to have to remember that one."

"Boy, you're nice," he said, turning to follow her back to the building. "Did anybody ever tell you that?"

At the door, she turned and smiled brightly at him. "I won Miss Congeniality in high school."

Awkwardly she tangled with the door, pulling and fighting to keep it open. Finally on her yank, he reached a foot out to hold the door so she could slide around him and get inside. He shifted the boxes in his hands so he could see the stairs. "Are you sure they didn't miscount or something?"

She looked back at him climbing behind her. "And now who's being nice?"

"Just trying to keep up," he said, shifting the weight of the boxes again as they rounded a landing and started up the next flight.

"You do that," she said as she turned slightly in challenge. "Just try to keep up."

He glanced up the stairs looming above them. "Like I have a choice."

Up, up, they climbed until at the top and down the hall, they all but fell into her apartment. A.J. set the new boxes by the others on the fireplace. Eve simply dropped the pillows and blankets in the floor and pushed her hair, now damp on the roots out of her eyes.

"You better go get that box," she said, resting her knuckles on her hips.

"Isn't there more to get?"

"Yeah, but I've got to rest for a minute."

"Oh." His bravado turned in a heartbeat to unease.

"You can just bring it back here," she said with a shrug. "It's not like I don't have the room."

"You sure?"

"Yeah, no problem."

Slowly he stepped to the door. "Okay, I'll be right back."

"I'll be here."

When he slipped out the door, Eve sighed with a smile on the edges of it. He was totally insane. Reluctantly she looked at the boxes on the fireplace and scratched her ear. Moving had to happen sooner or later, but suddenly sooner seemed much sooner than she had figured on.

"Might as well get started," she said with a sigh. She stepped over to the first box and tore the tape off of it. As she did so, she smiled at the memory of A.J.'s dramatic rescue. Kidding aside, this box would certainly have been the one to take the three flights down airborne. It wasn't until she reached inside and pulled the top item out that her breath snagged, and tears jumped to her eyes.

The crystal rose had never looked so fragile. Her heart swelled as ache scratched over ache. Looking at the delicate petals, memories flooded back through her, and she wrapped the rose into her chest knowing how close she had come to losing even it.

"Man, they need to rethink these corners," A.J. said, bumping through the door with the box. "They're impossible."

She jumped at the noise and spun toward him, forgetting for a second too long the tears sliding down her cheeks. The second he looked at her, all humor left his face. The box slid to the floor without so much as a backward look. Her gaze dropped to the floor as she sniffed and fought every emotion she had stuffed down for months on top of months. In the next heartbeat his arms were around her.

However, nothing could stop the tears. They flowed from every crevice in her whole body, overwhelming every sense she thought she had until it felt like she might drown in them. Hurt that she had been pushing down for more than a year suddenly had no weight on top of it, and it sprang to the surface like an unleashed coil. Everything hurt—head, body, heart, and soul. There was only throbbing pain. Tears slid down her cheeks and across her nose as she squeezed her eyes closed to stop them.

But this army would not be thwarted. They were too many and had been held down too long. The sobs pulled up more sobs until she wasn't sure there would ever be a bottom to them.

"Shh," A.J. said softly as the warmth of his arms melted into her. Illogically in that moment, she just needed someone to hold onto, and one arm went around his back lest he try to let her go. She gripped his shirt, crushing the soft jersey material in a clinch, knotting it, wrinkling it, and not really caring. In the safety of his embrace, the floodgates of her pain shattered, and all her mind could contemplate was how very bad she ached.

It was then that she felt the palm of his hand rubbing slowly up and down her back, and she couldn't remember ever feeling anything so amazingly gentle. Her head, resting in the middle of the space between his chest and his shoulder, felt completely sheltered from all of the horrible feelings gushing through her. Slowly they subsided although he never so much as moved to back away from her. Peacefully his palm continued its slow, methodical motion up and down her back until she thought she could just get lost in that movement.

Exhaustion pulled at her, wrapping around her like the tentacles of a massive octopus. What she wanted to do was simply lay her head down and go to sleep. What she did instead was sniff back the tears and pull away from him. When she looked up into his soft golden-bronze eyes, however, there was only concern gazing back at her.

"Sorry," she said softly as she swiped at the tears.

His smile, soft but sadness-and-worry-tinged, touched her heart just as surely as his hand was touching her arm. His eyes were serene. "No need to be sorry."

Something tugged at her heart, pulling her gaze from his down to her hands. "It's just that..." She beat back the tears that threatened again. "...Dustin gave me this, and I don't know what to do with it." The tears threaded through her as slowly A.J.'s hand slid up and down her back even though he was now standing next to her rather than in front of her. She could feel his gaze on her face although she couldn't bring herself to look at him.

"Then we've got to find an extra-special place for it," he said gently. He held out his hand, and ever so carefully she placed the rose in it. Once more he rubbed across her back as he looked up to the mantle just above them. "I think this looks like the perfect place, don't you?" With great care, he set the fragile crystal in the center of the mantle and stepped back to her side as he slipped an arm around her shoulders. "See, perfect."

For a long moment words failed her as the sight of the rose prominently displayed for all to see blurred in front of her. "I miss him."

Tenderly A.J. pulled her closer. "Nothing wrong with that. It just means you loved him."

"I did," she said as the tears washed over her. "I loved him so much."

A.J. held her there simply encircling her so she had a soft place to grieve. His heart hurt for her—for them. Life could be so utterly unfair at times. He wished he could do something more to ease her pain, but he also knew that to totally carve out the pain, the love would have to come with it. And so, he didn't even try to make her pain go away. Instead, he just created a safe space for her to feel it.

After several moments his gaze chanced up to the little rose, and it seemed to be looking down on her like a guardian angel from some realm beyond. A.J. smiled at the thought. Yes, Dustin seemed to be watching over her in ways A.J. couldn't explain; however, he felt them as if they were palpable.

In that moment as he gazed at the rose, he made a solemn promise to do his part to protect her in this realm if Dustin would simply agree to take care of her in the next. The pact was made in the silence of A.J.'s soul, but it could have been no more definite had Dustin been standing right there.

Slowly Eve moved back, and A.J. looked at her. Serenity he had never seen in her eyes crossed through them. "Yeah?" he asked, knowing she would understand exactly what he meant although he himself wasn't completely sure of the meaning.

Softly she smiled. "Yeah."

As the light faded from the gray-hued sky, Eve pulled an armload of clothes from the trunk of her car and handed them to A.J. Immediately his gaze took in not only the stack in his arms but also the pile still in the car.

"What?" she asked, seeing the bewildered look on his face.

"Are these all yours?"

"Yeah." She grunted as she pulled an armload for herself out and slammed the trunk. "This is about half of them."

"Half?" he gasped. He shifted the stack in his arms. "When do you wear them all?"

She laughed as they started across the lot. "I don't really know."

The bewildered look stayed with him all the way up the stairs. "I think you could have an outfit change every five minutes and not wear all of these in a year."

"It's one of the hazards of the job," she said. "You've just got to have the newest, cutest outfit the second you see it."

"Ugh. Give me an old pair of jeans and a T-shirt, and I'm good to go."

As they got to the third floor Eve looked at him in exasperation. "Comfort before fashion? Sounds like someone else I know."

"Oh, yeah? Who's that?" he asked just as they reached her door.

Instantly her heart fell. How did she always manage to walk right into that trap? She unlocked the door and pushed into the apartment, hoping the noise would drown out her answer. "Dustin."

"Huh, good taste in women and in clothes? Smart man," A.J. said without missing a beat.

She looked at him in disbelief, and instantly he stopped so that he was standing, arms full of clothes, in the middle of her living room. "What?"

Her disbelief melted into a smile. "Wait 'til you see the shoes."

Skepticism descended on his face. "I don't think I want to."

She laughed. "Smart man."

It was his idea to order pizza, and they were halfway through unpacking the last box when the pizza arrived. A.J. went to the door and retrieved the hot box. He paid quickly and brought his prize to the middle of her living room floor, smelling the hunger-inducing aroma with each step.

"Don't you love the smell of Canadian bacon?" he asked, folding himself on her carpet like a ten-year-old with a new toy.

"I wouldn't have known what it was, but it smells delicious." Leaving the box, she joined him on the floor as he laid the pizza box down and opened it. She picked up the two drinks he had set aside. "Mountain Dew or Pepsi?" she asked, holding the two cups up.

"Pepsi," he said, pulling a stringy piece of pizza from the box. He laid it on a napkin and handed it to her as she exchanged pizza for Pepsi.

"I am starving," she said as she put the drink between her legs and prepared to devour the pizza.

"You are? I had a fruit pie for breakfast like twelve hours ago." He bit halfway into his slice of pizza and chewed heartily.

Her hunger threw propriety out the window. Besides it was just A.J., there was nobody she needed to impress. Three bites were in her mouth by the time she came up for air. "Oh, man, that's good."

"Told you." A couple more bites and he started to reach for another slice. However, he stopped, looked around, and then dragged the box and his cup over to the wall. There, he resumed scooping another piece out. Taking his lead, Eve scooted over by the fireplace and leaned on the hearth. Another four bites were in her mouth before she realized no one had said anything for a solid minute.

"Okay, here's one," she said after she took a drink and swallowed the sweet but tart soft drink.

"What's that?" he asked still chewing.

She gulped the piece in her mouth down. "Pizza or hamburgers?"

"Definitely pizza."

"Thick crust or thin?"

"Thick."

"Stuffed crust or not?"

"Not." He stopped for a minute, and narrowed his eyes like he was trying to recall the detail of a crime. "As long as it has a lot of cheese on the pizza itself."

"I'm with you there," she said, tipping her cup at him in emphasis.

He took another bite. "How about this one: TV or movies?"

"Regular TV or like movies on TV?"

"Regular TV."

"Movies. Definitely movies."

"Me, too. I hate the stuff they have on TV these days. It's like the same old thing over and over again. Shoot 'em up cop shows or stupid sitcoms with lots of laugh tracks and no point. Except for cartoons, of course."

"Oh, of course," she agreed, grinning.

"Although now they can even mess up cartoons. Give me Wylie Coyote any day."

The laugh jumped to her throat as she reached for another slice. "You would really think he would figure out when to quit. Wouldn't you?"

"He's hilarious. All these dumb schemes, and they do the whole thing with two little sounds: mee-meep."

"I like the signs he holds up."

"I like that rock trick that he has like seventeen versions of— trying to drop this boulder thing on Road Runner."

"Yeah," Eve said. "And then half the time he's the one that ends up under that rock."

A.J. pulled another piece from the box. "Did you ever see the one when Road Runner is playing that dumb little piano thing, and the Coyote has it rigged to blow up on a certain note?"

She took a bite and shook her head. "I don't think I've seen that one."

"It's so hilarious. There's this music sitting up on the piano, and Road Runner keeps playing through it, but at the end of it there's this one note that he keeps hitting wrong. Of course that's the note that will blow the whole piano up. He plays it wrong like three or four times, and that last note is just so off. Then finally the Coyote gets so fed up, he comes out to show him how to play it…"

"…and it blows up on him," she finished, nodding. "I think I have seen that one."

"That just cracks me up every time. It's like, 'Here, move out of the way and let me show you how it's really done.' Then it just kabams everywhere."

"Oh, man, how true is that," she said.

"No kidding. As soon as I think I'm going to show somebody how to do something— KABAM! Never fails."

"You? Surely you've never made a mistake."

"*A* mistake?" He leveled a get-serious gaze at her. "Now who's underestimating me?"

"Oh, yeah? What's the biggest mistake you've ever made?"

His chewing slowed as he thought about the question. Then as she watched him, the smile fell from his face. "The times when I think if I would've done something different, somebody else might still be alive." He looked at the pizza in his hand as if it held no fascination for him. "The ones you lose are really hard."

Her heart softened toward him more than she'd expected as she gazed at him, suddenly so serious. That face that seemed in perpetual animation dropped away to reveal a despondency she hadn't known was even a part of him. "Yeah, but I'm sure you save a bunch of them, too. That's got to make you feel good."

The gold of his eyes traced over her face. "It never makes up for the ones you lose."

Strange, she thought as his gaze dropped from her face and he went back to his pizza, for the laid back, just have fun, no cares and no worries attitude he usually exhibited, she had never so much as guessed this side was underneath all that. She retreated into her own world and then wondered why she was so surprised. Compassion seemed as inherent to him as playfulness did.

In a different light, she looked over at him, sensing things she had never known were there. "You know, I bet the girls are all coming up with these life-threatening conditions just to get you to come over and save them."

His seriousness fell into dubiousness. "Ha. Yeah, right. They all take one look at me and run the other direction." Slowly he stretched his legs out in front of him and crossed his ankles.

"Oh, now I don't believe that one for a minute," Eve said. "Surely you've got some girl going into heart palpitations when you walk into a room. Like... what's her name... Melody."

"No, uh-huh. Melody and I decided long ago that friendship is as far as we want to go together. Of course that doesn't stop her from trying to fix me up with everybody that happens to walk by." He reached for the last piece of pizza and held it up to her in offering.

"You can have it." Eve wiped her mouth with the napkin and zeroed in on the previous topic. "So, does she have any particular body in mind?"

Exasperated misery slipped onto his features. "Any girl with a pulse I guess. The other night she tried to fix me up with this chick who thought getting plastered together was a good way to get to know each other."

"Eew, fun."

"Yeah, tell me about it. And she wasn't the worst one either. Do the words star charts or table dancers tell you anything?"

Eve's eyebrows raised on their own volition. "Boy, Melody must have great taste."

"Yeah, well, unfortunately I'm not much better."

"Oh? Why's that?"

Slowly he shook his head. "It just seems like every girl I hook up with is either so batty I want to throttle her after two dates or she has this thing about making me into someone I'm not. Ties, button-down shirts, froofy restaurants. Ugh! It's just not me." He took a bite.

Eve smiled in understanding. "Pizza and Cheetos."

He leveled an index finger at her. "There you go."

Nonchalantly she leaned back against the fireplace and looked around at the apartment. "Well, at least you get to go out once in awhile. I have a feeling me and these four walls are going to get to be really good friends."

His gaze traveled over to her quizzically. "What about Dante?"

She sighed and looked down at her cup. "Dante's sweet, but... It's like he wants the whole package, you know, marriage, wife, kids, the white picket fence. I don't know if I'm up for that anymore."

For a moment A.J. tucked his chin near his chest, then he looked at her. "With him or with anyone?"

With no need to hide, Eve looked at him although she didn't have a good answer for that question. "I had it," she said softly. "The whole dream package—well, without the picket fence and the kids... but... it takes so long to build, and it can all be gone so quick, and then you're left with starting over..." She shook her head so that the mop of hair waved across her face. "I just don't know if I can go through that again."

"So you'd rather sit here and look at these four albeit very lovely taupe walls for the rest of your life?"

She sighed. "It doesn't feel like I have a choice."

Gently he smiled at her. "You always have a choice. Now whether you want to make that choice or let the choice make itself is your call."

The weight of choices, made and unmade, descended on her

shoulders. "Right now, I feel like I've made enough choices to last a lifetime. This whole moving thing is about all I can handle for awhile."

He sat in silence for a moment. Then he looked around at the apartment. "I really can't believe Jeff isn't over here making sure you don't hurt your little finger carrying boxes that are too heavy."

Eve ducked her head and pursed her lips. "He doesn't know."

Instantly A.J. looked at her like he'd been sucker-punched. "You didn't tell them you were moving?"

She shrugged. "They would've just wanted to help."

"Hello. They're your friends. That's what they're there for."

Slowly Eve shook her head. "Jeff has work, and Lisa with the baby and all. She shouldn't be carrying stuff up stairs. Besides, I didn't want to put him through that."

"Through what?" A.J. asked although by the soft tone of his voice, she knew he already knew the answer to that question.

"Jeff… had a really hard time when Dustin… Being a fireman and all, it was really hard on him. I know he feels guilty sometimes for still being here when Dustin isn't. I can see it in his eyes. Today was going to be hard enough. I really didn't need them looking at me all scared and sad the whole day."

"So, you're just going to move and not tell them?" A.J. asked seriously.

Eve laughed. "Yeah, right. He'd probably hunt me down if I did that. No, I'll tell them… next week sometime when I'm unpacked and things get a little more settled." Once again she looked around at the empty walls. "It's just so hard to believe this is home now. It feels like somebody else's place and I'm just going to crash here for awhile."

"Yeah, on the floor," he said, nodding at the heap of pillows across the way.

She looked at her watch and sighed. "Yeah. I was going to go back to the other place tonight, but I think I've about decided just to call this good."

He mimicked her, and his eyes widened when he saw the face of his watch. "Oh, man! I didn't realize it was so late." He pulled up onto his heels as he threw the remnants of supper into the pizza box. She watched him, suddenly grateful that he hadn't just set the boxes down and left. His gaze chanced over to her and caught hers staring back. "What?"

"I thought today was going to be awful," she said with barely a breath behind the words. "But I think I lucked out when my white knight showed up."

His smile was a fusion of the two sides of him—playfulness and compassion. "Just be glad I had the good sense to wait around for you to show up."

His words went right to her heart and spread the warmth of his smile throughout her. "Trust me, I'm very glad."

Seven

"You didn't call us?" Lisa shrieked Wednesday evening when Eve finally got up the courage to call and tell them.

There were still boxes from the movers stacked everywhere, but the chance that they might just "happen" by her old place and panic when she wasn't there finally made her pick up the phone. She heard Jeff's muffled voice in the background, and she closed her eyes. "It wasn't that big of a deal. I got movers. They moved the big stuff…"

"She what? Let me talk to her," she heard Jeff say. Great. She should've called on a night he wasn't there. "Eve? Am I hearing this right? You moved by yourself?"

"I told you I'm a big girl. I can take care of myself."

"Well, everybody can use a friend— especially when you decide to do something like that. Why didn't you call us?"

A friend. The smile that traced through her pushed what would have been anger away. "Don't worry about it. Okay? Besides A.J. helped me."

That stopped him cold. She almost heard him slam into the name. "A.J.?"

"Yeah," she said, smiling at the memory of him standing on those stairs. "It was my lucky day or something."

"Well, you should've called us."

"Next time," she said gently. "Could I talk to Lis again?"

"Uh, yeah. Just a second."

The next voice she heard was Lisa's. "You really could've called us, you know?"

"I know," Eve said.

"But I know why you didn't," Lisa said softly. "Oh, and what's this about A.J. anyway?"

Again Eve smiled. "His sister lives about five doors down from me."

"And he just showed up?"

"Yeah, something like that."

"What about Dante?" Lisa asked, and the worry was back in her voice.

"I don't know. I haven't talked to him in a couple weeks."

"Did you tell him you moved?"

That was an idea Eve had never even thought of. "It kind of slipped my mind."

Slowly Lisa sighed. "I thought you two were getting along."

"We were. We are." Eve stopped. "Look, I know you want things to work out between us, but I'm just not sure it's going to."

"Of course it won't if you don't give it a chance."

"I'm not trying not to give it a chance. It's just… I think we're in two different places in our lives right now, and I don't want to force something that doesn't feel right."

"Have you told him that?"

"Not exactly. I just kind of hoped he'd move on, and I wouldn't have to."

"Look, Eve," Lisa started with a sigh, "I really think Dante could be good for you, but I can't make you date him if you don't want to. I do think you owe him a phone call though… so he doesn't think you just skipped the country."

Eve tried to think of a rational way around that, but nothing was coming. "Okay. I'll call him."

When she and Lisa hung up, Eve stared at the phone for several long minutes. Calling him was the right thing to do—at least to let him know she had moved if nothing else. But if it was the right thing to do, then why was it so hard to just pick up the phone and dial a few numbers? Another moment slid past her before she pulled the receiver up and dialed, trying not to think about what she was doing. On the other end the phone rang, and rang, and rang.

Then just before she hung it up, the answering machine clicked on. With a quick shake of her head, she replaced the receiver. She could always try again later, and with that thought she went into her room to get her things for her shower. Later sounded much better than now anyway.

The third Friday in November A.J. was in his room picking around on the old guitar he had bought in middle school. He'd never gotten very good on the thing although he could pick out the melodies to several songs. It wasn't like playing the guitar, it was more like killing time with a guitar on your lap. He heard the phone downstairs ring, but it was so seldom for him that he didn't think anything of it until his mother was at the bottom of the stairs yelling up at him.

He slid the guitar to the bed and raced for the door. "Yeah?" he asked, holding the door in one hand.

"Phone."

With an extra bounce on each step, he descended the stairs. "Who is it?"

His mother shrugged. "Some guy."

Confusion wrinkled across his forehead as he went into the kitchen and picked up the phone. "This is A.J."

"Hey, just the man I'm looking for." Jeff's voice sprang over the wires. "Listen, we put together a little poker party tonight, but our fourth hand bailed. You wouldn't be interested?"

Staring at a full stretch of night sitting in his room all alone with a guitar, A.J. saw no reason to decline. "Just tell me where and when, and I'll be there."

"Call," Jeff said as he leaned into the table staring at A.J. "What do you got?"

"Two pairs. Jacks and sevens."

"Yes! Three queens."

"Ugh," A.J. said, watching Jeff lay his cards on the table and then rake the money to his side. He looked over at Gabe who shrugged.

"I had a ten," Gabe offered as if that might help.

A.J. picked up his glass and downed the last of his soda. Jeff noticed the clink of ice as he began shuffling the cards.

"There's more in the refrigerator. Help yourself."

For a second A.J. thought about declining but decided against it. He stood from the table and ambled into the kitchen to the refrigerator where he pulled a can out just as Lisa rounded the corner from the back room.

"Oh, hi," she said clearly surprised to see him rummaging through her refrigerator.

"Hi," A.J. said, holding the can awkwardly. There was something about Lisa that always put him right on the edge. When he was around her, he had the feeling that one wrong move might banish him to her bad list forever. "I was just..." He held up the can. "Umm, Jeff said to help myself."

"Oh, yeah, that's fine," she said, and for a second he wondered why she was being so nice. It wasn't that she was mean, and there was no denying that she was beautiful. However, she always looked so serious.

As he poured the soda into the glass, he watched her go over to the cabinet and pull out a glass. When she turned, he was once again square in her sights.

"So, are you having fun?" she asked, crossing past him to the refrigerator.

"If your husband would let the rest of us win a few, it would be fun."

She laughed. "He's a hustler."

"Yeah, I noticed."

Slowly she poured some bottled water into her glass. A.J. felt trapped. He couldn't just leave when she was being so nice, and yet he was having trouble getting logical sentences past the fear to his brain. Careful not to spill it down the front of his shirt, he took a sip of the soda.

"So, have you talked to Eve recently?" Lisa asked as she leaned on the cabinet and took a sip of her own drink.

The gasp in his core sucked the soda down the wrong pipe, and when he started to answer, his voice squeaked. "No. Umm, not in awhile. Why?" He swiped at his chin, sure there was a trail of sticky brown soda sliding down it.

"Oh, she just mentioned you helped with moving her in and stuff. I thought maybe you had talked to her."

He shrugged. "That was a fluke." Heavens, the last thing he needed was for Lisa to think he was making moves on Eve when Lisa clearly had other ideas about who her friend should be with. "Have you talked to her?"

It was more to find something to talk about than an actual

question, but the look on Lisa's face made him question the sanity of asking.

"She sounded kind of down when I talked to her the other night," Lisa said.

"Yeah." And for one moment he forgot about the she-monster standing in the kitchen with him. Eve's face, vulnerable and hurting traced through his brain. "I just hope she's not sitting there alone in that apartment again tonight."

Lisa tilted her head to the side quizzically.

"She doesn't get out much— except for work," he clarified. "I think she just sits there most nights unless somebody calls and forces her to go somewhere."

"Hey, A.J.! We're decaying in here!" Gabe yelled.

"These cards won't play themselves, you know," Jeff agreed.

With a slight glance at Lisa to say he was sorry, A.J. slipped out of the kitchen and back into the living room. "Yeah right. You just want my money."

"That's what we're here for," Gabe said.

When the phone rang at nearly nine on Friday night, Eve considered letting the machine get it. However, as she hadn't spoken to a real live person in more than four hours, she thought that even a telemarketer would be a step up.

"Hello?" she said, swinging the phone to her ear.

"Hey, Eve-girl, what's up?" Lisa asked, and Eve dropped back into her chair.

"Not much. Just learning to hang drywall."

"Drywall?"

"The Do-It-Yourself channel. It's fascinating."

"Sounds like it," Lisa said unconvincingly. "Listen, Jeff had some of the guys from the station over to play poker, and I'm bored silly. Why don't you come over, and we'll find something to do?"

"Now?" Eve asked taken aback by the request.

"Well, yeah. Unless they're still playing tomorrow night, I don't think it would do much good to come then."

"Oh, I don't know. I was just going to kick back. Maybe go to bed early."

"Well, I figured that. It's just... I got these wallpaper books so

I could choose something for the baby's room, but I can't decide, and Jeff's no help at all."

"He's not into home decor?"

"He's not into anything other than a dumb deck of cards right now."

Eve heard the uproar in the background as something dramatic happened in the game. Leaving her pregnant friend to deal with a bunch of drunken gamblers really didn't sound like the most compassionate choice in the world. "It'll take me awhile to get ready."

"Hey, it's just us. Just come in what you're in."

"I'll be there."

The little silver Celica pulled up next to the curb, and the headlights snapped off. Eve stepped out and swept her hand through the straight dark hair that now draped gracefully down her back. The sides were pulled to the top of her head making her neck and face appear much thinner than they usually did. She readjusted her sweater so that one side dropped off the shoulder the way it was supposed to.

It was nice to be in something other than work clothes or lounge around the apartment clothes. Casual, with just a touch of class and a touch of daring mixed in, that was how she liked to look. Lisa would know she had changed, but in truth she knew Lisa wouldn't have wanted to see her in the stuff she was usually in at this hour.

At the door to the house, she reached down and rang the doorbell as she flipped the other side of her hair back over her shoulders.

"Who could that be?" Jeff asked with some concern when the doorbell rang. "Jeez. It's almost ten o'clock."

"Maybe it's Dante," Gabe said absently as he looked over his cards. "He said he might come if they got finished."

"I'll get it," Lisa said, crossing through the room.

"No, he said he couldn't make it when I talked to him," Jeff said as the concern in his voice grew. He laid his cards on the table and disappeared into the little entryway with Lisa.

Concern jumped into A.J.'s awareness. Clearly Jeff wasn't comfortable with this arrival, and that told A.J. it could be trouble. He listened for sounds to tell him what was going on in that entryway. At that moment Jeff came back into the room shaking his head. He sat down and picked up his cards just as A.J. got the question from his brain to his tongue. "Everything... okay...?" His gaze chanced up to the doorway, and the sight there pulled the rest of him up straight. One blink to make sure he wasn't dreaming, and A.J.'s heart stopped.

"Hey, Eve," Gabe said in greeting as he looked up and waved to her.

"Hey," Eve replied as her gaze landed on A.J. and froze there. He tried to smile, but it didn't quite make it that far.

"Come on," Lisa said, taking hold of Eve's arm to drag her past the card table. "The wallpaper's in here."

A.J. had never been so thunderstruck in his life. In fact, until that very moment he hadn't even really known the meaning of that word, but suddenly it was the only one that applied. Like grace itself she moved across the living room, the black of her outfit outlining and highlighting every curve. When she was gone, A.J. tried to refocus on his cards, but they were blurred by the image of her. "I didn't know Eve was coming."

"I think she just stopped by," Jeff said, studying his cards. "I'll open."

"I'm in," Gabe said as he flipped some money to the center of the table.

"Umm." A.J. scratched his eyebrow trying to remember the rules of the game. "Yeah, I'm in."

There were indeed wallpaper books—four of them. The only problem was that Lisa had conveniently forgotten to mention the fact that A.J. was one of the poker players. As she and Lisa flipped through one of the books, Eve's ears strained to hear what was going on in the living room. It was crazy. It wasn't like they had anything going on, and yet her brain couldn't quite get beyond the sight of him sitting at that table. The light blue cap, the blue, white, and gold plaid shirt. It wasn't runway material, but it certainly wasn't bad.

"Now, I like this one." Lisa pointed to a frilly lace pattern.

"But then I think, 'If it's a boy, I don't think he's going to want a frilly pink lace on his walls.'"

"Yeah, no," Eve said, fighting to follow the conversation. "You need something that will work with either. Unless you're going to find out early."

"Nope," Lisa said. "Jeff thinks it's better if we're surprised."

Eve smiled at Lisa, standing there in her maternity get-up, talking about Jeff like he was the hook that her whole life hung on. She had certainly come a long way from the drenched rat who had stood on Eve's porch the year before uncertain as to where her life was taking her. "Well, then we're going to have to find something neutral." She started to flip through the catalog.

"This is going to take awhile, isn't it?" Lisa asked.

"It could."

"Then, here, let's go sit in there. There's more light and a place to sit down." She picked up two books, leaving two for Eve.

With a sigh, she picked up the books and followed Lisa out into the living room. "Great idea."

"A straight," Gabe said, laying his cards on the table.

"A straight?" A.J. asked in exasperation. "How is that possible?"

"It's an ambush," Zack Jameson, the fourth hand, said, leaning over to A.J. as Gabe raked more money to his side, and Jeff shuffled and dealt.

"Tell me about it. Are they always like this?"

"Every third Friday night," Zack affirmed just as A.J.'s attention snagged on the woman gliding back into the room. Concentration and common sense slipped away from him.

"Let's get something to drink before we start," Lisa said as she laid the books on the couch.

"Okay," Eve agreed. As they walked past, A.J. couldn't help but think she seemed much taller today. When they were safely in the kitchen, he managed to ante up intelligently.

Each man laid cards on the table and received cards to replace them.

Gabe examined his cards seriously. "No way." He tossed his cards on the table and leaned back. "Fold."

"I'm out," Jeff said, throwing his cards to the table and leaning with his elbows on the table.

"I raise you a dollar," Zack said and flipped a dollar out to the table.

"I'll see your dollar, and…" A.J. meant to raise it a dollar, but the second Eve appeared in the doorway, it somehow came out, "I call. What do you got?"

"Two pair. Sixes and nines."

Logical thought seeped from A.J.'s mind. "Oh. Uh, a flush."

"A flush? You bailed on a flush?" Gabe asked in total disbelief. "What are you, nuts?"

"I just…" A.J. started as Lisa sauntered over to Jeff. She laid a hand on his shoulder and then ran it down across his chest. Instantly Jeff reached up, clasped her hand, and kissed it.

"Having fun?" Lisa asked.

"Yeah," Jeff said, smiling up at her. "You?"

"A blast," she said.

Not looking at the two women standing there was rude. Looking at them seemed like taking his life in his hands. When A.J.'s gaze caught on Eve's, she ran a delicate hand through the side of her hair, calling attention to her bright red nail polish. She smiled. "Hi."

"Hi," A.J. said, wondering where all the air in the room had gone.

"Having fun?" she asked.

"Always," he said although he wished his voice would sound just a little more normal and a little less breathless.

"You winning anything?" Eve asked.

"Never."

She laughed, and his heart laughed with her. Gabe dealt the cards, and the three others picked them up. A.J.'s hands didn't seem to be cooperating as he tried to pick up the cards and carry on a conversation with her simultaneously.

"You get all your boxes unpacked?" he asked as one card jumped from his hand onto the floor.

"I wish. Oh, Chelsea came by the other day. She got her box."

He retrieved the card from the floor and sorted through his hand. "Mom will be thrilled to hear that."

"Well, we better let you all play," Lisa said, giving Jeff one more squeeze. "Come on, Eve. Let's talk wallpaper."

One more small smile directed just at A.J., and Eve followed

Lisa over to the couch.

"A.J.?" Gabe asked.

"Yeah?" A.J. asked as he fought to sort out the cards in his hand.

"Cards?" Gabe asked, holding up the deck to ask how many new cards A.J. wanted.

"Oh… Umm, four." He laid three down on the table as Gabe dealt out four cards.

"Hey," Jeff said, "you don't get to pick which one you don't want after you see the new cards."

"Oh, sorry," A.J. said, suddenly seeing that he was going to have to bust up two pair because he wasn't paying attention. Reluctantly he threw another card onto the discard pile.

"You got to watch that boy," Gabe said with a shake of his head at Jeff.

"Tell me about it," Jeff said.

Yeah, watch him have a heart attack in the middle of the living room, A.J. thought. Only good thing was the other three players had some emergency medical training. The way this was shaping up, he might need their help before the night was over.

For nearly two hours, Eve and Lisa had talked about everything from lace and pearls to little toy boats. They had narrowed it down to teddy bears, Winnie the Pooh, or bunny rabbits.

"So this book is out," Lisa said as she transferred one wallpaper book to the other side of the couch. "And this one has the bunnies. This one is…?"

"The teddy bears with the toys. And oh, yeah." Eve picked the last one up and handed it to her. "Winnie the Pooh."

"We're down to three. Man, I was hoping I could take like three of these back."

"Well, get bozo over there to choose one, and you can," Eve said with a laugh.

"That's it," A.J. said, throwing his cards to the table and standing up.

"Aw, come on," Gabe said. "One more."

"I don't have any more money to lose," A.J. said, stretching his back.

"I'm done too," Zack said.

"Such wimps you invite," Gabe said to Jeff.

"And who was it who quit early last week?" Jeff asked.

"I had to get home," Gabe said in defense.

"And you don't this week?" Jeff asked.

"Nope. Ash went to see her folks."

"Why didn't you go?"

"Let's see," Gabe said seriously. "Ash's mom, three hour trip, work weekend. Ch-ching!"

"Well, enjoy spending my money," Zack said as he stood. He held a hand out to Jeff who caught it. "See y'all Sunday."

"Bright and early," Gabe said.

Zack exited as A.J. put a foot up onto the bar at the bottom of the chair. "So, do you guys invite unsuspecting suckers over a lot, or did I just get lucky?"

"No, most of the time Dante comes if he's off," Gabe said, "but he couldn't make it."

Eve's heart slid through her chest. At least Dante wasn't here.

"Yeah, I was racking my brains trying to figure out who to ask," Jeff said, "and then Lisa thought about..."

"We're down to three," Lisa said from Eve's side suddenly, and Eve jumped.

"Three what?" Jeff asked, leaning back in his chair to look at her.

"What do you think of Winnie the Pooh?" Lisa stood and brought the book over to the table.

"Wallpaper?" Gabe asked as if it was a rattlesnake poised to strike. "No way. I'm out of here."

"It's not that bad," Lisa said.

"I've got three days all to myself. Wallpaper is not what I want to be doing." Gabe stood and held a hand out to Jeff. "Besides Ash said I could call her after her parents go to bed..."

Jeff smiled teasingly. "Wouldn't want you to miss that."

Gabe laughed. "I wish. She'll probably just tell me the hundred and two ways her mother still hasn't changed."

They laughed.

"Well, we certainly wouldn't want you to miss that either," Lisa said.

"Take care," Gabe said, and he stepped over to the entryway.

"We've gotten it down to these three." Lisa laid one book on the table when Gabe was gone. "Winnie the Pooh..." She looked over to the couch where Eve still sat. "Bring those other two over here."

Reluctantly Eve grabbed the book handles and dragged them up with her. When she got to the table, she swung them up so that they hit the table with two thumps. Lisa sat down by Jeff who leaned over the book at least trying to look interested.

"I like this one," Lisa said, pointing at the old-style cartoon with the faded orange background. "But I don't really want the orange walls that Eve said would look good with it."

"Orange?" Jeff asked. "No, no orange."

"Then there's this one." Lisa grabbed another book and searched through it. "This one, right?" she asked, looking up at Eve who stood behind her, wishing she could disappear.

"Yeah."

"The rabbits are cute and everything, but I don't know," Lisa said.

"I like the other one better," Jeff said although he didn't sound terribly convincing.

"Okay, so bunnies are out." Lisa slammed that book and slid it to the floor. "The other one is… this…" She flopped the third book open and flipped through it. "Yeah. This one."

The teddy bears set against a pale beige background sat in groups of four or five each with a different theme. One held a bat and a ball, one had a floppy hat, a teacup and pearls, one had a basket of flowers, one a plastic dinosaur. Jeff turned the book around, and Eve noticed even A.J. leaned forward to get a better view.

"You could put a pale yellow, blue, pink sponge paint thing with that," A.J. said. "That would be really cute."

Both women stopped and looked at him. Instantly he shrank back and shrugged. "I used to paint houses. They did some of that in a couple of them."

"You know," Eve said, looking back at the book. "He's right. These three hues right in here would be really cool together."

Lisa looked at Jeff skeptically. "How good are you at sponge painting?"

"What is sponge painting?" Jeff asked with wide-eyes.

A.J. laughed. "It's not that hard although it does help to know what you're doing."

"Oh, yeah. That's helpful," Jeff said, looking at A.J.

77

skeptically.

Like he didn't care, A.J. shrugged. "Or you could always go with a straight pale yellow or blue. That would be easier."

"So you like this one?" Lisa asked, tapping the book.

"Yeah," Jeff said. "It's good."

"Then this one it is." Lisa lifted that book off the other one so Jeff could close the other choice. When she laid it back on the table, she looked at it and nodded. "Yeah, I like this one too. Good, then I can take these other ones back and get this ordered."

"Be sure to order a little extra," Eve said. "So you can match the pattern."

"Good idea."

For a moment no one said anything, and then A.J. pushed back from the chair. "Well, I'd better make tracks."

Eve looked at her watch. It was almost 12:15. "Me, too."

Their hosts stood. Jeff extended his hand to A.J., and Lisa hugged Eve.

"Thanks for coming," Jeff said.

"I would say thanks for asking, but..." A.J. replied.

"I'll be sure to keep you in mind for next time."

"Yeah, you do that."

Jeff turned his attention to Eve. "And you take care of yourself." He hugged her, and for the first time in a very long time, it didn't feel suffocating.

"I'll try." Eve started to the door, followed by A.J. and then Jeff and Lisa whose arms linked without question.

"Have a good night," Jeff called as Eve pushed through to the outside. "Behave yourselves."

"We'll try," A.J. said good-naturedly.

"Night," Eve called over her shoulder.

"Night," her hosts called back.

Six steps down the sidewalk, her senses picked up on A.J. walking right next to her and on the fact that the door still hadn't closed. Then just as they got to the curb, the door closed, and Eve's heart jumped forward when she realized they were alone. "Where's your car?"

"Down the block. There wasn't any place to park close," he said, and his gaze fell to the shadows at their feet.

"Oh," she said, deciding that's why she hadn't noticed it earlier. "I didn't know you were a poker player."

"I'm not," he said with a laugh. "But it sounded like something different."

"Ah." The closer they got to the little silver car, the slower her steps went. "So, you been hanging out on staircases saving poor damsels in distress lately?"

His smile slipped across her heart. "No, I've pretty much gotten out of that racket."

"Too bad," she said lightly. "You're so good at it."

He tucked his head to the side. "Yeah, well. It was fun while it lasted."

At the door to her car, Eve turned and leaned against it. "Well, I guess this is good night."

"Guess so," he said, glancing off into the darkness down the block.

She waited, not knowing what she was waiting for. "Well, drive careful."

"You, too," he said with a tight smile and a slight nod.

One more moment and she turned to unlock her car. She slipped underneath the steering wheel and smiled back up at him. "Night."

His half smile melted through her. "Night." And with that, he slammed the door.

As he stepped past the back of her car, Eve shook her head slowly and reached down to start the car.

Although A.J.'s steps carried him away from her car, his heart was still right at that door, saying good night, looking into her beautiful eyes, getting lost in the trance that was Eve. When he started his car, he watched as she pulled away from the curb, and he pulled out behind her. It would be her who had to pull off first this time, he thought with a smile. Too bad because it would make their journey together even shorter than the last time.

It was nice that Lisa had thought to invite her, and suddenly he felt like a dummy when his conversation with Lisa drifted through his mind. She had already thought about Eve before he opened his big mouth. In fact, Eve was probably on her way over at that very moment. Great. Now Lisa probably really wondered what his plans were where Eve was concerned. True, he would like to have plans, but reality was he didn't. Eve was so far out of his league, he was sure he couldn't even see her league with his good binoculars.

No, it was a nice fantasy when he really had no concern for reality, but Eve was Eve. He was A.J. They came from different worlds. He noticed her car slowing down, and for a moment he wondered why. Then he realized she wanted him to pass. His foot mashed the pedal, and in moments her bright smile was shining at him through her window. With a wave, she pulled off the freeway and into the darkness. He shook his head knowing he would never do anything to mess up their friendship. "God, keep her safe. Okay?"

Eight

"Hi. Is this Eve?" the voice said the Friday night after Thanksgiving. She had spent the entire day before at her parents' house simply trying to get through the next moment. By Friday evening Eve wanted nothing more than to go to sleep and forget about life for a few hours.

"Yeah."

"Oh, hi. This is Dante."

Guilt ripped through her. During two weeks of intense boredom, she hadn't once had a single good opportunity to pick up the phone and call him. "Oh, Dante, hi. I've been meaning to call you."

"Yeah, I tried your place, but… Jeff gave me this number. I hope you don't mind."

"No," she said, sitting down in the chair heavily, "I don't mind."

"Oh, good. I thought… Well, I kind of thought you were going to call me, and then when you didn't, and you moved and everything…"

More guilt. "I'm really sorry. It's just… I've been so swamped with the move and work and everything…"

"Yeah, I understand. You just… you didn't mention you were moving or anything…"

"I didn't know," she said hurriedly, and then she realized how flighty that sounded. "It was kind of a spur of the moment thing."

"I figured it must've been something like that because you never mentioned it."

There was a long moment of silence as Eve fought with her brain to come up with some topic to discuss that wasn't about her or moving or him or most of all them.

"Umm, I was just curious if you might be free tomorrow night," he said hesitantly. "If you aren't, that's cool. I know it's kind of short notice."

Eve squeezed her eyes closed, wishing her answer could be anything else. "No, I'm not doing anything."

"Really? Oh, good because I thought… Well, some of us are getting together tomorrow night. I thought maybe you might like to go."

She really didn't want to, but she also knew that just telling him that over the phone wasn't the way to handle it. "Tell me when and where and I'll be there."

On Saturday night, A.J. thought about calling her. That was silly of course. She didn't want to hear from him. It wasn't like they were any more than two people who happened to end up at the same place a couple of times. But the thought followed him all the way out to the drum set in the garage. However, after twenty minutes it became clear that even the noise of the drums couldn't hammer her out of his head.

Finally he gave up, shut the jam session down, and went into the house. He grabbed a couple of Oreos from the cabinet and munched on them slowly, trying to think of something else he could do not to think about her. In exasperation he picked the receiver up from the wall and dialed Melody's number. "Hey," he said when she answered. "You interested in going out?"

"Out?" she asked. "Why?"

"I'm bored."

"Sure. I'll be there in a hour."

"Sounds great."

Form-fitting, the wild, green, purple, and turquoise print dress replete with its own mini skirt sounded like a good idea when Eve had pulled it out of the closet. Granted she still hadn't found great shoes to go with it, but coupled with her hair in wavy curls and the anklet she had found earlier in the week, it looked really good. The problem was the halter-top bodice wasn't exactly the warmest thing she had ever worn, and the temperature picked that evening to plunge.

When she got out of her car at the restaurant where they had agreed to meet before heading over to the club, she immediately realized her error. For half a second she considered looking into the trunk to see if maybe she had left a jacket in there by accident. However, a big gust of frigid air sent even that idea skittering. Wishing she could run without either tripping or looking like an insane lunatic, she hurried to the door of the restaurant. Once inside she did a short chicken dance trying to get warm.

Just as her body returned to non-chill status, Dante opened the door and stepped inside. Instantly his eyes lit up. "Well, hello there." With no warning, he wrapped an arm around her shoulders. "Long time no see."

"Yeah," she said, tip-toeing slightly so he wouldn't bury her nose in the wool of his jacket.

He stepped back, and his gaze slid down her body even as his hand didn't move from the center of her back. Generally she liked having people look at her. In fact, that was the point of wearing this in the first place; however, something about his appraisal didn't feel wanted or natural.

"Nice dress."

"Thanks," she said as embarrassment seeped through her. She pulled at the bottom of it wishing the skirt wasn't as short as it suddenly felt.

His lips were next to her ear before she knew they were coming. "*Es muy bueno.*" When he pulled back, the smile in his eyes sent her hand up to the knot of material at her neck to make sure it was secure. She wasn't sure of anything anymore.

With a soft push, he led her over to the check-in table. "Two."

City Streets had a good crowd, and A.J. was glad. He followed Melody to a table and ordered a drink when the waitress made it to their table.

"So, what brought this on?" Melody asked, shaking out her layered medium blonde hair when the waitress left.

"Boredom. Complete and utter boredom." He leaned back in the chair and rested his arm over the back of it.

"Well, it's about time. I thought you were going to sit in that house and petrify."

The waitress set the beer on the table in front of him, and he paid for it and Melody's drink. He added a nice tip and a smile to the payment. "Thanks." When she was gone, he tipped the bottle up and took a drink. "You're not working tonight."

"I took the night off. Actually I had yesterday off too, but now I'm going to have to work Christmas."

"I had to work yesterday, so don't come crying to me." The tips of his fingers tapped out the beat to the song playing on the speakers. "Man, it feels like forever since I've just kicked back and forgot about everything else."

Melody laughed. "Maybe because it has been."

It seemed more logical for Eve to take her car to the club. After all, she thought, the point of this date was to break up with him, but when they exited the restaurant, he insisted on driving her.

"You're so independent," Dante said, shaking his jet-black hair, gelled and set to perfection.

"Is that a bad thing?" she asked, not sure if she should be offended or proud.

"With you, it's always a good thing," he said, and he leaned over to her and kissed the side of her cheek.

Her heart wanted nothing more than to cry. Why was this always so difficult? She glanced over at him, and nothing in her wanted to see Dante. When that was all she saw, she turned her head and looked out the window fighting back the tears. If she could just find a good way to tell him, let him go on with his life so she could go on with hers, then maybe her heart wouldn't have to break from the trying.

"Let's dance." A.J. grabbed Melody's hand.

"Dance?" she asked in surprise, but he didn't give her time to really protest. On the dance floor, he took her in his arms and swayed slowly. How was it possible that everywhere he looked, he saw Eve? Every head of long, almost black hair caught his attention, and they seemed to be everywhere. Of course none of them was Eve, and the second he got that message through to his heart it would throb in place. If he could just erase her from his memory or find something that would.

"Remember the prom?" he said to Melody.

"The prom? Ugh. Don't remind me," she said incredulously.

"No, the prom was fun."

"You forgot my corsage."

"I told you I was sorry about that, and I gave it to you the next day."

"It doesn't help the next day."

He danced four more steps. "Well, it was still fun."

"Yeah," Melody finally agreed. "It was."

"The guys have been hounding me to meet you," Dante said, wrapping Eve under his arm as the line inched forward.

"These are like guys... from the station?" Eve asked. In an instant the last fire station she had been in flashed through her mind, buckling the middle of her knees.

"Yeah. I've been telling them all about you."

She tried to smile, but it made the center of her ache. "Great."

That dance ended, and although A.J. was far less polished in rock dancing, he didn't want to go sit down. He reached over and spun Melody like he knew what he was doing, but they both laughed when he nearly cloths-lined her. His body moved in time with the beat when he let her go although cool hardly described it. Then they just got silly and started showing off what couldn't even be considered moves to each other.

Her top-this dance was followed immediately by his until they were both laughing so hard, they couldn't even dance. Falling together, laughing, they exited the dance floor and walked to their table.

"You're insane, you know that?" Melody asked.

"Why thank you," he said as if he was proud of himself. For one moment all thoughts of Eve slipped from his mind, but then his gaze chanced across the room, and one look stifled the laughter. He shook his head, knowing it couldn't have been her. His gaze returned to Melody, and he smiled. It was fun to have a night out with a friend.

"…And this is Eve," Dante said by way of introduction to the people surrounding the table. She didn't know any of them, and it hardly seemed fair to act like she and Dante were a couple when her only intention was to not be in a few hours. Nonetheless, she slid in next to Hunter, one of Dante's friends, and tried to look comfortable.

They hardly had time to order drinks before Dante took her hand as a slow song came on. His eyes were liquid when she looked at him. "Let's dance."

NO! her heart screamed like it was falling off the sheer face of a cliff. *Please, please no.* But he pulled her up and led her to the dance floor because her protest never made it to her voice. Once on the dance floor, his arms came around her waist, and she closed her eyes to block out the moment.

His voice was suddenly in her ear. "The guys are jealous."

"Yeah?" she asked, beating the pain down.

He smiled at her. "I would be too."

When A.J.'s gaze snagged on her wafting across the dance floor, he tried again to tell himself that he was just imagining things. However, if he was imagining things, he was very good at it. He tried not to stare although that was not as easy as it sounded. It was only when his brain registered who she was dancing with that his senses came back into focus. It was her. Her and Dante. Strange, he thought watching them, didn't she say something about not going out with Dante anymore? Or did he misunderstand that comment because some part of him wanted that to be the truth? It was obvious they were together…

"A.J., hello!" Melody said, waving her hand in front of his face. "Where'd you go?"

"Oh, nowhere. I'm here." He ripped his gaze from the dance floor and anchored it to his bottle.

"So, did you get it or what?"

"Get what?" he asked, trying to focus on what she was saying.

"Super Terrestrial War. You said you were going to get it the day it came out. That was today."

"Oh." He shrugged. "I might go get it tomorrow. I was kind of busy today."

"I cannot believe you missed its opening day." Melody shook

her head in exasperation. "You're growing up on me here, and I don't like it."

Yeah, he thought sullenly, join the crowd.

A few minutes, that's all Eve asked out of this night. A few measly minutes that Dante wouldn't have his hands on her or be whispering in her ear or be looking at her like a steak in the butcher's window. He wasn't doing it to make her self-conscious she was sure, but it didn't matter—that was the effect it was having regardless of his intentions. The third time they stepped off the dance floor, Eve was desperate to find some small reprieve—something to stave off the excoriating time at the table. On the bottom step down, she glanced over to one side, and the sight of the long angled nose and that smile that could be no one else's flooded through her. "Hey, it's A.J."

"Who?" Dante asked already turning the other way to their table.

"A.J." Eve yanked Dante in the other direction. "Let's go say hi."

Her feet carried her as if they had suddenly sprouted wings, and two tables before she got to his, she called to him, oblivious to the fact that she was dragging Dante through the crowd with her. "A.J.! A.J.!" She hadn't even considered the possibility that with the smoke and lights that it wasn't him, but when he turned, even those non-doubts disappeared. "Hey!"

He stood in surprise, and Eve wrapped both arms around him in greeting. Hesitantly his hand came around her back. It wasn't a long hug, but it did more to pull her spirit out of the blackness than anything else had in a week. She stepped back, and Dante's hand came around her even as he extended his other hand to A.J.

"What are you all doing here?" A.J. asked, clearly taken aback.

"Night on the town," Dante said.

"Cool," A.J. said, and then he glanced at the nice-looking but not stand-out girl who was obviously his date. "Dante, Eve, this is Melody."

Melody looked at them and held a hand out. "Nice to meet you."

"You, too," Eve said, wondering if there was a mystery date lurking somewhere around. "I guess you guys are out on the town too, huh?"

"He finally decided to get a life," Melody said in exasperation.

"I have a life," A.J. protested.

"Hours and hours behind a drum set blowing your brains out does not constitute a life."

"Drums?" Dante asked instantly interested. "I didn't know you played."

"A little," A.J. said, backing away from them. "I'm not terribly good."

"Don't let him fool you," Melody said sagely. "He almost made it big in L.A."

"Really?" Dante asked.

"Almost," A.J. emphasized.

Eve's gaze went to him in amazement, and total joy traced through her heart. "Well, if you can play, can you dance?"

"I'm not too bad," he said with an off-handed shrug.

Melody leaned over into Eve's space. "He's awesome."

"Well, how about I be the judge of that?" Eve looked up at Dante, not really caring if he minded but knowing she should ask anyway. "You don't mind, do you?" However, she didn't even give him a chance to say no, and Dante barely made a sound. "Great. Come on, A.J. Let's see your moves."

This must be a dream, A.J. told himself over and over as he followed Eve to the dance floor. There was simply no other good explanation. That was it. He was dreaming, and any second he was going to wake up. The piano led into the opening beats of "Old Time Rock 'n' Roll," and suddenly he really didn't care whether it was a dream or not.

"Do you jitterbug?" she asked over the music.

"I can try." He had seen a few people jitterbug in his lifetime. Not enough to know what to do, and certainly not enough to be proficient, but enough to at least get started. He took her hands in his, and they pushed back from each other three times. When she came back, he spun her under one arm and pulled her back through, danced a little, and tried it again. This wasn't too hard.

The next pass through, she said, "Here, grab my hand." She reached behind his back, and he managed to grab her hand; however, the second he had it, he realized they were in serious trouble as they were now back-to-back and going nowhere.

"Let go of this one," she yelled, laughing. When he let it go, she twisted back under his other arm.

"Sorry," he said as they started dancing again.

"'S okay." Three tugs and she said, "Try it again."

This time they at least didn't end up in a tangle.

"Not bad," Eve said as they continued to dance.

"Why thanks," he said when she came back to him. He spun her under one arm and back out again. Basics. That was good.

"Here, try this," Eve said, and before he had time to ask what she was going to do, she arched both of their arms up and over their heads spinning them back-to-back and then face-to-face in the span of a second or two. "See, easy."

Yeah, easy, except now the room was spinning. Trying to be really cool, he did the hands behind the back thing again, and unbelievably it felt almost natural.

"Boy, you're good," she said.

"I've been trying to tell you that."

"Over the head!" she yelled, and his hands swung up with hers. When he came back face-to-face with her, he laughed. However, before he caught his breath, she said, "Twice." Up and over, and up and over their hands went. If the room wasn't spinning before, it certainly was now. "Behind the back!"

His body followed her instructions, and then she was back in front of him. Three tugs and she said, "Here." She bounced both hands up even as she held onto his; however, she underestimated how high it was over his head, and her arm caught him square in the forehead.

Guilt and laughter collided in her face as she released his hands. "Sorry."

He put one hand to his forehead, but he was laughing too hard to really care.

"Maybe this would be safer," she said, putting her hands over her head to clap like the rest of the dancers.

Agreeing wasn't necessary. He lifted his hands and bounced along with the claps. Safer, he thought, looking at her, but not nearly as much fun. When the music came back up, he reached over for her hands, and pulled her in to him. A spin under his arm and back out again. Three tugs and he spun her behind his back like an expert. As the music faded out, he spun her twice and caught her with his other arm.

He laughed at the delight on her face. "I didn't say I was any good."

"You were great," she said as he righted her and stepped back. Her gaze went to his head. "Where's the cap?"

Nervously he reached up and ran his fingers through his hair. "I left it at home."

"I like it." A slow song started over the speakers. "How about one more?"

"I might step on your toes."

"Not if I step on yours first," she said.

A.J.'s breath caught in his chest as she stepped into the hollow of his arms. His head bent into her without him telling it to. The silky material of her dress slid under the palm of his hand. It could have been no softer had it been her skin. Her head rested in the crook between his shoulder and his neck, and feeling like the world must have just stopped turning, he closed his eyes and just floated right off of it.

The middle of his mind said she wasn't his date. She was a friend and barely that. Still the non-rational parts of him wanted nothing more than to make believe for that one moment they were together, that she was his, and he was hers, and everything else would take care of itself. Slowly they swayed together, and the smoothness of her hand in his felt like heaven.

Moments and moments until he forgot to count them all, they simply swayed together. Then as the music began to fade, he reluctantly opened his eyes and glanced over to the tables where Dante was presumably waiting for her return. All A.J. could see was darkness, but he knew Dante was there all the same. The song ended, and for one more lingering moment they held each other, and then he stepped back and was instantly caught in her gaze. "Thanks."

Soft, sad, and scared, her dark eyes gazed back at him. "Thank you."

He ducked his head and put his hand at her back to lead her back to the table. If only it was the two of them on a date… But A.J. jerked that thought up short. It wasn't. She was with Dante, and that was how life was. At the table, Dante stood, and it didn't take a tape measure to realize he was nearly a full nine inches taller than A.J.

"Thanks for letting me borrow her," A.J. said, guiding her back into Dante's arms.

"Yeah," Dante said, trying to sound cool, but not really succeeding. He looked down at Eve. "We'd better get back to the guys."

She nodded although A.J. never really heard her response.

"Nice to meet you, Melanie," Dante said, and he and Eve turned and disappeared into the crowd.

Wishing it didn't feel so bad to watch her walk away, A.J. sat down in a heap. Melody stared at him with skeptical but inquiring eyes.

"I'm thinking I've been looking for a date for you in the wrong places," she said. "I should've been looking on the runways."

"What does that mean?"

"That means, don't you think she's a little out of your league?"

"Eve?" He tried to laugh. "She's not my type."

"Yeah, you don't go for gorgeous, super model type older women."

He looked at Melody dourly. "Are you trying to make a point?"

Slowly Melody shrugged. "I'm not saying anything."

"Good," he said as he took a long drink from the bottle. He set it down, considered the whole general scheme of things for a moment, and then stood. "Let's dance."

Melody looked at him, and he tried not to see the pity in her eyes. "Okay."

Every time Dante asked her to dance the rest of the night, Eve's mind would go to A.J.'s face when she smacked him in the head with her arm, and the laugh came to her. Somehow that one single moment made the rest of the night bearable. She even saw him a couple more times—dancing with Melody or sitting over at their table. She wanted to go back over there and just sit and talk, but she was chained to the table with five firefighters and their wives and dates.

By the time Dante decided it was time to go home, the laughter in her spirit had all but died. Life was back.

A.J. saw them leave. He had seen little else since she had walked off with Dante, looking far too much like one half of a happy couple for his heart to take. When the silky print dress disappeared into the smoke by the door, he wished with everything he had that he could make her memory disappear as easily.

His thumb rubbed up and down the side of the cold beer in his hand. What he wouldn't give to go back and relive those few precious moments in her apartment. What he wouldn't give to…

"I think it's time to call it a night," Melody said, looking at her watch and yawning.

"Yeah," A.J. agreed. He slid off the chair. There was no longer a reason to stay.

Dante's thumb rubbed across her shoulder tenderly, and Eve fought not to shrug it off. If she could get through the next few minutes without killing one or both of them, she would be doing good.

"I really had fun tonight," Dante said in that low voice that pulled her nerves right to the surface. "I'm glad you wanted to go with me."

Eve sat there, never turning to face him, her gaze buried in her lap. The words wouldn't line up in her head, and worse they couldn't get past the lump lodged squarely in her throat.

"You are so beautiful," Dante said, sliding closer to her, and he leaned in to kiss her. However, at the last moment she turned her head and ducked away from him. Confusion traced over his face as he backed up and looked at her. "What's the matter?"

She tried to look at him, but the vulnerability in her heart wouldn't let her. "I can't do this." The rivets holding the pain in her chest weakened. "I mean you're really nice and everything but…"

He backed up further, staring at her in stunned bewilderment. "But I thought…"

"I wanted to tell you before." Her gaze bounced up to him but dropped. The words were no more than a whisper. "I didn't know how."

"Eve, what are you saying? I love you. I want to be with you."

Slowly she shook her head even as her eyes fell closed. "I can't make myself feel something I don't. That's not fair to you. And I can't keep pretending that this is working when…"

"No, don't say that." He took his arm from her shoulder and grabbed up her hands in his. "Look, I know, okay maybe you don't feel anything right now, but it's early in the game. You have to give yourself a chance. Please, Eve. You have to give us a chance."

She took a deep breath and looked at him, willing her heart not to crack right down the middle. "The game's over."

Lying on his bed as the deep night took full control around him, A.J. held the little Nerf football and tossed it into the air. What he wanted to do was find a way to forget about her—or at least not think about her for a few seconds running. However, nothing he came up with was working. He had tried the drums, but the middle of the night isn't the best time to cymbal crash your way past something. So he had retreated to his room, turned on his stereo, plugged in the headphones, and turned up the volume.

He tossed the ball into the air and caught it with the other hand. Light was pointless. It was so dark in his heart that the light wouldn't have made any difference anyway. He tossed the ball into the air, and as it fell back to him, his memory stumbled over the angle of her smile as it spun on the dance floor. She was beautiful—no doubt, but there was so much more to her beauty. He tossed the ball into the air. Her greatest beauty was in the strength she exuded despite the events of her life.

The ball went up into the darkness, but when it fell, his hand misjudged it, and it bounced away from him onto the floor. With a sigh he looked over at it, lying in the shadows. Slowly he shook his head. It was clear that whatever she thought of him—if she even did think of him, which was doubtful—her thoughts certainly did not include them together. Another sigh slid through him as he pulled the pillow under his chin. Sleep now. Tomorrow would be another day. Another day farther away from her. Another day for her to get closer to Dante.

"Melody's right," he said softly. "She's out of your league. Just get over her already." He flipped on his back and stared at the ceiling. If only doing it was as easy as saying it.

The soft cotton of Eve's latest pair of pajamas wrapped around her as she lay in bed long after she had gotten home. She should've been exhausted. In fact, after the roller coaster of emotions she had been on ever since Dante had called the night before, sleep should have been easy. However, every time she closed her eyes, a jumble of faces floated around her like an out of control kaleidoscope.

Lisa wouldn't be happy about Dante, and Jeff would be less so. Dante obviously was crushed, and although she wanted to do something to make the pain and confusion in his eyes vanish, every plan she thought of was doomed to make things worse. If she could just talk to Dustin, ask his advice, find out what she should do. He always knew the very best course of action when it came to her life. Even when she couldn't see it, he always could.

One more moment with him, she thought as her gaze bounced back and forth across the expanse of dark blue ceiling. One more so he could tell her what to do. "I'm just so confused," she said to the empty room. "I don't know what to do anymore."

The breeze ripped through her heart as once again she stood next to that coffin, saying good-bye to her best friend, her lover, her husband. She ripped her pillow off the bed and punched it hard. "I hate this! You know it? I really hate this! I don't want to live like this anymore. Do you hear me, God? I don't. It's not fair. You took him from me and You left me with nothing! How could You do that?" Her anger collapsed in on itself. "I just don't want to be alone anymore. I hate being alone."

"Hello," A.J.'s sarcastic voice traced through her. "They're your friends. That's what they're for."

An image of him trying to throw popcorn into her mouth blurred through the tears. "I just don't want to go on without Dustin," she said softly.

"Whether you make the choice or let the choice make itself is your call," A.J. said from sometime before time began.

He was right. She had been letting the choices happen to her instead of making them on her own. Even with Dante, she had been against that idea from the start, but it was too easy to let the choice happen.

"Okay, I give up. I don't want to be miserable anymore. Show me how to do what I need to do."

Nine

"What is your problem?" Lerone asked when A.J. climbed back in the ambulance after their fourth run of the day a week into December.

"Nothing."

"Yeah, nothing. You do realize that semi never saw us at that intersection."

A.J. started the ambulance and put it into gear. Two more hours and he could go home and mope alone. "I saw it."

"Sure, you saw those big red letters as they went past. Hello, semi. Good-bye world."

"It wasn't that bad."

"It wasn't going to hit your side either." For emphasis, Lerone buckled his seatbelt. "And let me tell you, I don't think that the guy in the wreck appreciated being dropped either."

"I didn't drop him."

"No, you dropped the gurney he just happened to be attached to."

"It must be your incessant talking," A.J. said angrily. "I can't concentrate."

"Oh, it's my fault. Cool, I'll be sure to say, 'Sorry' to the next one you drop."

As he drove through an intersection, A.J.'s brain said it really wasn't as bad as Lerone was making it out to be. The truck was a good four feet away, and the guy couldn't have dropped more than a couple inches at the most. He probably didn't even feel it. Even so, A.J. thought, pulling the excuses up short, he needed to get his head screwed back on straight or he might have to go back to the auto parts store. Not a good thought. No, he needed to buckle down, forget about everything else, and do his job. People were counting on him, and he couldn't let them down because of some personal ghost problem that existed only in his mind.

"Calling any units in the vicinity of 2430 Maple Street."

Lerone looked at A.J. seriously. "You sure you're okay."

"I'm fine. Just answer the call."

The mall was jammed top to bottom with Christmas shoppers two Saturdays into December. When she was little, Christmas was always Eve's favorite time of year. It was the one time that her mother lifted her "limited mall access" rule. Back then buying was out. It was more the sheer joy of getting to try on hundreds of outfits and dreaming of the day she would be able to purchase them at will.

Truth was, she still couldn't buy them at will, but it never hurt, even now, to dream. For this trip, she had roped Lisa into coming too. They had talked nearly every night since the club scene although they hadn't seen each other since the wallpaper selection event. As assumed Lisa wasn't thrilled with the news about Dante although Eve could tell she wasn't exactly surprised. And life had gone on as it always found a way to. However, by the time Eve suggested the little outing, the four "albeit lovely walls" of her apartment were starting to close in on her.

"Three hours," she had begged the day before. "Surely Jeff won't miss you too much in three hours."

And so now they were here shouldering their way through the crowd and trying to have a nice day together.

"So, did you get the wallpaper in yet?" Eve asked as they walked slowly past the windows adorn with ivy and red ribbon. In the center of the square stood a huge Christmas tree complete with lights, bows, and ornaments.

"I called them yesterday. It should be here next week."

"Cool. Have you decided on the paint yet?"

Lisa scratched the base of her ponytail. "I really liked A.J.'s idea, but I don't think I'm talented enough to pull that off. Especially not looking like Moby Dick." She spread her arms out to the sides and then laid her hands across her growing belly.

"You look beautiful," Eve said sincerely. "You're pregnant. That's not a bad thing."

"Yeah? Tell that to my thighs," Lisa lamented. "They're never going to be the same."

Eve looked at her friend, and for all the softness in her heart, there was a little twinge of jealousy. "You're never going to be the same."

Slowly Lisa shook her head. "I just hope I'm ready for this. Jeff is so excited I think you could hit him with a stick and he'd burst. But every time I think about this baby, and getting it here, and what happens after it's here… and the fact that they're going to send me home with it and say, 'See ya later. Good luck.' I just don't know…"

"You'll be fine. Besides it's not like you can't call Aunt Eve to come over and baby-sit once in awhile."

"I'm sure Aunt Eve will have better things to do with her time."

"Than hold that baby? I don't think so." Eve glanced into a window and caught sight of a brown-beige teddy bear. "Oh, look! That would go so great in baby's room. You could sit it in that little rocking chair you were talking about. Come on, we've got to get it."

"Jeff is going to shoot me if I get any more presents for this kid," Lisa said, dragging her feet as Eve pulled her to the store's entrance.

"Then I'll get it. My present."

"Then Jeff might shoot you," Lisa said seriously.

Eve laughed. "Like he hasn't wanted to before. Come on."

"A.J., you busy tonight, man?" Jeff asked over the phone wires the next Friday.

"Uh-oh," A.J. said, having heard this set up before. "Let me guess, you're short a hand and looking for another wallet."

"Something like that," Jeff said with a laugh. "How about it? You in?"

All the good reasons to say no slipped through him, but they weren't good enough. "Your place?"

"Eight o'clock."

All evening as they played, A.J. listened for the doorbell, but for all his mental telepathy, it was silent. That was okay, he told himself. Seeing her again would be too hard. It was better if she didn't show up. However, just the fact that she might show up took what was left of his sanity and dumped it out the window.

"A straight," Gabe said, laying his cards on the table.

"Ugh! Three of a kind," A.J. said, lamenting the death of the best hand he'd managed to acquire all evening.

"Darn," Gabe said as he pulled the money into his pile. "Aces, too. You've got to hate that."

"Yeah, I'm so sure you're just heartbroken," A.J. said, rubbing his sweating hands on his pants.

"I am. Don't I look heartbroken?" Gabe turned his best dejected face to Jeff who laughed.

"Miserable."

Gabe smiled triumphantly as he turned back to A.J. "See, told you."

"Oh, by the way, speaking of miserable," Jeff said as he began shuffling the cards. "Thanks to your brilliant idea, I'm now sponge painting tomorrow."

"Me?" A.J. asked incredulously when Jeff's gaze landed on him. "What did I do?"

"I think these three colors would look great sponge painted, Lisa," Jeff said in a sweet voice, and he shook his head as he dealt the cards. "I finally get a day off, and now I get to paint a whole room—pink, yellow, and blue. Oh, joy."

"Hey," Gabe said. "Don't rag on him. You were the brilliant one that was so excited about having a kid. Remember?"

"Well, no one told me I'd have to paint!"

A.J. laughed. "It's really not that bad. Won't take more than a couple hours tops."

"Not for you maybe," Jeff said, throwing his money in. "Me on the other hand will have to figure out how to get the paint where it's supposed to be and not everywhere else, which is probably where it will end up."

"I'm telling you it's not that bad," A.J. said as he tossed a dollar into the pile, laid two cards aside and took the two Jeff dealt him. "I'll even come help you if you're that desperate."

"Sure you will," Jeff said as he dealt Gabe a couple cards.

"I will. Just tell me when to be here."

"I'm in," Jeff said.

"Not me," Zack said, folding his cards.

"I'm in," A.J. said, and he looked at Gabe.

"Okay, I'm in."

They went once more around the table, with both Jeff and A.J. staying in.

"Nope," Gabe said when it came to him. "Too many for me."

Jeff looked across the table at A.J. "I raise you a dollar."

"I see your dollar and raise you another."

A smile of triumph slipped onto Jeff's face. "Call. What you got?"

"Four of a kind," A.J. said barely holding the smile back.

"Ahhh, no!" Jeff groaned. "Full house."

"Oh, darn," A.J. said as he happily raked the money to his side. "Don't look too heartbroken over there."

"Yeah. Yeah. Yeah," Jeff said mockingly angry. "That'll cost you a wall."

"I told you I'd help."

"I thought you said that so I wouldn't be paying attention."

A.J. laughed. "That too."

"Fine. Just for that, you get two walls. Be here at nine, and bring your paintbrush."

"We're going to try it," Lisa said over the phone wires as Eve sat near her fireplace soaking in the warmth. December was living up to its name. "At least I think we are. Jeff sounds less sure about this every time I talk to him."

"He's a guy. He just doesn't want to do the work," Eve said.

"Yeah, well, unfortunately he's it. I don't think I'm going to be too much help."

"Well, if you really need someone to come keep him in line, I could always round up my brushes."

"That sounds scary," Lisa said. "You and Jeff with paintbrushes? My poor carpet might never recover."

"And just Jeff?" Eve asked skeptically. "Your walls might never recover." The fire waved in front of her happily just as she heard the shouts in the background. "Uh-oh. Friday night poker game?"

"It's a curse," Lisa said.

"Sounds horrible."

"It is," Lisa said, but there was too much happiness in her voice for that statement to be taken at its meaning. "But seriously, you wouldn't mind coming to help?"

"Mind? I'd love to. Just tell me what time to be there."

Eve and Lisa were busy plotting out their strategy the next morning when Jeff walked by the room decked out in old sweats and a T-shirt fresh from his morning shower.

"I think we should use this as a base," Eve said, referring to the pale yellow. "The other two can play off of it."

One second and then Jeff poked his still-wet head around the corner. "Eve?"

"No, Godzilla," she said with a laugh.

"Lis, you didn't tell me Eve was coming," Jeff said, and Eve couldn't quite read the tone of his voice.

"She's better with color than I am," Lisa said off-handedly. "Besides she brought her sponges."

"Oh, great," he said slowly, but it was clear by the tone that it was not great. "Umm, Lis, you don't happen to know where the donuts are, do you?"

"I think they're still in the refrigerator."

"I don't think so," he said. "I looked there when I got up this morning."

"Oh. Well, maybe they're in the cabinet."

"I looked there too." A pause that stretched on a little too long. "Could you come help me look?"

Lisa looked up at him in confusion. "Now?"

He flashed a timid smile at her. "Please?"

Less than happy, Lisa sighed and walked to the door to follow him out. Eve tried not to read too much into the exchange, but every indication screamed that her presence was not welcome. She considered leaving, but Lisa had asked, and Eve hated to abandon her. Then she heard the whispers in the kitchen. Definitely not a good sign.

She remembered those whispers. Dustin was good at fighting so no one else heard. Apparently it was a guy specialty. Their intensity escalated. Then just as Eve gathered the nerve to simply leave, the doorbell rang, and the whispers stopped abruptly. Had there been a back door other than in the kitchen, she would already have been out of it. She could always claim a headache. It wouldn't be that far from the truth. A minute, two, and suddenly there were voices in the hallway. Unfortunately they were missing a distinctive feminine quality, and her nerves jumped to the surface.

"We were just looking for the donuts," Jeff said. "We'll bring some in as soon as we find them."

"Cool," A.J. said, turning the corner, but the instant he saw Eve, he froze. With his brown cap turned backward, pale green button down shirt over a tight white T-shirt that stretched over every muscle on his chest, and light brown pants, he looked incredible.

Eve tried to catch her breath, but there was no longer oxygen in the room.

"I'll just be... in the kitchen," Jeff said hesitantly, and he turned and took off back down the hallway.

They stood, looking at each other, and not saying a word for a long moment.

"Hi," A.J. finally said as he slowly set his long roller and paint pan on the floor.

She wanted to smile, but the bafflement jamming her brainwaves wouldn't let her. "Hi."

A.J. straightened, and a smile traced through his golden-bronze features. "Jeff didn't say you'd be here."

"Yeah, Lisa didn't mention you were coming either."

Slowly Eve rubbed one hand over the other, wishing she could wipe off the moisture there without looking totally obvious. A full thirty seconds he stood there, then his gaze dropped from her to the paint cans sitting next to her.

"That the paint?" he asked, pointing at them.

"Oh, uh. Yeah." When he stepped over next to her, she thought she might actually pass out. Electricity poured off his body as he picked one can up and read the printing on it, and although she wanted to back up lest she be irrevocably caught in its force field, not one molecule of her could move. She tried to refocus her attention where he was reading, but the pull of his face being so close to her would have scrambled the words anyway.

Her gaze snagged on the soft but strong features just a foot away. Somehow she had never noticed how heart stopping he was until that moment.

"You think that'll work?" Lisa asked, ambling into the room

behind them, and with one jerk, they both turned as if they had just been caught doing something illegal.

"Oh, yeah," A.J. said smoothly, and Eve couldn't help but think she liked that voice as much as she liked everything else about him. "It looks great. How were you planning on doing this anyway?"

"Eve thought the yellow would be a good base and then the other two could be sponged over it."

"Sounds good," A.J. said, glancing over at Eve, but it happened so quick, she didn't even get a good look into his eyes before they were gone.

"Donuts!" Jeff announced, sidling into the room with a plateful of food.

"Ah, the magic words," Eve said with a laugh, and the other three looked at her in surprise. Timidly she shrugged. "For A.J.," she clarified although it clarified nothing. "You feed him, he'll do anything."

Instantly two disbelieving stares hit her head on, and the one next to her sank to the floor and didn't dare look over at her. She dug her hands into the pockets of her jeans wishing she knew what to say to take those words back. "Umm... I just mean I gave him pizza, and he helped me move," she said, fighting to get out of the hole she was digging for herself, but that didn't help. Finally with no other option she dropped the subject altogether. "Sure, I'd love a donut." She reached over and pulled one off the top. For good measure she took a large bite. "Umm, that's good."

Jeff looked at her like she had lost her mind, and although Lisa looked much closer to laughing than shipping her to the funny farm, she certainly wasn't jumping in to help her friend salvage the wreck.

"You got chocolate?" A.J. asked from behind her, and Eve jumped involuntarily.

"Light and dark," Jeff said, offering the plate to A.J.

Just as Eve took another bite, A.J. reached past her to the plate and snagged a donut for himself. However, she felt the proximity of his hand near her back, and the room started swimming around her.

"Nothing like a nutritional breakfast," A.J. said as though she hadn't just totally embarrassed him, and she managed a grateful glance over at him.

"Are we going to eat or paint?" Lisa finally asked as Eve popped the final piece of donut into her mouth and wiped her hands.

"Let's rock and roll," Eve said.

"Tunes," Jeff said, setting the plate down and departing.

In seconds from the living room, the piano lead in for "Old Time Rock and Roll" started, and Eve had to stifle the laugh.

"Hope you don't mind Segar," Jeff said when he came back in the room.

"Great dance music," A.J. said, pinning Eve with a smile, and her heart soared.

"Okay, what's first?" Jeff asked, slapping his hands together.

A.J. and Jeff taped off the walls and then applied the first coat of yellow with the rollers as the women decided which other color would be best with the sponge patterns they had available, and then they oh-ed-and ah-ed over the wallpaper. Up and down the ladder A.J. went painting first the top by the ceiling and then the bottom by the baseboard. It quickly became apparent that Jeff was not kidding about not having much experience painting, so A.J. had given him free rein on the center of the wall while A.J. worked on the top and bottoms.

Two walls were finished and drying when the trips up and down started to take their toll on A.J.'s cooling system. "Man, you'd think with it being December it wouldn't feel like an oven in here." He shook his top shirt to get some air before wiping the sweat from the band of his cap with the hand holding the paintbrush.

"I could turn the air conditioner on," Lisa offered.

"No, I don't want the rest of you to freeze." He climbed down, moved the ladder and climbed back up again.

"They've got curtain material that goes with this," Lisa said to Eve, "but I'm afraid my sewing would be worse than Jeff's painting."

"Thank you for that comment," Jeff said.

"You're welcome," Lisa said sweetly, and Jeff looked up at A.J. and shook his head in exasperation. A.J. laughed as he returned his attention to the wall; however, the closer he got to the ceiling, the hotter it got.

"You know I'm not so bad with a sewing machine," Eve said. "I used to make my own clothes in high school. What kind of curtains did you have in mind?"

The lilt of her voice drifted over him, and suddenly A.J. wasn't sure if it was the ceiling or something else making his temperature rise.

"Something simple," Lisa said. "A valance in this material and then maybe a shade in the blue."

"That would be cute."

A.J. tried to wipe the heat off his forehead, but it was going nowhere. Finally in desperation, he set the brush in the pan and jerked off his top shirt.

"Nice and toasty up there?" Jeff asked as A.J. wadded up the shirt and threw it into the center of the room.

Instantly Eve's gaze chanced on him and stopped. He scratched one ear in embarrassment and returned his attention to the wall. "Yeah, something like that."

The yellow base was drying, and rather than waste time with the four of them making lunch, Eve had gallantly offered to stay and help A.J. with the blue sponge paint design. It wasn't difficult to see what Jeff and Lisa surmised by the offer, but Eve didn't really care. Ever since he had shed the outer shirt, all she wanted to do was get closer to him.

Far from the little kid he looked like most of the time, he now looked stunningly mature. The paint tray rested on the top of the ladder between them as she stood on one side and he on the meager rungs of the other.

"You were a painter, huh?" she asked as they worked the sponges randomly over the wall.

"Eighteen months," he said, focusing on the wall.

"Why'd you quit?"

"Too many hours not enough pay."

"So you became a paramedic for the money?" she asked incredulously.

"No, then I flipped burgers for a couple months until I moved out to L.A." He backed up to gauge the evenness of the pattern.

"Yeah, Melody said that. You were a drummer?"

He shrugged off-handedly. "I tried."

"It didn't work out?"

"I guess I wasn't good enough." He added two more impressions and nodded in satisfaction.

"I find that hard to believe," she said, watching him even as she put on the paint.

He descended the ladder. "Why?"

Without asking she picked up the paint tray and stepped off the ladder. She backed up as he moved the ladder to the un-sponged part of the wall.

"Well, you really must've liked playing if you went to L.A."

He set the ladder down and climbed his side before he reached for the paint tray from her. He set it back on top. "Yeah, well, liking it and being good at it are two very different things."

She climbed her side as her gaze traced over him. "Do you still play?"

He shrugged. "Sometimes. When I get the chance."

"So, do you have your own set?"

"In my garage, but I've got to be careful. One of the neighbors called the cops on me one time."

Eve snickered at that. "Now that I would've liked to see."

He looked at her incredulously.

She lowered her head and her voice authoritatively. "A.J. Knight, you are hereby under arrest for disturbing the peace." She glanced at him wickedly. "Sounds just like you."

"Hey. I'm a nice guy. Remember? Nice and quiet and well-behaved..."

"And totally insane?"

His face fell although a smile immediately jumped into his eyes. "Now who's being nice?"

She struck her best model pose. "Miss Congeniality, remember?"

He shook his head ruefully. "I'm really going to have to find out who stuffed that ballot box."

"Why?" she asked, tilting her head at him teasingly. "You wouldn't have voted for me?"

"For Miss Congeniality? Yeah, right."

She returned to her painting. "Well, then what would you have voted for me for?" It was a joke, but when she felt his gaze slide across her, the teasing dropped away.

"Most annoying," he finally said.

"Ah! Now that was mean!" Without thinking she reached over and whacked the side of his arm. However, the sponge in her hand was full of paint, and suddenly he had a pale blue sponge pattern streaking down his arm. Realizing what she had just done, she pulled back the smile and tried not to laugh. "Oops."

He looked down at his arm. "Yeah, oops." He dipped his sponge into the paint. Then in the next second he reached across and tapped her cheek with it. "Oh, oops."

Her mouth fell open in incredulousness. "Hey now, mine was an accident."

He shrugged as he returned to the wall. "So was mine."

"Oh, yeah, accidentally on purpose."

"You started it."

"That's no excuse." She reached down and got more paint on her sponge. With one motion she reached over and streaked blue paint from the bottom of his cap to his chin.

"Hey!" he said, trying to duck away from her, but not succeeding because he would've had to fall off the ladder to totally avoid her advance.

She smiled sweetly. "Oh, sorry. It was an accident."

"Oh, yeah? I'll show you an accident." He jumped off the ladder and grabbed her, easily lifting her off her side.

"Hey! Stop it! Put me down!" Like she weighed nothing at all, he wedged her under one arm and carried her kicking frame over to the yellow paint bucket that was still open on the other side of the room. When she saw it, incredulousness flooded over her so that she couldn't even fight anymore. "Oh, you wouldn't."

"You're going to learn, Miss Congeniality."

"No, I didn't mean it," she said, laughing. "I didn't. I'm sorry! I'm sorry! I won't do it again! I promise!"

"Oh, now she's sorry." Reaching down into the paint bucket, he pulled up a finger of paint and angled it at her face.

She looked at the paint on his finger. "You wouldn't."

"I wouldn't?" he asked as if he was questioning the universe. "Yes. Yes, I would." With that he wiped the paint down one side of her face and then down the other.

It was much colder than the blue paint, and she squealed as he wiped it down the side of her neck. With one more kick she broke free. Laughingly he looked at her in triumph. "Nice make-up job."

"Oh, yeah? How's this?" Her right hand caught him square

across the face with the blue sponge.

"Oh, oh…" He reached down to the yellow, and scooped up three fingers of paint. "You're going to pay for that!"

Her eyes widened at the seriousness on his face. "Is it too late to say, 'I'm sorry'?" she asked as she backed away from him.

"Way, way too late," he said, pursuing her step-for-slow-step.

"Because I am, you know," she said still backing.

"You are what?"

"Sorry. I really, really am." At that moment her foot met up with something she at first thought was the wall, but the second she saw the horror on his face, she knew it wasn't the wall. He gasped and put out a hand to stop it as Eve screamed and covered her face. However, his heroics saved only the ladder as the pan filled with baby blue paint slipped from its perch. A.J. lunged to catch it before it hit her, but he was only half successful, and after one bounce that managed only to cover them both with paint, the pan fell at their feet.

Ice-cold paint slid down her hair, down the back of her neck, and onto her arms. She gasped. "Oh, that's cold." She started laughing and couldn't quit. "Oh, it's so cold." With one hand she pulled her lime green T-shirt, now drenched in paint away from her body. A.J. was busy wiping the paint off his arms, hands, and the front of his once-white T-shirt.

"Hey, I thought you two were supposed to be… painting…" Jeff turned the corner, but when he saw the two of them drenched in paint, he stopped.

"Yeah," A.J. said, turning to the door. "Well, we decided the splatter look would be quicker."

Eve couldn't believe he could keep from bursting out laughing. She put her hand over her mouth ostensibly to wipe away the paint but it was really to stop her own giggling. A.J. tried to wipe the paint off his face nonchalantly, but the paint on his hand mixed with it and left two nice green streaks right down the edge of his face.

"What's going…?" Lisa asked, and when she turned the corner, Eve noticed A.J. take a slow backward step. Lisa put her hands on her hips and surveyed the mess. "What did you two do?"

"It was my fault," Eve said, stepping in front of A.J. "It was. I'll clean it up."

Jovial incredulousness crossed over Lisa's face as she looked at her friend, the paint streaming down her hair and onto the front of her shirt still dripping. "You look like those guys at the football games."

Jeff looked at Lisa skeptically as Eve and A.J. stood totally busted and knowing it.

"What guys?" Eve asked as she shook her hands off.

"You know those guys that have like nothing on except two beers in each hand and paint all over their faces." At that moment she could hold it no longer, and Lisa burst out laughing. She shook her head. "It's a good thing we didn't put you two in charge of something really important."

"No, kidding," Jeff said, realizing she wasn't totally mad and joining Lisa's laughter. "Now remind me again, whose good idea it was to put the tarp on the *whole* floor."

"It's a good thing," Lisa said as she reached over and laid a hand on his shoulder. Her composure was no longer hers. Every time she looked over at them, her laughter consumed every place on her face. "But who knew we'd have The Three Stooges over to paint for us?"

"You mean the Two Stooges," Jeff corrected, doubling over into her.

"Yeah, the Two Stooges," Lisa agreed.

Eve's composure broke before A.J.'s, and she reached up to push her streaked hair out of her face. However, she only managed to transfer more paint into her hair as she broke into laughter. A.J. looked over at her clearly not as comfortable with how funny the situation was as the other three. The second he looked at her, though, the humor hit him.

"Here, you've got some paint right here," he said as he reached over and wiped her face with his sponge.

"Where don't I have paint?" she asked, holding her hands out to the sides.

"This is true," he said, the guilt sounding in his voice.

Then Eve glanced at the wall, and splattered was a good word for it. The bottom third had light blue streaks all over it. "Oh, no."

"Quick get a sponge," A.J. instructed when he looked at it. Without question she grabbed her sponge. "Just go over the splatters." Oblivious to the fact that his brown cap now had streaks of blue and that they had an audience, he grabbed his sponge and started working on the wall.

In less than a second, Eve joined him. Every splatter she found, she covered with her sponge so that the splatters became only recognizable sponge patterns.

"We should've done this to begin with," she said. "Saves a lot of time."

"Here, I need some more paint," A.J. said, and before she could ask, he turned to her and dabbed his sponge against her back. He transferred that paint to the wall. Again he retrieved paint from her body and put it on the wall. "You sure make a good paint bucket. You know that?"

"Why thank you," she said, wiping her sponge on him. "So do you."

"And you thought they might be making a mess," Lisa said to Jeff from behind them. Eve glanced behind her as the wall's owners, still laughing, tip toed out.

A.J. touched her face with the sponge. "I think they thought we had messed something up."

"Imagine that," Eve said as she retrieved paint from the center of his chest. "See, I said I'd clean it up."

A.J. glanced behind him and then returned to the wall. "Thanks. I thought Lisa would blow a gasket."

"Lisa's cool," Eve said, getting more paint off his chest.

"She's scary," he said, leaning over closer to her to get paint from her shirt but more so his voice wouldn't have to carry far.

"Scary?" Eve asked incredulously. "I don't think she's scary. I'm more scary than she is."

He took a swipe across her face but stopped when he looked at her. "In that get-up, I'm not going to argue."

Laughter jumped squarely into her soul, and she shook her paint-streaked head. "You're insane."

His eyes shone. "I try."

Ten

"Oh, I love it!" Lisa said when she crossed into the room late into the afternoon. "Look at all these colors."

"Yeah, they kind of blended together," Eve said, stepping back to examine the last part of the last wall. "It's kind of a rainbow effect, huh?"

"It's great."

One more print and Eve stepped back for good. She had taken a shower before they ate lunch. A.J. was taking one now. Jeff had done his best to get him to take one earlier, but A.J. said that helping wasn't helping if you found every excuse you could to get out of it. Granted he would probably have to use turpentine to get the paint off of himself after all this time, but Eve hadn't minded painting the whole afternoon with Bozo the Clown.

"You don't look half bad either," Lisa said, walking over to her friend who had opted to keep her jeans but traded in her baby blue paint shirt for a cleaner one of Lisa's. However, she did notice that Lisa's shirt wasn't exactly new. Practical, Eve thought. Smart, and very practical, just like Lisa herself.

"Too bad I couldn't keep those blue streaks, huh?" Eve said, running her fingers through her damp hair. "What a fashion statement."

"Yeah, then everybody would be having paint fights."

"Sorry about that," Eve said. "It got a little out of hand."

"Oh, really? I didn't notice."

"Well, considering you had a hand in setting it up, I'm thinking you should have."

Lisa looked at her serious but worried. "We didn't. I swear."

"Yeah, right."

"I swear. Jeff about had a heart attack when you were here this morning. He figured you'd think we were trying to set you up, but honestly we weren't. He told A.J., and I told you, and well… it just kind of happened."

Although she knew it was setting a dangerous precedent, Eve really couldn't be mad at her friends—even if they had set up the day by dubious means. "Okay, but don't let it happen again."

"I promise, I'll warn you next time."

Their own clothes were in plastic bags when Eve and A.J. stepped out into the late December afternoon. He had borrowed a pair of light blue jeans and a light gray T-shirt from Jeff, and Eve was still in Lisa's shirt. Lisa and Jeff had begged for them to stay, but after cleaning up the mess, they really didn't feel like intruding any longer.

"So, what did you think?" Eve asked, looking over at him as they walked slowly to the cars.

"It's cool. All those colors mixing together. It's like a new pattern everywhere you look."

"Yeah," she said thoughtfully. "You know, I think that's why I don't have a favorite color."

His gaze jumped to her face incredulously. "You don't?"

"No, I just really like it when they can all fade and blend and work together to make something really awesome."

He smiled. "Yeah, forget conventional."

"Exactly," she said as they stopped at her car. She turned and leaned against the door. Then she laughed when she caught sight of the blue paint flecks still in his hair. "You missed some." Carefully she reached over to his hair as he watched her hand. She pulled a piece out and showed it to him.

"I'll probably be finding them for the next year."

"You? I washed this stuff four times, and there's still streaks in it." She ran a set of fingers through her hair.

"Tell you what, how about I make it up to you?"

She dropped the hair and looked at him skeptically. "That sounds scary."

"No, seriously. How about this? I can pick up a couple movies. You order pizza, and we'll all meet at your place say 45 minutes or so."

"Canadian bacon?" she asked.

He smiled at her. "Your choice."

"And who gets the prize for best timing in the whole world?" Eve asked as she carried the pizza not to the dining room table which was in clear view of the television but rather to the center of the living room floor between the two recliners.

"Me, of course," A.J. said, popping one of the movies into the player.

"What'd you get anyway?" Eve asked as she opened the box lid and breathed in the heavenly scent of fresh pizza.

"Mission: Impossible."

"Cool." She pulled one slice out for herself and pushed the box across the floor to him when he sat down next to the other recliner.

He hit the remote button. "Nope, no previews. Ugh. Hate previews." Without really looking, he grabbed a piece and pulled it out of the box.

Eve was too busy eating to really care what they were watching. As long as it wasn't horror, she could deal with it.

"Ahh," A.J. said, sinking back against the recliner footrest as he took his first bite. "This was a good idea."

"Yes, it was," Eve said wholeheartedly. "My white knight saves the day once again."

His gaze traced over to hers. "You're so lucky."

"Yes, I am."

"…and then we watched movies 'til like midnight," Eve said Monday evening when Lisa called wanting "all the details."

"And?" Lisa asked leadingly.

"And, what?" Eve mimicked. "And then he left."

"Well, did you kiss him? Did he kiss you? Did you like sit in the same chair at the scary parts or something? Did he really leave at midnight? Come on, Eve. I'm dying here."

"No. No. No. And yes," Eve said with a laugh.

Lisa growled. "It was supposed to be yes, yes, yes, and no."

Eve shook her head slowly. "It's not like that, Lis. I'm telling you, it's not. He's a nice guy, a wonderful guy. He's funny and sweet, and I have a lot of fun when he's around, but it's not like we're going to rip each other's clothes off every time we see each other or anything."

"Well, did you at least make another date? Like are you going to see each other again sometime?"

"Not unless somebody sets me up without telling me again," Eve said warningly.

"I didn't…"

"Oh, no. Of course you didn't, and Jeff had no idea either. Give up the innocent act, you are so busted."

"We really didn't plan that."

"Yeah, and you would be mortified if it happened again. Right?"

"Well, it's not like you're helping things along."

"There are no things to help along. I'm telling you. There is nothing going on between A.J. and me. We're friends. Besides he's like five years younger than me anyway."

"So? There's no rule that says you have to be the same age."

"And he's not the most stable person in the world either. Did you know he packed up and moved to L.A. to be a drummer?"

"It could be worse. He could've not come back."

"Lisa!"

"Eve," Lisa said, managing to stretch the single syllable into two. "Look, you dumped Dante because he was all love-marriage-family. Why can't you have some fun with A.J. who's not focused on all of that?"

"That's just it. I am having fun. But I'm not going to push things into something that's going to make us both miserable."

"Why would it make you miserable?"

"Because things are nice just like they are right now."

"Well, what if it doesn't make you miserable? What if it makes you happy?"

Eve pushed that question away from her heart as she looked up onto the center of the mantle. "Just don't push it, okay, Lisa? If things work, they work. If they don't, I really want to have him as a friend."

Lisa said nothing.

"Okay?" Eve asked again.

"Okay," Lisa finally said reluctantly.

"And tell that husband of yours the same goes for him."

The you-may-not-set-us-up-under-any-circumstances plan lasted until two days before New Years.

"Don't tell me you already have plans because I know you don't," Lisa said when the subject of their party came up.

"And don't tell me this isn't a set up because I know it is," Eve retorted.

"It's a party, Eve. Lots of people have them on New Years."

"Yeah, and I'm sure no one who lives in your house just happened to think up this brilliant party idea as an excuse."

"It's a party, Eve."

"Oh, yeah? Who's going to be at this party?"

"Just some friends, work friends, people."

"One people in particular whose name just happens to start with A and end with J?"

"It's a party. We're inviting people—lots of different people."

"How many people?"

"Ten, twenty. I don't know something like that."

"So, it's not just going to be the four of us, conveniently dwindled to the two of us?"

"It's a party, Eve."

The good news was, it was indeed a party. The bad news was, Eve only knew about six people there. She couldn't be positive that was planned, but it looked mighty suspicious.

"Hey, Eve," Gabe said, holding out a hand to her when she walked in the front door. "Happy New Years."

"Hey," she said, happy to see someone that she knew. She angled her way over to them.

"Wow!" Ashley said, appraising Eve's straight black cocktail dress with the spaghetti strapped top. "You won't have any trouble catching flies with that outfit."

"Nope, no fly catching for me tonight," Eve said, smiling. "I'm just here to have some fun."

"Here's an extra Smirnoff I got for Ash," Gabe said, holding a bottle out to Eve. "But she wimped out after one. She's my designated driver."

"Oh, no thanks," Eve said quickly. "I'm my own designated driver tonight."

Gabe shook his head slowly. "You two are way too kind to all those poor pathetic slobs who have to be out working all the wrecks tonight."

"I think I'd like to stay in one piece if that's okay."

He shrugged and set the bottle back behind him. "Suit yourself."

"Hey, what are we standing around here for?" Ashley asked. "This is a party, remember?"

It had been a long day at work. A.J. hated the holidays. The only thing worse would've been drawing the short straw and having to work that night. Not only was it the worst night of the year to work, he really wanted to go to the party at Jeff's.

He had fought with his hair for an hour, but finally gave up and grabbed one of his black ball caps. It didn't look too bad with the black and gray diagonal shirt—although it made him look a good six years younger than he wanted to. Oh, well. Tonight the fantasy would come crashing down anyway. There was no way that Eve would show up dateless, and the fact that he hadn't gotten up the guts to call her to ask her to go with him, pretty much solidified the fact that they wouldn't be together tonight.

As he climbed into the Civic, his mind traced back over his time with her, and he couldn't help but smile. For as prim and proper as she looked on the outside, there was a life force inside her just waiting to jump out. It wasn't hard to see—unless they were with someone else, and then she retreated back into her who everyone else seemed to think she should be shell.

In fact, he had fallen for that lie at first too—until he watched her throw popcorn in the air and giggle with joy when she caught one, or when she sat in the floor to eat pizza, or when she was covered with blue paint and seemed not to mind at all. No, she was not the same person that she showed the world, but he was sure the glimpses he'd had of her would not be on view tonight.

When he pulled up to the party, it was nearly 11:30. Had it not been New Years Eve, he might not have even bothered to come. Well, that and her, he thought as he raced up the sidewalk to the front door. He rang the doorbell and turned to look out at the assembled cars. The only one he really cared about was a little shiny silver one; however, before he located it, the door swung open.

"A.J.," Jeff said happily swinging a hand up to catch A.J.'s. "You made it."

"Sorry I'm late."

"Just in time," Jeff said.

Eve was beginning to regret her little speech to Lisa. Okay, so she didn't like the idea of being set up, but she was beginning to think she didn't like the idea of *not* being set up either. Her gaze jumped to every person who walked through that little entrance arch, and had it not been for Ashley and Gabe who managed to include her in every conversation, she might have just sat and stared at the opening all night.

"... my parents have this cabin out in New Mexico," Ashley said. "We wanted to go for Christmas, but *somebody* had to work."

"I'm telling you, win the lottery, and I'll gladly quit," Gabe said seriously.

"Anyway, we're wanting to get up there in January. Maybe over the long weekend. The snow's perfect this time of year."

"Oh, I bet it's gorgeous," Eve said, drifting away on the thought. "I haven't been skiing since..." Her gaze dropped to her cup. "It's been a long time."

When she looked back up, Ashley's gaze was soft and sad. "Hey, why don't you come with us?"

Eve's eyebrows arched skeptically.

"No, I mean we already asked Jeff and Lisa, and they're in, but of course, Lisa can't ski. It'd be fun to have somebody else to ski with other than the guys. Come on, Eve. It'll be fun."

"Oh, well, I really..."

"Just say, 'Yes' and come. You know you want to," Ashley coaxed.

"Well, okay, but..."

"Hey! Look who the cat dragged in," Gabe said, noticing the doorway.

Eve's gaze jumped to the door, and with one slam, her heart stopped.

"Hey, A.J. over here!" Gabe called.

She watched him walk across the room like it was some dream that couldn't possibly be real. No one should look that good, but for as good as his clothes were, the best part of his whole outfit was the smile in his eyes.

"Hey, all," A.J. said, catching Gabe's hand in the air as Gabe stood. "Well, you can still stand. That's a good sign, and you don't even look too plastered yet."

"I'm getting there," Gabe said, raising his glass. He wobbled slightly.

"Yeah, I can tell." A.J. glanced past Gabe at Ashley and smiled. "Hey, Ash. How's it going?"

"Hey," she said warmly.

Then his gaze floated over onto Eve, and he smiled softly but said nothing.

"Eve," Gabe said, leaning toward A.J. "Her name is Eve."

"Yeah," A.J. said as a smile exploded onto his face. "Seems like I remember that."

"Here," Ashley said, scooting away from Eve. "Have a sit down."

"Oh, okay," A.J. said, but he hesitated as if he was unsure she would want him anywhere around her.

Mesmerized but still partially conscious, Eve scooted the other way to make room for him. When he sat down on the edge of the couch, her breathing joined her heart in thudding to a stop. The shimmering gray material gracing his arm only inches away called to her hand, but she held one hand with the other and dared not let them move.

"You ever been skiing?" Ashley asked A.J., resuming their conversation without missing a beat.

"A couple times." He leaned back into the couch. "Some buddies of mine talked me into going to Breckenridge once. It was great, but if you ever get a chance to night ski at Keystone when it's ten below, skip it."

"Night skiing?" Gabe asked in trepidation. "Isn't that a little dangerous?"

"No, it's not too bad unless you lose track of the trails with lights," A.J. said.

Ashley laughed. "Extreme sports, huh?"

"Yeah, like extremely stupid."

"Well, if you can ski with the lights off, can you ski with the sunshine out?" Gabe asked.

"I'm not too bad," A.J. said. "Why? Who's going skiing?"

117

"Us and Lisa and Jeff," Ashley said. "But we're looking for a few to round out the trip."

"Cool. When?"

"We were thinking over the long weekend in January."

"Count me in," A.J. said without hesitation. "I'd love the chance to eat up some black diamonds again."

"Fab. Then it's just the six of us," Ashley said.

Eve wanted to protest, but she was having trouble breathing normally.

"Six?" A.J. asked, stopping on the number. "Who else is going?"

"Eve," Gabe said as if that should be obvious. "She's our designated driver. Isn't that right, Eve?" He raised his glass to her just as A.J. turned to look at her cowering into the couch and feeling her cheeks turn rosy. If she made a sound, she didn't know if it would signal confirmation or negation.

"Oh, cool," A.J. said although he didn't sound at all thrilled.

"Okay, okay, we've only got five minutes!" Lisa called to the room as she poured champagne for each guest. "Everybody get your glass."

Wishing her life made any sense, Eve reached for her glass of water and drank the rest of it.

"And Gabe," Lisa said, pouring him some. "And Ashley, and... oh, A.J. you made it."

"Yeah a little bit ago," he said awkwardly.

"Oh, and Eve," Lisa said a little too loud for Eve's senses. Couldn't the world just overlook the little fact that he was now sitting by her? It wasn't like she'd planned this or anything. Then again, it wasn't like she planned anything in her life anymore.

Jeff turned up the television as the ball in Times Square began its slow descent.

"Ten," everyone in the room said right together. "Nine, eight, seven, six..."

Eve looked around, and for all the happiness of being with her friends that should have been surrounding her at that moment, all she could feel was utter loneliness at the absence of the one who wasn't there. "One," she said softly, and she looked at the champagne in her glass. She should've just stayed home. This moment would've been much easier where she could've cried in peace.

"Happy New Year!" the partygoers yelled, and the noise was deafening.

If she could've disappeared right into the couch cushions she would have. The very moment of the anniversary of the first time Dustin kissed her. The thought tore through her and left her staring at the pale gold liquid in her glass. She had been so happy at that moment, so sure it would last forever. But it hadn't lasted forever. It hadn't lasted even a sliver of forever.

"I wouldn't drink it either," A.J. said, leaning closer to her. He wrinkled his nose in disgust. "Jeff's as good at picking out good champagne as he is at painting."

Eve looked at him numbly and tried to smile. "I guess you're an expert at champagne now too?"

"Yep, champagne and rescuing nearly airborne boxes—my specialties."

The middle of her heart dove right over that balcony as her soul crumpled over itself. "I'll be back." With that, she jumped to her feet and pushed through the revelers, fighting to find the back door before she broke down completely.

Concern ripped through A.J. like a machete. He hadn't meant to make her cry, and yet just before she jumped up, he had seen the tears. He stood and set his drink on the table.

"What's the matter with…?" Gabe started.

"Excuse me," A.J. said, rushing past them and following her. He paid no attention to the curious stares he got on the way to the door that led out to the little back patio. Just as he got to the back door, he met up with a bewildered looking Jeff and Lisa who stood in the kitchen, looking at the door that had just slammed shut. "I'll get her," A.J. said, pushing past Lisa who started for the door.

She stopped and then retreated back to Jeff's side.

When he pushed through the door and saw the outline of Eve standing there in the darkness, head down, shoulders slumped, A.J. took a breath and asked for the right words. Quietly he let the door swing back closed, and he shut it for good measure. Slowly he walked over to where she stood by the little white railing. When he was only a couple inches away, he stopped and took one more breath. "It's got to be hard sometimes," he said softly.

She sniffed. "What?"

"Trying to get through these things like it's not killing you."

Her head fell forward even farther.

"I know," he continued. "I remember Christmas the year after my dad left. Mom put up a brave front and everything, but it was still hard. I remember sitting there under the tree with all my presents, just watching the door and waiting for him to walk in. Somehow I kept thinking if I just waited long enough, he'd be there, you know?" A.J.'s breathing constricted around the words. It was the first time he had thought about that morning in years. "I'd always loved Christmas until that year, but it just wasn't any fun anymore. It hurt too much."

One inch at a time she turned to look at him, and tears glinted on her lashes. "New Years Eve was the first night he kissed me," she said softly. "It was more of a dare than anything. He was there. I was there. We weren't there together. We just happened to be talking when the clock struck midnight. But his friends started giving him a hard time about it, like it was New Years and he was sitting there not kissing anybody. You wouldn't have thought Dustin was shy, but he looked so scared, I thought he might seriously be sick." She laughed at the memory. Then her face crumpled into it. "But the second he kissed me, I knew…"

"That's so amazing to me," A.J. said as his soul absorbed the story. "I mean it's almost like fate just turns the page or something."

Her gaze snagged on his questioningly.

"One minute you're all happy to be on your own, and the next minute, wham it hits you that things will never be the same." A soft smile traced over his features. "Dustin was a very lucky guy."

She looked down at the champagne in her glass. "It's just so hard to believe that this year he'll have already been gone for two years. Where does the time go? I sit there sometimes, and I think there's no way I'm going to make it through the next minute. Then all of a sudden it's been an hour, and then a day, and then a year, and then… I wonder sometimes if one day I'm just going to wake up and it's been so long that I've forgotten."

A.J. shook his head. "Not possible."

"I read these books, you know, and they all say the same thing that eventually you have to let go of the hurt, but I don't think I want to do that. If I do, I might forget him altogether."

It was then that he reached one hand over and cupped it

across her back. "How many times have you relived that moment?"

"A million," she said without questioning which moment. "Every minute of every day, I relive it. I don't think a day's gone by that I haven't wondered what I could have done to make it turn out differently. If I just would've been there, if I just hadn't left, if I just hadn't listened to him and gone to Dallas, then maybe at least that morning when he left, he would've kissed me on the cheek trying not to wake me up and I would've pulled him back into bed, and he would've told me that he needed to get to work and how late he was going to be, and I would've laughed and told him he could go if he wanted. But I wasn't even there when he left, and now I'll never have another one of those mornings."

As her tears overflowed their banks, A.J. took her in his arms gently. Her grief slid down her cheeks making her sniff rather than breathe.

"And how many times have you relived the good moments— not because you regretted them but because of how wonderful they were?" he asked after a long moment.

She sniffed twice and backed away from him. "What do you mean?"

"I mean Dustin lived more than that one day. Surely there are a lot of days you remember that are about him living rather than about him dying."

However, her features were still baffled by the statement.

Gently A.J. continued. "Like what did he like to call you?"

She smiled at the thought. "Mrs. Knox. It sounds like an old lady name, but he loved saying that. To begin with, I got mad at him, but then I figured out he wasn't going to stop, so…"

"And what was his favorite color?"

At that, she outright laughed. "Anything but pink. Even I stopped wearing it after awhile. He always said it made him dizzy, and I figured he was dizzy enough as it was."

"Why?"

"Well, he was always doing this stuff… sneaking up on me while I made supper, twirling me around for no reason, pulling me up out of chairs so I had to sit on his lap. He just always seemed to be having such a good time. I figured it was safer if I didn't push him right over the edge." She stopped, adrift in the memories.

"Have those times gotten lost?" A.J. asked, tilting his head so he could look in her eyes.

Slowly she looked down, spun the liquid in her cup, and took a small sip. "Yeah, I guess they have."

"He wouldn't want you to be miserable forever, you know."

"No, he wouldn't." Her gaze caught his. "Are you telling me I have a choice?"

"What do you think?"

She smiled at him teasingly. "You always have a choice. Whether you make it or you let it make itself."

Her soft smile lit the corners of his heart. "And what is it that you're going to choose?"

She took a deep breath and exhaled slowly. Then she took her champagne and tossed it out onto the lawn. "Not that stuff. Bleck. That's awful."

He laughed. "Should we go back in and see if they have something a little less awful?" His hand came up in offering to hers. She looked down at it and smiled as she placed her hand in his.

"Lead the way."

As they sat on the couch long after most of the partygoers had left, the moments just after midnight slipped away from Eve. Peace had overtaken the sadness, and tranquility was now at the center of her heart. A.J.'s hand hadn't left hers since they'd come back in, but that didn't feel frightening or awkward—just really, really nice.

"We're thinking about flying to Albuquerque and renting a couple of cars," Ashley said as the six of them sat in the living room. No one was in the mood to clean the debris scattered around them. "It's only a couple hours away from the cabin."

Jeff looked at Lisa with concern. "Are you going to be able to fly?"

"Four days," she said with a nod. Then she looked at Ashley. "If you wait 'til the next weekend, I'm grounded."

"Then we have to make it that weekend," Gabe said as though his was the final word.

"I can get your tickets Friday if you're serious," Ashley said.

Lisa looked at Jeff. "I think we're in."

Ashley's gaze turned to A.J. who didn't appear to even be listening as he sat next to Eve who really wasn't.

"How about you guys?" Ashley asked.

A.J.'s head dropped to the side, and he looked at Eve questioningly. She looked at him and thought for only a moment. Then she smiled. "Yeah, we're in."

Their hands never let go until they got to the little silver car. Jeff hadn't even made his "you take care of her" speech nor had he so much as grilled Eve about calling the second she got home. They simply said goodnight and see you in two weeks, and then they closed the door. Gabe and Ashley said good-bye at the curb, and Eve noticed how A.J. waited to make sure that Ashley was driving.

Then they walked to her car and stood in the halo of the streetlight.

"Thanks for tonight," Eve said, letting go of his hand and wrapping her arms around herself. She really needed to start being more sensible about what season she chose to wear certain outfits.

"No, thank you." He pulled her into his arms and held her for a long moment. "You going to be okay getting home?"

"I didn't drink the champagne, remember?"

He laughed as his one hand rubbed across her back. "Yeah, seems like I remember that part." Then he backed up slightly and gazed into her eyes. "But you're all right?"

"Yeah," she said, ducking her head and then lifting it to meet his gaze again. "I'm all right."

For one miniscule instant, she thought he was going to kiss her. His eyes said he was. His body said he was. But then, at the last possible second, he smiled and backed away. "I'll follow you?"

She couldn't have stopped the smile. "You'd better."

When A.J. waved to Eve as she crossed off the freeway onto her exit, he wondered about the sanity of letting himself fall for her. The fact that she wasn't over Dustin yet was abundantly clear. What was not clear was whether she ever would be. He thought back to that night that seemed so long ago, and the images were right there in front of him.

"This suit has got to go," the other paramedic had said as he hooked up the IV's and fought to stabilize the lifeless figure lying face down on the gurney. The acrid smell of seared skin and plastic filled the air, and the motion of the vehicle under his feet swayed. "Hey! Keep it steady up there! This is hard enough as it is. Get that suit off."

The cold metal of the scissors wrapped around his fingers as A.J. started at one tear and worked as quickly as he could to remove the strips of charred fire suit that still clung to the figure. At that moment as he fought to maintain his balance despite the overwhelming attack on his senses, all he could think about was Jeff, sitting in the front of the ambulance, dazed, frightened, and overwhelmed with worry about his friend. At that moment there was no way A.J. could have pictured her sitting somewhere in a far away hotel having no idea how her whole life was about to change. Slowly the scissors worked until the right side of the suit had fallen away, revealing deep red wounds that seemed to not even be flesh.

Wailing. He remembered the wailing of the siren, and only now did he know that's how her heart sounded the moment she had heard the news.

"It's not coming off," he said to the other paramedic who was busy filling a syringe.

"Don't pull it!" The words still echoed through his head. "You'll make it worse. If it comes off, let it."

Instantly he watched as his hands let the crunchy material fuse back to the wound that was oozing blood. He did his best to find places that would just come off, but there weren't many.

"Cripes, how much farther?" the other paramedic had asked. "We're going to lose him before we even get there."

Nine minutes. The next day A.J. had driven back to the scene and timed it. Nine minutes from the front door of the apartment building to the emergency door of the hospital, and yet it had felt like a lifetime…

A.J.'s senses came back to the reality of the freeway, and for a moment nothing looked familiar. Then suddenly he realized why. He had missed his turn some fifteen minutes before. Shaking his head to force it back to the here and now, he pulled onto the exit and made the U under the bridge.

"How many times have you relived that moment?" some deep part of him asked. Tears clouded his vision as he pulled back onto the freeway. "A million," he said to the darkness around him.

Eleven

"Let me get that." A.J. reached out for the carry-on bag Lisa had on her shoulder as they followed Jeff to the line in the airport.

"I can get it," she said, but his hand stayed on the strap.

"Let him have it," Eve said from Lisa's side. "It'll make him feel important."

"Yeah," A.J. agreed with a grin, "otherwise, what's the use of having me around?"

For a second Lisa held the bag, and then she relinquished it to his care. He took it, shouldered it, and looked around the airport as the three of them joined their leader.

"I wonder where Gabe and Ash are," Jeff said, looking at his watch through the sunglasses he hadn't had enough hands to take off. Besides the sunglasses, he looked like a pack animal. "They were supposed to be here."

"They'll be here." Lisa shifted her weight awkwardly. "Gabe probably lost his goggles or something."

"Or something," Eve said with a laugh.

Jeff looked at his watch again as the black leather of his jacket slipped over the white button-down shirt. "Well, I hope they get here soon."

"They'll be here," Lisa assured him as she attempted to reach down to readjust her shoe. "Ugh. These shoes are killing me."

"Why'd you wear them then?" Eve asked.

"Because my boots don't fit anymore. Nothing fits anymore."

"Just think, five more weeks, and you'll be able to wear whatever you want," Eve said.

"Could we make those five weeks go a little faster?" Lisa asked as they all inched forward in the line.

"Let's not," Jeff said seriously.

"A little nervous, are we?" A.J. asked Jeff as he tilted his head playfully under the backward, black New York Yankees's hat he wore.

"Nervous? I wouldn't say that," Jeff said. "Petrified would be much closer."

Eve laughed. "Now's not a good time to decide that."

"Who decided?" Jeff asked, moving two suitcases forward and kicking at the other one. "She said, 'I'm pregnant,' and I passed out."

Both A.J. and Eve laughed, but Lisa shook her head seriously. "He's not kidding."

"Hey, guys!" a voice called from behind them, and all four gazes turned to it.

"Well, we were beginning to think you all chickened out on us," Jeff said, extending his hand to Gabe. However, Gabe's normally quick come back didn't come.

"Bad news," Gabe said, and Eve noticed that Ashley wasn't with him.

"Where's Ash?" Lisa asked.

"Her mom had a heart attack last night," Gabe said. "It was slight, but Ash is with her right now."

"Oh, no," Lisa said.

"Is she all right?" Jeff asked.

"They think she's going to be fine, but they're going to do a few tests today to find out what went wrong." Gabe's face fell even further. "So, I guess that means we're out."

"Crud," Jeff said, and he sighed, letting a carry-on slide off his shoulder. "Well, I guess that means trip's off."

"No, hey." Gabe held up a hand. "You guys go. I brought you the key and some directions."

"We can't go without you guys," Lisa said.

"Ashley insisted," Gabe said. "She said to go and ski a run for her."

Lisa looked at Jeff who looked back at her with concern and uncertainty. Neither Eve nor A.J. said a word. This decision wasn't up to them, and they knew it.

"It'll be the last time you guys get to go without bottles and diapers and pacifiers for who knows how long," Gabe coaxed. "Call it our early baby present."

"I don't know," Lisa said. "It doesn't seem right to go without you."

"Ashley will be crushed if you don't," Gabe said, pulling the stuff out of his pocket. "You've got your tickets, the place is yours until next weekend if you decide you don't want to come back." He held the items and smiled at Jeff. "Except you, Mister. You better be on that truck Tuesday morning, or you'll be on KP duty for a month." Gabe put the stuff in Jeff's hands. "Have fun, and ski a couple runs for us."

"Tell Ashley we'll be praying for her and her mom," Eve said.

Gabe smiled at her. "I will. Have a safe flight."

The four of them waved as he turned back for the door.

"I hope Ashley's okay," Lisa said as the ticket clerk called them forward.

"Me, too," Eve agreed as Jeff stepped up to the counter.

"New Mexico," A.J. said, settling into his seat next to Eve and across the aisle from Jeff and Lisa. "I've never been to New Mexico. Mexico, yes. New Mexico, no."

"You've been to Mexico?" Eve asked, surprised by every single thing she learned about him.

"Juarez," he said. "Once for like half an hour. We went to El Paso for this school trip. It was fun until two of the guys got busted for trying to smuggle alcohol back across."

"Two guys, huh? And one of them's name wasn't something Knight. Was it?"

He slid another two inches down in the seat. "Nope, I was a good boy. All I wanted was a knife that had a hollowed out handle."

"A hollowed out handle? What good does that do?" Eve asked skeptically.

"You put alcohol in the handle, and you put the knife in your pocket," Jeff said from across the aisle. "Two birds with one stone."

Lisa jabbed Jeff. "And how would you know that?"

"People talk. I listen," he said, shrugging innocently.

Eve's eyes widened in disbelief. "And you wanted one?"

A.J. shrugged. "I was sixteen. You want a lot of dumb things when you're sixteen."

"So, did you get it?"

"No, the chaperone guy wouldn't let me."

"Huh, smart chaperone," Eve said.

"Tell me about it. My mom would've flipped out."

"And the fact that you were going to wig your mother out never crossed your mind while you were thinking about purchasing this double-edged sword?"

"I just thought it looked cool."

"Well, remind me what cool means to you the next time we're shopping."

A.J. smiled at her as the plane taxied to the runway. "I'll be sure to do that."

"What do you think, two cars or one?" Jeff asked A.J. when they were standing in line for the rental counter. The women had decided to find a nice place to sit down and guard the luggage.

"I don't know. How are we planning on doing this anyway?" A.J. asked.

"Well, I had thought we'd go skiing one day and the girls would go the next, but that's not going to work. And I don't want to leave Lisa at the cabin without a vehicle."

A.J. shrugged. "Then I guess we get two."

"Okay. Two it is."

Eve wasn't exactly sure how the car thing had happened, but suddenly she was sitting in the passenger's seat of a Dodge Ram pickup watching A.J., who was sitting next to her, pull out of the Albuquerque airport as he followed Jeff in a little blue Camry.

"I just love the mountains," Eve said as she put her head back on the headrest and gazed out at the white snow-capped mountains in the distance. "It's all so fresh and clean and new up here."

His glance over was only that. "So, you've been skiing then?"

"Oh, yeah, we went on Spring Break right after Dustin and I got together. He spent the whole day pulling me out of the snow. I don't think I even got off the lift without falling that day." She shook her head. "It was awful. But then the next day, I stopped being like, 'Ahh. Ahh.' every time the skies started sliding. I did better that day. We went a couple times since then."

"Well, at least you had someone to help you. I had six guys going, 'Hey, A.J., there's a jump. Come on, man. Go for it.'"

Terror jumped to Eve's heart. "A jump?"

"It was really this little incline out of the snow, but it was enough to get you airborne."

Her eyebrows reached for the ceiling as her head came off the headrest and her gaze drilled into him. "You didn't jump it, did you?"

"Sure I did," he said with a shrug. "I had to. They were all sitting there watching me. Besides they dared me to, and I couldn't go back on a dare."

She laughed and let her head settle again. "On your first day you were ski jumping?" It was strange how wonderful it was to simply be able to sit and look at him.

"Well, I wouldn't exactly call it ski *jumping*. It was more like ski *crashing*, but hey, I tried it."

"You are crazy." Eve shook her head and looked out the window, feeling all the tension from the trip drop away from her. "Okay," she said, turning back to him. "What's the dumbest thing you've ever done on skies?"

He looked over at her skeptically. "You don't want to know."

"Yes, I do." Turning, she pulled her knee onto the seat between them. "What's the one thing that to this minute you really cannot believe you did."

His gaze squeezed into total uncertainty, and he shook his head. "You're going to think I'm insane."

"I already think that. Come on. What is it?"

With one more I-really-wish-you-would-just-drop-this-topic glance, he sighed. "I skied down the entire hill with a beer in my hand."

She looked at him questioningly. "That's not so bad."

"Buck-naked."

Her eyes widened in shock, and she collapsed laughing. "Oh, no. You're kidding, right?"

"Like I would tell you something like that and be kidding," he said as just under his cap flushed red.

"You...? Why would you do that?"

He shrugged, and together they both said, "They dared me

to."

Every time she tried to stop laughing, the giggles would hit her again, and she doubled over. He looked over at her and laughed. "I can't ski Copper Mountain anymore."

"I wonder why! Oh, that's awful."

"No, they wanted me to go down a black diamond like that, but there are some things you have to draw the line about."

Her hand came up to her forehead as she tried to stop the laughing. "I cannot believe you would do something like that."

"I don't think they believed it either. They didn't dare me much after that."

"Can you blame them?"

"I tried to, but the ski patrol wasn't exactly interested in my motivation."

"I can imagine."

"So that's my one dumbest thing on skies," he said. "What's yours?"

"Oh, man, I don't have anything close to that."

"Yeah, but surely there's something you did that wasn't exactly brilliant."

She ducked her head, and two strands of hair fell across her face as one image jumped into her head. With a push she strung the hair behind her ear. "I knocked the ski pole rack down in the rental place."

"How'd you manage that?"

"Well, I didn't exactly realize how long the skies were, and the guy put them on me and left to go get the phone or something. My ear cover thing was on the chair, and I was afraid I was going to forget it, so…they really shouldn't put those racks in the middle of the store."

"Big mess?"

"Uh, yeah, you could say that."

"Where was Dustin?"

There was only the smallest of pangs. "I don't remember. All I remember is that was the first time of the next hundred thousand that he picked me up that day. Let me tell you, those poles are a lot harder than they look."

A.J. laughed softly. "I can see you laying in the middle of these hundreds of poles, 'Dustin, help!'"

Sheepishness crept over her. "Oh, yeah. And I was trying to

act all cool and everything too. We'd only gone out like a few times at that point. He must've thought, 'Well, hello, Miss Grace.'"

His glance sideways at her made the center of her heart do strange things. "Funny, you don't look clumsy."

She rolled her eyes. "Oh, brother. You don't know me very well then. Once I get it, I'm fine—like roller blading, that's cool, but if I've never done it before, look out!"

Instantly he was interested. "You roller blade?"

"I love it. Almost as much as skiing now."

"So you got over the 'Ahh. Ahh.' point?"

"Heck, by the third day I could even stand up off the ski lift."

"Impressive."

"Okay, granted you were probably doing black diamonds by the third day…"

"Second," he corrected.

She looked at him in amazement. "Are you afraid of anything?"

"Haven't found it yet," he said.

"Yeah, I noticed." Nothing about her thought that was frightening. Somehow it was comforting to know he wasn't afraid of the boos in the night. "Does Jeff know what he's gotten himself into?"

A.J. raised his eyebrows wickedly. "I'm not telling him. Are you?"

"Hey, he deserves everything he gets if he goes skiing with you!"

The twists and turns through the mountain pass were enough to make her mortally queasy. "Are we almost there?" Eve asked as A.J. took one sharp turn banked by a drop-off on one side and solid rock on the other.

"How am I supposed to know? Do I look like I have a map?"

"You don't know where we're going?"

"I didn't think to look at the map, but that's okay. All we've got to do is keep up with them, and we'll be fine."

"Oh, yeah. All we've got to do… Does he know where we're going?"

"I sure hope so."

Eve pulled at the neck of her oversized off-white sweater. She had brought half of her closet, but she wasn't sure if she would have enough clothes to survive a whole night in a lost pickup. Thinking that discussing what happened if they got separated might send her anxiety mechanism into overdrive, she searched for something else to talk about. "Okay, how about this one: pickups or cars?"

"Define cars."

"Sports cars."

"Define pickups."

She really didn't have much expertise in that area. "Umm, this one."

"Probably sports cars. They really handle curves well."

"Huh, that would be nice about now." The acceleration of the pickup increased past her comfort level. "You know that speed limit sign said 35."

He looked down at the speedometer which read, 30. "Oh, good," he said, pushing the pedal to the floor.

"No. No!" She tapped one foot on the floor to keep her nerves inside her body. "Okay, I'll shut up now."

With one glance over at her, he slowed down and said, "M&M's or Crunch bar?"

"M&M's."

"Brown or green?"

"Brown."

"Isn't that funny?" he asked, shifting the position of his leg. "They're the very same except for the outside color."

"But they wouldn't be half as much fun without the colors." She took her mind and gaze off the road as they rounded another sharp corner. "If you could come up with a new color for M&M's what would it be?"

"Purple."

"Why?"

"I don't know. I like purple I guess."

"Purple, is that your favorite color?" she asked.

"I don't really have a favorite color. I like black, and red, and blue…"

"And purple."

"I like whatever's clean."

"And if nothing's clean?"

He glanced over at her. "Then whatever doesn't smell."

"Good plan."

At that moment ahead of them, the Camry slowed and turned left off the highway just in front of three large boulders. The gravel road it took didn't look exactly inviting, but A.J. turned, and they bumped their way up the first ten yards.

"Did Ashley mention how far from nowhere this place was?" Eve asked as the highway disappeared into the trees behind them.

"I don't remember anyone asking that question," A.J. said. "I just hope Jeff knows where he's going or we're going to wind up in somebody's lake."

"There's a nice thought."

The pickup was in a steady uphill climb, and Eve finally leaned back into the seat to keep her stomach with her. "I sure hope Lisa's okay."

"That makes two of us."

At a bend in the road, the taillights of the Camry came on for a moment and then it veered off to the right. A little way up that road, back in the midst of the tall pine trees looming in all directions, sat a cabin. A.J. waited a half-second before he turned the pickup and followed Jeff to the path on the side of the road. There was a driveway, but it was stacked three feet in snow and thus inaccessible.

When the vehicle came to a stop, Eve took a solid breath. She reached for her door handle and stepped out into the crisp late afternoon air. It smelled just like she remembered. Ahead of them, Jeff got out and stretched his back.

"That was fun, huh?" he called to Eve.

"Fun isn't the word I would use," she said as she walked over to Lisa's door. When the door popped open, Eve offered her friend a hand up. "Careful, it might be a little slick."

"Okay," Lisa said, pulling up, watching for ice, and looking around at her new surroundings all at the same time. "Okay, now I'm glad we came."

"I'm hoping someone thought to bring a snow shovel," A.J. said from where he had just slammed the pickup door. "This isn't exactly valet parking."

"Gabe's notes say there's one in the garage," Jeff said, swinging out of stand-and-stretch mode into let's-get-serious-about-how-we're-getting-inside mode. "You up for a little exercise?"

"Ready when you are," A.J. replied.

Jeff grabbed the key and the instructions from the dashboard of the Camry, and as the women stood at the car and watched, the men crunched their way through the snow. At places their feet slipped through farther than they had realized nearly pulling them all the way to the ground. Crashing into each other while trying to maintain balance they made their way through the snow. When they finally reached the cabin steps, both of them had snow up to the knees of their pant legs.

"This is the right cabin. Isn't it?" A.J. asked, looking around from his new vantage point.

"Let's hope so." Jeff worked the key for a second, and the door slid open. "Presto."

They disappeared into the cabin.

"How long do you think this is going to take?" Lisa asked as she wrapped her arms around herself.

"Long enough to know we should get back in the car," Eve said. She helped Lisa back in and walked carefully around the back to the driver's door. Once inside, they waited, watching the cabin for movement. "So you survived the ride?"

"I was beginning to wonder on a couple of those turns," Lisa said. "How did you guys do?"

"Good," Eve said, thinking back to the skiing stories.

Lisa looked at her but didn't ask the question in her eyes. At that moment A.J. appeared on the deck with a shovel.

"Ah, our white knight has arrived," Eve said with a smile.

"He's our white knight?" Lisa asked teasingly. "Oh, boy. Are we in trouble."

If she only knew, Eve thought, watching him. If she only knew.

Almost an hour of hard work later, the path to the cabin was cleared, and all four of them had made it inside with luggage.

"It's colder in here than it is outside," Eve said, shivering for emphasis.

"We turned up the heat," Jeff said. "It'll take it awhile."

The men transferred the luggage to the three bedrooms as Lisa and Eve searched through the cabinets, trying to determine what they would need when they went to the little grocery store they had passed in town what seemed like hours before.

"We're going out to turn on the water," Jeff said, crossing through the living room to the bedroom A.J. had disappeared into.

"Okay," Lisa said. Then she looked at Eve. "I think our first problem is what to eat tonight."

"That'd be a good place to start."

"Is Gabe always this organized?" A.J. asked in surprise. Everything right down to the hiding place of the flashlight was exactly where it said it would be in the notes.

"Him or Ashley," Jeff said as the two of them walked through the musty underbelly of the house to the water valve.

"Ashley," A.J. said.

"I don't know. You might be surprised," Jeff said. "People aren't always what they seem at first."

At the valve, Jeff turned, and it took two good jerks to get the valve unstuck. When that was finished, he turned to A.J. "All systems go."

"I guess we're going to have to drive back into town," Jeff said, clearly not excited about that idea as he stood in the kitchen minutes later.

"We should've stopped on the way through," Eve said.

"Yeah, but who knew we'd be stuck in the middle of nowhere?" Lisa said, and she winced and shifted position in the little stool at the bar.

"I can go," A.J. said, and the three others looked at him. "What? I've bought groceries before."

"Yeah, but how are your navigational skills?" Jeff asked, not entirely teasing.

A.J. shrugged. "They let me drive the ambulance."

"The man's got a point," Eve said. "Tell you what, we'll go in and get the stuff. You guys take it easy for a while. Lisa, you put your feet up, and Jeff, you make sure she does."

"We won't be long," A.J. said as he grabbed the list from the counter.

Back in the pickup Eve wondered about her sanity. The sunlight was fading behind the mountain, and the temperature had dropped since their last foray outside.

"It's a pretty nice place," A.J. said as he turned the pickup around on the road that was too small for the large vehicle frame.

"Once it gets warm and livable," Eve said.

"Wait until you get to those slopes."

"That's what I keep telling myself."

They bounced out to the highway in silence as Eve tried to figure out how he knew the way so easily. She was sure if it was her, they would've ended up in Arizona by the time she realized it was the wrong direction.

"Scale of one to ten, how good of a skier are you?" A.J. asked.

"One is what?"

"Can't get off the lifts without falling down."

"Ten is what?"

He smiled at her. "Me of course."

She shook her head incredulously. "Ten and a half. I'm better than you, but I don't do moguls, black diamonds, or ski jumps."

"Bowls?"

"Or bowls," she corrected herself.

"Ten and a half on blues and greens." He shrugged. "Not bad."

"I'm sure you'll be bored silly with me."

He glanced over at her, and his smile lit his eyes. "Not likely."

It was official. Eve couldn't have made it back to the cabin if her life had depended on it. Twists and turns and curves and inclines—they were enough to make her think that she couldn't even ride the trail much less drive it.

"You okay?" A.J. asked with some concern as they crossed past the three boulders and lurched across the potholes leading to the final turn.

"We're almost there?"

"Almost."

"Good." Pitch blackness surrounded the pickup beyond the headlights, so that all she could see was directly in front of them. "You think they're worried about us yet?"

"I doubt it. Jeff, Lisa, alone, cabin off in the woods? You do the math."

"True," she said although that didn't make her feel exactly comforted.

He rounded the last corner, and the lights of the cabin came into view. "Well, at least they left a light on." The pickup stopped behind the Camry, and he killed the engine.

Eve crawled out and shivered at the onslaught of the chill even through the parka that was now standard with her outfit. Quickly she grabbed two bags and headed down the little trail. Before she even got to the steps, he was right with her.

"Careful, the steps might be slick," he said, bracing his body behind hers lest she not negotiate the steps successfully. At the door, she slid it open and stepped inside, grateful for the warmth. Jeff sat on the couch reading, but he looked up at the sound.

"We're home," A.J. sang out.

"Shh," Jeff said, standing quickly and striding over to take the bags from Eve. "Lisa's resting."

"Is she okay?" Eve asked, not totally liking the tiny note of concern she heard in Jeff's voice.

"She's fine. Just a little tired from the trip." He set the bags on the counter. "So, what'd you get?"

After the dishes were cleaned, Jeff and Lisa decided that bed sounded better than socializing, and they excused themselves and retired to the large bedroom off to one side of the cabin.

"Party poopers," A.J. said, collapsing onto the sofa and grabbing the remote.

"Do you blame them?" Eve asked as she sat carefully on the other side.

He smiled. "No." Slowly he flipped through the channels until with only four flips, they were back to where they started. "Ah, simplicity," he said sarcastically.

On her side, Eve yawned and pulled one of the pillows from the couch so she could hold it to her chest.

"We've got a shoot 'em up show," he said as he flipped again through the channels. "News, another shoot 'em up show, or..." Although the next picture was dark, the sounds emanating from it clearly announced what that show was about. "Hmmm." A.J. tilted his head curiously and arched an eyebrow. "This could be interesting."

"Give me that," Eve said in annoyance. She swiped the remote from his hand and hit the power button. "How about we talk?"

"Talk?" he asked, wide-eyed. "About what?"

"About you."

"Me?" His eyebrows arched further, and then his face dropped in mischief as he ratcheted himself lower on the couch. "What do you want to know?"

"Besides skiing, what do you like to do?"

"Play the drums."

"Okay, besides play the drums and ski, what do you like to do?"

He narrowed his gaze thoughtfully. "Eat."

With one swipe she whacked him on the top of the head with the pillow. "Besides that, ding-dong."

Instantly his hands went over his head as if for protection, but the attack was already over. "Jeez. I didn't know I was being interrogated."

"Wait 'til you see what I've got planned next," she said seriously.

He looked at her with skeptical fear. "I don't think I want to."

"You're right. You don't. Now answer the question."

"What do I like to do?" He resumed his former position on the couch. "Hmm, I don't sing, and I don't dance very well, but I like the clubs as long as I'm not supposed to be impressing the girl I'm with. I like to play cards, but I lose more money than I ever win." He shrugged. "I don't know, mostly I like to hang out or do stuff I've never done before."

"Like what?"

His eyes lit from a spark inside him. "Ski diving. I'd love to do that sometime. Bungee jumping. I almost got to do that once but the guy who said he'd do it if I would backed out on me. Fly a plane, surf, go scuba diving, rock diving, swim with the dolphins, climb Mount Everest..."

"Climb Mount Everest? Are you serious?"

Slowly his head rolled to the side until he was gazing at her. "No, probably not, but I think it sounds like fun."

She shook her head in bewilderment. "You're unbelievable. You know that?"

"Why?" he asked, looking over at her. "What would you like to do?"

"Not climb Mount Everest. That's for sure."

The gold of his eyes softened as his gaze burrowed through her. "Well, what's your Everest?"

"Hmm." She thought for a moment, her mind sliding through doors she had thought had long since been slammed shut. "Water skiing."

Interest burst into his eyes. "No kidding? I love to water ski."

"You would," she said with a slight note of fear in the back of her voice.

He sat up and spun a knee around to face her. "You know what's really cool?"

In fear she shook her head.

"Wake boarding. Oh, man. That's the ultimate."

"What does that entail?"

"It's like snowboarding except you're on the water."

"On the water?"

"Yeah. You've got this board and it's strapped to your feet. You jump up in the air and flip around, and hopefully land upright. It's just so awesome." He spun around so that his back was on the couch again as he reveled in the memories. "You'd love it."

Eve's gaze dropped to the pillow in her hands. She had seen two opportunities to water ski pass her up—more to the point she had forced them to pass her up as she sat in the boat saying, "No, no. I don't want to." Truth was she did want to, but fear of either crashing or totally humiliating herself or both took her desire right out of the game. "It must be nice to have so much courage."

His gaze chanced on her again. "It's a choice." He shrugged. "You make the choice, the courage will come."

Softly she smiled, thinking that she wished it was so easy.

Suddenly he yawned and stretched his arms high above his head so that the arm of his basketball jersey slipped down revealing the tanned skin stretched tightly over the solid muscle. "Man, I am beat."

"Yeah, me, too," she said, taking his cue.

Together they stood, and he walked behind her to the little hallway leading to their rooms. As she stepped into the hallway, the light behind her snapped off plunging the space into complete darkness. Her steps slowed lest she meet up with something she didn't know was there. At that moment, she felt the warmth of his hand find the small of her back, and her entire body sprang to attention. Waves of feelings gushed through her with that one simple touch, and she had to beat them back down.

At the end of the hallway, she could just make out the tiny shaft of light from her room, and just as she reached the door, she turned to lean against the wall. "Good thing I'm not scared of the dark."

"Yeah," his voice whispered through the darkness.

Although he was no longer touching her, she could feel him barely inches away, and desire in a form she hadn't felt in a long time caught her breath. "Well, sleep well."

"You too," he said, and she felt him move away from her. However, at his door he stopped. "And if the dark gets too scary. I'm just across the hall."

"I'll remember that," she said, her voice fighting not to sound breathless. When his door closed, Eve's eyes closed with it and she exhaled. He was A.J. A.J., not Dustin. What was she doing? She couldn't be attracted to someone like him. He was young and out to have fun. He didn't know about the world and all the heartache it could hold. It was just being that close to a man again, she rationalized as she stepped into her own room. She could have fun with him—as friends and that was as far as she wanted this, or any other relationship to ever go again.

When she climbed into bed, her thoughts drifted over A.J., sitting there in his basketball jersey and reversed hat. He was such a little kid. Then her thoughts snagged onto Dustin, and clinging tightly to that image, she fell asleep.

Twelve

"You got everything?" A.J. asked as Eve, barely able to move for all the clothing she had on, climbed carefully into the pickup.

"If I don't, I'm not going back in there to get it," she said. "I may die of dehydration before we get there the way it is."

"Well, we wouldn't want that," A.J. said with a laugh. "Here, at least take the coat off. It's going to be a little while before we get there." He reached over and helped her remove the purple parka, wondering briefly at the color choice. No, she already had that parka packed long before they made their first trek up the mountain. When she was down to her stretched thermal shirt and her black ski suit, he appraised her. "Better?"

"I'll live."

"That's the spirit."

On the long drive to town, A.J. spent the majority of it willing his gaze to stay on the road and not take too many trips across the seat to her. Her black hair stood out in contrast to her purple ear warmer, and the white of her shirt made the tan of her face even darker. It was really too bad that friends was all they would ever be, but in his heart, he was grateful for even that much.

When they got to the slopes, they ambled their way up to the rental place and got in the short line. As they were moving forward toward the counter check-in spot, he leaned over to her. "There are the ski poles, don't get too close."

"I'll try not to," she said, and his effort was rewarded with a broad smile.

His selections were made long before hers were. First her boots were too small. Then there was a latch broken on the next pair. By the time they had all of their things together, it was easier to just put their stuff together in one locker than to find two empty ones that worked.

"You ready?" A.J. asked when she pulled herself up from the little bench.

"As I'll ever be."

The day was beautiful. Light, fluffy white clouds floated across a crisp clear blue sky as the ski lift swayed upward to the top of the mountain. A.J. had offered to let her do a few experimental runs on the bunny slope, but Eve knew he would be bored stiff if she made him stay at the bottom, so she opted to throw caution to the wind and start at the top.

"Look at that range," A.J. said in awe. "Man, how anyone can look at that and say there's no God is beyond me."

Eve's gaze transferred itself from the mountain to the angles of his face set in perfect contrast to the scene beyond. Even his headgear, that black cap turned perpetually backward seemed in perfect proportion. The only thing out of place was that comment.

"What?" he asked as he turned to her questioning stare.

"I didn't know you were into God and stuff."

"Yeah, me and God go way back," he said with a soft laugh. "I prayed one time that he'd help me find my hamster. Two hours later, I found him, and I've been on pretty good terms with God ever since."

She continued to look at him in amazement. "You know, I have the hardest time figuring you out."

"Why?"

"You just seem so young and carefree sometimes, and then it's like you're this wise old guru with all the answers."

"Nope," he said, refocusing his gaze from her to the approaching lift station. "I'm just a guy who likes to play life by ear."

She shook her head. "Well, you're sure good at it."

He nodded to the lift station. "Here we go."

One more moment, she looked at him. Then she too, got ready to dismount.

At the top of the first run, A.J. stopped and waited for Eve to come abreast of him. "Just like riding a bike. Right?"

"Something like that," she said, pulling at her glove.

"You want to go first or should I?"

"I think I'd better," she said. "I might not be able to keep up with you."

"Then lead the way, my lady," A.J. said, sweeping a hand in front of him. With a breath, Eve pushed off from the top and angled her way first to one side and then the other. Purple and black ski suit, black hair and purple ear warmer. It was a view he could definitely get used to. With no effort he pushed off and followed her down, thanking Ashley and Gabe and God above for getting the two of them on this mountain together on such a beautiful day—anything more would be gravy.

For two runs down the mountain, Eve chose the green trails so she could get her ski legs under her. Twice she had managed to get far enough ahead of him to be able to stop and watch him come down the slope behind her. There was something so easy about the way he skied. In her experience she was usually one, small miscalculation away from disaster, but to see him, it looked like there was no such thing as a miscalculation.

At one point she had stopped to watch, but when she turned around, there was no bright green parka to be seen. Then, like lightning, it flashed from amidst the trees, flying off of a jump that got bigger because of the angle he had chosen to take down the mountain. For one second fear clutched her chest, but then he landed like a bird on its nest and slid down right to her side, spraying her with the top powder when he stopped.

"Having fun?" she asked, barely containing her amazement or her amusement.

"Always," he said with a huge smile as he readjusted the sunglasses disguising the softness of his golden-brown eyes.

She missed those eyes, but something about the sunglasses was appealing enough to not complain too much.

"You ready for a blue?" He nodded to the sign just above her head.

"I guess so."

"We can stay greens if you want," he offered, leaning on his pole to do an impromptu stretch.

"No, blue's fine." She gathered her courage and sent up a

silent prayer that it was a blue more akin to a green than to a black. "You ready?"

That smile flashed across his features. "Your lead."

All day long they had managed to stay on semi-easy blues, which A.J. was glad for. She didn't have too much difficulty, but he could tell the tougher blues were testing the limits of her ability. More than that, the beauty of the morning hadn't lasted as just after lunch a cold front had moved in over them, and a light snow had begun to fall. With each passing hour the snow had increased until it was falling in regular patterns from the gray sky above. As they went down just after three, Eve's motions had become less decisive and much more determined.

He could see her right leg fighting to get swung around with each and every turn she made, and it was clear that she was getting tired. When they pulled up to a stop at the top of the slope overlooking the chair lifts at the bottom, A.J. noticed the tired tilt of her head over the ski poles.

"You about ready to call it a day?" he asked.

She fought with her clothing until she could see her watch. "It's only a little after three. We can still make a couple more runs."

The pros and cons of arguing ran through his head, and finally he decided to voice at least one. "I'd hate for you to be too sore to move tomorrow."

"Me?" she asked incredulously. "I'd be more worried about you. I'm sure Jeff's got his sights set on those black diamonds I've been avoiding all day." However, she was still leaning against her poles, trying to catch her breath even as she said the words.

"Then maybe we'd better stop for my sake," A.J. said, hoping his concern for her didn't sound in his voice.

"How about we go one more and then call it a day?"

He thought for a minute but decided if they took it easy, which they had plenty of time to do, one more run didn't sound so awful bad. "Your choice."

A playful smile traced across her face. "Race you." And with that she pushed off.

A.J. laughed as he followed her down. Beating her would have been a breeze, but it was more fun to follow behind and let her think she was beating him. At the lift, it was clear that the weather had already sent many of the ranks scurrying for cover as they waited only five chairs before catching theirs. Carefully he transferred his poles under his leg so he could have a few moments of rest. Without thinking, he swung his feet, heavy with the skis and boots back and forth as the ground virtually disappeared beneath them.

"Don't you just love snow?" he asked when they found themselves enveloped by it as the rest of life disappeared.

"Love it? Uh, no. There's a reason I live in Houston," Eve said, trying to get her glove off while holding her poles.

"Here." A.J. reached over and took her poles from her.

"This dumb glove's had something in it all day," she said, pulling the outer layer off with her teeth. "It feels like a pin right by my thumb."

As she worked to get the under layer off, A.J. looked out to where they had once been able to see skiers. "Man, it's really coming down."

"Yeah, no kidding." Eve shook the glove out, but it did no good. "Crud. Whatever it is, it's not coming out."

He looked at her as she shook the glove harder. "You know if you drop that thing, I'm not going to jump out and rescue it."

Her face fell in incredulousness. "I wouldn't put it past you."

"No, even I have to draw the line somewhere."

"Good place to draw a line." Giving up, she pulled the glove back on. "It's just going to have to hurt."

"No pain. No gain."

She looked at him in annoyance. "Like I said, you can be so wise sometimes."

"Hey, I try."

The lift bumped over another lift support with three jerks. Eve looked up at it. "I hate those things."

"Why?"

"I'm always afraid they're going to dump me out." Finally she got the outer glove back on. "And I'm sure you wouldn't bother to jump out and rescue me either."

"Glove. Eve." A.J. balanced the poles like a scales. "Glove. Eve. It's a tough choice."

With the back of the glove that was now on her hand, she reached over and whacked his shoulder. "Hey!"

Rubbing his shoulder, he lifted his eyebrows. "But that choice is getting easier all the time."

She shook her head as through the now solid snow, the lift station came into view ahead. Holding out her hand, she said, "Poles."

He arched his eyebrows once again. "I'm not sure it's safe to give them to you."

"And if you keep making mean comments like that, it won't be."

With a laugh, he handed her poles and retrieved his own from under his leg. "Man, I hope we don't run into somebody in this mess."

"Yeah, you and me both," she said as she prepared to disembark. "I'm thinking it's a good thing this is the last run."

"I'm thinking I'm agreeing with you there." The chair slid over the dismount area, and the two of them slid off, him going in a wide arc around the outside bank and watching to make sure she had a smooth path as well. At the trail edge, she stopped.

"You following me?" she asked.

"Right behind you."

They pushed off, and in seconds A.J. realized that the downward path of the snowfall looked much more horizontal and menacing when skiing into it. It took only the span of the first downhill slope for the iciness of the snow to start freezing the stubble that had appeared on his face since the night before. Ahead of him she slid side-to-side through the snow slowly although the thought occurred to him that he'd better keep up with her lest she disappear completely.

At the bottom of the first slope she waited just long enough for him to bottom out before she started down the next one. This one was far steeper than the last one, and she was having to make wider arcs so as not to crash. Down, down they went. Then just off to the right, A.J. caught sight of something that didn't look quite right—unmoving colors amid the white of the snow. Since it seemed to be on Eve's path when she made the next turn, he decided to ski directly over to it to check it out.

Expertly he pulled up on the scene and even managed to throw no snow across the two skiers making up the multi-colors. One was bent over the other, and it didn't take more than one look to know that whatever happened wasn't good.

"Get it off. Get it off," the voice of the skier still in the snow begged. "It hurts!"

"How?" the other one asked, panic flooding through his voice. "How do I get them off?"

With two clicks, A.J.'s skies were off, and he ran through the snow to the downed skier. Every step confirmed his worst fear. Without asking if they needed his help, he reached down and snapped off first one then the other ski of the person lying in a tangled mess in the snow. He knelt next to the person he now realized was a woman not so much because he saw her but because of her voice. She was too wrapped up in clothing to be visually identifiable.

"What happened?" A.J. asked even as he helped her roll up out of the snow, the skis no longer forcing her legs to stay in odd, unhealthy angles.

"She was coming down," the man said. "I think she got her skis tangled, but they didn't pop off like they were supposed to."

"A.J., what's wrong?" Eve asked as she skied up to the wreck.

"It hurts! It hurts!" the woman moaned, near hysterical with pain as she clutched her right knee and swayed.

"What hurts?" A.J. asked, his focus totally on her rather than on the two bystanders.

"My knee." She gasped and started crying when she tried to move the leg.

"Where on your knee? Show me where."

Weakly she ran her hand over the inside of her knee and yelped with pain the second she tried to move it.

"Can you stand?"

Fear jumped into her breathing. "It hurts so bad."

"Okay, okay," A.J. said, breathing for her. "We're going to get some help." When he looked up, his only clear visual was the snow. He assessed his options quickly. "Just stay here for a second. I'll be right back." Leaving her, he stood and stepped over to Eve who had panic carved into her face. "You're going to have to go down and get the ski patrol."

"Me?" Eve asked incredulously as she transferred her gaze from the woman in the snow to him.

"I need to stay here and help as much as I can, and I don't want her partner to go. She might need him. That leaves you."

"But what do I tell them? I don't even know where we are."

A.J. realized that in her panic, Eve was going to need clear instructions from someone she trusted. Like it or not, that person was him. Gently he took her shoulders and turned her just enough so that she was looking at him rather than at the woman still crying in the snow. "Ski down to the bottom. In this blizzard, you'll never find an emergency phone out here. When you get to the bottom, go to the first aid center, tell them there's a skier down with a knee injury about two-thirds of the way down on Bear Run. Tell them we're going to need an emergency sled to get her down."

Behind him the woman screeched in pain and then whimpered, and Eve tried to look past him. However, A.J. recalibrated her shoulders so that she was looking only at him. "Hurry, but don't do anything stupid. Okay? We need you to get to the bottom in one piece."

Clearly dazed, she nodded.

"I'll ski down with them and meet you at the first aid center."

Slowly she nodded. Then she closed her eyes, took a deep breath, and when she looked at him again, he knew she would be all right.

"I'll meet you down there," she said softly.

Carefully Eve turned her skis and started down the mountain, and A.J. watched her until the purple parka disappeared into the veil of snow. Then he turned his attention back to the other two.

"I'm A.J. by the way. A.J. Knight," he said as he knelt down in the snow next to the woman. "I'm a paramedic, and my friend is an experienced skier, so if you had to crash and get yourself in this pickle, you sure picked a good day to do it."

Through the tears, the woman laughed and then winced in pain.

"So, where are you guys from anyway?" A.J. asked, knowing that waiting while she focused on the pain would make it that much more excruciating. Medically, there wasn't much he could do, but that wasn't the only area in which he had skills.

"Oklahoma City," the man said.

"No kidding. I have a cousin who lives in Oklahoma."

At intervals as Eve descended, her mind stumbled across the pitiful figure lying in the snow, crying in pain. She knew they had to do something, but had she been the one to have to come up with the what, they would've been in big trouble. Then just as her mind threatened to slip off into fear and panic again, A.J.'s stern face snapped into her field of vision. He wasn't panicked. No, he was very clear on what needed to be done and how to do it.

Maybe that was why he wasn't panicked—he knew what to do. It was a possibility, Eve thought as she bottomed out on the next slope near the sign pointing greens from blues from blacks. Blues would be faster, but if she got on a really steep one, the seemingly extra speed would be canceled out by her need for wider arcs. There wasn't much of a decision as she turned her skis down the green trail. They were up there, and they needed her. His determination and confidence flowed through her so that suddenly it felt like she was virtually flying down the mountain.

There was a good chance that she had already broken her speed record today before this run, but this time how fast she was going didn't seem to be a problem. She was in control, and she was on a mission. The fear factor would have to take care of itself.

"We'd already decided it was our last run," A.J. said as the snow continued down around them. "But I think Eve just wanted to get me really sore for tomorrow."

"What's tomorrow?" the woman asked. It seemed that as long as she didn't move her leg, and as long as they had something to talk about, the pain was at least bearable.

"Me and another friend are going to do the kamikaze thing, but I think Eve's strategy is get me sore today so I'm not a lunatic out here tomorrow," he said with a laugh.

"Smart woman," the woman said with a wince.

He shook his head. "You have no idea."

When she crested the last slope, Eve didn't so much as slow down. The few skiers left at the bottom of the mountain made for very simple obstacles, and in no time she was down. Quickly she clicked off her skis, stood them next to the center wall and tromped over to the first aid door. A patrol officer stepped out just before she got there.

"We've got a skier down," she said, quickly striding the last few steps to his side.

Concern washed over his face. "Where?"

149

"Two-thirds down Bear Run on the right if you're coming from the top."

"What kind of injury?"

"Knee, and it's pretty bad. They're going to need help getting her down."

The patrolman nodded and stepped off to the side to grab a phone. The confidence dropped away from her as Eve wrapped her arms around herself and looked up at the mountain, now completely invisible in the snow. "God, please help them."

"A teacher?" A.J. asked, wishing he could look at his watch, but knowing that would destroy what small hold he had built on the situation. "What do you teach?"

"Second grade math," the woman, who he had long before learned was Gayle Everett from Oklahoma City, said. Since Eve's departure, he had learned that Gayle was relatively new to skiing. She'd only been on blue trails three times. She had two small children at home. Her husband's name was Gregg and he had only been skiing one day—this was her brilliant idea. They were finished for this trip as soon as they made it down this time. So much for that.

"Whoa. You are a real thrill seeker," A.J. said. "Forget black diamonds—second graders would be enough for me. How many kids do you have at a time?"

"Between 20 and 25, but I have five different classes a day."

"You must be exhausted by the time you get home."

"Sometimes," she said, as A.J. heard the faint sounds of the snowmobile. He waited a moment to decide which trail they were on. Then Gayle heard it and looked up the mountain. "They're here, huh?"

He smiled at her. "Sounds like it." He stood as the patrol pulled up.

"What happened?" the patrol asked as A.J. stepped over to shake his hand.

"Knee injury. It's probably twisted pretty good. The skis didn't pop off."

The patrol looked at him questioningly.

"A.J. Knight, I'm a paramedic from Houston. I just happened to come across them."

"Oh," the ski patrol person said, and then he zeroed in on his patient as he stepped past A.J.

It was then that A.J. noticed Gregg standing helplessly off to the side. As the ski patrolman started asking Gayle questions, A.J. stepped over to Gregg and held out a hand. Gregg never really looked at A.J. He kept his gaze on the figure in the snow.

"Thanks for stopping," Gregg said as he shook A.J.'s hand. "I didn't know what we were going to do."

"They'll be bringing the sled pretty soon," A.J. said, preparing Gregg for the next step in what A.J. knew would be a terribly long afternoon for them from this point forward. "They ski pretty fast when they take somebody down. Would you like me to ski with them or with you?"

"I'll be fine, but would you mind staying with Gayle?" Gregg said. "I'd hate for her to be alone when she gets to the bottom."

A.J. nodded. "Not a problem."

People would walk past Eve into the warmth of the center, but she was stationed outside at the corner of the building, and until they came down, she wasn't moving. For a while the snow lightened, and she prayed that they would be coming soon. She wondered how long it took the patrol to find them and if they had already. Alternately she would think about the woman and then about A.J.

How he was able to stay so calm, she couldn't quite tell. Had it been just her, she would probably have freaked out. However, every time her spirit dipped toward freak-out mode, his voice slid through her, calm and in perfect control. "Hurry, but don't do anything stupid." Somewhere in the middle of her, that picture met up with the one of him, minus clothes skiing breakneck for the bottom. He knew the depths of stupid, and yet, when it counted, he seemed far older than most people twice his age. The kid and the guru, her mind said again just as through the dense snow, the figure of the ski patrol became visible.

Instantly Eve straightened from her position, trying to make out the green parka as well. It took less than another second, and she saw it too. Breath returned to her body. Swishing side-to-side they sliced their way down to the flat place and then trekked over to the little barn next to the first aid center.

"We're almost there, Gayle," A.J. said even as he judged his speed with regard to the ski patrol's as they negotiated the final flat spot. "We're going to go into a little barn thing so we won't have to fight the snow." His commentary had started at the top and had not stopped all the way down even though he wasn't even sure that she could hear him. "That second hill was fun, huh? Whew. They ought to put you on the bobsled team after that one."

The little barn was dim and difficult to see in at first when they entered it, but A.J. fought through the darkness so that when they began to unbuckle her, he was the first to see her. He smiled. "Hey, you look like a mummy."

"Gee, thanks," she said obviously fighting off the pain. "These straps are killing my legs."

"And I'm sure the rest of the sled's like a four-star Marriott bed," A.J. said as the patrolman worked to unbuckle her. "Okay, Gayle, you know how you got in that thing? Well, now we're going to have to get you out of it."

She looked at him as if she'd rather be boiled alive. "That four-star bed is looking better all the time."

"Yeah, I bet."

The last buckle was off, and A.J. reached down for her hand as the ski patrolman assisted to make sure she didn't fall. A.J. could tell she was in a great deal of pain, but she only whimpered. With her arm tucked under his, she hopped two steps.

"It's right through here," the patrolman said, leading them into a bright yellow room.

Once inside a nurse directed them to a bed, and A.J. helped Gayle to it. Leaning against the bed, she slowly unwrapped herself from the outer clothing and the boots just as an anxious-looking Eve walked up.

"Gregg's going to be coming down," A.J. said, focusing on Gayle. "I'll go outside and make sure he gets here okay. This is Eve, she'll stay with you until I get back." When he looked at Eve, there were questions in her eyes, but she voiced none of them. As he passed her, he laid a hand on her arm. "I'll be right back."

"I'll hold you to that."

The clock in the base of the hill square was edging it's way to 4:30 when skis and poles in hand, they tromped their way off of the mountain.

"You think she's going to be okay?" Eve asked.

"Six months of great physical therapy fun, but she'll be all right," A.J. said, suddenly sounding very tired.

Eve smiled at him. "Bet you didn't think you'd be working on your vacation."

"That's part of it," he said with a slight shrug as they got to the steps leading down to the rental store. They retrieved their things from the locker, returned Eve's items, and stored A.J.'s. As they walked out to the parking lot, the snow had thinned so that visibility was much improved.

In her heart, Eve had something to tell him that felt more real than anything had in a very long time. Gently she let her hand brush across his, but when he didn't respond, she took hold of his hand, liking the strength she found there. "I'm glad you were up there with me today."

He looked over at her in surprise and confusion. Then his gaze dropped to the slushy snow at their feet.

"I would've fallen apart without you," she said honestly as she tried to look at more than his profile. However, his gaze stayed down and the best she could see was half of his cap, the sunglasses, and the edge of his face. "They were lucky to have you there too."

Reluctantly he glanced at her. "I didn't have a choice."

"You always have a choice," she said purposefully swinging her steps into his. "Remember?"

He smiled at her shyly. "Yeah, seems like I remember that part."

They reached the pickup, and A.J. went to her side to help her in. Once inside Eve's hand suddenly felt cold without his there around it. When he jumped in on his side, he whipped the sunglasses off and threw them to the dash before he looked over at her with playful eyes. "What do you say we go get a couple movies?"

"Either that or I get to interrogate you again," she said, falling deftly in step with his cue.

"Movies. Definitely movies."

Thirteen

The farther up the mountain toward the cabin they went, the more A.J. realized they should have taken the car. It wasn't that the car would've been better for them, but if Jeff had needed a vehicle, he and Lisa should've had the pickup. Without alerting Eve to the small seed of worry in his heart, he tried to keep the conversation light. She had been through enough trauma without worrying about something that probably wasn't even an issue.

"So, how sore are you going to be?" A.J. asked, glancing over at her.

"Not too bad, except for this puncture wound in my hand." She looked at her hand with concern.

"Let me see," he said. Without hesitation, she reached her hand across the seat into his line of vision. True concern for the skinned gash drove into him. "Your glove did that?"

"I told you it hurt," she said as she pulled her hand back to examine it.

"Yeah, but you didn't tell me it was eating right through your hand."

"I tend to underestimate these things," she said.

"I can tell. When we get back to the cabin, I bet they have some first aid stuff or something. I'll get you fixed right up."

Her eyes twinkled at him. "Ah, my own personal doctor."

"A.J., your faithful white knight, at your service."

She let her hand drop to her leg as she leaned back tiredly on the headrest. "How much longer?"

"A good twenty minutes," he said, having timed their descent by the clock on the dashboard. "Why don't you close your eyes and take a little nap?"

"I might just do that," she said, and her voice was already fading out.

Careful not to jar her with the sound, A.J. reached down and flicked on the CD he had brought and put in the stereo. It hadn't been played yet because until now, he just liked talking to her more than listening to music. The first strains of music filled the pickup which was winding its way slowly up the gray-tinged highway. Unconsciously his fingers caught the beat of the drums, and they beat it out on the steering wheel.

Had it not been for the dull concern that Jeff and Lisa might need some transportation, A.J. would've been perfectly happy to drive forever with Eve's beautiful eyes closed peacefully at his side. It was all he now asked from the universe.

"Is this going to sting?" Eve asked with concern as they stood together in the tiny bathroom doctoring her hand.

"A little," A.J. said seriously. Carefully he dumped the peroxide over the wound and into the sink.

Instantly Eve jumped back even as he held her wrist steady. "Ow!"

"I said a little."

She shook her hand even in his to get the stinging to stop. "A lot! A lot!"

"You have a high pain threshold, huh?" he asked teasingly.

"Yeah, and you have a propensity for lying." She stopped shaking her hand.

"One more," he said, holding the bottle over her hand. Quickly he dumped the liquid, and she started hopping from foot to foot again even as he held her wrist.

"The next time, I'm not calling you."

"The next time I'll bring anesthetic."

"Good plan."

With the cut now fully cleaned, A.J. grabbed the wound cream from the cabinet and applied some. Then with a rip through his teeth, he opened an extra-large Band-Aid and placed it on her hand. "All done."

Instinctively she pulled the hand up by her heart. "And how much will that cost me?"

"One pizza and movie night. Your choice of venue," he said as a broad smile slipped onto his face.

"That doesn't surprise me," she said with a laugh. "You'll do just about anything for food."

He laughed as he started to hand her the gloves. Then he stopped "What was in this thing anyway?" Carefully, he turned the glove inside out and examined the black material by the thumb. He couldn't see anything, so he rubbed his thumb across it. Immediately something jabbed into him. It was then that he realized what it was. "This nylon thread's broken." Quickly he reached into the first aid kit and pulled out the little scissors. With one snip, he set it back on the sink. He ran his thumb back over the material and smiled. "All better." He handed the glove to her.

"I guess this means I get to supply the Cheetos, too."

"Hey, a trade's a trade."

She laughed as he backed up far enough for her to cross in front of him and out the door. However, he stayed just long enough to clean up the medical supplies and put everything back together. With a snap of the light, he left the bathroom and went down the hall to join the others who were congregated in the kitchen.

"A.J. was great," Eve was saying as his steps slowed toward the end of the hallway. "I'm afraid I would've fallen apart."

"Oh, you never know," Jeff said as he worked to put the finishing touches on supper. "You might be more helpful than you think."

As A.J. walked into the room, Eve held her hand out to him from the little stool where she sat by the bar. Although the gesture would've seemed perfectly natural had it just been the two of them, with Jeff and Lisa there to analyze it, it felt anything but. Nonetheless, he crossed the room and took Eve's outstretched hand so that he could stand behind her. With no pretense she held onto his hand and leaned back into his chest.

"Well, I don't want to find out. I'm just glad he was there," Eve said, and when she looked up into his eyes, his heart turned over.

"How was your day?" A.J. asked, trying to turn the conversation away from him and Eve.

"Good," Jeff said. "Very relaxing for a change."

"No 15 million phone calls," Lisa agreed, taking a sip of the apple cider in her cup. "I think I could stay here forever."

"Nope, just through next weekend," Eve said, tugging A.J.'s arm around her shoulder and over her body. "Then Gabe will come kick us out, remember?"

Lisa shook her head. "I can't even stay that long or we'll have to drive back, and I don't think Jeff wants to put up with me in a car that long."

"Put up with you?" Jeff asked, choosing his words carefully. "I wouldn't call it that."

Slowly Lisa took a sip. "Yes, you would. You're just too afraid to say it."

"Smart," Jeff said, tapping his head with the handle of the spoon. "They call it being smart."

A.J. felt Eve laugh.

"They call it being married," Eve corrected.

Jeff pointed the spoon at her. "You got it."

A.J.'s gaze traveled down to her. It was like holding a piece of his soul close, and for a moment he was afraid the word might send her skittering from him. However, she pulled his arm tighter around her, and he didn't move to protest.

"So, how was the snow?" Jeff asked.

"Great powder," A.J. said. "If it keeps snowing all night, we should have perfect snow tomorrow."

"Too bad Gabe couldn't come," Jeff said as he banged the spoon against the side of the pan. "He's going to be sorry he missed this."

"Yeah, I hope Ashley's mom is doing all right."

"You know, we brought our cell phone," Jeff said. "We could always call them if there's a tower within shooting distance of here."

"Hey, I've got mine in my suitcase, too," Eve said as though she had just thought about it. "I could go get it."

"After supper," Jeff said. "This is ready."

"Cool. I'm starving," A.J. said.

"And we're all so surprised by that," Eve said with a laugh.

He grinned down at her. "Hey, you're the one who only let me have 15 minutes to eat lunch."

"Ah." Eve rubbed her hand up and down his arm, causing

chill bumps to crawl their way up his spine. "Poor baby. Don't you feel sorry for him?"

Lisa looked at Eve, and they laughed as Lisa said, "No."

"Anybody want some popcorn?" A.J. asked, holding the giant serving bowl over Jeff and Lisa who sat together on the couch fast-forwarding through the opening previews of the movie A.J. and Eve had brought.

"Sure," Jeff said as he reached up for the bowl, but A.J. yanked it away.

"Hey! I said *some*."

"He offers and then he yanks it away." Jeff shook his head. "Indian giver."

"And who's surprised?" Lisa asked as A.J. turned from the couch and met Eve returning fresh from her shower.

Her hair was pulled up in a high ponytail although straggled down her face were the pieces that hadn't made it into the ponytail. In a white tank top covered by a gray and blue patchwork button down shirt that she hadn't bothered to button and fitted gray jeans, she looked like she was planning to go out to some club rather than simply sit around and watch movies.

"Surprised about what?" Eve asked, folding herself onto the ground next to one of the chairs as A.J. went into the kitchen and tried not to watch her figure as she moved.

"A.J.'s being stingy with the food," Lisa said.

"And you've been around him how long?" Eve asked, laughing so that even fifteen feet away in the kitchen A.J.'s heart tripped forward a step.

"I didn't say you couldn't have *any*," A.J. said, coming back over with two more bowls. "I just said you couldn't have *mine*." He dumped a good amount of popcorn into each of the two bowls and handed them over the couch. Then he took the big bowl and swung a leg over Eve so he could sit down in the chair that she was sitting in front of. Carefully he set the bowl next to Eve and took a handful.

She took his cue and grabbed some for herself. Playfully she threw a piece in the air and leaned over to catch it, but it landed next to his foot. He leaned over her shoulder to get some more popcorn.

"Nice shot," he whispered softly.

Her gaze slipped back to his, and suddenly his soul was spinning through the depths of her eyes. She didn't say anything. Her smile made words unnecessary as she threw another piece of popcorn in her mouth.

"Sure, he won't share with us, but he'll share with her," Jeff said as if he was annoyed although there was too much happiness behind his tone to think that he really was.

Eve's gaze snapped away from A.J.'s although it left only in the physical realm. In his memory, it was still right there.

"What are you jealous?" Eve asked Jeff just as Lisa landed an elbow in the soft part of his stomach.

"I… was just saying…" Jeff started, but Lisa cut him off.

"Just be quiet and eat your popcorn."

Jeff's eyebrows arched upward. "It was a joke."

"The movie's starting," A.J. said, willing Jeff to take the women's advice and shut up. He really should've gotten Eve her own bowl. Somehow that simple thought hadn't occurred to him. Once more he reached down and took a handful of popcorn, but this time he was extra careful not to touch her or in any other way give the two people across the way reason to give them a hard time.

"Oh, and before you say anything, A.J. picked this one, so it's not my fault," Eve said, and when she reached down for more popcorn, her arm brushed across the loose material of his pants. Heat ripped through him. He couldn't be sure if she had done it on purpose or not, but it really didn't matter, that one brush brought his breath to a standstill.

"Great. Now you tell us," Lisa said dramatically.

"Fair warning," Eve said with a shrug as she munched on the popcorn.

A.J. wanted to say something in his defense, but his brain could concentrate on nothing other than Eve's shoulders inches from his leg and likely to touch him again at any second. He shrunk back in the chair, hoping the others would drop it, and knowing there wasn't a single thing he could say that wouldn't get him in deeper than he already was.

At that moment Jeff caught A.J.'s gaze without the other two noticing, and Jeff's smirk said far too much. Whether that was the original plan or not, he was in this thing far deeper than he knew he should be. A.J. knew it. Jeff obviously knew it. It was hope only that kept Lisa on the side of not knowing, and Eve was a question A.J. couldn't even allow his brain to consider.

It would've been nice to just ask her, but that option was fraught with more peril than it seemed. If she wasn't interested, he could ruin the friendship. If she was interested but couldn't because of Dustin, that might throw A.J. into a tailspin of doubt and uncertainty that he might never recover from. And then there was the possibility his heart seemed most concerned about, what if she was interested and ready? No part of him was sure he was. More than that, there were things she didn't know about him, things he couldn't tell her. The whole thing was a lose-lose-lose proposition. To his way of thinking, it was far better to just not look too closely at it, and maybe it would all quietly go away.

His attention snapped back when the other three burst out laughing. Thankfully he had seen this movie several times before, so he knew they were laughing at the movie and not at him. Nonetheless, he was sure they would in fact be laughing at him if they could hear the thoughts running through his head. It was silly, ludicrous really, that he could ever have even a chance with Eve. Fighting that thought away from his soul, his gaze fell to his hands and brushed across the loose spirals of black waves inches away.

She was his friend, and that was enough.

"I don't think I've ever laughed so hard," Eve said as she lay on the floor, looking up at the ceiling. Her hands lay across her stomach as her body wound down after the long day. In the chair looking down at her A.J. sat, and at that moment she was immensely glad that he had been there to share the day with her. "That goofy lady selling squirrels. You... should... have... bought... a... squirrel..." The memory of the movie scene brought the laughter back to her. "Man, I knew they were in trouble when they didn't buy that squirrel right away."

Gazing down at her, he looked so serious. "So you liked the movie?"

"Yeah, you don't have such bad taste after all," Eve said teasingly as she let her hand drop over to his ankle.

"Well, thank you very much." He tilted his head, and slowly his gaze became even more serious. "I had fun today."

"So did I," she said, exhaling so that everything in her relaxed into a peacefulness she hadn't felt in months.

However, the intensity of his gaze dragged concern to her.

"Sorry about before," he finally said softly as he glanced at the closed door Lisa and Jeff had disappeared into.

Eve's heart fell with concern for the sad regret in his eyes. "What before?"

His gaze snapped from the door to hers and then landed on his hands. "I didn't mean for them to think... to make you... I should've thought farther than that."

A moment she looked at him. Then with a push, she sat up and faced the chair, folding her legs Indian-style beneath her as she put both hands on his ankles. "Hey, they were teasing."

The gold of his eyes stayed far away from her face. "Yeah, but I know you aren't... I mean you didn't..."

Her face softened as a gentle smile slipped onto her lips. "I'm not mad. I kind of thought it was funny."

He surveyed her face as the light flickered in the depths of his eyes. "You did?"

"Yeah. Besides if I listened to them, I'd already be married to Dante." Revulsion wrinkled across her nose. "Now there's a scary thought."

"What was so bad about him anyway?" A.J. asked, tilting his head to the side in that way that made him look terribly young and vulnerable.

"Ugh. He was so serious all the time with all the museums and the French restaurants. He even wanted to take me to the opera."

"I take it you don't like the opera?"

"I don't like movies with subtitles much less whole performances where I have no clue what's going on." Slowly she shook her head. "Besides, I don't need somebody to impress me, to sweep me off my feet, and carry me away to some castle in the sky." Her gaze dropped to his socks. "I never did."

For a moment silence descended across the room.

"Then what do you need?" A.J. asked so softly she almost didn't hear the words.

Looking up at him should've been hard, but her heart led the way to his eyes. "A really good friend."

A gentle smile played across his golden-tan features. "Then I guess you got what you're looking for."

Fourteen

"You know," A.J. said the next morning as he and Jeff sat at the little bar by the kitchen hurriedly munching breakfast, "I think it'd be better if we take the car and leave the pickup here."

Jeff chewed his toast as he looked over at A.J. questioningly. The last thing A.J. wanted to do was to alarm his friend, but the concern in his chest needed to be voiced. However, to soften the impact he shrugged. "If the girls need to go down for some groceries or something, they'd be better off in the pickup."

Understanding slid through Jeff's eyes, and he nodded. "That's probably a good idea."

"And I was thinking," A.J. said, treading carefully across the thoughts that had slipped into and out of his consciousness all night, "since you have a cell and Eve has a cell, maybe we should take yours—you know, just in case. Not that we'll need to use them or anything."

Jeff nodded. "That's probably smart. It's a good thing we know there's a tower somewhere out here."

The call to Gabe the night before had gone smoothly, and to A.J. that was a good sign. Lisa's door snapped open, and the two men looked back to her.

"Morning," she said although she didn't look fully awake. "I was afraid you might have left already."

"Nope, just grabbing some breakfast," Jeff said, and he hugged her when she stepped into his arms. "We got some more new snow last night, so those first few runs should be unbelievable."

"Well, don't let them be too unbelievable. I'd like it if you come back in one piece." She hit him softly with her hand. Then she looked over at A.J. who was trying not to intrude on their moment. "Don't let him do anything too dumb today."

A.J. smiled at her, hoping Eve hadn't let her in on all of his secrets. "I'll try to make him behave."

"I'd appreciate that," Lisa said with a small laugh. She broke away from Jeff and walked around the counter to the cabinets. "Is Eve still sleeping?"

"She had a pretty rough day yesterday," A.J. said. "I think I wore her out."

An amused glance from Lisa landed on him, and instantly he wanted to take the words back.

"Skiing can be so tiring," Jeff said just before he tipped his bowl up and drank the rest of the milk.

Quickly A.J. stood and took his dish over to the dishwasher. "I'm going to go get my stuff." He took off down the hallway, the conversation behind him fading.

"Would you be nice to him?" Lisa asked softly.

"I am," Jeff protested.

"No, you're not…"

A.J. closed the door to his room quietly. The only good thing was that Eve hadn't been privy to that little scene. In fistfuls he yanked up the gear he needed to take and stuffed it into his bag. At least flying down a mountain, they wouldn't have a chance to talk. He would just have to make sure Jeff didn't get a chance, or he knew what his friend suspected about his feelings would be verified in a heartbeat.

Taking his gear, he went back out to the kitchen, listening for voices, but hearing none. A step into the kitchen, he realized why. Only Lisa remained, sitting at the bar drinking from a mug.

"I take it you don't like to sleep late," A.J. said, figuring the best defense was a good offense.

"Not these days," she said with a laugh. "Too much action around my mid-section."

"So, how are you feeling?" A.J. asked as he sat down two seats over from her and went about inspecting his gear.

"Pretty good," she said. "A little tired since we've been up here though."

"Thin air," he said knowingly. "I'm surprised your doctor let you come."

"Well, I go back the day after we get home. I just hope I'm not too jet-lagged that he'll notice."

A.J. looked at her, gauging the meaning of that answer although he knew it wasn't his place to ask. "We're going to take the cell phone, and you all can have Eve's. That way if you need something, you can get in touch with us."

"Oh," she said in surprise. "Okay."

"And we're leaving the pickup here," A.J. said suddenly wondering if leaving was such a good idea. "Did you get the directions to a doctor here?"

Lisa shrugged. "Some old guy with a little clinic in town."

"What's his name?" A.J. asked, not sure how she would take the inquiry but not really caring.

"Breely. Horace Breely," she said without hesitation. "I even saw the clinic on the way in."

"But besides the tired thing, you're feeling all right?"

"I'm fine," Lisa said as Jeff tripped over his duffel bag when he came out of their room.

"You know, skiing would be a whole lot more fun if you didn't have to lug 700 pounds of junk along to do it," Jeff said, throwing the things out from the doorway into the room before closing the door behind him.

"Don't strain yourself," Lisa said in amusement.

"You're one to talk," Jeff said, righting the duffel bag by the door. "Miss I-Brought-Everything-In-My-Closet-Just-In-Case."

Lisa shrugged good-naturedly. "You never know what you're going to need."

"Now you sound like someone else I know," A.J. said as his heart swooped forward.

"Don't encourage her," Jeff warned.

"It doesn't matter," A.J. said. "They do it with or without encouragement."

"Hey, that's a two-way street there," Lisa said, ambling over to Jeff who was still fighting with his gear by the door. When he stood, any pretend animosity dropped away from between them.

"You have our number, right?" Jeff asked, and Lisa nodded. "Oh, man. What about Eve's? How are we going to get in touch with you?"

Lisa shrugged. "We'll give you a call when she gets up."

"Are you sure?" Jeff said as he leveled a serious gaze at her.

Lisa laughed. "I can remember to make one phone call. Baby hasn't eaten that many brain cells."

"Okay, but you take care of yourself," Jeff said gravely.

"I will," Lisa laughed again. "And don't you go flying off of any mountains or into any trees."

"Just a couple," Jeff said teasingly.

Lisa pulled him to her for a hug. "Well, at least you're smart enough to bring a paramedic along."

"Can't be too careful," Jeff said, and then he kissed her. "Love you."

"I love you."

"We'll be back about 5:30 or so."

"Thanks for the warning." She let him go, and he gathered up his things. Then gently she put a hand on his back, and when she turned to A.J., he saw the trace of concern in her eyes. "Take care of him for me."

"Will do."

"Okay, what's up with you and Eve?" Jeff asked from his perch in the driver's seat. The fact that they had made it halfway to the ski slope had seemed like such a good sign until that very moment.

"Up?" A.J. asked, examining his fingernails like they held the final key to solving world peace. "Why?"

"Okay, you're dumb, but you can't be blind too," Jeff shot.

"Gee thanks."

"Seriously are you interested in her or what?"

"Who wouldn't be? She's gorgeous," A.J. said off-handedly.

Slowly Jeff shook his head. "No, it's more than that. I see how you look at her, and I think she's happier when you're around, too."

"I wouldn't know. I've never seen her when I'm not around."

Jeff drove down around four sharp corners before he looked back over at A.J. "Look, I don't have to tell you that Eve is like a sister to me, and I also don't have to tell you how hard on her Dustin's death was. But I think you need to know that I see something when she looks at you—something that hasn't been there in a long time. Just don't shut the door on the possibilities, okay?"

A.J. knew far more about what was possible than Jeff ever would. Eve had told him outright. "I'll keep that in mind."

"We're supposed to call them and give them your number," Lisa said when Eve stood in the kitchen making herself breakfast at just after ten.

"Why?"

Mischievousness traced through Lisa's eyes, and she dropped her voice seductively. "A.J. said he didn't want to go even an hour without hearing your voice."

"Ha. Ha." Eve sat down at the bar.

"No, I think they're afraid I'm going to go into labor or something," Lisa said as if that was silly.

"Okay, that's not even funny."

"I didn't think so either, but I figured we better humor them or they're going to be coming back up here every hour to check on us." Lisa started for Eve's room. "Where is it?"

"Right side of the suitcase," Eve said as she poured milk over her Cornflakes.

In minutes Lisa was back, talking, and a smile crossed Eve's heart. Jeff and Lisa—the two most unlikely people to hook up in the whole world. Yet, here they were, a month from the second miracle of their lives.

"But no black diamonds, right?" Lisa asked. "And don't let him talk you into any bowls either... Okay, just a second, I'll get it." She pulled the phone away from her ear. "Phone number?"

Eve quickly relayed the digits, almost wishing that Lisa would think to let her talk to A.J. She should've been smart enough to get out of bed this morning to tell him good-bye, but the dream she was having held her in a vice grip. Even here, over a bowl of cold cornflakes, it was right there. There was something about that dark hallway, something about being so close to him, and yet knowing that throwing logic to the wind wasn't an option. Over and over her brain would put her there as her heart willed her to make a different choice.

However, the choice is, was, and always would be the same. It had to be. Lisa beeped off the phone. "I think they're going to go do the black diamonds."

Eve shrugged, looking at the phone Lisa laid on the counter. "I thought that was the plan."

"Yeah, but blacks? Ugh. That's so dangerous."

Before she thought about it, Eve laughed. "That's nothing. I think A.J. and danger are like one in the same." Her brain caught up with her mouth just as the words left, and she looked over at the mortified face of her friend. "But I'm sure they won't do too many dumb stunts. Jeff's smart enough to keep A.J. in line."

"I hope so," Lisa said as she sat on one of the stools. She looked over at Eve. "It's getting worse."

"What?" Eve asked with concern.

"Letting him go. It was bad enough when it was just me, but now…" Her gaze fell to her rounded stomach. "It's so hard to watch him walk out that door."

Compassion washed through Eve. "A.J.'ll take care of him."

Lisa seemed to consider that a moment. Then she looked at Eve, and the subject changed in the middle of her eyes. "So…?" Lisa asked leadingly as she leaned onto the counter.

"So, what?" Eve asked innocently as she spooned cornflakes into her mouth.

"So what happened last night?"

"We watched a movie," Eve said with a shrug. "Remember? You were there."

"Not the movie. A.J. Were there fireworks after we went to bed?"

"We talked for awhile," Eve said, holding the truth closer to her vest. She hated the fact that A.J. was so sensitive about the teasing. She felt responsible for that. If she would've just been a little cooler about the whole thing when they got home, maybe Jeff and Lisa wouldn't have embarrassed him so much. However, the strange thing was, it seemed he was more concerned about her than about himself, and she couldn't quite figure that out.

Lisa exhaled in frustration. "You two should be on Oprah for as much as you talk."

Eve shrugged. "We're friends."

"Uh-huh, and that whole sitting next to his chair when there was one across the room thing? What was that about?"

"The floor looked comfortable."

"Come on, Eve. Why don't you just admit you like him? I mean, what's there not to like? He's sweet, and he's cute, and…"

"You're married."

"Yeah, but you're not." The words superceded any thought on

Lisa's part, and her enthusiasm deflated with them. "You know what I mean."

"Yeah," Eve said softly. "I do. Look, you don't have to sell me on him. I'm already sold. He's great, but as a friend..."

"Is that the only word you know?"

"It's the only one I want to know. Come on, Lis, I come with more baggage than a 747. He doesn't deserve that. He's free, and he's having fun. I don't want to drag him down."

"But he cares about you, and not just as a friend either."

Panic surged through Eve. "Why? Has he said something? Did he say something to Jeff?"

"He doesn't have to say anything. It's not about words. It's about how he looks at you and how you look at him, and the fact that for the first time in a very long time you're letting someone get close to you. That's real, Eve—whether you want to admit it or not."

Slowly she shook her head. "He's just being nice."

"Because he likes you."

"We're..."

"Friends. I know. You told me that." Lisa sighed slowly. "Look, remember when Jeff and I first got together? Oh, man, panic city. But you kept telling me how he was different around me than he was around any other girl he'd been out with. Well, I'm telling you that about yourself now. You're different when you're with A.J. When he's around, you look like you want to live again. That's something special, and I don't want you to throw it away because you think you can only be friends or that you have to stay friends because of the past."

Eve wanted to protest, but no words came out of her mouth.

"You know," Lisa said thoughtfully, "you told me once that if you ever had the chance to do it all again, you'd do it in a heartbeat. Well, maybe this is your chance."

"But I had it. I had my chance, and it's gone."

"No," Lisa said gently, "only Dustin is gone. A.J. is right here."

As that thought ran through Eve, Lisa jumped slightly.

"Oh," she said, laying a hand on her stomach.

"What?" Eve asked, instantly glad for the diversion from her thoughts but uneasy about the form it came in.

A moment and then Lisa shook her head. "Sometimes those

Braxton-Hicks contractions get serious." She breathed a couple more times before she relaxed. "Listen, Eve, I think I'm going to go lay down for a little while. Do you mind?"

"Do what you need to do. I can find something to keep me busy."

Carefully Lisa slid off the stool. "Think about what I said."

Eve nodded and watched her friend cross the full length of the living room. When Lisa had gone into her bedroom and closed the door, Eve thought about Lisa's words. Dustin was gone. The man she thought was the only one she would ever love had been stolen from her grasp, and now in front of her stood someone new. Someone who felt so close to her own soul that it scared her breathless.

She put her dish in the dishwasher, grabbed a pillow from the couch, and flopped into the chair he had occupied the night before. Her gaze went to the snow falling gently outside the window as she let her mind drift—to him, to A.J., and for the first time, she placed no limits on where those thoughts could take her.

"A black diamond?" Jeff asked skeptically.

A.J. looked over the edge. "It's an easy one."

"And you're going to explain the broken leg to Lisa?"

"Hey, you heard her. You're with a paramedic. How much safer could you get?"

Reality swirled away from Eve, and suddenly she was back in the dark hallway, sensing him barely inches away from her. Only this time she wasn't hoping he would turn and go into his room, no, every piece of her wanted him to step next to her, to take her in his arms. As she closed her eyes, she felt the warmth of him closing the space between them, making time stand still.

"Are you sure?" his voice asked softly.

"Yeah," she breathed, willing him to make the space between them vanish.

"Eve," a voice outside her head said, but it wasn't his. "Eve?"

Instantly she was awake, and the dream fell away from her. "Lisa?" With one glance, reality surged forward. "What's wrong?"

Lisa stood, hunched slightly with her hand on her stomach. "I think we need to call somebody."

"Call...?" Eve sat up in the chair. "Who?"

"The doctor," Lisa said just as she doubled over.

"The... oh, my gosh. The baby?" As Lisa nodded, Eve vaulted from the chair and over to her friend. "Contractions? You're having contractions?" Again Lisa nodded. "Oh, gosh. Oh, gosh." Air failed. "Phone... phone... where's the...?" In the middle of her panic, she found the phone on the bar. "What's his number? Do you have a phone book?"

Lisa leaned back into the couch as the contraction subsided. "The number's in our room. In my black carry-on."

Without asking any more, Eve raced to the open bedroom door and scanned the room. "Black carry-on." One swipe and it was on the bed. She pushed the strands of hair out of her face as her hands searched.

"Side pocket," Lisa called from the living room.

"Got it," Eve said, yanking the paper from its hiding place. She fought to breathe, to think as she crossed with the number back out into the living room. Quickly her fingers dialed the number as panic flooded through her. The phone clicked. "Yes, is this..." She looked at the note in her hand. "...Dr. Breely's office? Okay, good. Listen, my friend just went into labor. I need to know what to do."

"How far apart are the contractions, Ma'am?"

"I... How far apart are the contractions, Lis?"

"About four minutes I think."

"About four minutes," Eve said, pushing the hair back from her face as she watched Lisa's face and body contract again. "Oh, no. Here's another one. Lis." She knelt down by the couch and laid a hand on her shoulder, wishing she could do something more to help her friend.

"How far away are you from the hospital?" the lady asked.

"The hos... Umm, we're about 30 minutes from town," Eve said, fighting to keep rational with her.

"Okay, the hospital is on the far east side of town. Once you get to town, you'll see the signs. I'll have the doctor meet you there."

"Oh, okay."

"What's the patient's name?"

"Lisa... Lisa Taylor." When she signed off, Eve's brain

immediately ran into six different problems. "I've got to get the directions back down. Where would they be?"

"I think he put them in our suitcase," Lisa said, trying to get comfortable but obviously not succeeding.

"Okay." Eve took half of a calming breath and raced back into the bedroom. "Suitcase." She headed for it and grabbed the top clothing. "Crud. Where are they?"

The gasp from the couch did nothing to settle her nerves. "Lisa, are you okay?"

But there was no answer.

"Please, God. I can't do this alone. Where are they?" Deciding at the bottom of the suitcase that the directions weren't there, Eve redirected her search to the dresser drawers. She was making a huge mess, but there weren't enough brain cells to care. "Papers." With one hand she grabbed the sheaves from the top drawer. "Thank you, God." Her feet traced back out into the living room. "I found them."

"Could we call Jeff?" Lisa asked, and her voice was filled with the panic that laced Eve's entire body.

"Yeah, I'll call them. I've got to get my boots." Dialing even as she ran to her room, Eve's mind was so jumbled, she wasn't sure that what was going to come out of her mouth would have any basis in reality. She yanked one boot on as the phone rang. It rang again. "Oh, come on." She grabbed the other boot and pulled it on, still the phone rang. "Come on. Pick up the phone!"

The moan from the living room yanked her attention away from the phone, and she hit the off button. Back in the living room, she surveyed the situation and prayed sincerely for divine help—she certainly needed more than she had.

"We're going to have to get you to the pickup," Eve said like a drill sergeant. "Where are your shoes?"

"Bedroom."

Eve headed back to the bedroom, her mind sliding through her previous two visits looking for the shoes before she got there. She threw the clothes at the end of the bed back into the suitcase in a heap and yanked the shoes from the floor. Her legs carried her into the living room where she slipped the shoes on Lisa, and she stood to survey her friend. "Coat?"

"Back of the door," Lisa said as another contraction clamped over her.

Torn between staying with her friend and getting things ready so they could go, Eve finally chose getting ready. Sitting here wasn't going to help, and it was obvious that Lisa needed more help than Eve could give her. She grabbed the coat and Lisa's purse for good measure.

"You okay?" she asked, knowing it was a dumb question.

The pain subsided from Lisa's face. "Did you get the guys?"

"We'll call them from the pickup," Eve said, not wanting to panic her friend. She went to the couch and did her best to help Lisa up. Sanity clicked in long enough to grab the keys from the counter, and they started for the door. They had a scant four minutes to get to the pickup. "Okay, I know you don't want to hurry, but I don't think contractions in the snow sound like much fun, so…" At that moment Eve pulled the curtain back on the double sliding doors to reveal a winter wonderland of white and gray.

"Oh, sheez. Okay," Eve corralled her own alarm as she slid the door open, "we're going to have to be real careful down these steps." Already little tufts of snow had accumulated on the steps. One slow step at a time they descended. "How you doing? You okay?"

Lisa nodded, clearly not wanting to use precious energy on speaking.

"Good. Good girl." Finally they reached the bottom. "Careful, some of this might be deeper than it looks." She was breathing through the seconds, ticking them off in her head with every step they took. They were running out of time to get to the pickup door. She looked at Lisa. She would've liked to tell her to hurry, but hurrying wasn't a great idea either. "A little further. Just a little…"

"Oh. Oh!" Lisa gasped as she grabbed for Eve.

"Six more steps," Eve coached.

In that same second Lisa's eyes crumpled on the pain as she moaned.

"Breathe," Eve said, stopping in utter helplessness. "Just breathe." She had no idea how to do baby breathing, and the truth was she wasn't breathing either, but somewhere in the back of what little she knew about having a baby, there was something about breathing. Lisa's fingers wrapped into Eve's arm as Eve stood, watching, powerless to help. After many agonizing seconds,

Lisa finally nodded and straightened enough so that Eve knew they could get the rest of the way to the pickup.

With a swipe, Eve cleared the stacked snow from the passenger's door. It was a struggle to get Lisa up into the cab, but when she was in the pickup, Eve breathed a sigh of relief. "Just get her to the hospital. Everything will be fine."

"Race you down," Jeff said as he stood at the top of the steepest example of a black diamond they had encountered so far that day.

"I thought you didn't do black diamonds," A.J. said with a laugh.

"I thought I didn't too." With that, Jeff jumped off the top, swinging his skis expertly side-to-side over the moguls. Slowly A.J. shook his head. Lisa would surely kill him if she ever found out.

"I've just got to get this thing turned around," Eve said as the immensity of the pickup's frame suddenly became very real in her consciousness. She put a hand on the gearshift and pulled it into drive. With the first pressure of the gas, the tires spun underneath them. Focusing on her breathing if only to keep herself sane, Eve turned the pickup wheels to the side, and the pickup bucked forward.

"Oh, easy," Lisa moaned.

"Sorry." The windshield wipers swiped across the windshield, causing Eve to jump. "Come on." Cautiously they angled across the road, but the banks on either side came up to the pickup's grill. She drove as far forward as she could, then put the gearshift into reverse. However, when she turned around to look out the back, snow was all she saw. She threw the pickup into park. "Just a second."

With just more than a swing, she got into the pickup bed, and the snow crunched right over the top of her boots. Quickly she wiped off the fluffy white mess covering the back window. Then she jumped back to the ground and crawled in just as Lisa pulled her shoulders forward to her knees.

"Another one?" The only reason for the question was to reassure herself that some part of her short-circuited system still worked. She put the pickup in reverse and started backing just as the full impact of the contraction hit Lisa.

"Owww!" Lisa screamed, and for one second too long Eve's attention went to her friend. In the next split second she felt the backend of the pickup sink.

When she looked into the windshield, it wasn't road that she saw—it was trees. Quickly, she shifted gears to go forward; however, the pickup did little more than spin. "No. No. No. Come on." Rocking her body in a desperate attempt to get the vehicle to move, she fought off insanity.

"Oh, no," Lisa said in fear next to her, and Eve looked at her. Blank numbness gazed back at her. "I think my water just broke."

"Uh… oh." Desperately Eve rocked forward, but the tires did no more than spin. After another frantic moment, rational kicked her in the head. The pickup wasn't going anywhere. Guilt washed over her as she glanced at Lisa. "Well, I guess we go to Plan B."

Trust because there was no other option was in Lisa's eyes. "What's Plan B?"

"I have no idea."

"Man, those clouds look worse than they did yesterday," A.J. said, appraising the clouds sliding over the mountains in the distance. The thick, dark, gray clouds had no trouble completely obscuring all traces of the majestic peaks. The lift ascended higher, drifting up toward their destination.

"Isn't that where the cabin is?" Jeff asked with some concern.

"Yeah."

"You know, we haven't heard anything from the girls since this morning. You think they're okay?"

"Wouldn't hurt to check," A.J. said, feeling that same vague unease he had the day before as he looked at those clouds. Ominous hardly described them.

Jeff needed no more prompting. He pulled the little cell phone out and looked at it. "Oh, man. It was off."

"Off?"

With short punches Jeff clicked the phone on and dialed the number. "It must've gotten shut off in my pocket."

That news didn't help the apprehension in A.J.'s chest. His whole focus went to his friend's face as they waited. Concern turned to confusion and then to fear the longer Jeff sat without talking. A.J.'s gaze went back up to the invisible mountain as he tried to think through the situation.

Finally Jeff hit the off button. "They don't answer."

"Don't answer? That doesn't make any sense. They'd have to hear it."

The other side of the conversation dropped away as Jeff redialed the number. He waited. A.J. waited, fighting not to let the fear crawl into his gut. Jeff shook his head slowly, waited a moment more, and then hit the off button. "Nothing."

A.J. looked at Jeff and then at those clouds. He wanted to panic, but that wasn't going to help Jeff who had already paled to three shades of white. "We'll call them again at the bottom. Maybe there's something in the way up here." Granted that didn't exactly seem possible, but it was the most plausible excuse he could come up with. Besides, he knew Jeff already knew the score. One look at his face was enough to verify that. Closing his eyes, A.J. willed his strength into Eve just in case she needed it at that moment. However, when he opened them, all he saw were those clouds, and fearful anxiety twisted inside him.

Fifteen

"Two more," Eve said as she carefully balanced both her and Lisa back up the front porch steps. "Good girl." She went to the sliding door and opened it, realizing she hadn't bothered to lock it on their departure.

"Oh!" Lisa's hand grabbed onto Eve's arm, and the fingers dug further than they had the last time.

"Okay, breathe… breathe…" Eve said as they stood on the front porch, the swirling snow whipping around them.

"I can't. It hurts," Lisa said in breaks and breaths.

"You have to. Listen, you have to concentrate on breathing. Think about breathing."

Agonizing seconds slipped by until finally Lisa's body relaxed slightly.

"You ready?" Eve asked, and she waited for Lisa to nod before she helped the bent and huddled frame through the door. "That one was closer than the last one, wasn't it?"

"I've got to lay down," Lisa said, gasping through the pain that hadn't totally receded.

"Okay, let's get to your room." Helping her step-for-step, Eve's mind was like a laser. Just get her to that bed, and somehow they could deal with everything else. In the room, Eve worked to get the bed ready for Lisa to get into. "Careful up."

Lisa had hardly collapsed into the pillows when the next wave of pain hit her. Instantly Eve huddled at her side and did what she could to ease the searing pain screeching its way through her friend. As that contraction slipped into the past, Eve began to seriously consider what her next move was. She looked around the room really hoping that something would tell her exactly what to do next. When she found nothing, she straightened and assessed her options. There weren't many, and none of them made her feel at all calm.

"I want Jeff," Lisa said, her voice somewhere between weak and pleading.

"Okay," Eve said, seeing a break in what she could do. Her gaze swept the room. "Dang it. I left the cell phone in the pickup. I'm going to go get it. You'll be okay?"

Lisa nodded with barely enough energy behind it to accomplish that.

"Okay, don't move."

"Don't worry."

"No answer," Jeff said as A.J. stood at his side at the base of the ski slope.

A.J. exhaled in frustration as he looked up at the clouds now moving in over them, whipping the snow with it. Skiing was no longer so much as a consideration. "Would they have gone to the hospital?"

"I don't know," Jeff said, his face registering panic at the very thought. "Maybe."

"Eve would've been smart enough to get her to the hospital," A.J. said, sounding far more sure than the pit of his stomach felt. "Let's go get this stuff back."

Jeff looked less than assured. With a tight smile A.J. clapped him on the back. "I'm sure everything's cool. We'll just go check."

When Eve retrieved the phone from the front seat of the pickup, her first thought was to call the guys. However, she knew that getting the doctor was more important, so her first call when she got back into the cabin was to the clinic. Unfortunately the doctor was already at the hospital, so then she had to call there. It was like playing phone tag with an invisible target.

"Busy," Jeff said in irritation as they stood in the rental shop waiting to return their gear.

"Well, at least we're getting through now," A.J. said, sincerely hoping that was a good sign.

"No, we don't have another way down," Eve said as her mind spun toward the black hole of desperation.

"Which direction are you from the town?" the receptionist asked.

"Umm, we're… I don't know. Left from if you're coming in from Albuquerque."

"Left? North?"

"Yeah, I guess so."

"It's snowing pretty good up there," the receptionist said. "Are you on the main highway?"

"No, we're off, back in the trees," Eve said, hearing the panic in her chest jump through the words as Lisa screeched in pain from the other room.

"I don't know. That country's pretty treacherous if we don't have really good directions."

"Directions," Eve said, catching on the word. "I have some directions." Instantly her search mechanism lurched into gear. "Where'd they go? They were here… The pickup. Just a second. I've got to get them." Adrenaline carried her right out of the cabin and to the pickup where she ripped the door open and grabbed the pages. "Here… Here they are…"

"Yeah, north," the receptionist said, her voice fading back in. "I'm sorry, Ma'am. The doctor says it's too dangerous to make that trek in this weather."

The pages blurred in front of her. "But we need him."

"He understands that, but in this weather, it's too likely that he'll miss a turn or take a wrong one."

"No, no. You don't understand. I can't do this alone!" Eve pleaded as another wail came from the bedroom. "Lisa needs a doctor."

"If the weather breaks…"

"No, by then it'll be too late! Please!"

"You can call us back when the contractions get a little closer."

"Closer? No, they're…"

"Good luck." And the phone clicked off.

"Here, let me try," A.J. said, taking the phone from his friend when they got into the parking lot. There wasn't much more that he could do, but the way Jeff looked, he would be a poor translator of even the most benign news at the moment.

The net beneath Eve's high wire act dissolved, and she looked down at the phone in shock.

"Eve!" Lisa cried. "Is Jeff coming?"

"Jeff…?" Eve asked, snagging on the name with no understanding. At that moment the cell phone in her hand rang, and she looked at it for a miniscule second before pushing the on button. "Yeah… hello?"

Terror twisted through A.J. at the first hint of the fear in her voice. He put a finger in his ear to block everything other than her voice out. "Eve? What's wrong? Where are you?"

"A.J.?" He heard the panic in the two letters. "A.J., is that you?"

"Yeah, what's going on?"

It was then that he heard the cry, and he knew.

"What is it?" Jeff asked, pulling at the arm of his shirt. "Is Lisa okay?"

"It's Lis," Eve said through the phone. "She's in labor."

"Are you at the hospital?"

"No," Eve said, and tears crowded over the word. "I got the pickup stuck. I can't get her out of here." She was hardly breathing through the words and the emotions.

"The doctor?"

"He can't come. He won't come. The weather's too bad."

"What did she say?" Jeff asked in wild-eyed panic. "Is Lisa okay?"

A.J. brushed him off, knowing he had to make a choice between them. He started the little car, realizing that sitting in the parking lot wasn't getting them any closer any faster. "Eve, listen

179

to me. Where's the doctor's office?"

"No, no. He's not there. He's at the hospital."

"Are you sure about that?" He backed out and turned toward the front gate which was nearly invisible in the snowstorm.

"Yeah, I just talked to him… well, not to him, but…"

Another agonizing moan, and A.J. calculated them in his head. "Okay, listen to me. We're going to go get the doctor, and I'll call you back as soon as we're headed that way."

"No, A.J., don't leave me. I don't know what to do."

"Help her breathe," he said, slowing his own breathing to corral the panic in his heart. "Keep her calm. Give her ice chips if you have any. I'll call you back in a few minutes."

"O… Okay," she said unsteadily but no longer hysterical.

"I'll talk to you in a minute." They signed off as he pulled onto the highway. Snow hit the windshield so that visibility was cut to nearly nothing.

"It's bad, huh?" Jeff finally asked, barely breathing.

"She's in labor. We just have to get a doctor up there, and we'll be okay."

"Crud." Jeff hit the dashboard full force as his face crumpled on the news. "I knew I shouldn't have left."

A.J. glanced over but only for a brief second. "You can't be with her every second. She's going to be fine. Just hang onto that. Okay?"

Fighting the fear that looked more like anger, Jeff shook his head. "We've got to get up there."

"We will. I promise."

"Everything's fine," Eve said in her best lying voice as she brought a cup of ice into the bedroom just as Lisa fell back into the pillows, spent from the last contraction. "I brought you some ice. They said you can suck on it for awhile if you want."

"Are the guys coming?" Lisa asked, and her eyes held far more fear than they had when Eve had left. Her hair was damp from the sweat, and her chest rose and fell without taking in much air.

"They're on their way."

"And no reports of broken bones or anything?"

"Not a single one. Jeff must've taken it easy on A.J."

Lisa smiled weakly. "I'm sure Jeff is the one you were worried about."

"You never know," Eve said. "Him and Dustin could make hanging shoe racks look dangerous."

A picture of Dustin fighting to keep the rack on the closet door while Jeff worked with the screw gun floated through her mind. Funny, that may well have been the first time she had seen Jeff. She couldn't really remember, there were too many other images to be sure. Nonetheless, Jeff's frantic attempts to get the gun going in the right direction as Dustin struggled with the metal tubing brought a smile to her face even now.

"Shoe racks?" Lisa asked with a raise of her eyebrows.

"Haven't I ever told you that one?"

"I don't think so," Lisa said, relaxing for the first time in more than an hour.

"We need to speak with Dr. Breely," A.J. said, not trusting Jeff to be coherent at this point. They had already worked their way through a mini-maze of receptionists and nurses, and very few had been anything close to helpful.

The nurse at the desk looked at him as if she would rather eat a raw fish.

"We have to talk to him right away," A.J. said, not willing to take the no in her eyes as an answer. "It's an emergency."

The skepticism didn't leave, but she picked up the phone and paged the doctor. A.J. looked at Jeff and nodded in encouragement. Minutes ticked by. Impatiently A.J. looked at his watch. 2:30. He wished he knew more about how long Lisa had been in labor. He had known for nearly 20 minutes, but before that… His brain worked through the time they had been on the slopes. How long had Eve been trying to call? Or had she just started?

"May I help you?" the voice said from behind them, and when A.J. turned, the antipathy he had felt toward the doctor when Eve had told him Breely wasn't coming dissipated.

"Are you Dr. Breely?" A.J. asked the tiny man who looked like he had to be getting close to 90.

"I am." With white hair, sun-bleached wrinkles, and eyes hidden behind thick, black-framed glasses, Dr. Breely looked far more like a patient than a doctor. "They said it's an emergency."

"Yes, Sir," A.J. said, taking one look at Jeff and forcing himself to calm down enough to make their case. "We have a woman in labor. She's up in the mountains. She's only about 36 weeks along, and they can't get her down here."

"This seems to be a pattern today," Dr. Breely said, wrinkling his forehead further, but A.J. could see that the statement was not bitter but of great concern for the doctor. "We had a young woman call in earlier..."

"That was probably Eve," A.J. said, putting the pieces together. "She's with Lisa..."

"Taylor," Dr. Breely said.

"Right. Lisa Taylor. This is her husband, Jeff. We were skiing, and Eve called us. They're stuck up there. The vehicle they had got stuck."

The doctor pushed up his glasses in concern. "I wanted to go, but I don't see as good as I used to anymore."

Options flowed through A.J.'s head. "We can take you."

Consideration traced across the doctor's face. "Let me get some things together."

"Great. We'll be here."

During the contractions, Eve did her best to hold Lisa's hand and help her through them. Four minutes was a thing of the past. They were now at a shaky three, and Eve wished she knew at what point things were going to get really serious. She had managed to get Lisa out of her clothes and into her gown. She had also corralled all of the towels from the master bathroom and had them stacked near the bed ready.

Strange what little tidbits of information came up in the middle of a brain fraught with chaos. Towels, breathing, hot water. She wasn't at all sure what to do with any of them, but she assembled them anyway. Nonetheless, at each contraction, she ran back to the room—fearing that the baby might make its appearance on any one. What she would do if that happened, she wasn't at all sure, but staying busy made that possibility seem less imminent.

When the phone rang, Eve slid off the bed to answer it. "Hello?"

"Eve, how is everything?" A.J.'s voice cut over the line, and she sucked in a ragged breath as she glanced at the sweat-soaked exhausted figure of her best friend.

"We're hanging in." She stepped out of the room. "Where are you?"

"We just picked up Breely, and we're headed up there."

"You're still in town?" she asked, having sincerely hoped that they would be only ten minutes or so from the cabin by now.

"We just left. The snow's pretty bad, so I don't know how great of time we're going to make."

Lisa's cry of pain yanked Eve's attention back to the room, and she raced back in. She took Lisa's hand as panic surged through her again. "It's okay, Lis. Breathe. In... out... breathe. Good girl."

"How far apart are they?" A.J. asked.

"We're getting down to about three minutes each," she said as tears of helplessness washed over her.

"Listen, I'm going to put the doctor on so he can tell you what to do in case the baby comes before we get there."

"Before... No, A.J." She stood from the bed and walked out to the living room pushing all the hair up to the top of her forehead in consternation. "Look, I don't do blood. Okay? I'll pass out. I will. I can't do this by myself. You've got to get up here."

"Eve, listen to me," he said calmly. "If she doesn't go really fast, we should get there in plenty of time, but there's a chance that we won't, so I want you to talk with the doctor..."

"No, A.J., I'm telling you I cannot do this. I can't. Do you understand me? I can't do this!"

"Eve," he said, cutting into the panic. "Look, you don't have a choice here. Lisa needs you."

Tearful panic swept through her system at the thought of what he was telling her even as the moans of agony sounded from the bedroom. "I thought I always had a choice."

"Yeah, well, this time, your choice is: do it, or find a way to do it."

The choices, or lack thereof, wound through her until her brain wrapped around his words, and she realized he was right. She had to pull it together—there was no other choice. "Okay."

"Good. Okay. Here's the doctor."

A.J. handed the phone into the backseat, praying that whatever instructions the doctor gave Eve wouldn't totally freak her out. She was on the verge of losing it, and every word was more like a time bomb than a simple set of letters. As he guided the car around another hairpin curve that was only semi-visible through the snow, he glanced over at Jeff who sat in dumbfounded silence.

"She's at three minutes," A.J. said.

"I should've been there. I shouldn't have left."

"Hey, man. This stuff happens. Babies aren't on the same schedule as the rest of us."

When Jeff looked over at his friend, the helpless anguish there tore through A.J. like a knife blade. He had seen that same look before—on a sidewalk under the canopy of an inferno. That time he had failed his friend, miserably. This time, he was determined not to. Solidly he reached across the seat and gripped Jeff's shoulder. "We'll get there. I promise."

Jeff's eyes spoke of "I hope so," and "I don't have a choice but to believe you." However, the overwhelming distress was still there.

"Umm, Mr. Taylor," the doctor said from the back as he held the phone over the seat. "Mrs. Taylor would like to speak with you."

Gingerly Jeff took the phone as A.J.'s heart went with it.

"Lis?" Jeff asked, but the name barely made it from his lips. "Hey, Sweetheart, how're you doing?...Yeah, we're on our way. We'll be there as soon as we can... I know. I love you, too..."

When A.J. looked over, he watched as utter helplessness washed over Jeff's face.

"I'm so sorry, Baby. Hold on. Okay? We'll be there..." He wasn't even breathing anymore as A.J. reached over and took the phone from his limp fingers.

The screams of pain still reverberated through the airwaves, and A.J. had no question as to why Jeff's whole countenance had frozen dead with horror.

A.J. righted the phone on his own ear as the noises on the other end stopped completely. "Hello? Hey, is anybody there?"

"Yeah, yeah, I'm here," Eve said, not totally panicked but certainly not calm. "Running out of great advice to give myself though. You know, think positive and all that junk. Believe me, it's highly overrated."

A.J. laughed softly. "Just remember, God'll never give you more than you and He can handle together."

"Oh, yeah? Then I'm thinking we're going to have to have a serious sit down about that one..."

The line snapped in two as A.J. drove around another corner. He looked down at the phone, sighed, and hit the off button. The wipers beat back and forth so that he really needed both hands for driving anyway. Whether she knew it or not, Eve was far from the weakest-spirited person on the earth. She would do whatever she had to. His job now was to get them there so she wouldn't have to do it alone.

The feeling of being totally alone swept over Eve when the line went dead; however, all it took was recalling the soft calmness of his voice to remind her that she wasn't alone. She hit the off button and set the phone on the dresser. The doctor had given her enough instructions to give her something to do.

"I think I'm going to hit Jeff over the head when he gets here," Eve said as she went about clearing everything that wasn't nailed down away from the end of the bed.

"Why's that?" Lisa asked as if she were hardly there anymore.

"He was all happy about getting a relaxing vacation yesterday. It's just like a man to leave me with moving all the furniture." She heaved against the chest at the base of the bed. When it didn't move, she went to the other side to pull on it.

"Don't hurt yourself," Lisa said with blurry concern.

After another futile attempt, Eve opened the trunk and started pulling stuff out. Pile after pile she set over in the far corner. "That'd be good. Then they could take both of us to the hospital."

"Four people and a pregnant lady in one little car? I don't think..." Pain closed in on Lisa before she knew it was coming, and instantly Eve dumped the contents in her hands back in the chest. She took Lisa's hand, which tightened around hers until her fingers turned white, but she hardly noticed.

"Breathe, girl. Breathe. You're doing great. Short breaths. Work through it." Eve pulled her watch up to check the seconds that passed between the first hint of contraction and the end. Why that was particularly important, she wasn't sure, but it was one of the things the doctor had said to find out, so find out, she would.

"How much longer?" Jeff asked, glancing at his watch as his leg jumped up and down on the seat.

"How long since we left town?" A.J. asked. He didn't want to take his gaze off the road for even a moment. On one side he could see the mountain, on the other, he knew there was a drop-off, but he couldn't tell where the road stopped and the freefall began.

"Almost an hour. It shouldn't be taking this long," Jeff said. "Are you sure we didn't miss the turn?"

A.J. glanced down at the speedometer. The car was going barely ten miles an hour. "It's the snow. I'm afraid to go any faster."

"No, no. I know, you're right," Jeff said although he didn't sound happy about that fact. "It's too dangerous to push it too hard."

Nonetheless, praying it was a good decision, A.J. pressed the accelerator down a fraction of an inch so that the meter crossed up to 15 and then near 20. Precious time was sliding by, and with every passing minute, they got just that much closer to being too late.

The slow blink of Lisa's eyes made Eve wonder if she would have the strength to make it to the end of this road. Towels soaked with blood lay on the bathroom floor in direct line of sight from where Eve was as she sat down on the bed to retake Lisa's hand. She couldn't think of them. She couldn't think of anything other than making it to and through the next contraction, and what she needed to do as soon as it was over.

"You look absolutely exhausted," Eve said as she ran her hand over the cold washcloth she had laid across Lisa's forehead longer ago than she could remember.

Lisa's hazy gaze traced over her friend as she reached up and clasped Eve's hand. "Thanks for being here."

Eve smiled, hoping it didn't look like she was sitting by a deathbed. "Hey, where else would I be?"

A jerk, and Lisa shrieked in agony as her body bowed over itself again. There was hardly a reason to time them anymore. By the time one stopped, the next was only a minute away anyway. As

Eve did her best to coach the hunched figure through the pain, the phone on the dresser bleeped to life. Wishing her arms were long enough to reach it without letting Lisa's hand go, Eve took two seconds to grab the phone before she returned. "Yeah."

"How's Lisa?" A.J. asked without introduction.

"She wants to push," Eve said, the doctor's admonition from earlier to keep her from doing that still rang through her head. "I don't know how much longer we can keep this up."

"We just passed the lake, so it shouldn't be much longer," A.J. said, and Eve's mind went about calculating how long "not much longer" could take. "But the doctor wanted an update. I'll let you talk to him."

Eve blew the hair up out of her face as she waited for the phone transfer.

"Eve?" Dr. Breely asked. "What've we got going?"

As concisely as she knew how although she didn't know the exact language, Eve relayed what she knew.

"We must be getting close then. We can't wait any longer," Dr. Breely said in resignation when she had completed the update. "Okay, if she gets ready to push again, I need you to get ready to deliver this baby."

Eve's breath caught. Towels, breathing—she could do those, but delivering a baby? That was far beyond her realm of comfort or knowledge. The rational part of her brain wanted to protest, but before she could, the doctor started going through the procedure, and the protests vanished into concentrating on his instructions.

"You got all that?" he finally asked when her mind had spun completely away from her on all of the information.

"Yeah, I think so," she said as Lisa curled forward again. Struggling to focus on three things at once, Eve put the phone to her other ear and bent to comfort her friend. "Could I talk to A.J. again?"

"Sure," Dr. Breely said.

She breathed through the thoughts of the coming minutes.

"A.J. here," he said with worry but firmly.

"You're going to be here as soon as you can, right?" she asked, trying to keep her voice calm and level.

"You know I will."

187

Sixteen

A.J. hit the off button and looked at Jeff. "Looks like you're going to be a daddy a little sooner than you thought."

Jeff's face was the color of paste when he looked at A.J. "Man, this is making those black diamonds look like the bunny slope."

At least he wasn't passing out, A.J. reasoned. "Tell me about it." He guided the car around two more turns and then just ahead, the boulders came into view. "Hang on, guys. We're almost there."

Through the next two contractions, Eve worked to get things set up as the doctor had instructed. The last of the fresh towels from the other bathroom were stacked at the end of the bed, pillows from every available source were on the floor waiting for Eve to get to the point that doable meets "it's time." Finally she knew she could wait for them no longer.

The gasp from the head of the bed jerked Eve's attention to it because this was no scream but far more urgent.

"Eve," Lisa's astounded voice said as she clawed backward. "I think this is it."

"Okay," Eve said without so much as a moment of decision. "We're going to have to scoot you down to the end."

Carefully she worked Lisa's frame to the end of the bed even as she put the pillows behind her for support. At the end of the bed, she set first one foot then the other on the two chairs she had swiped from the dining room. Her foot crunched over the shower curtain that was now lying on the floor beneath the end of the bed.

"Do you know how to do this?" Lisa asked.

"I was hoping you did," Eve said with the slightest hint of a laugh under the statement.

"Remind me next time to keep A.J. here with me. Maybe he would at least know what to do," Lisa said obviously trying not to focus on the impending occasion.

Eve couldn't have agreed more. "Okay," she said as she grabbed another towel and took up position at the end of the bed. "The doctor said on the next contraction, you take a deep breath, hold it, and push for ten seconds. Then you rest. If the baby's head gets here, then you're going to have to pant instead of pushing."

Concerned compliance crossed through Lisa's tired eyes. Some part of Eve wished there wasn't quite so much trust in those eyes because if this ended badly, she knew who she would blame forever. *Don't think about that*, she coached herself. *You can do this. You have to.*

A gasp, and Eve's inward coaching turned outward. "Here we go. Deep breath, hold it. One, two, three, four, five..." Had she been watching this on a video, Eve was quite sure she would've passed out; however, there weren't enough brain signals left to shut her system down. "...ten. Okay, stop."

Head and shoulders, Lisa collapsed into the pillows. "I think skiing would've been more fun."

"You think?" Eve asked as she pulled a fresh towel up from the stack on the floor. "Ready to try again?"

"If I said, no, would it make any difference?"

Eve laughed without making much of a sound. "I doubt it."

"Then I guess I'm ready." When the next contraction hit, they fell in line like a well-timed marching band—Eve coaching and Lisa pushing.

"I see the head," Eve said as her breath stopped. "Pant. Pant."

Just as that contraction subsided, Eve heard the noise by the front door. However, she stayed with her job until in unison the three men burst through the door. Without any real discussion, they each took their place around the bed.

"Lisa, Baby, I'm so sorry," Jeff said, racing to take Lisa's hand and wrap her overwhelmed body as best he could in his arms.

"I'm so glad you're here," Lisa said. Genuine tears traced down her face as she reached a hand up to clasp his.

A.J. helped Eve up from the floor even as she gave the update to the doctor who took her position. "I just saw the head," Eve said. "I've got towels and water…"

The doctor surveyed the situation and nodded to her. "I may have to sign you up for my nursing staff."

A smile started on Eve's face just as the next contraction hit. Instantly she and A.J. sprang into action to assist the doctor. A.J. grabbed the doctor's bag and started laying out the instruments that they would need. Eve stood, ready and willing to do whatever the doctor decided he needed her to do.

"One, two, three…" Eve started counting as though that was her assignment—the one thing she could still do after she had done so much.

"We've got a crown," the doctor said excitedly.

When Eve got to ten, Lisa relaxed, gulping in air as her shoulders went limp.

"Eve," the doctor said, and she snapped to attention. "I want you and Jeff to hold Lisa up on this one. Make a back for her to lean on."

Instantly Eve stepped past A.J. whose countenance was pure concentration. She sat down on the bed as Jeff pulled Lisa up off the pillow. He sat behind her so that her shoulders rested on his, and Eve's place evaporated. Quickly she grabbed Lisa's hand, and her excitement burst through her. "Hey, I saw the head. It's like right there." As she looked at her friend, it occurred to her that the one person who should be happiest at the moment was the one that was too exhausted to feel anything. Gently Eve patted the hand she held. "You're about to be a mommy."

Weakly Lisa smiled at her as a contraction wrenched through her body.

"Deep breath," Eve coached. "Push. One, two, three…" She was simultaneously watching Lisa and the doctor.

"Don't stop," the doctor called as he worked with the baby. "Here's the head! Great. Great. The head's out. Okay, Lisa relax for a minute. You're doing so good."

"Black hair," Eve told her, and Lisa's eyes went liquid.

A moment and the doctor exhaled. "Here we go again… this is it."

In the briefest span of time she had ever experienced, Eve's gaze caught A.J.'s and he smiled at her in awe and excitement.

Then their attention snapped back to the experience happening around them.

"...Seven, eight, nine..." Eve counted as overwhelming wonderment gripped her.

"It's here," the doctor said as his hands worked quickly, "and we have a baby boy." At that moment a loud wail emanated from the tiny form in the doctor's hands. "And he has a good set of lungs, too."

Relief flooded over Lisa who collapsed into Jeff. Quickly the doctor set about his work on the new life that had made such a grand entrance.

"A boy," Jeff gasped as he hugged Lisa to him. "Oh, man, it's a boy." His face buckled into relief and joy. "We have a boy."

The pent up fear and determination spilled over Eve's lashes as relief flooded through her system. "You did it, Lis. You did it, girl." She squeezed the hand that was still in her own and then looked over at the little bundle that the doctor laid into the clean towels A.J. was holding.

Carefully, A.J. cleaned the child, and then he stopped and gazed down in complete wonder. "Oh, he's beautiful, Lis." A.J. stepped over to the side of the bed with the baby cradled perfectly in his hands. As he passed the baby to Lisa, Eve got her first glimpse—lots and lots of jet-black hair. Once the transfer was made, A.J.'s hand found Eve's shoulder as the four of them gazed at the form that whimpered in Lisa's arms and then let out a loud cry.

"Oh," Lisa said, resting into Jeff who was smiling so big he looked like he might in fact burst. As Eve watched her friend, the tears slid into Lisa's eyes as she looked at the little creation in her arms. Gently Lisa stroked the baby's cheek with the edge of her finger. "Hi, little one. How are you?"

The baby let out another cry, and the four of them laughed.

"He's so incredible," Jeff said, mesmerized by the sight. He pulled Lisa's head back into him and kissed the top of her hair. "Oh, man." His gaze went back to the tiny infant. Then he glanced up at A.J. and seemed to remember the others in the room. The fringes of his lashes were laced with the emotion pouring from his heart. "Thanks, A.J., man." He reached over to shake A.J.'s hand.

A.J. shook Jeff's hand even as he said, "Hey, Eve's the one you should be thanking. All I did was drive." Gently he laid his hands on her shoulders, and that simple gesture felt incredible.

When Jeff looked at Eve, "thanks" was all-but unnecessary. She reached over and put her hand on his forearm. "You've got one brave lady here," Eve said as her hand slid from Jeff's arm to Lisa's. "She did all the real work." However, Lisa was in a world unto herself as she gently stroked the tiny cheek.

"Isn't he amazing?" Lisa asked in complete awe. "I have a baby. Oh, my gosh." Emotion, relief, and overwhelming concern for her new role slid through her voice. She looked at Eve as if she couldn't quite figure out where she was. "I'm a mom." Then the tears took over.

"And a beautiful one at that," Eve said as she leaned over and put her arms around Lisa. Head-to-head they looked at the tiny figure whose eyes were blinking open. "Oh, man. We did it. I can't believe we did it."

When the initial excitement waned and fatigue once again took over Lisa's features, A.J. stepped away from the bed and set about cleaning the room. Luckily Eve had done a good job of getting ready. He took the chairs back into the dining room and came back as the doctor took the baby to do a more thorough examination.

Working quickly A.J. removed the shower curtain from the floor and stacked it with the two pans of water next to the bed. Room in that bathroom was at a premium so he took the items to the other. He had just emptied the first pan into the tub when he felt Eve's presence behind him. He glanced over his shoulder, and his gaze caught hold of her standing in the doorway, hands in pockets watching him. "Can I help?"

"You sure?"

She shrugged. "I made it through the delivery. Maybe I won't pass out now."

"We need to get the sheets on the bed changed," he said, not letting his overwhelming desire to grab hold of her take him over.

"Okay. I'll get that done." And she was gone.

A.J. couldn't quite find his breath back. He had thought she was the most incredible person he'd met long before now, but the second he had been given the chance to see her stand face-to-face with fear and pound it into submission, whatever denials about his feelings that he'd managed to muster to that point had disintegrated. She was strength personified. Compassion, understanding, and beauty all rolled into one.

His heart turned over every time he thought about her voice on the phone—scared out of her mind and totally unsure of her own ability to handle the crisis. He laughed softly at the thought as he ran the water over the shower curtain. One thing was for sure, after today if there was a crisis in his life, he wanted Eve right there beside him.

"You want me to wash these?" she asked from behind him, and he jumped at the sound of her voice.

"Yeah, we need to."

She turned to leave.

"And the towels too," he called.

Her form reappeared in the doorway. "I thought I told you, I don't do blood."

"Yeah, seems like I remember that part," he said with a laugh, and once again she was gone. Love, there was simply no other word for it, swept over him, and all other thoughts vanished. Somehow he had to find a way to tell her because sooner or later his body was going to get away from his mind, and at that point there was no telling where this would go.

Dr. Breely had taken his instruments to the other bathroom, and Eve was busy wiping the master bath floor when A.J. returned. She heard him in the bedroom although he didn't know she was there.

"Hey, Mom and Dad," he said, knocking softly, and Eve's heart jumped into her throat at the gentle sound of his voice. "How's the newest member of the family?"

"Great thanks to someone," Lisa said softly.

She didn't have to see his eyes, Eve knew how serene they would look by heart.

"Thanks for keeping Dad here in one piece," Lisa said as she reached up to put a hand on Jeff who sat beside her on the bed.

"Oh, so you didn't tell her about the black diamonds then?" A.J. asked with a laugh.

"Shhh," Jeff said instantly. "That was supposed to be a secret."

"Some secret," Lisa said, and Eve heard the fatigue in her friend's voice. "If you wanted that one to fly, you should've taken

Eve. Isn't that right, Eve?"

Her heart snagged as she stood and stepped over to the door. "I certainly would've been safer."

When Eve's gaze caught on A.J.'s smile, her heart did a somersault right through her chest. She pushed the hair up out of her face as she ducked back into the bathroom and threw the rag in the sink. Without question she knew they could see straight through her when she looked at A.J., so she quickly decided it was best not to so much as glance in his direction when she walked back into the room. However, with his light gray sweater and happiness beaming from that sweet face, that wasn't exactly easy.

"So," she said, focusing on the little family of three rather than on the figure standing on the other side of the bed, "what's this little miracle's name anyway?"

"Alexander Jeffrey," Lisa said lovingly.

"Alexander," Eve repeated as she smiled and brushed a gentle hand over the baby's head. "That was Dustin's middle name."

Lisa smiled at her. "It was my grandfather's, too."

"It's a beautiful name," Eve said as tears came to her eyes. "Just like he is."

"Yeah, and I wonder where you got the Jeffrey part," A.J. said teasingly. "Must be the milkman's name or something."

"Hey, you better watch it over there." Jeff pointed a warning finger at A.J., but he laughed long before the statement had a chance to sound serious.

"Alexander Jeffrey," Eve said softly as she gazed at the tiny scrunched up face. Then the name jumped through her. "A.J."

"What?" he asked.

"No," she said, laughing. "That's his initials—A.J."

"Oh, no," Jeff said in mock distress. He looked down at Lisa. "Is it too late to change our minds?"

She didn't bother to even respond to the comment. Instead she looked down at the little face and smiled. "You hear that, Alex? You're named after four heroes."

Undiluted joy slipped over A.J.'s features even as Eve tried not to watch him. Slowly he shook his head as he took in the scene. After a moment, noise at the door brought the four gazes to it.

"I think we should let the new mama have some rest," Dr. Breely said clearly not wanting to break up the party.

"Yeah," A.J. said softly. "I think things are clean enough. We can do the rest later."

Eve and A.J. started for the door.

"Is it okay if I stay?" Jeff asked, sounding unsure.

Dr. Breely smiled. "They're all yours."

They walked out into the living room, and A.J. shut the door quietly behind them. Midway across the dining room the doctor turned to him.

"Thanks so much, Doc," A.J. said, suddenly feeling far older than he ever had before. "We were lucky to have you."

"I think they are lucky to have such good friends as you two," Dr. Breely said.

A.J. glanced at his watch. "You want me to take you back down?"

"Actually," the doctor said with a glance out the window that was now cloaked in falling darkness, "I thought maybe I'd stay up here tonight, and tomorrow we could transport the two of them back down to the hospital. I'd really like the pediatrician to check the baby out."

"Okay," A.J. said, working through that plan. "You can have my room. I can take the couch."

"He could have my room," Eve said, stepping forward from where she was leaning on the back of the couch.

"Oh, no. I'm not going to make a lady sleep on the couch," Dr. Breely said. "Even my dear wife, Charlotta, God rest her soul, sent me to the couch when someone was banished there. No, I couldn't take your room."

"It's settled then," A.J. said.

"You know we really probably need to think about something for supper," Eve said, sighing slowly.

"It's not hospital food," A.J. said to Dr. Breely, "but she's not too bad of a cook."

Eve shot him an I-can't-believe-you-just-said-that look.

"Well, if she cooks like she nurses, we're in good shape," Dr. Breely said.

"Why don't you go get settled?" Eve asked. "I'll get something started."

A.J. waited for Dr. Breely to turn back for the other bedrooms, and when Eve turned for the kitchen and brushed close to him, his sanity went with her. Scratching his head to beat the desire back down, he turned and followed them.

Adrenaline. It was the only logical explanation of how Eve was still awake as she and the three men spent the meal getting to know one another. Dr. Breely found A.J.'s stories of the big city trauma scene fascinating, and although a few of them threatened to make her sick, she too was enthralled. It wasn't the stories themselves, but how calmly he seemed to handle them and how no matter how horrible they were, he seemed to have a way of thinking through a situation so the best thing could be done. From the little girl stuck in the drainpipe to the day that he and Jeff had met on a windy bridge—trying to pull a life back over the side—the stories solidified what she was beginning to see so clearly: There was far more to this soft-spoken gentle soul than she had ever given him credit for.

"Well, it sounds like Houston's mighty lucky to have the two of you in its service," Dr. Breely said with a note of approval in his voice. "Macho's a dime a dozen these days, but real courage is getting harder and harder to come by all the time."

A.J. shrugged as his gaze focused on his glass. "I guess you do what you have to do."

"Yes, you do," Dr. Breely said.

Eve's gaze went to the downcast, thought-filled eyes she knew by heart. The heroism he exhibited wasn't about showing off to the world, it was based in a genuine desire to do whatever he could to help. Right or wrong. Whether it turned out well or not, he was going to be right in there helping, doing whatever he could to make a difference. She had thought him so young, and yet it had nothing to do with being young. He had seen the horrors of the world, and he chose to live despite them. It was a standard she wished she had the courage to reach for.

A moment of silence wrapped around the room, and then Jeff pushed back from the table. "I guess I'd better go check on them again. Make sure they haven't escaped or something."

Instantly Eve snapped back to reality as she, too, stood and grabbed for dishes. "Yeah, I'd better get this cleaned up."

"Here," A.J. said, stopping her hand with one touch as Jeff left. "I'll get these. You go relax."

"I can get them," she said, not wanting him to think her weak.

But his smile wafted through her tired soul. "I think you've done enough for today."

"Oh, you think?" she asked as mischievousness slipped from his eyes to her heart.

"Never argue with a man who's offering to do the dishes," Dr. Breely said earnestly, and both gazes went to him. "That was the mantra my Charlotta lived by."

"Well, Charlotta was a smart woman," A.J. said, gazing right into Eve's eyes.

Her spirit felt like it might float right off the earth as Eve released the dish in her hand to his care. "Well, I could use a shower."

"There you go," Dr. Breely said, standing. "Now, you go get comfortable. Us men can handle a few dishes."

She stopped for one more moment as if to give them a chance to change their minds.

"Go on," A.J. said with a slight nod. "We'll still be here when you get back."

"You promise?" she asked as fate turned a page right before her eyes.

"You know it."

When Eve came out of the bathroom, A.J. took his turn. After a quick shower, he stood at the mirror. Without bothering too long with styling his hair, he ran some gel through it and called it good. He didn't even bother to grab a cap as he headed out to the living room. This wasn't about impressing her, it was simply about wanting to be with her every single moment that was available to him. However, when he stepped back out into the living room, only Dr. Breely was there, sitting in the chair reading.

"Shower's free," A.J. said, not totally feeling in the same league with the good doctor.

"Ah, okay," Dr. Breely said, looking up at him. Then he returned to his reading. "Snow stopped. It's a nice night out."

"Oh, really?"

The old man's face lit with a soft smile. "I think you should go see for yourself."

With a question, A.J. looked over to the sliding door. He

stepped over to it and pulled the curtain back. There on the porch white sweater draped gracefully over a set of black jeans stood the best dream he'd ever had. Slowly, quietly he slid the door to the side, stepped out, and pulled the curtain and the door closed behind him. She was leaning on the railing with her elbows, gazing down past the pine trees into the hollow beyond. Peacefulness slipped into his spirit as he stepped to her side and laid his own elbows on the railing next to her.

She never so much as glanced at him. "Dustin would've liked it here," she said as if drifting on a dream.

A.J.'s gaze floated over her—face, hair, gorgeous eyes. "You did good today."

"He always said you couldn't judge somebody by what they say, but when they show you who they are, you should believe them." Her head dropped on the memory, and then just as A.J. thought he was going to lose her to the memories forever, she turned and caught his heart in her gaze. "I couldn't have gotten through today without you."

Her eyes brightened with the tears, and he saw every emotion from fear to pain to joy slide through her eyes. Gently he turned to her, and she slipped into his arms—gripping him as though she was grabbing onto a lifeline. "I was so scared, and then the pickup, and they wouldn't come and help us, and I didn't know what I was going to do."

His arms tightened around her, fighting off the nightmares of the afternoon that seemed to be clinging to her spirit.

"Lisa kept looking at me like I knew what I was doing, but I didn't," she continued through the tears. "I didn't have a clue, and I just knew I was going to mess something up or do something that was going to hurt her or the baby." With a sniff, Eve wiped the tears as she pulled back from him. "But the whole time I just kept thinking about you, and about how you didn't even question that I could handle it." She looked at him, searching through the depths of his eyes for his soul. "Every time it got really bad, I could just hear you in my head saying, 'You can do this, Eve. You can do this.' And somehow I did."

The honesty pouring from her heart became too much to allow her to face him, and she turned and gazed far out into the darkness. For a moment the only sound was the whisper of the wind in the trees amidst her sigh.

"When Dustin died, I didn't let anyone see the real me. I couldn't. They looked at me, and they saw this rock. They thought I was handling everything so well. Somehow I knew I had to be strong, keep it together, so they wouldn't have to worry about me. What they didn't know was that I was really freaking out. There were days I couldn't even walk across the room without falling in the middle of the floor and laying there for hours. I couldn't go into our bedroom, I couldn't look at pictures, I couldn't even hear a siren without breaking down. I couldn't do anything. But the thing I really couldn't do was show that to anybody. I couldn't be who I really was with them."

Her words faded out as he heard her soft breaths through the tears. "Today on the phone, with you, that's who I really was. I was scared and terrified and panicking, but you didn't think I was weak because of that. You made me believe I didn't have to not be weak to be strong. I could be scared out of my mind, but that was okay because I could be that and still do what needed to be done."

Gently he laid his hands on her shoulders and after only a moment she leaned back into him. His arms wrapped around her as they stared out into the night together. Her hair brushed across his cheek causing emotions he'd never felt to surge to the surface. Just holding her this close made logic, reason, and reality slip away from him.

"You know, sometimes weakness isn't such a bad thing," he said softly. "Sometimes it's in our weakest moment that we find out how strong we really are."

She shook her head. "I don't know how you do that every day. Going out there into situations you have no control over every day. It's like putting who you are in the middle of the highway knowing you could get run over whether you make a wrong move or not."

"It happens." His mind flashed back to the sound of sirens and screams in the deep middle of a Houston night, and he took in a shaky breath. "Sometimes you do get run over."

"But how do you do that? How do you get yourself to stand out there the next time?"

That was a question he had been asking ever since he had found out the fireman he had treated that night hadn't made it. "Well, first you have to have a lot of faith. You have to believe that you did your best, and then sometimes it helps to have a really short memory."

She shook her head incredulously. "You laugh," she said, tilting again on the fear. "But I just keep thinking if something would've happened today, I would never have forgiven myself."

All laughter evaporated from his soul as his head fell. The air suddenly felt like a serrated edge to his burning lungs. "I didn't say it was easy."

A deep need to understand was lodged in her eyes when she turned to him, and her gaze burrowed into his. "Were you scared today?"

Had he wanted to hide, there was no place to go, and the question hit him so fast that honesty was the only option. Like an avalanche that starts with one rock but picks up frightening speed in mere seconds, the emotions he'd been holding down ever since the first time they didn't answer the phone cascaded over him. "Terrified." His eyes fell closed as the stinging pain of helplessness flashed through him. "I just kept thinking I should have known. I should have made it a point to call on every run. I could've driven faster, gotten up here sooner. I wanted to help Lisa. I wanted you not to sound so scared. I wanted to do something to help Jeff because he looked like his world was crashing down around him, but there was nothing I could do to help any of you."

A tear escaped from the edge of his eye and traced its way down his cheek like a single perfect raindrop. Then like the brush of an angel's wing she reached up and ran her thumb over it before tracing down his face to just past his lips.

"So white knights get scared too?" she asked softly, and when he opened his eyes, there was only a simple understanding in her eyes.

"Yeah," he said, sniffing back the other tears. "They do."

When her hand came to rest on his chest, the gap between his soul and hers disappeared, and as he gazed into her soft brown eyes, so did everything else. Softly his hand slid up to the place where her sweater fell from her shoulder. At first it did little more than brush the skin there, but in a rush one touch was not enough. The palm of his hand slid under her hair and cupped around the slenderness of her neck. The trust in her eyes was the last thing he saw as his own fell closed.

A brush, and only that, as the space between them evaporated in their need to be closer. Once, twice his lips touched hers. Then need, want, and desire flashed through him in a blinding rush. He was no longer breathing, only living for his lips to be on hers. Deeper he meshed his soul with hers, wanting only to go deeper still until they were no longer two but one and the same.

Time and space skipped a beat as heart, body, and soul he slipped through their bounds and flew with the angel in his arms. One hand slid down her back to the hollow at her waist as the other ran its way up and down the soft fabric covering her back, sensing the smooth silkiness of the skin beneath it. Ecstasy itself couldn't have felt as good.

When his sanity corralled his body long enough to pull him back, he was still spinning on the passion flooding through him. In fact, he couldn't quite tell how his legs were still standing at this point. The last few moments in her arms made every death-defying stunt he'd ever pulled feel like sitting in a chair snoozing. Her gaze caught his, and he could see she was as blown away as he was. He tried to smile, but it didn't make it that far as it vanished into the breathlessness clutching his body. Then the smile fell into a well of confusion and concern as he searched her eyes trying to surmise if he had just made a huge mistake. However, there was no indictment in her eyes only unconditional trust.

"You shouldn't do that to me," he finally said, pulling sanity back to him with a gulp of the chilled night air.

"Me?" she asked in surprise. "What did I do?"

His smile returned. "Standing out here, looking all warm and inviting. You really shouldn't do that."

"Yeah, I noticed you didn't bring a coat."

"With you around, who needs one?"

She slipped into the shelter of his embrace again. "You know, they're going to try to take the credit for this."

Softly he laughed as the middle of his soul opened up to the unqualified way she seemed to be with him. The barriers had collapsed. Friends had given way to something he had only allowed himself to hope for in the middle of his deepest dreams. "I'd say it's an even trade."

And the tightening of her arms around him only solidified that belief.

Seventeen

They had managed to get Daddy Jeff, Mommy Lisa, and Baby Alex bundled up, and into the car, which was no small feat considering Daddy was behaving like he'd lost his mind, Mommy was still in a lot of pain, and Baby Alex chose every other semi-sane moment to make sure no one had forgotten he was around.

"We'll take Dr. Breely and follow you," A.J. said, wondering at the sanity of letting Jeff drive.

Jeff, A.J. was learning was not always the take-charge, I-can-do-anything firefighter he had met that first day on the bridge. That day he had thought Jeff had a handle on everything. Today, however, he was quickly learning how wrong that impression was.

"You're coming right now though, right?" Jeff asked.

A.J. glanced over the top of the car as he watched Eve help Dr. Breely into the pickup that A.J. had spent most of the morning digging out of the snow. He smiled at the sight of her. "Yeah, right now."

"I'd really rather have the shoulder strap," Dr. Breely said when Eve stopped to wait for him to scoot over.

"Oh," she said taken aback, "okay." She slammed the passenger door and went around the pickup just as A.J. stepped over from the car. Her heart smiled for her. "Looks like you get to sit by me."

Mischievousness flashed through his eyes. "That could be dangerous."

She arched her eyebrows at him. "Tell me about it." Then

with a jump, she vaulted into the pickup and settled in the middle of the seat. When he crawled in after her, Eve's senses went on an all-points alert. The feel of his lips on hers still reverberated through parts of her that she had thought had long since ceased to exist. Standing on that porch, his arms wrapped around her, she could've stayed there forever. Unfortunately life, it seemed, had other plans.

"You know, they're going to need a car seat," Dr. Breely said as if he was talking to himself when the little convoy had crossed onto the highway. Instantly Eve pushed the hair out of her eyes and looked at him. He shrugged. "I'm assuming they're going back to Houston at some point."

Eve looked over at A.J. whose countenance fell in concern.

"They don't have any of their baby supplies either," Eve said.

"Let's get them to the hospital in one piece then we'll worry about shopping," A.J. said, and Eve smiled at him as she rammed her shoulder into his.

"Just what you wanted to do today, huh?"

He smiled at her as one of his hands dropped from the steering wheel onto hers, sending pulses of heat up her arm. "Sounds like fun to me."

"Do you know anything about car seats?" Eve asked as she rounded the metal racks of the Taos Wal-Mart that was stacked with them.

"Probably not as much as you do," A.J. said, following her with the cart that already had several items for Lisa in it.

"Oh, boy. That's not what I wanted to hear." Eve finally stopped when she reached the place she had started at. She set her hands on her hips and surveyed the choices. "Newborn, so these sitting up things are out."

"Yeah, his head would look like them dumb dogs in the backs of people's cars," A.J. said, bobbing his head back and forth.

"I'm sure Alex would be thrilled. He's not even a day old and already you're making fun of him."

A.J. shrugged. "Hey, he's part of the family. It comes with the territory."

"What's the difference between these two?" Eve asked, indicating two carriers on the top rack as she examined them.

"Looks like about $40."

"Yeah, but what makes one $40 better? Or do they just think some dumb sucker like you might not look and pay the $40 extra without realizing it?"

"That was harsh." A.J. laid his hand on his heart even as he examined the two carriers. "Oh, this one has that turned handle thing. The other one doesn't."

"Hmm, I wonder how much difference that would make."

He stepped back. "I wouldn't have a clue."

She stood for a moment deciding and then reached for the more expensive one. Carefully she set it in the cart, but it didn't really fit. "It's for Alex. He's worth 40 extra dollars."

"Now what?" A.J. asked, placing a hand over the box to steady it as he followed her out of that aisle.

"Diapers and burp rags and pacifiers and clothes…"

"You know, there's only so much room in that pickup," he said, pushing and holding the unwieldy object simultaneously.

"Yeah, right, you just don't want to shop."

"I didn't say that."

She turned into another aisle. "You didn't have to." When she stopped in front of the display of various baby paraphernalia, she surveyed it. "Just think of this as the ultimate black diamond of existence."

He looked at her skeptically. "Uh-huh. I thought that was shoes."

Despite the fact that she was sincerely searching for just the right items, Eve laughed. "No, that would be the bowls."

"Oh," he said, stretching the syllable out past its length.

"Besides, I can't wait to see what little booties they have for him."

Gamely A.J. walked up beside her and examined the display. "So what are we looking for anyway?"

"Diapers," Eve said finally finding the tiny stack of newborn diapers. She pulled one out and handed it to him. Then she calculated the time until they got back to Houston and pulled another one out. "Better make it two."

Dutifully he put the diapers under the car seat.

"And we need socks." She reached out and grabbed a tiny blue pair. "Look how little these are. Aren't they precious?"

He took them from her and held them up. "How can anyone

have feet this small?"

"And here's wipes and a bib. Oh, look at this bib. Mommy's Little Angel. Isn't that just precious?"

"You're not getting any ideas, are you?" he asked with concern.

In mock annoyance she reached over and hit him with the bib. "You really want to go through that again?"

"Not any time soon," he said doubtfully.

"I didn't think so," she said, but barely got the words out before she was drawn over to the baby clothes. "Oh, look at these." She pulled one out and held it up. "Isn't this just the cutest thing you've ever seen?"

"Second cutest," he said with a grin. Then his gaze snagged on the rack of tiny hats just above the clothes. "Oh, man, look at this little baseball cap. We've got to get this."

"Yeah, now who's got the fever?"

"Now that you mention it, I am feeling kind of faint." A.J.'s steps swayed to the side as he put his hand to his forehead. "Oh, Eve, catch me. I'm delirious from shopping fever."

"You're delirious all right, but I don't think it's shopping's fault," she said as she sidestepped his antics to get to the next rack.

He stopped incredulously. "You're not even going to catch me?"

She held up another little outfit. "Shopping. A.J.," she said as she balanced the words with her hands. "Shopping. A.J." She shook her head. "It's a tough choice."

Before she could react, he reached over and grabbed her around the waist. "I think you should pay for that comment."

"Hey, now," she said, dropping her face into seriousness. "Remember the blue paint incident."

He looked around. "I don't see any paint."

"Oh, yeah? There's some right here." Her finger traced its way from his temple down his cheek. "And right here." She reached across and traced down the other side.

"And here?" he asked as he leaned toward her and found her lips with his.

The fact that they were standing in the middle of the baby section of Wal-Mart escaped from her consciousness. All she knew, all she wanted to know was the feel of his lips on hers. When he broke the kiss, he gazed at her and then shook his head.

"I never knew shopping could be so much fun."

"You just weren't shopping with the right person until now."

He exhaled. "I think you're right."

Knowing that she needed to put distance between her and the feelings he pulled up in her, she turned around and reached for another outfit. However, he never left as he wrapped his arms around her and rested his chin on her shoulder. She held a blue and white sleeper and a blue and gold sleeper up for his inspection. "Which one?"

"Doesn't matter," he said, and she felt him burrow into her hair to get to her neck.

"Hey!" She hit the top of his head with the hanger. "Pay attention."

"I'm trying. Believe me, I'm trying."

She shook her head. "I find that hard to believe."

"You think this is a bad, just wait 'til we get to the shoes," he said and buried his face into her hair.

She couldn't help but laugh out loud, and after a second he let her go as she went back over to the cart.

"Oh, you know what else we need?" she asked.

"What's that?"

"A shower curtain."

"For what?" he asked not entirely sure of where that idea was headed.

"To put in that other bathroom," Eve said as she pushed the cart backward out of the baby stuff.

"Why?"

She scrunched her nose at him. "Because… ew."

"I washed it."

"And I'm sure you did a very good job, but I'm not leaving Ash with a shower curtain that's seen that much of life." She pushed the cart down the main thoroughfare and turned into the household goods aisle.

He shrugged. "Maybe we should get them new towels too. The towels didn't exactly cover their eyes."

"You know what? That's a good idea. There were a couple that I really couldn't get the stains out of."

"No, I was kidding. That was a joke."

"Ha. Ha." She held up two shower curtains. "Which one?"

By the look in his eyes, it was clear he had no idea. "Umm,

that one."

"This one it is." She put his choice back on the shelf and the other one in the cart.

"Hey!"

"Hey, what?" she asked with a shrug. "Women's intuition—whatever the man says, do the opposite."

"Now, you know, I didn't hear you saying that yesterday."

She smiled at him. "Yeah, well, yesterday you knew what you were talking about. Today, you're on my turf."

"Oh. I see how you are."

"Besides," Eve said playfully, "there was a rip in that one I could see from the back."

Incredulously he shook his head. "You are something else. You know that?"

"And just what that something else is, we haven't quite figured out yet," she said, running a hand over various towels on the display. Finally she made her choice.

"All done?" he asked when she didn't immediately take off for another section of the store after placing the towels in the cart.

"Yeah, I guess so," she said, scrawling down her mental list. As they backed out of that aisle, Eve saw him pick up his shower curtain choice and turn it over. With a smile he shook his head and put it back as he caught up to where she was. "I told you."

His hand found the small of her back, and he leaned in close to her. "Next time I'll listen."

When she looked at him, teasing and unfettered happiness met in her chest. "Smart man."

"And these two little sleepers," Eve said, pulling them out of the sack for Lisa and Jeff's inspection. "We couldn't decide so we got both of them." She laid them to the side as her hand reached down into the bag for the final item and she smiled. "And this was not my idea…" Slowly she pulled out the little hat, and Lisa melted with one look.

"Oh, a little baseball cap. It's so cute." Lisa took it and set it on Alex's head.

"Umm, no. That's not quite right," A.J. said with a soft laugh. "Here, let me fix it." He reached over and turned the cap around on the tiny little sleeping head. "Perfect."

"Oh, no," Jeff said, smacking himself on the head. "What have we done?"

But Lisa looked at A.J. with no joke in her eyes. "It's perfect. Thanks."

"You're welcome," he said barely getting the words out.

Eve's gaze traced over him, and vulnerable joy was all that was written on his face. Quietly she stepped over to his side and wrapped her arm around his back. "If you need anything else, we now know where Wal-Mart is."

A question ran between Lisa and Jeff for a moment, and then Jeff spoke up. "It's going to be at least Wednesday before we get out of here, and then we're going to have to drive back. You guys really don't have to stay."

"But... oh," Eve said, having not realized they wouldn't all be going back together. "I didn't... yeah, I guess you're right." She looked at A.J. with the unspoken questions.

"I'm on shift Wednesday morning," he said. "I'd love to stay, but I probably should be getting back."

"Well, since it's like short-notice and everything, if you need to use our tickets to make up the difference," Jeff said.

A.J. held up a hand. "No, hey, that's cool."

"No, we insist," Jeff said seriously. "We won't be able to use them for awhile anyway. They might as well be put to good use."

"Okay," A.J. finally said, accepting for the both of them. "Thanks."

"No," Jeff said as he reached out for A.J.'s hand. "Thank you."

The brilliant stars shone above them as Eve and A.J. sat out in the hollow on the felled tree they had ventured down to upon their return to the cabin.

"You know," Eve said, leaning back into his arms as he leaned on the upright roots, "I always wondered why people seemed so different after they had a baby." A.J.'s arms moved slightly around her, but he said nothing. "I mean, I had friends who were like go out every weekend and party all night, and then they'd get married and have a baby, and they were... gone.

"I'm sure my friends thought that about me with Dustin, but we still did stuff, you know. Go out, have fun." She ran her fingers over the small rope of her belt. "But when that baby comes, it's like everything else just doesn't matter any more."

For a moment A.J. just breathed. "Why didn't you and Dustin ever have kids?"

"I'm sure we would have eventually, but he was getting his career started, and I was getting mine started, and the baby thing just got put on the back burner."

"Do you wish… now?"

"Sometimes," she said with a small smile. "I've thought about it, but me, with a baby? Now, there's a scary thought."

"I don't know." A.J. pushed her far enough away with his shoulder so he could look down at her. "I think you'd make a great mom."

Rather than protest she watched her hand slip down that rope. "I hope so."

He leaned into her so that his lips were right on her ear. "I know so."

She turned to look at him, and never would she have doubted that he would tell her anything other than the truth. "How did I get so lucky to find you?"

"I didn't think you were looking."

"I didn't either." Any doubt left in the scattered recesses of her mind drifted away the moment she released herself into the power of his arms. She was sitting there, barely balanced on the scratchy trunk of a tree, and yet she knew in his arms, she would never fall. He would never let her.

The feel of his lips on hers melted through her so that she wondered how she could ever have seen him as anything other than the man he was. Strong, capable, solid. Her dreams were no match for the reality that was A.J. Knight. He wasn't Dustin's replacement. He wasn't Dustin. He was A.J., and that was all she ever wanted him to be.

When his lips left hers, he gazed into her eyes. Her body couldn't have moved if it had wanted to—which it didn't.

"I don't ever want to leave," she whispered, and his soft smile slipped through her.

"So, you're ready to try those black diamonds, huh?"

One hand ran its way down the angles of his face. "I think I'm on one right now."

Gently he bent toward her. "First you jump off the top." He

kissed her forehead. "Then you slide down that first incline." His lips slipped over her temple. "Then that heart-stopping moment when you think there's no way you can hold on to control." In a breath his lips were on hers, and there was no doubt anywhere in her what that moment felt like. A moment and then another, and then he pulled back to look at her. "Tell me this isn't a dream."

"If it is," she said softly, "I never want to wake up."

He pulled her up into a hug so tight that her breath, had it been in her control, had nowhere to go. "Man, I wish this was a movie," he finally said when all the oxygen in her system was gone.

"Why?" she asked, catching her breath when he released her.

"Because do you know how easy it would be to take you up there and finish this scene?"

"Finish this...?" She choked on the question. Confusion dove through the happiness. "That's not what you want?"

"Are you kidding? I want it more than anything, but I saw what throwing caution to the wind did to my mom, and I don't want that for myself—or for you."

"Your mom and dad?"

"They tried, I think, and maybe at first they really thought it could work. But I promised myself a long time ago that my life was going to be different. That I wasn't going to fall into the trap that they had. And that was easy..."

"Until now," Eve finished for him as the compliment washed over her.

"Yeah, until now." His gaze fell from her face. "You probably think that sounds really lame and childish."

"No," she said sincerely. "I think you're smart enough to know where that line is for you. That's anything but childish." She wrapped an arm over his shoulder. "Besides it's not like I'm complaining or anything."

Soft uncertainty wafted through his eyes as that statement wound through him. "Are you sure?"

"Yeah."

Eighteen

"Here, I've got it," A.J. said, grabbing Eve's carry-on bag out of the overhead compartment.

"It's heavy. Be careful," Eve said as he pulled it out.

The bag came out with a thud against his shoulder. "No kidding what's in here anyway? Rocks?" Carefully he readjusted the luggage in his arms as they started down the aisle to get out of the plane.

"I can't tell you what's in there. If I did, you might know all of my secrets," she said as she purposely stopped walking one step so that his body would shadow hers a little closer. She couldn't explain it, but she really liked the safety of being so close to him.

Mischievousness flashed through his eyes. "I don't already?"

"Not by a long shot," she said with a smile. "Not by a long shot." Reluctantly she turned and followed the other passengers out of the door and across the sky cab until once again they were standing in Houston, Texas. "It's good to be home."

"You didn't like the mountains?" he asked, and she heard the hint of vulnerability under the teasing.

"The mountains, the stars, the snow... When are we going back?" she asked as they started out of the gate.

He looked up at a monitor. "First flight to New Mexico leaves in... two hours."

Her arm wound through his. "Boy, Lisa and Jeff would be surprised."

"Not half as surprised as my boss would be tomorrow."

"Ugh. Work." She flipped her hair back so she could lay her head on his shoulder. "Maybe home isn't such a good thing after all." They stepped onto the escalator marked Baggage Claim. "So, you think they'll make it back all right?"

"I just hope Lisa's had some psychological training," A.J. said. "Jeff wasn't exactly calm and cool about the whole situation."

"Oh, so, you noticed that too?"

Incredulously A.J. shook his head. "I always thought he was so together…"

"Jeff?" Eve asked incredulously. "Mr. I-Can't-Get-Two-Words-Out-To-Save-My-Life?"

A.J.'s face scrunched in disbelief. "Jeff?"

"Oh, my gosh. You should have seen him with Dustin that first time we all went out. You would've thought he was part of the wallpaper."

"I would never have pegged him for shy."

"Ugh, no. Shy would've been a major step up."

"Jeez, what happened to him? I mean I don't know that he's exactly out going, but he's certainly not bashful."

Eve smiled, remembering Lisa's words from the cabin. She tightened her grip on A.J.'s arm. "He found Lis." They walked up to the baggage return and stopped. No part of Eve ever wanted to let go of him again. A.J. dropped one of the bags to the floor.

"I guess love can do amazing things to a person," he said, draping an arm around her when he straightened. That arm felt better than anything had in a very long time.

"Yes, it can," she said as she laid her hand on his chest, and nowhere in her was there any hesitation.

It wasn't until they got to the little silver car in the parking garage that A.J. felt the full brunt of being home again. Her bags were stowed in the trunk. At her door, knowing they weren't going to the same place, his heart yanked up into his throat.

"Well," he said, reaching for her hand between them, "you drive careful."

"You, too," she said, gazing into his eyes as though her only hope was that he would find a way not to say good-bye.

"I'll see you?" he asked suddenly unsure of what was going to happen when he turned and walked away from her.

"Yeah. I owe you a pizza, remember?"

Softly he smiled. "Yeah, seems like I remember that part." A moment and he could stay away from her no longer. As she slid into his arms, even staying in that steamy parking garage forever seemed preferable to the alternative. He closed his eyes, imprinting her on his memory. Finally the hug broke, and he looked at her uncertainly. "Can I call you?"

"You better."

What he wanted to do was to take her into his arms and tell her the rest of the world would just have to deal with it. What he did was lean into her and brush her lips with his. It certainly didn't help, but to just leave, to just walk away was certain to kill him, too. "I'll see you later?" he asked, leaning down so he could see her eyes as she ducked her head.

She nodded and then turned to the car. He waited until she was in the driver's seat before he smiled and slammed her door. His car was on a different level, so he stood and waited with one small wave as she backed out and headed out of the parking garage. As his gaze fell to the two lone bags at his feet, ache traced through his heart. Their perfect weekend was over, and here he stood on the other side wondering if the magic in the mountains could possibly survive in the real world of life.

Reluctantly he picked up his bags and headed for his own car.

One day. It didn't seem like that big of a deal when Eve had called in to work to tell them she would be a day late. However, the moment she hit work the next morning, it was clear that one day made more difference than she had ever realized.

"The spring show is Saturday," Mary Jo said as Eve sat in the conference room Wednesday morning. "Saturday. And we are not ready. We've got run-throughs tomorrow, and the way this is looking, we'll be lucky to have half of the show ready by then. So that we don't have to waste time in assignments, I've written them all out here." She handed a stack of papers out to the people on either side of her. Eve took one for herself and passed them on.

As Mary Jo continued her diatribe, Eve's gaze took in how the hours of her life from now until the weekend would play out. Somehow this job hadn't looked like so much work when she'd first gotten it. The others began standing around her, and Eve's concentration came back to reality.

"And Eve," Mary Jo said as the others began to disperse.

"Yeah?" Eve asked.

"I want you to be point person on this. Make sure that everyone else gets their part done. If they don't, do it."

Eve nodded even as her mind traced through the tasks that was going to mean would fall to her at the last of the last minutes.

"I'm thinking about talking to the store manager about moving you up if you make this work," Mary Jo said.

"I'll... keep that in mind," Eve said shakily. The ramifications of where "up" could be shook her to the core, but she buried that. "I'll do my best."

A.J. hated rain—especially the kind that liked to fall when he wasn't totally sure where a call was located. True, he knew most of Houston by heart, but there were still a few streets that didn't just jump forth in his head when he heard them come over the radio, and a few that were so closely named that they interlaced in the files in his mind.

"Are you sure this is right?" Lerone asked when they turned at an intersection. He looked behind him. "I think that sign said, 'Commerce?' We need 'Congress.'"

"Commerce, Congress? Aren't they both right here?" A.J. asked, fumbling through the memorized maps in his head as Lerone worked with the perpetually obnoxious GPS that had never worked quite right.

"I think Congress must be the next street over, or two streets over," Lerone said as they got to an intersection clogged with vehicles.

"Which way?" A.J. asked.

"Umm, south, I think."

Sirens going, A.J. turned and fought his way through the traffic as he peered helplessly through the driving rain to see the next sign. His mind didn't have to see it, his heart felt the time sliding by. "Fra... Franklin. Crud. That's not it."

"It's this next one," Lerone said, pointing ahead of them and giving up on the GPS completely.

A.J. picked his way forward and relief poured over him at the sight of Congress Street. They turned into the traffic, stacked in all directions at a mid-afternoon standstill.

"Go around them," Lerone said.

"There's not room."

Slowly the vehicles in front of them exited to the sides affording space by little bits.

"What's this block?" A.J. asked, not wanting to take his gaze off the rain-streaked road.

"We've got two more blocks," Lerone said. "Yep, there's the lights."

"Thank God," A.J. said, wondering how much more his nerves could possibly take.

The ambulance came to a stop six cars back from the melee that had not so long before been a simple intersection. Throwing it into park, A.J. grabbed his bag, jumped from his side, and followed Lerone who was already several strides ahead of him on the sidewalk. Police, fire trucks, emergency workers were running in all directions.

"Over here," one of the firefighters yelled, directing A.J. into the center of the storm. "This one needs help."

A.J. banked to the right even as Lerone ran on. The woman who sat, leaning against the stoplight pole had bloody trails streaming down her face as the firefighter kneeling next to her fought to keep her calm. For a moment A.J. wondered why the other two paramedic crews weren't attending to her. Then he realized that there were at least four cars smashed in the rain-blurred intersection. Multiple victims. How many and how bad—that was for others to sort out. His mission at this moment was to help this woman in front of him.

"What do we got?" A.J. asked, bending down as the rain slid through his hair.

"Head gash," the firefighter said as A.J. sat on his heels to examine the victim. "A.J.?"

He looked at the firefighter in full gear, and the face and voice slipped through his consciousness. "Gabe." Recognition, and then something else. Not one part of him liked the look in Gabe's eyes.

"Please," the woman wailed, pushing against Gabe's hands. "Please, I have to get to my baby!"

A.J. refocused on the task in front of him. "Okay, listen, I need you to calm down, Ma'am."

"Her name's Serena," Gabe said, and as much as A.J. hadn't

liked the look in his eyes, he liked the tone of his voice even less.

"Okay, Serena, I need you to take deep breaths for me." He tried to look at the gash across the right side of her head, but she wouldn't sit still.

"I'm fine. Please, help them," she cried. "Please. I'm fine."

"It's deep," A.J. said to Gabe who continued to pin the semi-struggling woman to the pole.

"No, please. Don't worry about me. Help them."

"We need to clean this up so we can see what we need to get done," A.J. said as the blood streamed down his gloves. Then for a split second, his mind registered the long, black hair and the angle of the nose. He shook his head to clear it of Eve's face. It wasn't Eve. Carefully he worked with the wound, fighting to get the bleeding stopped.

"Have they gotten them out yet?" the woman asked A.J., and the terror in her eyes ripped his heart out.

"They're working on it," Gabe said.

"They have to get them out. They have to."

A.J. pursed his lips so that his mind would stay on the task at hand. Through the hair it was hard to tell how deep the gash was, but from the blood pouring out it was a fair guess that it was far more than a scratch.

"They said they were getting them out," she said, grabbing at A.J.'s hands. "But I haven't seen either of them yet. Can you see if they've gotten them out? Please."

"I'm sure they're doing all they can," A.J. said. Without a breakdown of the actual accident, his mind worked through the details. Gash on the right, she was probably in the passenger's seat. Someone ran a red light, and the other car hit hers in the driver's door. He could see the spidered glass of the passenger window although he didn't bother to look. That's why they had gotten her out first. She was the easiest. But who else was in there? He fought not to think about it as his hands worked to stymie the blood.

"I think we'd have a better shot at this if we weren't on a street corner," he finally said to Gabe.

Lerone ran by headed back to the ambulance.

"Hey, Lerone!" A.J. called to him. "We need help here."

"She's yours. We've got a mess up there," Lerone called back even as he kept running.

A.J. looked around and realized he was the help.

"What do you need?" Gabe asked, looking up to him for guidance.

"We've got to get her back to the ambulance."

"Just tell me what to do."

"No, not pink," Eve said in frustration. "I said fuchsia. Don't you know what fuchsia is?"

"I'll work on it," the girl who looked half of Eve's age said, buckling backward.

"Do that." Eve glanced at her watch. It was after three, and she hadn't had so much as a Cheeto since before seven that morning.

"Ms. Knox, they told me I was supposed to tell you that one rack went through a mud puddle on the way in. They need to know what to do about it."

"A mud puddle? Oh, come on. What do they think this is, California? Haven't they ever dealt with rain before?" She stomped off to solve the latest dilemma, grateful only for the fact that her dilemmas involved only mud-caked one-of-a-kind outfits instead of irreplaceable lives.

"How's her husband?" A.J. asked when they shut the doors so that the paramedic that had just arrived could work on the woman. Being 45 feet closer to getting out, she was better off going with that crew.

"Bad," Gabe said as they made their way back to the wreck. "I'm not sure he's even got a chance, and the baby's worse."

A.J. glanced back at the closed doors that were slowly disappearing into the crowded street. "The baby?"

"He was in the back," Gabe said as they made their way back up to the scene. "Driver's side."

The little family picture from a cabin bedroom deep in the woods crashed into A.J.'s mind as his gaze took in the scene ahead of them. Rain slid down his face, soaking into his soul.

"A.J.!" Lerone called from where he was kneeling next to one of the victims. "We need you, man!"

Without waiting for more of an update, A.J. raced to the middle of the rain-soaked street. "I'm here."

"Take over the chest," Lerone said as his hands worked to get air into the victim through the hand breather.

A.J. dropped to his knees on the other side of the immobile figure and found the compression area. "One, two, three…"

"Two models are out," Mary Jo said as she strode through the room where Eve was busy sorting through what could be washed, what couldn't be washed, and their options from there.

"Out?" she asked through the pencil in her mouth.

"Asian Flu."

"It's only Wednesday, maybe they'll be better by Saturday."

"And maybe six more will go down between now and then."

"That's not even funny," Eve said, looking up from where she knelt on the cold concrete floor.

"I'm not laughing," Mary Jo said.

"One, two, three,…" A.J continued to count as the rain dripped off his forehead onto the open shirt of the man lying on the street. Minutes and minutes had elapsed since A.J. had heard a heartbeat. In truth there hadn't been one since he'd started, but still he worked, willing his own life into this body. He bent down to listen between the artificial breaths.

"There's no pulse," the EMT that A.J. had taken over for said.

"We need to get him into a transport," Lerone said.

"One, two, three…" A.J. pushed his determination into the task as in his mind a plea for assistance from above slipped through him.

"A.J., man, they're here with the transport," Lerone said. "A.J.…"

He knew what backing up meant. "…Ten, eleven, twelve…"

"A.J., that's enough, man. Let's get him in the transport."

"Fourteen, fifteen." A.J. said as tears blurred through the rain.

"Let's get him on this," a paramedic A.J. knew he should know instructed. "On three. One, two, three."

The man was transferred to the gurney, and the emergency workers continued to work on him as they wheeled him away. A hollow emptiness filled the center of A.J.'s chest. Promises, some sincere, some meant only to calm an inconsolable person, flowed through his soul. "We'll do everything we can." "He's in good hands." "We'll take care of him." They weren't promises, they were lies. All of them.

"A.J., they've got two out on the other side. Let's go," Lerone said, clapping him on the back as he knelt in the street now awash in rainwater.

Pushing through the overwhelming fatigue dripping off his soul, A.J. pulled first one leg then the other under him. Hazy numbness overtook him as he stepped up to the group knotted on the other side of the cars. His mind wouldn't think, and worse, he couldn't really tell that it wasn't.

"No," someone from the knot said. "There's no use. He's gone."

When they backed up, A.J. saw the tiny form, looking all but lost in the sea of giants surrounding him. His heart collapsed over the sight. How old, he didn't know, but certainly not old enough to die like this. Tears and emotion collapsed over him. Suddenly he couldn't breathe.

"A.J.!" Lerone called from farther up the street. "A.J., man, get in the game! We need you."

Squelching all of the pain, he sniffed back the tears, pulled indifference to him, and raced over to where Lerone was working.

"This makes no sense," the young girl holding the three outfits up for Eve's inspection said at just past seven. "I can't find these on the schedule anywhere."

"Maybe they're extras," Eve said, her energy long since gone.

"I don't think so. They were with the show clothes."

"You have your list?"

"Right here." The girl handed the list over to Eve.

"Marsha? You coming?" another employee asked as she walked by.

The young girl holding the outfits looked around. "Oh, yeah." Without so much as asking, she hung the outfits on the end of the rack. "Let me get my purse."

"But..." Eve started as she looked up from the list two moments too late. She looked at the outfits, then at the list, then at the completely empty room around her. Slowly she shook her head. "I sure hope 'up' is worth this."

A.J. had been home almost two hours, but nothing held his attention. Television was a waste of time, he'd burned himself cooking a TV dinner in the microwave, even the drum set had no beat. His heart hurt. Every piece of him hurt. He tried to call Jeff's place, but of course, no one was home. He called Melody, but she was working.

Finally he rolled across the bed, grabbed the phone and after dialing, he ran his fingers through his hair that had dried in no discernable pattern. The click of her machine snapped through him, and her voice, soft and gentle, washed through his soul. He considered leaving a message, but what could he say, "I need you"? That was completely lame. So quickly he hung up vaguely wondering where she was. She hadn't mentioned any big plans she had for the evening, but then again, he hadn't asked.

In fact, he wasn't even sure that now that they were back home what anything that had to do with her meant to his life. Were they a couple now? And if they were, did that give him the right to ask where she would be when? It wasn't so much that he wanted to know where she was to keep tabs on her. It was more that he felt empty not knowing.

Trying to block her and everything else out, he closed his eyes and forced himself to drift. However, he hadn't gone very far when images began to collide in his brain. The street. Lisa's smile as she held Alex for the first time. The woman bleeding and yet begging for him to help her family. The tiny bundle on the street. Jeff holding Lisa and thanking A.J. for all he had done. And then further back to long before he really even knew Lisa. He remembered how scared her voice was on that phone call, how he had wished he didn't have to tell her that Jeff was bad, that she needed to come to the emergency room right away.

Then suddenly he was back on a darkened street, feeling the sheer invincibility of someone who had yet to lose a patient on their watch. What a joke that was. What a cruel hoax. That night he hadn't hesitated to assure Jeff, but it wasn't so much the promises as much as his own belief in them that now cut him to the core.

"He's in good hands. I promise we'll do everything we can." The promises, although vague, held out a thread of hope that A.J.'s soul now said was simply a stark lie. For when everything they could do wasn't enough, what then? When hope surrendered, what then? When they packed up their medical supplies and went home, what did they leave for those to whom those false promises had been made?

Although he didn't want to think about it, he knew. He knew because she had told him. "I'd lie there in the floor for hours and cry." She thought he was so courageous, that he could do the all-but-impossible—her white knight. That was the cruelest joke of them all. He was no white knight, swooping in to save the day. No, he had failed her. Even before he knew her, he had failed her.

His mind slipped back to a graveyard and the sight of the coffin resting for a time over a newly dug grave. All the what ifs attacked him at once, but they all led him right back to had he done things differently, the image of that beautiful face, fighting back overwhelming tears might never have happened. Guilt spread through him, and in a poor attempt to thwart it, he rolled off the bed.

He was the only one who knew—if she knew what he knew, she would never want to see him again. And he didn't blame her one bit.

At eleven-thirty Eve sighed in resignation. There was simply no more she could do tonight. With her purse tucked in one hand and her pepper spray in the other, she exited the building and crossed to her car. Once inside, she punched the button on the player and revved the engine. What was that little drumming thing that A.J. did with his fingers while he drove? She tried to tap out the beat, but couldn't quite catch it. Despite the futileness of the attempt, she smiled.

Through the nighttime Houston streets she drove, feeling in her heart that somehow he would call tonight. Or maybe he already had, and he'd left a message. She couldn't wait to talk to him, to tell him about her day, to hear him assure her that she could in fact make this work. That would be nice because right now, it seemed almost as daunting as delivering a baby in the very center of nowhere.

However, when she got home, there was no message. Sad, but trying not to be, she went to the refrigerator and pulled out some ham. He had work today, too, and it wasn't like she had told him to call her. In fact, as she thought about it, she wasn't even sure he had her number. Well, sometimes you have to do things yourself, she thought as she pulled the phone book from the drawer. She sat down at the table and ran a finger down the listings for Knight.

Unfortunately she didn't know his mother's name, and there was no listing for A.J. or even A. After three trips down Knight and the names on either side of it, she gave up. It was after midnight anyway. Tomorrow she would find him—if her body was still moving by that point. And with that thought, she went to take a shower.

The next night when Eve arrived home long at after one in the morning, elation surged through her when she saw the blink on her machine. However, when she punched the button, it wasn't A.J. she heard, but Ashley.

"Hey, Eve, we're meeting over at Jeff and Lisa's tomorrow night at seven for a surprise welcome home party. Of course you're invited. Hope to see you there." And she was gone.

Yeah, Eve thought, I hope to see me there too.

Three times in two days A.J. had squandered the opportunity to leave a message on her machine. He simply didn't know what to say. There were the feelings from the mountain that still brought a smile, but underneath those was the distinct possibility that his first words to her would come out, "I'm so sorry. You have every right to hate me." Every time her voice drifted over the lines, his rational instinct took over, and he hung up. So, he was at least mildly excited when Ashley called to tell him about the welcome home party.

It was a given that she would be there. Nonetheless, what he would say and how he would say it kept him awake long into the Thursday night as the Nerf football made its arcs into the dark night around him.

"I didn't say, seven. I said, seven hundred," Eve said into the phone at six o'clock on Friday evening. "No. How are we supposed to feed 200 people with seven slices of ham? Turkey? Yes, they ordered turkey, too… Well, my list clearly says turkey. What are we going to have to go down this thing item for item?"

She put her hand to her head as the frustration from the previous three days came to the surface in a growl. "How about we just start over? Would that help? Fine. Great. Let's start over."

"Surprise!" the three of them semi-yelled when Jeff appeared at the front door of their house.

"Hey!" he said as a smile that knifed through A.J. crossed onto his face. "I was wondering when we'd see you guys."

"We couldn't stay away," Ashley said. She reached up from her stance on the top step and hugged Jeff. "Now where is that baby?"

Jeff laughed and pointed through the entryway. Then he held out a hand to Gabe.

"Somehow I knew you were going to figure out a way to get out of coming back on time," Gabe said, clapping a hand over the elbow attached to the hand he was shaking. "And now, I'm guessing you're going to want your two weeks off, too."

"You know it," Jeff said, laughing. "Come on in."

Timidly A.J. stood at the bottom step, the gift he had been forced to get and wrap on his own tucked under his arm.

"A.J.," Jeff said happily, and then his smile fell into concern as he looked around the otherwise empty sidewalk. "Where's Eve?"

He shrugged as the same question traced through him. "Ash invited her. I figured she'd be here."

More concern traced through Jeff's face, and then he forced a brighter look onto his face. "Well, then, I'm sure she's on her way. Come on in."

"And Eve about flipped out," Lisa said as Gabe and Ashley sat on the couch, her arm over his leg listening to the winding tale of Baby Alex's arrival.

"I don't blame her," Ashley said. "Ugh, I would've been a basket case."

"How far along were you?" Gabe asked, clearly calculating in his head.

"36 weeks," Lisa said, readjusting the pacifier in Alex's mouth.

"Man, I would've been doing more than flipping out," he said. "Them babies aren't supposed to be coming that early."

"Yeah, that was the first thing Gabe said when you called,"

Ashley said. "He was like, she had to be like four weeks early, and four weeks at that point can make a huge difference. How much did he weigh anyway?"

"Five and a half," Lisa said, "but everything is perfectly wonderful."

Ashley smiled. "I can see that."

"Okay, emergency training is one thing, but that's like in a whole 'nother ballgame," Gabe said skeptically. "Didn't you guys freak out?"

"I did," Jeff said from his recliner as he looked over at his family now safe and sound. "But A.J., man, he never so much as blinked."

Gabe smiled over at A.J. who was having trouble keeping himself from running far and fast. "That doesn't surprise me. A.J.'s like, 'Blood? Ah, no big deal.'"

"Could we not say the 'b-word'?" Ashley asked obviously sickened by just the thought.

"Sorry," Gabe said to her as he laid an arm over her shoulders.

"No, you should've seen him," Jeff said. "Okay, first we do this. Then we do this. Let me tell you, if I'm ever in need of emergency help again, he's the one I'm going to call."

The image of a woman pleading for her husband's life met in the middle of the rain-streaked image of a man who A.J. had no power to bring back. "Lisa and Eve did it all. I didn't do that much."

"He kept me sane," Jeff said, tipping his glass at A.J.

"That's enough to test anybody," Gabe said.

"I'm not arguing," Jeff said. Then Jeff's face fell with concern. "By the way, where is Eve?"

"I don't know," Ashley said. "I called her and left a message. I tried calling her again last night late, but she wasn't home."

A.J. caught the worry in Lisa's gaze when she looked at Ashley. "You didn't get a hold of her?"

"I just figured she'd be here," Ashley continued.

Lisa's gaze jumped from Ashley to A.J., and suddenly he realized what she was asking him with no words.

"I tried too," he said, tripping over the words, "but I never could get her." There was a long moment of silence as A.J. realized he should have tried harder—much harder. "I'll go try again." He felt the four gazes follow him out.

"No, don't even!" Eve warned. "We've got less than 24 hours and now you're telling me that we're down to five models, and one of them is iffy?"

"We called as soon as we found out," the agent said. "They were all on that shoot together last weekend. They must've gotten something from the water."

The water? That was the very last excuse she wanted to hear. "Okay, let me get this straight. The show is tomorrow, and I'm down to four models who may or may not have been exposed to this thing." She growled in utter frustration. "Let me make some calls, see who I can round up, but if I can't come up with enough, I'm calling you back."

"What am I supposed to do?"

"Find me some models!" She hit the off button, fuming. "This is not happening." Her hand grabbed for the phone book and flipped through the Yellow pages to the listing for Models. How she wished she lived in Hollywood or New York. There she could've come up with models by squeezing the woodwork. Here, it wasn't nearly so easy. Her finger traced down her options just as her cell phone bleeped to life. Absently she hit the button. "Knox."

"Jeez. If I didn't know any better, I'd think you were delivering another baby," A.J.'s voice said over the air, and without hesitation she leaned back in her chair and breathed in the sound.

"If I didn't know any better, I'd think I was too," she said with a smile.

"We thought you'd be here," A.J. said, and Eve looked at her watch in resignation. 9:45.

"Oh, man." She sat forward. "Believe me, I wanted to be."

"Where are you?"

"Working. This stupid spring show is tomorrow morning, and I'm beginning to wish I had the Asian Flu."

"Hey, don't say that. The hospitals are filling with it."

"Tell me about it. They took half of my models hostage already."

"Ah, man, what a drag."

She shook her head. "I'm afraid I'm out for tonight. You're going to have to celebrate without me."

"That wouldn't be much of a celebration," he said, and she heard the disappointment in his voice.

As strange as it was, that made her heart skip a beat. "How are Jeff and Lisa?"

"Good. Wondering where you are though."

"I wish I could be there, but the way this is looking I may have to pull an all-nighter the way it is." Thankful for the distraction after three solid days of problems, she leaned back in the chair. "How are you?"

"Cool. Thing's are right back to normal."

"I thought about calling you the other night, but I didn't have your number."

"You were going to call me?"

"It was midnight, and I didn't have anything better to do."

"Have you ever heard of a little thing called sleep?"

"Hmm, seems like I remember that part, but at this point it's been so long, I don't think I'd even know how to do that anymore."

"You need a break."

"Tomorrow I'm on all day. Sunday I'll think about taking a break."

"How does roller blading sound?"

"It's January."

"Less traffic on the sidewalks. I can pick you up if you want."

"You need directions?"

"Na, I'll just follow the sound of, 'Help!'"

"Very funny," she said laughingly. "If I was there, I'd hit you."

"Then I'm very glad you couldn't make it tonight."

"Oh, that was cruel. You wait."

"Believe me, I have been," he said, and his tone yanked the smile right off her face.

"Me, too."

When they signed off and Eve hung up the phone, she wondered what kind of strange power he had over her. Just hearing his voice could pull her back from insanity's brink. She looked over the project on her desk, and although not one thing about it had changed, she now had a point to focus on beyond tomorrow morning. Sunday. She couldn't wait.

"That one on Wednesday must've been rough," Jeff said as he and A.J. stood in the kitchen rounding up snacks for the others. When

A.J. looked over at him in confusion, Jeff nodded out to the living room. "Gabe told me."

A.J. scratched the back of his head. "Yeah, it was." He pulled cookies out of the bag he was holding as he felt the words trace across his soul. "Sometimes it gets to me," he said, feeling like he needed to tell somebody that before it exploded inside of him. "Being out there, wishing I could do more, and knowing there's nothing I can really do."

Jeff's gaze lost all the teasing in it. "You can't do everything every time."

"I wish I could."

"If you didn't, you wouldn't be out there in the first place. You know, sometimes it's in the cards. Sometimes it's not, but you just have to do the best you can with what you're dealt."

"Then I wish the dealer was always on my side. Sometimes I get the feeling that He isn't."

The smile Jeff gave him was sympathetic. "We all do. We all wish every call could turn out perfectly, that we could save everybody, but just because we can't, that doesn't mean He isn't with us on every call. It's just that sometimes He has a different plan than we wish He had."

Slowly A.J. arranged the cookies on the plate. "So, have you ever regretted… doing this?" He needed an answer—a reason to go on or better yet, a reason to quit.

Jeff glanced over, and then his gaze found the countertop. "Once."

A.J. nodded, fully comprehending the depth of that single syllable. "I wish I could go back and do that night all over again."

"Yeah, you and me both," Jeff said. Then he shook his head. "But going back isn't what life's about. You've got to do your best with right now and let the past take care of the past. Like last week, I would've totally lost it if you hadn't been there."

"I didn't…"

"Yes, you did. For me and my family, you did more than we could ever even thank you for." Jeff's gaze burrowed through A.J. "And just so you know, while you're busy remembering those that didn't work out, be sure to remember the ones that did. Okay?"

After a moment A.J. nodded, hearing the wisdom in that but knowing it wasn't that simple.

"Man, that looks really good," Gabe said, slapping A.J. on the back and causing him to jump. "But you know where it would really look good?"

"Where's that?" Jeff asked.

"Out here where the rest of us can eat it!"

"You better watch it," Jeff said, turning with the tray of food in his hands. "You're starting to sound like A.J."

"You say that like it's a bad thing," Gabe said, and this time he didn't sound like he was teasing at all.

Nineteen

"Is that your traffic-stopping shirt?" A.J. asked when he and Eve were sitting on the park bench lacing up their roller blades.

"You don't like my shirt?" Eve asked, pulling the fluorescent orange shirt out from her body.

"I'm not getting close to you. They could land airplanes on that thing."

"Oh, yeah? You better be nice to me or else... or else..."

"Or else what?"

"Or else."

His gaze slipped over to her skeptically. "Oo, I'm scared."

"Well, you should be." She pulled one roller blade out of her pack and bent to put it on.

"Orange?" he asked, stopping his own lacing efforts incredulously.

"What's the matter with orange?"

"You have shoelaces that match your shirt."

"That's a problem?"

"My shoelaces don't even match each other!"

"That doesn't surprise me," she said, lacing quickly. "Clothes aren't exactly your top priority."

"Not high enough to get shoelaces on my roller blades to match my outfit, they're not."

She set about tying the second one. "Yeah, you're doing good if your pants match the rest of your outfit."

"Outfit? Hmmm, I never thought about this being an outfit." He put on his sunglasses and stood from the bench, barely catching his balance. Flailing his arms, he finally stopped. He struck a half-pose. "A.J.'s ensemble today is a fetching pair of baggy jeans with frays in all the right places. Now not machine-made frays mind you, but real, honest-to-goodness he's worn these things a million times frays. Coupled with a trendy yet casual jersey from the University of North Carolina." He held out his hands as if to show off his clothes, but his skate slipped again, and he almost went down as he turned his shoulders to model his shirt.

"Oh, and don't forget the ever-popular, yet so seldom worn right accessory—the ever-present backward baseball cap," Eve said with amusement as she stood from the bench and checked her own balance.

"Of course. What outfit would be complete without it?" he asked, holding his balance by the throat.

She looked down at herself. "Ah, man."

"What's the matter?" he asked in instant concern.

"I forgot mine." Her gaze jumped to him as she skated the two steps to his side. "I guess I'll just have to take yours." With that, she whipped his hat off his head and took off down the sidewalk.

"Hey! Hey!" he yelled barely keeping his balance as he tried to turn, lunge for the hat, and catch her at the same time.

"You want it?" she asked, skating backward tauntingly. "You're going to have to come get it." She slipped it onto her head, pulling her hair back and down with it as she put it on backward.

"Well, then slow down," he said obviously trying to get his skating legs under him.

"What's the matter? This can't be any harder than moguls, and you're an expert at those."

"I've never actually done this before though," he said.

"You haven't roller skated?"

"When I was seven!"

She shrugged, liking how out-of-control he looked. "It's just like riding a bike."

He managed to stay upright although he didn't look like a natural as he followed her down the sidewalk. "You should've warned me."

"About what?"

"About the fact that I was stupid enough to ask a world-class skater out to roller blade."

"Ah, poor A.J. Finally met his match."

"Just wait until I get you on some water skis, then we'll see who's met their match."

Slowing down a fraction she closed some of the distance

between them. "It would help if you'd pick up your other leg."

"I am."

"No, up. This isn't up." She demonstrated his contrived form of skating.

"Up? Like this?" He did as instructed; however, he jerked his body to get it done which threw him off balance. "Ahhh!" In the next second he face planted in the grass.

Laughing, she clapped as she switched directions and skated back to him. "Well, that was graceful."

"Hey. Did I say I was good at this?" he asked, rolling over and reaching up for her hand.

"If you did, you were lying." She reached down and pulled him to his unsteady feet. In an instant her comprehension pulled in the fact that he was only inches away—closer than he had been since they'd left New Mexico.

His smile slipped through her heart even as he held onto her for balance. "Nice hat," he said, gazing up at it.

"I thought so." She reached up and touched it.

It wasn't that she thought about it before that exact moment, but she simply couldn't take the distance between them any longer. Leaning just far enough so that she could find his lips, she brushed across them. However, one touch only brought a need for more. Suddenly all she wanted was to get closer to him, and for one second too long that desire took over the laws of physics as she pressed into him. By the time her brain kicked in to warn her, it was too late.

"Ahh!" she yelped, fighting to keep her balance even as they went down.

In the next second they were lying on the grass next to the sidewalk. Embarrassment, humiliation, mortification—they should've been yanking her up off of the trail, off of him. But none of them were anywhere to be seen. In fact, who happened by to see them, she really didn't care. She wanted to shout to the world how she felt, and this was as good of a way to do that as any. Gently she ran a hand over the spikes of blonde toned hair.

"That was graceful," he said as one of his arms came around her back.

"You thought so?" she asked with no hint of anything other than intensity. "How about this?" No other move she had ever made with a guy had been so bold as she draped herself right over his body, making it nearly impossible for him to even move. Her skate clunked on the concrete as she meshed her lips with his. A moment, another, until she was spinning on the feeling of his lips on hers, his body cradled in the protection of hers, his hand sliding up and down her back in perfect rhythm to the day around them.

When she pulled back and looked at him, what she could see of his face held pure disbelief. "I think we should go skating more often," he said.

"Oh, yeah? Why's that?"

"It's kind of fun watching an expert at work."

"Watch and learn," she said as she pressed her lips to his again.

A.J. could've stayed right there the rest of the day and not had any complaints. However, his senses finally kicked in when he heard the jogger's footfalls on the sidewalk.

"Okay," he said, pushing up from the ground as he pushed her off of him. "Break's over."

"Ah," she pouted. "I was enjoying the break."

"Yeah, well, if you're really lucky I might just go down for good next time."

She laughed as she rolled away from him. "Want some help?"

"No," he said as he struggled to his feet. "I think I'm perfectly capable of crashing on my own."

"Chicken." Casually she dusted off her pants when she was back on her skates.

"Smart," he said, catching his balance. "They call it smart."

She laughed. "Then here, how about I teach you to skate?"

His gaze slid across her skeptically. "Do I dare trust you?"

"Do you have a choice?"

Laughing, he put his hand in hers and turned his skates up the sidewalk with her. It took several strides, but his body finally caught onto the cadence of hers, and his strides lengthened. "So, how'd the show go?"

"Oh, jeez. Let's put it this way, for awhile there, I thought I was going to have to call you to come model."

"Me?" His skate slipped, but he caught it. "You couldn't be that desperate."

"You didn't see me yesterday." She skated with no hesitation.

"I hated to miss the party. How are Gabe and Ashley?"

"Glad they didn't come with us, I think."

Questioningly she looked at him.

"Ashley has this thing about blood."

"Ahh," Eve said with complete understanding. "I used to know someone like that."

"Oh, who would that be?"

"I think you know her," she said. "She's this really cool person. Skates like a dream, skis like a… well, we won't talk about that."

"Likes to shop and take people's heads off while they're dancing?"

"Oh, so you know her?"

He couldn't have squelched the smile had he wanted to. "Yeah, I think we've met."

It was after seven when they made it back to Eve's place, pizza and movie in hand. She pulled a piece out for him as he worked with the player.

"Have you ever noticed how much better pizza tastes when you aren't sitting at a table?" she asked as she took a bite of his and then handed it to him when he sat down next to the chair.

"Hey, you ate mine."

"Sorry," she said. "I was hungry."

"Good thing I didn't wear you out too bad, or I might not get anything."

"I have a feeling that would never happen," she said, sliding over so that she could lean against the same footrest as he was using. "I know how you are with food."

"Yeah, the same way I used to be with hats until somebody stole mine."

"I look better in it than you do," she said as she reached up and ran her hand over the black cap.

"That wouldn't be hard."

"Shhh, the movie's starting."

Midway through the movie, Eve had given up and laid down on the floor, using A.J.'s leg for a pillow. Where it flowed out from

233

under the cap, her hair streamed over the frays in his jeans, and his heart missed a beat every time he noticed it. Jeff was right. All the beauty that she possessed was nothing compared with the woman that she was inside.

Without asking permission, his hand laid on the bright orange sleeve and ran itself down the length of her arm just past her elbow and then back. Just touching her like this made the rest of his senses stand up and take notice.

After several minutes he felt her relax, and then her shoulders dropped for the last time. He didn't have to look to know she was asleep. She'd had a hard week. He couldn't blame her for being exhausted. He thought about her skating like she was born on roller blades, and he smiled. She seemed to have no qualms whatsoever in trying something new, and more astounding no hesitation in being with him. It was a feeling he could get used to.

At that moment, his gaze slid from her to the television, and then it snagged on the crystal rose looking down at them from the mantle. Funny, he didn't remember it looking quite so ominous the last time he was here. His hand stopped its exploration of her arm.

"You know this wasn't my idea," he said under his breath to the rose. "I didn't know this was going to happen…"

"Look at her, A.J. She trusts you," the rose said in the back of his head. "And what've you done? You've lied to her over and over again. Just being with her like this is a lie."

"I didn't lie. I just… haven't told her everything."

"Haven't? Like you ever intended to. Face it, you lied, and you know it. Look at her. She thinks you're this goody-goody white knight riding in to rescue everybody. What a joke. That's why you don't want to tell her the truth. She might see what you really are."

"What?" he asked fearfully.

"A coward. That's what. A coward who had the chance to save the man she really loved, and what did you do? You let him die."

"I did my best."

"Well, your best wasn't good enough, was it? Dustin's the one who should be with her right now—not you. You don't deserve her. You don't deserve her trust or her love. And you know it, too. That's why you won't tell her."

"I will," he said pleadingly. "I will tell her."

"Yeah, right. Once a coward, always a coward. Besides what

makes you think she won't hate you forever if you do?"

"Because she believes in me now."

"No, she believes in who she thinks you are, but you haven't had the guts to show her who you really are, have you? No, look at you, you coward. You won't even tell her you love her because you're afraid of what she would say. You're afraid she'd laugh in your face, and you know what? She probably would."

A.J. tore his gaze from the rose, and it fell to her. The sight burned his lungs. As much as he wanted to bury that voice, run a sieve through it and drop it off a cliff, he knew it was right. Dustin should be here, camped out in the living room floor, holding his wife—not him, some poor imposter who was an inferior substitute at best, a bald-faced liar at worst.

He didn't want to wake her up, but he had to get away before the lies between them pulled her down with him. Carefully he moved one leg that instantly screamed in pain. His chest filled with sticky cotton, clinging to every air space available when she moaned in protest.

"Shh," he said, bending over her and willing her to go back to sleep. However, she rolled over to her back when her head was on the floor and looked up at him blankly.

"Where are you going?"

"Home," he whispered.

In confusion she turned her head and looked at the television. "The movie's not even over yet."

"Yeah, but you need some sleep."

Blearily she smiled. "I was."

"I noticed." His smile was weaker than hers as he brushed the hair back from her face. "Get some rest. I'll call you."

"Promise?"

"Yeah, I promise," he said, not meaning a single word. Gently he bent and brushed his lips on hers, knowing it was good-bye, feeling that good-bye slice him in two. Then, knowing he had no other choice, he pulled back, stood, and let himself out, not trusting even a backward glance.

Just after two, Eve awoke again, and for a moment she thought his departure was only a dream. However, she could feel the emptiness of the apartment around her. Slowly she pushed herself upright, stood, and walked to the television that was still flashing incoherent pictures. With a sleep-heavy hand she snapped it off, and the little nightlight on the mantle snapped on in the darkness.

Solemn peace slipped through her as she gazed at the rose. "You know I never planned on this," she said, running a gentle finger over the iridescent colors. "But I can't deny it anymore. I love him, Dustin. I think I have for a long time. I know he's not you, and he never will be, but with him I think I can finally move on."

"Life is yours to live, Eve. Don't miss this chance living in the past with me. This moment is as precious as that one we had."

Her gaze dropped to the darkness at her feet. "I won't forget you."

"Hey, it's not good-bye," Dustin said softly. "It's never good-bye. Only until I see you again, remember?"

The warmth of the smile spread through her. "I love you, you know that?"

"I know. That's why I have to let you go. You deserve to live."

"With A.J.?"

"With whoever you choose."

"I choose A.J."

"Then he's one lucky guy."

The whole world felt so heavy to A.J. Without her, there was a denseness that hadn't been there before. It hurt to simply put his feet on the floor the next morning, and the ache had nothing to do with yesterday's skating excursion. At the mirror, he ran a hand over the scratchy stubble covering his jaw line. No one had to tell him he looked like a mess. He was, and he knew it. Thing was, at the moment he couldn't have cared less.

"Well, after Saturday, I would've thought you'd look like the devil," Mary Jo said when Eve breezed into the room on her way to her drawing table Monday morning.

"It's a wonderful day, don't you think?" Eve asked, swinging her briefcase to the table.

Mary Jo looked at her skeptically. "A wonderful day? Okay, who are you and what have you done with the real Eve? You know her, the one who usually looks like death barely warmed over?"

"She decided to come back to the land of the living."

"By choice?"

Eve smiled throughout her whole spirit. "You always have a choice."

A.J. tried not to think about her. In the garage he turned the music up to the point that hearing loss was more than a possibility. The drumsticks reverberated through the nerves in his hands as he pounded on the drums in front of him. But no matter how hard he beat, she was right there every time he closed his eyes. In stone-faced denial he switched over to the hardest heavy metal CD he owned and poured himself into the beat.

All through supper Eve sat watching the phone, willing it to ring. She couldn't wait to talk to him, to tell him about her upcoming promotion to head her own department. Girls' footwear and leisurewear. There was something appropriate about it, she thought with satisfaction. She couldn't have been more than seven or eight when she first started dreaming of being the one who decided what went on those racks. Now here she was living her dream in more ways than she could ever have imagined.

"You're not going out tonight?" A.J.'s mom asked when he flopped on the couch to watch television with her on Wednesday night.

"Not planning on it, why?"

"You just haven't been here much lately, and now I can't get you to leave. I figured you'd be itching to get out of here—go out on one of your adventures."

He tried to settle in on the couch. "Nope. I'm not going anywhere anytime soon."

"No L.A.?"

"Nope, no more L.A.'s. I've learned my limitations."

Concern descended across her features. "Limitations? I've never heard you use that word before."

"Well, there's a first time for everything."

When Jeff called on Friday night begging for a fourth hand, A.J. wasn't about to give in to the overwhelming temptation to throw rational out the window and just go. No, for her sake he wasn't going there again. She deserved better, and he was determined that she would have it.

"I can't," he said, rushing through the words. "I've got plans."

"Oh," Jeff said, and A.J. knew what Jeff thought those plans were. "Well, have fun."

"Yeah, I will." The phone dropped back to the cradle, and A.J. looked at it with a hard, cold stare. With a yank he pulled it up to his ear and dialed the number. "Mel, hey! You got plans tonight? Well, you do now."

By Friday evening when Eve got home, she knew something was drastically wrong. He hadn't called, and it had been more than five days although it felt more like five lifetimes. The phonebook was pointless; information wasn't any better. Finally her heart needed to know that he was all right more than her mind needed to not feel like an idiot. Standing by the door down the hall, she took a deep breath and reached up and knocked on it.

Her gaze traced back to the steps, and again she prayed he was all right. Quickly she knocked again.

"Yes?" the half-inch of face lodged between the door, the frame, and the chain asked uncertainly.

Eve cleared her throat. "Hi, umm, you probably don't remember me, but I live just down the hall. Umm, I'm the one A.J. left that box with that time."

"Yes?"

"Well, I just wanted to know if you've heard anything about him. I'm a little worried."

"About A.J.?" the face said. "Why?"

"Well, he hasn't called me. He told me he would, but he hasn't. I don't have his number, and I just wanted to make sure that... that he was okay and everything."

Doubt was all Eve could see.

"He lives with my mom."

"I know, but I don't know her name, and he's not listed in the phone book. Umm, I just remembered that he was your brother, and I thought maybe you might know something..." She realized this conversation was headed nowhere. "That's okay. I just thought..."

The door slammed closed, and her heart slammed with it. Then she heard the chain, and hope flooded through her when the door opened.

"Please, come on in," Chelsea said softly, and Eve's heart went out to her. A young girl out on her own for the first time. Eve knew what that was like.

"Thanks," she said as she ducked into the apartment. When the door closed, Eve pulled her hair back from her eyes and faced Chelsea—the resemblance to A.J. threatened to rip her in two. "Umm, I know you probably think I've lost my mind, and maybe I have, but... A.J. was here on Sunday, and he said he'd call. At least I think he said he'd call, but he hasn't and I was wondering if something happened to him or something."

Chelsea's petite, soft features fell with concern. "Well, I haven't talked to him in awhile. I talk to Mom mostly, but she never said anything."

"Oh, well, I'm sure everything's all right. I just... I don't have his number so I couldn't call and ask for myself."

"Oh, I can give it to you." Chelsea grabbed a piece of paper from the cabinet and scrawled the number on it. Then just before she handed it to Eve, she stopped and surveyed her seriously. "You aren't the one he went skiing with, are you?"

"Yeah," Eve said, and just the memory brought a half-smile to her face. "I am."

"Oh," Chelsea said knowingly. Then she smiled. "Then I know he wouldn't mind." She handed the number over to Eve whose gaze snagged on a picture on the wall just beyond Chelsea. It was of Chelsea and A.J., younger by about ten years. Until that moment Eve hadn't realized the depths to which she had missed that face.

"A.J. is really a great guy," Chelsea said, hinting very carefully. "He seems all run-out-and-do-whatever-you-want, but sometimes he can be so sweet, he'll blow you away."

"Yeah," Eve said, staring at the picture, wondering why he hadn't called, and knowing exactly what Chelsea was talking about. One more moment, and she wished she could take that picture with her. "Well, I'd better get going. Thanks for the number."

"Anytime," Chelsea said as they made their way to the door. "Oh, and stop by and talk sometime. I have a feeling we won't just be neighbors forever."

Although Eve said thanks, she wondered at that statement. Five days ago, she had hoped that was exactly where this was going. Today she was far less sure. Number in hand she went back to her apartment and slipped inside. She wouldn't let him slip away quite so easily.

"Isn't this great?" A.J. asked, tipping his third bottle of beer up at their table when Melody's two friends had left with other guys to go dance.

"Yeah, great," Melody said obviously not thrilled. "You know, it's not that I don't like going out with you or anything, but what's up anyway? You haven't called me in like weeks, and now all of a sudden you have this burning desire to go out partying."

A.J. looked at her, his eyes already blurring from the alcohol. "I'm sorry, Mel. I should've called. It's just... I've just been busy with... other things."

"Other things? Uh-huh, and this wouldn't have anything to do with that girl we saw here that night, would it?"

"Me and a girl?" He tipped the bottle up again. "Come on. You know me better than that."

"I thought I did," she said quietly as he stopped a waitress to ask for another beer. "You know, I warned you about that one."

"You know, Mel, you're not exactly helping here."

The waitress set another bottle in front of him, and after paying for it, he downed about half of it without coming up for air. Melody's face sank further into confusion.

"We could talk about it, you know. Video games aren't my only specialty."

"Talk? There's nothing to talk about. Besides I'd rather dance," he said, standing and trying not to wobble.

She hesitated another second and finally shook her head and stood.

"Hello, Mrs. Knight?" Eve said into the phone shakily. "I was wondering if A.J. might happen to be there."

"No, I'm sorry. A.J. left a couple of hours ago with Melody

and some of her friends. They were going out partying or clubbing or whatever they call it nowadays."

"Oh," Eve said as the air in her lungs vanished.

"I could give him a message if you want."

She wanted to, more than living to the next moment, she wanted to. However, it was abundantly clear that he was fine, and he had her number, and he had chosen not to call for a whole week. "No, that's okay. Thanks." When she hung up the phone, Eve folded herself into the chair as anger and hurt flooded over her. She wanted to tell herself it was okay, that he'd just forgotten, but how could that be when every single waking and even many non-waking moments she was thinking about no one other than him? How could he just forget about her?

"You always have a choice," his voice floated over her. He had a choice, and it was obvious that he had made that choice. Why? She couldn't find an answer to that question, but denying it made sense to nothing other than her heart. As the thoughts streamed through her, she curled up tighter in the chair and sank into the misery.

"I'm fine," A.J. said, swaying dangerously when they exited the club at just after two. "Why? You think I'm wasted or something?"

"I'm doing more than thinking it," Melody said, practically carrying him across the parking lot. Her friends had gone home hours before, but A.J. had insisted that they stay for just one more, which turned into seven or eight more. That understanding was no longer in his memory—neither was anything else.

"Here, give me your keys," Melody said, holding out her hand.

"My keys?" he asked incredulously. He held them just out of her reach. "My keys, my car, my drive."

"I don't think so." She tried to grab them, but that move threatened to land both of them on the asphalt.

"Why not? You don't think I can drive?" he asked teasingly, and then something far down reached up and grabbed him. "What? You don't trust me?"

"Not in this shape I don't," Melody said.

"That hurts, Mel. It really does."

"Yeah? Well, tough. Give me your keys." She lunged after them again, falling into him in the process. He caught her under one arm.

"You know, if I didn't know better, I'd think you wanted more than my keys," he said, turning sad, drunk puppy dog eyes on her.

"Hardly." Her body caught his as he stumbled into her.

"Why not? It wouldn't be the first pass you made at me."

She fought to keep him upright as they crossed between two cars. "I was four," she said irritably, "and it was a mistake even then. Besides, right now, you're not exactly a catch." Her hand grabbed him and stayed his movement as a car passed by in front of them. "Now give me your keys before you get us both killed."

"What? You don't like me now? Is that it?" he asked, and anger flashed to the surface.

"If I didn't like you, I would let you drive," she said as they reached his car. "Now give me those keys."

He staggered to the driver's door as Melody managed to slip between him and it. For a moment words went through his head with no real destination, then through the slow blink of his eyes, he looked at the girl standing in front of him. Images slashed over images so that he couldn't be sure who she was. "Please don't be mad at me," he said softly as he reached up and ran a hand over her bleach-blonde locks. "I didn't mean for it to be like this." Clumsily he leaned forward, but she was far too fast for him as she moved out of the way.

"Man, she really did a number on you."

"Who?" he asked as the thread of conversation evaporated from in front of him.

"Your model-perfect girlfriend," Melody said, and in the brief moment that he forgot about the keys, she grabbed them. "Come on. Let's get you home before those beers start really taking affect."

It was at least her seven hundredth game of solitaire, but Eve was no longer counting them. He was out with Melody. That wasn't terribly bad. It was the two friends they were with that bothered her. Maybe Melody fixed him up again, and he couldn't tell her no. But that didn't explain Monday, Tuesday, Wednesday... She snapped another card out of the deck.

She wanted to be mad, to be furious, to hate him forever and go on with her life. The only problem was, she couldn't do that. He now had a place inside her, a place she couldn't just deny no matter how much she wanted to. Then again, what more did she expect? She knew from the beginning that he wasn't exactly stable. Jumping from job to job, and what was that whole L.A. thing anyway? Who just picks up and moves out there for no good reason?

Another card snapped out of her hand, and hit the table. Her finger tapped up and down on the table like a bored woodpecker as her mind searched for a place to play. He was jerking her around, that's what he was doing. Playing with her, toying with her. Sure, she hadn't wanted more than a friend to begin with, but that was no longer the case. Humiliation ran over her when she thought about her actions in the mountains. He probably thought it was hilarious how she had practically thrown herself at him.

Then there was Sunday... Ugh. She couldn't even think about that. How could she have let herself fall for someone so obviously not ready for commitment, so obviously immature as A.J. Knight? He was a kid. He always would be, and she would be better off if she just found a way to put him out of her head and her heart for good.

From the moment A.J. opened his eyes to the sunshine the next morning, the world was set on permanent spin cycle. "Ugh," he moaned, draping an arm over his stinging eyes. With the other hand he managed to take hold of the curtain and pull it across the window. However, his hand continued long past the stopping point, and when it landed, the lamp didn't quite move out of the way quickly enough. The resulting crash echoed through his head like a gong. "Ugh."

Two tons of bricks couldn't have felt heavier as he rolled to one side and pulled himself up off the bed. When he looked down, he realized he was still in the same clothes from the night before—only now they smelled much worse than he remembered them. Flashes of pictures jumped through his mind in no real pattern as he swayed forward on the bed. The bar. He remembered that part. And dancing. Vaguely he remembered that. And then there was something about Melody that he couldn't quite catch onto.

Pushing that and everything else away, he stood and made his way across the hall into the bathroom. His mouth felt like someone had stuffed it full of cotton. If it was possible, he looked even worse than he felt, he thought when he glanced into the mirror. He fought with his eyelids to keep them open although he wasn't really sure why that was such a good idea. It would be so much better to simply let them have their way and go closed permanently. Knowing that he couldn't go downstairs in this shape, he turned on the shower, but before he could take even a stitch of clothes off, his hand found the wall as the spinning recommenced. Slowly, carefully, he slid down the wall and laid his head on his knees. Hollow tears slid from his burning eyes, and he couldn't get enough energy up to even care why. All he wanted to do was to sit right there and hurt forever.

Twenty

The moment he drove up to the grocery store, A.J. knew he was in trouble. First of all, according to the radio report there was only one victim—a cardiac arrest with possible head trauma from the fall. However, one ambulance was already parked out front along with a fire truck. So either it was worse than the radio said or he had just driven through noon traffic for nothing.

"I've got the stuff," Lerone said, grabbing the bag and sliding from his seat.

With the precision that comes with a lot of practice, A.J. threw the vehicle in park and jumped out his door. He was racing up to the automatic doors just as the stretcher came out the Exit on the other side. In the next heartbeat, Lerone followed it out.

"They got it," Lerone said in annoyance.

"That's it?" A.J. asked. "What's up with the fire truck?"

"They were here on a routine walk-through inspection when the guy keeled over in produce."

"Talk about good timing," A.J. said, turning with Lerone for the ambulance just as two firefighters walked out of the store behind them.

"Well, fancy meeting you here," Gabe said, clapping A.J. on the back before A.J. even knew he was there.

"I should've guessed," A.J. said, laughing. "I'd pass out too if I saw you walking by."

"Such a funny line from such an unfunny person. What's going on? I hear you and Eve are burning up the town these days."

Confusion flashed over A.J. as they walked up to the fire truck. "Who told you that?"

"Hey, A.J.," Jeff said, sneaking up from behind him and goosing him in the ribs. "Long time no see. You hibernating at

Eve's these days or what?"

"I... Umm... You guys are going to put me out of a job showing up on calls like this," he said, totally clueless as to how to answer their other questions.

"Not likely," Gabe said, swinging a leg up into the truck. "Captain Fearless here can't even count to fifteen."

"It's not my fault they kept coming on the loudspeaker. 'Ding, spill on aisle seven. Ding, price check on aisle two,'" Jeff said.

"Like I said," Gabe said to A.J. as he jumped back to the asphalt, "don't quit your day job."

A.J. laughed although something warned him not to let them draw him in.

"Hey, you know, we haven't had a chance to take your money in a long time," Gabe said. "What's up with that?"

"Oh, I've been... busy," A.J. said, stumbling on the excuse.

Jeff smiled knowingly as A.J.'s heart fell into his shoes.

"Well, I'm not one not to notice a lovely lady when I see her," Gabe said. "And believe me, Eve's about as lovely as they come, but you can't hang out with her all the time—the rest of us might get jealous."

"You're just saying that because you want my money."

"No, I'm... well, okay, I am. But what do you say? Tomorrow night? Jeff's about eight-fifteen or so? There'll be snacks."

He wanted to say no. He knew he should say no, but instead he nodded. "As long as you let me win a few."

"Let you win? That's hardly..."

"A.J.," Lerone called from the ambulance door, "we've got another call."

"Gotta go," A.J. said with a wave. "See you guys tomorrow night."

"See ya," Gabe called.

"Take care of yourself out there," Jeff called, and A.J. waved again just as he jumped into the ambulance.

Work was the only thing keeping her sane. Over and over, Eve told herself how important it was to get started on the right foot in this new position. She didn't want the employees under her or the new manager over her to think she wasn't capable and committed to doing the job to the best of her ability, and so it was easy to rationalize the extra hours spent at the store. It wasn't hard to bury herself in the work and pretend like there was no rest of her life.

In fact, she had done such a good job of it that when she got home with only a week to go in February, she never so much as questioned the blinking red light on her machine. She punched it and then walked into the kitchen where she slipped off her shoes.

"Hey, Eve girl. Long time no talk," Lisa said from the machine, and Eve's spirit crashed to the ground on the sound. "Give me a call. We need to catch up, and I want to hear *everything*. Oh, and poker night tomorrow night. Come on over. I promise I won't make you wallpaper."

Lisa signed off, and Eve sat down at the table with the small bottle of water. Lisa wanted to hear everything. Everything. That explained why Lisa hadn't been beating down her door—she still thought everything was great with her and A.J. Better than great by the sound of that message. The ache in Eve's chest knifed through her throat. Telling Lisa would do one of two things: either confirm Eve's worst fears that A.J. wanted nothing to do with her or make two of his good friends hate him forever. As angry as she was at him, she didn't want him to suffer just because he didn't want to go out with her. There were far worse offenses in life than that.

And so, she decided that making that call could wait—at least until Lisa called back and demanded answers. That moment would come eventually, but it wasn't here yet, and at the moment that was all that Eve really cared about.

Seven-thirty wasn't that early, but A.J. knew he should've at least taken something other than the short cut to get to Jeff's. As he stood on their front porch and rang the doorbell, the question of what he was doing here at all streaked through him. The fact that someone was bound to bring up the whole Eve subject was more than a distinct possibility as was the fact that Lisa already knew the whole story and was waiting on the other side of that door to pounce.

That thought turned him back down the steps just as the door came open.

"Hey, there," Lisa said, and A.J. knew there was no escaping now. When he turned, the sight of her holding Alex and bouncing him softly tore through him. "Look, Alex. It's A.J. Remember him?

He's the one that gave you your favorite hat." Then she stopped talking to the baby and looked at A.J. with a smile that held no animosity. "It's good to see you again. Come on in."

When he made the top step, Lisa reached over and put her free arm around his neck. He hugged her quickly and then stepped into the entry way as embarrassment heated its way into his ears.

"I tried to clean up, but nothing stays clean anymore. Sorry," Lisa said, leading him to the living room. "But have a seat anywhere you can find one."

Sheepishly A.J. folded himself onto the couch and shifted when the emptiness of the house invaded his consciousness. "What'd you do, shoot Jeff?"

Lisa laughed. "No, he went out for snacks. Seems he had this silly idea that I was capable of going to the grocery store with fifty pounds of baby stuff to lug along. He'll be back in a few minutes."

A.J. nodded, fighting to think of something else to say. Something normal. Something...

"I'm surprised Eve didn't come with you," Lisa said before he came up with what that something was.

He looked for words, but none came.

"I guess you two've been tearing up the town since you got back." However, the affirmation of that statement that she had obviously expected wasn't forthcoming. "I mean I haven't talked to her in like three weeks, so I figured..."

For all the screaming in his brain, the best his body could do was to sit there and rub his hands together as the sweat poured off of them. Her meandering sentence slipped into oblivion.

"Is Eve all right?" Lisa finally asked.

"Yeah," he said quickly. Then his gaze fell to his hands. "I mean I guess so. I hope so."

"You hope so? What'd you guys have a fight or something?"

He couldn't face her. The guilt in the middle of him dragged his gaze to the carpet. "No, we didn't have a fight... exactly."

"You didn't have a fight exactly. What does that mean?"

"It's just... I don't know." He shrugged. "I think Eve deserves somebody better than me."

"Somebody better...? What?"

Despite the guilt, he glanced over at Lisa, and instantly tears stung his eyes. He shook his head as his gaze fell. "She doesn't really know me. She thinks she does, but..."

Lisa shook her head slowly as if it was spinning. "Okay, I'm lost. When you left New Mexico you looked like you were about two steps from the altar, and now you're telling me that she could do better? How do you figure that?"

"It's just..." His hands were rubbing together at a fever pitch. "She thinks I'm this invincible hero, that I can do anything, that I always know exactly what to do, but if she knew the real truth..." He shook his head slowly. "It's all such a lie. All of it. I'm not invincible. I'm not a saint. I'm not even much of a hero. I can't do the impossible—even when doing anything else means that somebody is going to die because I couldn't."

"A.J., nobody's asking you to do the impossible," Lisa said gently. "We're just glad you do what you can."

Slowly he shook his head. "You wouldn't say that if you were Eve."

"Why not?"

"Because I... Because Dustin..." The memories yanked the tears from his eyes. "I was there the night Dustin died. I rode the ambulance with him. I was new at the time, and I didn't know what I was doing. I should've done something more to help him, something so he could've gone back home to her, so he'd be here for her now." He clamped his lips together to stop the tears. "She doesn't know...about that night." He glanced over at Lisa but could hardly make out her face through the tears. "I can't tell her now... I can't tell her she lost her husband because I didn't know what I was doing."

Slowly Lisa stood from the chair and stepped over to where he was on the couch. He sniffed back the tears, fighting to get them to stop, but still they came like soldiers over the battle lines. Carefully she sat next to him and laid a hand on his shoulder that was hunched forward.

"Believe me, A.J., Eve knows how hard it is out there. She knows you do your best on every call and she'll know you did your best that night."

"She loved him so much, and I let her down. I let you all down."

When Lisa spoke again, there were tears welling in her voice. "You know what I remember from that night?"

He shook his head.

"I remember getting a call from a young guy who knew that

Jeff needed somebody there with him because he was in pain, and he was scared, and he was sitting in that hospital all alone with no one to lean on. I really can't imagine how scary that was for him, knowing how bad Dustin was, and how much pain he was in himself. But I remember walking in and being so grateful that you'd taken time out to call me. You certainly didn't have to. You could've just left him there like that, just gone on with your work and let the hospital sort it all out, but you didn't do that. You cared enough to go out of your way to help, and I know I'll forever be grateful for that."

Lisa sat for a long moment trying to collect herself. "There are things we can do, and there are things only God can do. You did what you could. Don't beat yourself up because you couldn't do His job."

All the hours he'd spent ripping into himself about what he could've done or should've done suddenly felt very heavy. "But how can I tell her now? I mean she trusts me, or at least she did until I stopped calling. I think she's just going to hate me now no matter what I do."

Softly Lisa laughed. "You underestimate her. Besides Eve is smarter than that. She knows a good thing when she sees it."

"A good thing? Ha. I'm hardly a catch," A.J. said, sniffing back the last of the tears. "Besides she's so gorgeous, and I'm such an idiot."

"Strange, weird, bizarre, yes. An idiot? I don't think so."

The crash of the door brought their attention to it as Jeff walked in, two sacks in each hand. Instantly A.J. jumped to his feet. "You need some help?"

"There's more in the car," Jeff said.

"I'll get it," A.J. said, thankful for the interruption. As he walked out to the car, he berated himself. What had he just told Lisa? Lisa, of all people. Sure she seemed understanding and not at all angry, but still. He must've completely lost his mind at some point in the past. That was the only explanation.

The ringing of the phone pulled Eve out of the long, hot shower she was enjoying, and quickly she wrapped a towel around herself and grabbed it. She sat down on the bed. "Hello?"

"Hey, Eve-girl," Lisa said lightly, and Eve wished she had just let the machine get it.

"Hey, Lis." She pushed the wet hair from her face. "What's up?"

"Just checking up on my favorite nurse."

"Oh, then you must have the wrong number."

"No, I don't think so. So, how's life? We haven't seen you in awhile."

"I figured you'd be bleary-eyed trying to take care of two babies at one time," Eve said just as in the background she heard the card-playing commotion, and her heart sank. She wanted to ask who was there, but it seemed a ridiculous question. More than that, if he was there, it would confirm that he was indeed just fine and going on with life without her.

"That's what I was calling about," Lisa said. "I'm in desperate need of a shopping break. This house is driving me crazy."

"Have you been back to work yet?"

"I went in for a couple hours this week, but mostly it's been the staff."

"Ah, trusting."

"Scary, huh?"

"So, what? Are we going to take Alex?"

"Shopping? I'm not that brave yet. No, Jeff's off, and he's generously agreed to stay home."

"And you're not worried he's going to have a keg party while we're gone?"

Another cry of defeat in the background.

"No, that's tonight," Lisa said with a laugh. "Come on, Eve. Save me. Please."

"Well, if it's life and death and we are talking shopping therapy, I bet I could pencil you in."

"That's what I wanted to hear," Lisa said.

All evening A.J.'s heart listened for the doorbell as his gaze kept vigilant watch over the entryway. For some illogical reason he had expected Lisa to invite Eve over. True, he didn't want to see her or his mind kept saying that he didn't. Yet, his heart simply wouldn't get in line. It wanted to see her. It did, and that's all there was to it.

So, it was with soul-bending confusion that he walked out of their house at one and drove home. The memories of her smile at

70 miles an hour drilled through him. If he could just find a way to tell her… But what words could he use now? They all seemed so empty, so meaningless in the face of this. Shaking his head at even considering the impossible, he drove past her turn off and sighed. No, she was better off without him, and he would just have to find a way to live with that.

All night, A.J. was right there in Eve's dreams. Standing on the cabin porch, holding her, skiing, that first night on the couch at Gabe's. Over and over so that when she awoke the next morning, she was almost surprised that he wasn't actually beside her. It was absurd to let herself go down that path. He wanted nothing to do with her, and what choice did she have but to abide by that decision?

With that unbelievably difficult understanding, she crawled out of bed and went to get ready for the shopping extravaganza with Lisa. "God, help me get through this in one piece," she prayed as she reluctantly pulled a gold-orange tank top with matching sweater and a form-fitting off-white skirt out of the closet.

"How are you with directions?" Jeff asked as A.J. sat in his kitchen the next afternoon, having been summoned by his mother from the garage.

"Driving directions?" A.J. asked in confusion.

"No, putting things together directions."

"Oh." A.J. shrugged. "Not bad. Why?"

"Because I wanted to surprise Lisa with this baby bed, but between feeding Alex and killing my thumb with this stupid screw gun, the only thing that's going to surprise her is the mess."

A.J. laughed. "Trust me, I don't think she'll be too surprised by that."

"Ha. Ha. Seriously, are you busy?"

"Blowing my brains out with a stereo."

"Well, come on over here, I've got some headphones you can use to blow your brains out while you work."

"How is it I always get to work when I'm around you?"

"You're just too talented."

"I am. Aren't I?"

"Yeah, bring that big head and your talent, and get over here already."

"I'll be there."

"I hate this!" Lisa called from the other side of the dressing room door.

"The dress?" Eve asked with concern.

"No. That I'm never going to fit in anything again."

"It's only been a month."

"That's my point. I hate this!" With a snap Lisa stomped out of the dressing room leaving the dress in a heap. "Let's go get some ice cream."

Eve arched her eyebrows but said nothing as she followed her friend out of the store. "We could always go see a movie or something."

"No, right now, I just want a big bowl of Rocky Road ice cream."

With a shrug Eve followed Lisa to one of the mall's food booths. Before she could protest, Lisa bought them both ice cream and handed her one. They found a little table and sat down.

"So, tell me about this new job," Lisa said.

"Insert piece 37 into the hollow end of A and snap together," Jeff read from his position on the floor where he was holding Alex in one hand and the directions in the other.

"Piece 37," A.J. said, trying to hold the directions in his mind long enough to accomplish them.

"Into the hollow end of A and snap together."

Carefully A.J. tried it one way then took it apart and tried it another. "You know, Alex, if you would just stay in that bassinet thing, we wouldn't be in this mess."

"Tell me about it," Jeff said as he bounced his son softly on the cradle of his bent leg. "And you thought painting was bad."

A.J. mashed his face in concentration as he pushed the two pieces together finally causing them to snap.

"Done?" Jeff asked.

"Either done or broken."

"Let's hope it's not broken or we get to start over."

"Why didn't you get one that was at least semi-together?"

"Saving money," Jeff said, peering at the next directions.

"At this rate we're going to have to use what you saved on a mental hospital."

"Slide the side panel together with the foot panel at notches."

"I really should have my head examined for agreeing to this."

Jeff smiled at A.J. in victory. "Too late. Slide the side panel…"

Eve had waited for the A.J. bomb to hit all afternoon. Once when Lisa had mentioned sending Dr. Breely a thank you card, Eve had known it was coming. But it hadn't. She couldn't quite figure that out until just after five, they pulled back into Lisa's driveway, and parked conspicuously at the curb was the Civic.

"Jeff's never going to believe I only bought one dress," Lisa said, acting like she hadn't even noticed. "He'll probably search the car for the rest of the loot."

"I could let you hold my shoes, then he'll think you got more than you did," Eve offered even as her alert mechanisms screamed at her not to go into that house.

Lisa stood from the car and gathered her things. "There's an idea." Without question she started up the walk as Eve's feet padded slower and slower behind her.

She wanted to think of an excuse, but the only phrase that was complete in her head was, "He's here!" On Lisa's yank, Eve caught the door and stepped slowly into the house, wondering where he was and willing herself not to do anything stupid when she saw him.

"And the mattress goes in," A.J. said, swinging the cushion over the now completed frame. "Done!"

"Cool," Jeff said, nodding in satisfaction just as Lisa strode by the door. A heartbeat and she stepped back into the doorway.

"Am I seeing what I think I'm seeing?" she asked in awe. She stepped over to the now-fully-assembled crib. "Oh, it's perfect. It's so perfect. Just a second, I'll get the bedding."

"Alex is sleeping!" Jeff half-called as she raced from the room, and she waved to indicate she had heard.

"Very nice work," Jeff said, holding his hand out to A.J., but the gesture vanished into the vision that was suddenly standing in the doorway.

He had told himself that she was nothing more than a dream, that he could live without her, that she couldn't have been as incredible as he had thought she was. But with one glance at the slender frame, and those solemn, uncertain eyes, all those lies disappeared. Slowly Jeff turned to where A.J.'s gaze was nailed, and he smiled and stepped over to her to give her a quick hug.

"Hey, Eve. Have you been out spending all of our money?"

She looked down at the white bag in her hand and held it up. "Shoes."

"Figures," Jeff said jovially even as he kept his arm around her.

"Here we are," Lisa said, pushing by the two of them with a giant plastic bag of baby bed items. Without pretense she unzipped it and dumped it on the floor. She picked up one long padded piece of cloth and threw it to the side. "Man, where do you start with this stuff?"

"Don't look at me," A.J. said in mock fear. "I put the bed together."

"I thought you were going to put it together," Lisa said, looking at Jeff teasingly.

"He *helped*," Jeff said, directing a warning look at A.J.

"Well, I'm glad somebody did," Lisa said as she sorted out the rest of the bag. "You need all the help you can get."

"She's got a point," A.J. said, knowing his only salvation was in interacting with Jeff and Lisa and not focusing on the heart-stopping beauty across the room.

"Hey!" Jeff picked up a pillow and threw it squarely at A.J.'s chest.

"What? She does."

"Here, Eve, help me with this," Lisa said, and A.J. noticed how reluctantly she moved from the door. When she took the sheet from Lisa, A.J. took a step backward away from the crib.

He watched as she leaned over the railing to pull the mattress out; however, it was heavier than she had anticipated.

"Here," A.J. said, instantly jumping to help her. Her gaze grazed him when he bent to help her, and the sad helplessness in it knocked him backward. Carefully he pulled the mattress out as she put the sheet onto it. However, the sheet was barely big enough, and it slipped off a corner she had already finished. He reached for it just as she did, and in a flash, they both jumped back from the touch. For one unbelievable second her gaze locked with his, and then she buried her gaze in the remainder of the task.

"Done," he said, dropping the mattress into the bed. He hadn't wanted to hurt her, but he had. That much was too utterly clear for words.

Lisa handed him another piece of the bedding. "That goes by the bars."

Trying not to get tangled in Eve's sights again, he worked quickly to attach first one piece and then another until the bedding was in place. Just before he proclaimed the project finished, a small cry sounded from down the hallway. Jeff started out, but Lisa was too quick and slipped past him. In the next second, they were gone.

"What about this?" Eve asked, and he heard the anger. She lifted a bumper pad.

"It goes on the headboard," A.J. said. He reached out for it. "Here."

"I can do it," she said, yanking it away. In rapid motion she attached the pad and stepped back.

"See, Alex," Lisa said as she walked back in. "This is your new bed. Isn't it great?"

A.J. wanted to be proud of the accomplishment, but it was clear that at least one other person in the room was less than impressed. Reluctantly he put his hands in his back pockets and tried to fade into the sponge paint on the wall.

"How does steak sound for supper?" Jeff asked, slapping his hands together.

"Oh, I've got…" A.J. started.

"I'm supposed to…" Eve started.

"No, now I'm not taking no for an answer," Jeff said firmly. "We owe you guys. Besides, I'm cooking."

"And that's a good thing?" A.J. asked, fighting to find any sense of joking in his heart.

"It's a very good thing. Trust me," Lisa said.

"Okay, I'm in," A.J. said, not daring to speak for Eve.

"Eve?" Jeff asked.

She shrugged. It the best they were going to get.

Twenty-One

They were talking, Eve noticed when they finally finished supper. They were—just not to each other. Although they sat on the same side of the table, there might as well have been the Gulf of Mexico between them. The one time their hands had touched, the butter knife had actually landed on the floor.

"Let's go sit in there," Lisa said when the food was gone. "Jeff'll get these dishes later."

"Me?" Jeff looked at her, and then he looked back at them solidly. "Yeah, I'll get these later."

They weren't overly subtle, Eve thought as she stood, making sure not to look in need of assistance from anyone. In the living room she chose a seat in the little chair that was neither Jeff's nor Lisa's nor the intimidating couch where A.J. sat.

"Here, Eve," Jeff said, handing her Alex. "You look like you haven't been spit up on in awhile."

Despite the awkwardness of the situation, Eve smiled. "He wouldn't spit up on me. Would you, Alex? Would you? No, you wouldn't."

Jeff threw a spit up rag at her. "Just in case."

"Gee, thanks."

"So, how's work?" Jeff asked A.J., who readjusted his seat on the couch.

"Slow."

"The slower the better," Jeff said.

"Very true."

"Eve's got news," Lisa said, jumping into the conversation.

"Oh, yeah? What's that?" Jeff asked.

She waited as long as could be considered polite before she got the words out. Then she put the fakest smile she'd ever felt on her face. "I got a promotion."

"A promotion? That's great. Congratulations," Jeff said, and Eve saw the same words flashed across A.J.'s face.

"I survived a model meltdown." She shrugged. "I guess that's promotion worthy."

"A model meltdown? There can't be that much to melt, can there?" Jeff said, and Lisa reached over and whacked his shoulder with a spit up rag. He looked at her in surprise. "What?"

Eve laughed. "No, the models didn't melt. Well, not really. They got sick, and I had to come up with replacements like two minutes before the show went on. It was a nightmare."

"Ugh, yeah. Sounds like an absolutely horrible job," Jeff said, acting like he was sympathetic, but Lisa hit him again because he really wasn't. "What? Interviewing models sounds like really grueling work. Doesn't it, A.J.?"

"Better than fighting rush hour traffic with nothing but a dumb siren to help," A.J. agreed.

"Well, at least they move out of your way," Lisa said. "It took me two hours to get home the other night. Two hours. I don't know how I'm going to do this when I go back for real."

"When are you going back?" Eve asked.

"Two weeks. Then real life begins. Oh, joy."

"I told you we should've stayed in New Mexico," Jeff said, leaning over to Lisa. She smiled and kissed him.

"And leave us here with all the work?" A.J. asked. "You would."

"Yeah, like you didn't think about staying there, too," Jeff said, smirking.

The smile and all the color drained from A.J.'s face. He ducked his head and put his hands over the dark blue material of his cap. "They couldn't do without me here."

"Yeah," Jeff said. "Like you're so important. You decide to show up when the job's already finished."

"Hey, now, they didn't tell us somebody was already on that call."

"And you were just heartbroken when someone was," Jeff said. "Darn."

"Well, I'll tell you, I'd a lot rather show up when they didn't need us than when they really do."

"Ugh, I hear you there. I never feel like my head's above board on those calls. It's like just fight to survive and drag as many with you as you can."

"Tell me about it. Man, sometimes I'd pay for someone who actually knows what's going on. It's, 'We need you over here!' 'Hey, we need help!' 'Can't you work any faster?' It's chaos sometimes."

In all her time with Dustin, Eve had never heard the guys talk so much about the happenings in the field. It was fascinating in a strange kind of way. It was like being let in on a secret society bent on keeping you out for your own good.

"You just wish you could help everybody at the same time, but you never have enough hands," Jeff said. "And the big ones are the worst."

"What's the biggest one you've ever worked on?" Eve asked, feeling completely at ease in asking the question.

Instantly Jeff looked at Eve like he had forgotten she was listening and then over at A.J. who had frozen at the question. For a second Jeff stumbled, and then he found a plausible disaster to relate. "Well, there was that pile-up that time out on Southwest. You worked that one, didn't you?"

"Yeah, I did," A.J. said softly although he never really looked up.

"That one was tough."

Silence slipped over the room as Eve's gaze went to A.J., and suddenly she was tired of being a spectator with no control. She was tired of being the only one in the room he wouldn't talk to. "How about you, A.J.? What was the worst one you ever worked?"

A moment slid over the next as he sat without saying a word.

"I think I should get those dishes," Jeff finally said as he stood.

"Yeah, I'll help," Lisa said, standing. She walked to Eve's chair and held out her hands. "Here. He's got to be ready for a diaper change by now."

A.J. glanced at his watch and stood. "I really should be getting home."

Anger and hurt collapsed on Eve as Baby Alex went back to his mother, and she was left holding nothing. It felt like no one wanted her to be a part of the conversation—like her friends would've preferred that she hadn't bothered to even be a part of it in the first place. "What?" she asked as the other three busied themselves away from her. "What did I say?"

They didn't answer. In fact, no one was even looking at her.

"You can tell me, you know," she said in anger. "I'm not an idiot."

In slow succession Lisa and then Jeff looked at her with dread written all over their faces.

"What?" she asked in desperate exasperation. "Tell me. It can't be that bad."

It was the instant before the anger reached her feet that A.J. turned to her, and eyes full of fear and sadness, his gaze traced over her. "The worst was the night we lost Dustin."

The words flitted over her mind without stopping, and her spirit sank on the confusion. "Dustin? But...? You were there?" Some irrational part of her wanted that answer to be no although she could tell from every face in the room that it wasn't.

A.J.'s gaze fell to the ground, but he managed one glance up at her. "I was on that call. I was with him on the trip to the hospital."

"You...?" She fought to make some sense of how that fit with everything else, but all it did was blow the whole picture to smithereens. "I don't understand."

In the ensuing seconds, it was clear that A.J. couldn't get the words strung together to help her understand.

"When we brought him out," Jeff finally said from across the room, and her gaze went to him, "the first team there was A.J.'s, and I was glad because I knew A.J. would do everything he could to bring him back."

"Bring him...?" Air lodged at the top of Eve's throat going nowhere. "You were there?" she asked A.J. again.

Almost imperceptibly he nodded.

"Why didn't you tell me?" she asked as answers to that question that she didn't want to hear fell like bombs in her brain.

"I wanted to..." he started. "I really did..."

"But...?" Images crashed over her, sending her senses scattering. Finally her understanding system gave way to her run mechanism. She shook her head to get sanity back, and then she fought to look at Jeff and Lisa. "Thanks for supper. I think I'd better be going."

"Eve," Jeff said, reaching out to stop her, but she raised her hands to thwart his effort.

"I'll be fine. I'm fine." And with that she raced out to her car swathed in darkness down the street. With every step and every movement, she tried to get her brain wrapped around the picture of A.J. in the ambulance with Dustin. At the car door, she yanked it open just as A.J. raced out of the house after her.

"Eve, wait! Don't…"

But she slammed the door, ignited the engine, and roared away without so much as a backward glance. One part of her said she should be grateful that Dustin was in good hands that night, but another just couldn't get beyond the question of why he had never told her he was there. He was there. Those words stuck like a glitched CD in her mind, playing over and over as hot tears began to fall.

The little Civic zoomed under the flashes of amber streetlights, flying to keep up with her. If he could just catch her… What? He asked himself. If he could just catch her, what? How could he make her understand how sorry he was for the whole thing? The only thing running through his mind was, "Catch her. Hold her. Make sure she's safe."

At that moment the flashing of something other than amber lights swept across his car, and in surprise he looked up to find a black and white patrol car in his rearview mirror.

"Oh, great."

When Eve made it into her apartment, her head throbbed with the memories. That first phone call, Lisa's panicked, heartrending voice, the long drive to the hospital, knowing the whole way that her world would never be the same. The memories slid through her like water over smooth rocks. Then slowly those images were replaced with the funeral, holding herself in check even when what she really wanted was to collapse on the hard church floor and lie there forever, to kick and scream at the world, to ask God to just take her too.

All of life in that moment had stopped. The next months were a blur, hardly recognizable even now. Long minutes melting into long hours until one day couldn't be discerned from the next. Then the memories became clear again, and the center of every one was A.J. Right there. So close she could reach out and touch him. But he was a dream, an illusion that she had wanted to see so badly, she had convinced herself that he was the one she'd told herself that she didn't want to find.

Ache scratched through her at the admissions she'd made to him, talking about Dustin, about losing him. Crying in his arms when she should've been running in the other direction as fast as she could go. He wasn't a white knight. He was a predator. Waiting to swoop in and sweep her up at her weakest moments.

What little logic that was left in her brain, protested that line of thought of course, but the humiliation was too strong. He wasn't the man she thought he was—not even close, and from that point forward, she wanted nothing to do with A.J. Knight ever again.

By the time A.J. pulled into the La Paloma parking lot, he knew his only hope of talking to her would be to actually go knock on her door. That option was out. The headlights of the Civic swept the parking lot and landed squarely on the little silver Celica sitting forlornly in the darkness. He looked at it, trying to decide what to do, but in truth, there was no decision. She was home, and she was safe. That's what he had come to make sure.

The words he wanted so badly to say jammed into the brick wall in his head. She didn't need him. Probably she never had. What was it that she said, "I'm a big girl"? A soft, sad laugh escaped from him at the thought. She was a big girl. She could take care of herself. She certainly didn't need him hanging around like some stupid little lost puppy. With tears raining down over his heart, he turned out of the parking lot and headed home.

She was better off without him although he wondered if he would ever again be whole without her by his side.

Twenty-Two

By mid-April life was getting back to whatever had passed for normal before the entrance of A.J. in Eve's life. She hadn't seen him since she'd left Jeff and Lisa's. He hadn't called, which she told herself was fine with her. The outward animosity she had felt at being the last to find out the earth-shattering news had dimmed into a dull ache although she still couldn't quite understand why he hadn't told her. Nonetheless, she had accepted the fact that they simply weren't meant to be together.

The two times that Lisa had ventured out onto that limb, Eve had cut her off succinctly. And once Lisa had started work again, even that reminder had disappeared. In fact, she hadn't seen or heard from either Jeff or Lisa in more than a month. So when the phone rang just after nine o'clock on the 23rd of April, Eve never so much as thought about who would be on the other end. "Hello?"

"Hey, Eve-girl," Lisa said happily. "How goes it?"

She swallowed everything else. "Great. I made it through my first official season change without any major screw-ups, so maybe I'll have a job tomorrow."

Lisa laughed. "That's good to hear. We've been swamped. I pulled in this new hardware store account a couple weeks ago. It's been nuts."

"Hardware? I didn't know you knew anything about hardware."

"Neither did I, but I'm learning fast."

"Nails, screws, tool belts, hot guys. Sounds fun to me."

"Well, I've yet to see the hot guys part, but I've seen enough nails and screws to last me for awhile."

"I'll bet. How's Alex?"

"Growing. He's almost thirteen pounds already. You lay him on the floor, and he'll hold his head up like those dumb bobbing dog heads in the back of a car."

The reference, which should have been funny, only sucked the air right out of Eve. "I bet he's a doll."

"He is. I wouldn't trade him for anything."

Alone coiled around Eve as she thought about Lisa's life. Lisa didn't come home to an empty house that sounded like a mausoleum every night. No, she had family—people to count on, people to count on her. Tiredly Eve laid her head back in the chair. "How's Jeff?"

"As insane as usual. He decided to hang a ceiling fan in our bedroom. 'Bout blew himself up in the process."

"Is he all right?"

"Yeah, he'll live although he does still buzz from time to time."

In the background, Eve heard his voice. "I heard that!"

"You were supposed to," Lisa sang out, and Eve smiled. "So, we were wondering," Lisa said, coming back on the line, "what are you doing this Sunday?"

"This Sunday? Why?"

"Gabe and Ash invited us out to Astroworld. She got a discount on some tickets or something."

"Uh-oh," Eve said, smelling a set-up. "This wouldn't have anything to do with a certain person trying to rope me into seeing another certain person. Now would it?"

Silence, and Eve knew.

"Umm, well, actually Jeff did ask A.J., and I think he's coming, but…"

Concern raced through Eve at the tone in Lisa's voice. "But what?"

Lisa sighed slowly. "He's bringing a date."

"Oh." It was the only thing Eve could think of to say as her mind spun on the words.

"So, if you want to bring somebody too, that's cool," Lisa said quickly.

"Oh, I don't know…"

"Come on, Eve," Lisa said, and there was genuine pleading in her voice. "I never get to see you anymore, and Astroworld's a big place. We won't probably even see that much of them."

Still, the thought of being there with him being with someone else tore through her like wildfire.

"Please, Eve. You don't even have to ride any rides if you don't want to."

Huge parts of her wanted to say yes, but the mere thought of seeing him with someone else kept her from the word. "You know, Lis. I think I'm going to have to take a rain check on this one."

"Oh, Eve. Come on. I wouldn't have told you if I thought you were going to bail on me. Please. I'm asking you. I'm begging you."

The ache tracing through her was sniffed away with one breath. "I really don't think it's a good idea."

"But this isn't about him. This is about me, your friend, asking you to come and spend a fun afternoon with me. We can eat cotton candy and funnel cakes and caramel apples…"

"I hate caramel apples."

"Then we'll get you the candied kind. Come on, Eve. It'll be fun."

Although it sounded anything but fun, Eve sighed. She really did want to see her friends again, and she was getting sick of looking at the apartment walls. "I'll tell you what, if I can find a date, I'll come."

"Yay!" Lisa shrieked. "Then I'll call you tomorrow night. If you haven't found one, I'll find you one."

"Oh, great. There's a scary thought.."

"Seriously. It'll be fun, so don't flake out on me here. Bribe somebody. Blackmail them. Hog-tie them if you have to, but come. Okay?"

Despite the doom in her chest, Eve laughed. "I'll try."

As they drove to Astroworld in the little Civic, A.J. looked over at Melody and smiled. She was truly a good friend. For the last two months she had been unwavering in her quest to help him get over "Demon Woman"—her choice term for Eve. At first he had tried to tell her that Eve wasn't so bad, but Melody insisted that anybody who could make A.J. look so sad deserved the title. In his heart, he knew that it was he who deserved the term, but convincing Melody of that was hopeless, so he had finally given up.

"Man, it's been so long since I've been out here," Melody said. "I think the last time was just after we graduated. Jeez, that's been a long time."

"You feeling a little old over there?" he asked teasingly.

"Old?" she asked, wrinkling her face at the word. "Don't ever use that word around me. My mom is old. I'm just getting started."

"Granted we don't know what *on*..."

"Hey, speak for yourself. I'll have you know, I'm starting management classes in the fall."

Instantly the bravado fell from his face. "Management? You?"

"Yes, me. I talked to Farin the other day, and she thinks I'd be perfect to take over for her when she moves on in a couple of years. But to do that, I have to have a degree, so I'm going to go back to school."

Soft incredulousness flowed through him as he looked at her. "That's cool, Mel. It really is. I think you'll be great at it."

"Yeah," she said, crossing her arms. "I do too." She sat for a moment and then glanced over at him. "So, what about you? You planning on doing the search and rescue thing forever?"

He shrugged. "I haven't found anything I like any better yet, so..."

Slowly she shook her blonde locks. "Look at us. A couple of slackers who've actually made something out of ourselves. Pretty unbelievable I'd say."

"Yep, pretty unbelievable."

Although she hadn't had to hog-tie him, Eve was glad when Blaine the new guy in men's wear had said yes to her request with no more than a few moments of decision. Granted, she'd never seen him in anything other than a suit and tie, but the long khaki shorts and tank-T-shirt weren't half bad. His dark hair and surfer-boy looks weren't half bad either although he really could've ditched the aren't-you-so-lucky-to-be-seen-with-me attitude.

She couldn't count the number of times he'd run his fingers through his hair to feather it back, and by the time they got to the park, he had looked in the rearview mirror more than he had at the road. The sunglasses he donned when they got out to the car didn't help, but he had come, on ultra-short notice, so she wasn't going to complain. Besides, what had Lisa said about not even seeing each other all that much once they were at the park?

"They said to meet them by the gate," Eve said as she readjusted the waistband of her white shorts pulled smartly over the navy and white swimsuit top. The braid running from the top of her head down past her shoulders swung over her shoulder as she adjusted her own sunglasses. She looked at her watch. "We'd better hurry, or they might leave us."

Blaine swiped a hand through his hair and reached for her hand. "Hate to keep them waiting."

"You guys go on in," Jeff said as the six of them stood at the gate. "We can wait for Eve."

"Yeah, it's silly for us all to stand out here," Lisa said, shifting nervously. She hadn't looked comfortable since the moment A.J. had walked up with Melody at his side, and the longer they stood, the more distressed she looked.

"Well, I say we go on in," Gabe said. "We could at least get in line for something before it gets terribly crowded."

"I'm sure she'll be here any…"

"Oh, hey, speak of the devil," Gabe said as his gaze swept the parking lot beyond.

When A.J. turned, his heart hit the bottoms of his shoes. Of course she was gorgeous. That was a given. But the sight of her hand tucked firmly in Robocop's made jealously leap to his fists.

"Hey!" Lisa said, stepping over and giving her friend a hug. "You made it!"

"We're here," Eve said, returning the hug.

Lisa stepped back and surveyed the medium-tall, well-built guy standing next to Eve. "And who's your friend?"

"This is Blaine Donovan. Blaine, this is everybody."

"Hi, everybody," Blaine said in a mid-baritone pitch. The others returned the greeting.

"I don't want to be rude," Gabe said, jumping in. "But could we do the introductions in line?"

They laughed and followed Gabe and Ashley into the short line to the gate.

Eve was having a hard time finding a place to look that didn't include the lithe but rock solid frame she had felt only in her dreams for nearly two months. His face hadn't changed although the lightheartedness that had lit his golden eyes seemed to have dimmed since their last meeting. Without much watching, she could see that her hopes for his date to be someone he'd just met and asked out were less than real. No, he stayed close to her. His hand on her back guiding her forward. Always aware and concerned for her comfort and safety. Always the gentleman even at a lowly amusement park.

Still, something in the back of Eve's mind said she had seen her before. Somewhere…

"I say we hit the Serial Thriller first," Gabe said from the front. "The longer we wait, the worse that line's going to be."

"Oh, boy. Count me out," Lisa said. "I don't do roller coasters."

"Don't do roller coasters?" Gabe asked, and then he looked at Jeff. "Why'd you bring her along anyway?"

"To drive home," Jeff said with a shrug, and Lisa hit him up side the head. He ducked away warily. "It was a joke."

"Not a very good one," she said.

"I've heard Batman The Escape is awesome," Blaine said from behind Eve, and she jumped at the sound of his voice.

"Yeah, I want to hit that one, too, but I think that's like way at the other end of the park," Gabe said. He grabbed a map from a receptacle and opened it. "Yep. It is. I say we start here and work our way around."

"Sounds good to me," Jeff said. "How about you guys?"

A.J. looked at his date who nodded enthusiastically. "Sounds good to us," he said.

Even the sound of his voice hurt. Eve put her head down and did her best to disappear. He was happy. She was miserable. Yes, life was definitely back to normal.

From his place in line beside Melody, A.J. watched Eve sitting with Lisa and Ashley on the bench beside the Serial Thriller. His spirit hurt to look at her, and yet his gaze wouldn't tear itself away. All he wanted to do was go over there, put his arms around her, and have everything be back the way it was on the mountain. In exasperation he sighed and looked back at the coaster he was about to get on with Melody.

Then carefully she leaned in to him. "You know, a smile wouldn't kill you."

Despite the ache in his heart, he smiled. "I thought your only specialty was video games."

"Oh, you'd be surprised," Melody said, and he felt the soft touch of her hand on his back. She was a good friend, and he was glad he'd asked her to come. He would never have gotten through today without her.

The previous coaster rolled to a stop, and they all stepped forward to get on.

As she watched the coaster loop through a series of inversions, Eve's heart went with it. She had seen the private exchange they had shared, and it did more to solidify his place with his date than anything previous.

"Melody seems nice," Ashley said from beside Lisa. "She's just A.J.'s style."

Eve felt the silent conversation pass behind her back as a sad acceptance washed over her. Melody. Of course, that's where she had seen her before. "Yeah," Eve said softly when no one said anything else. "I guess they were more than friends after all."

When she turned with a tight smile, the other two women were looking at her with sympathy in their eyes.

"Well, there's nothing wrong with Blaine," Ashley said, trying to cover her gaffe.

Reluctantly Eve's gaze traveled back to the coaster. No, nothing was wrong with Blaine—except for the fact that he wasn't A.J.

"I say we do the Dungeon Drop next," Gabe said excitedly as they sat around the table eating lunch.

"That thing that drops you off the tower?" Jeff asked as if it would drop you right into hell.

"Yeah, that looks mind-blowing," Gabe said.

"A little too mind-blowing for me," Jeff said, chewing on a

fry. "I don't do heights."

"Is that why your knuckles are permanently white?" Gabe asked.

"Coasters I can handle. Dropping out of the sky? I don't think so."

"You should see this guy," Gabe said, not giving up as he clutched the table in front of him. "I don't think he ever let go of the bar once today."

"I did once," Jeff said.

"Yeah, right, that first time when we took off." Gabe held up his hands and then jerked forward and grabbed for the table.

"Dungeon Drop sounds like fun," Eve said, having gotten her fill of watching the others have fun without her. The shops that Ashley and Lisa went into held no fascination for her. All they had was overpriced junk as far as she was concerned. For most of the morning she had chosen to tag along, waiting just long enough to not get on the ride before Lisa and Ashley found a store to go into. Then Eve was forced to sit and watch as the others twisted and turned their way to utter bliss.

As she sat listening to them regale each pitch and turn, she made up her mind that she'd had enough of sitting on benches. So when Jeff looked at her like she had two heads, she shrugged. "What? How bad could it be?"

"You're mighty brave all of a sudden. You wouldn't even ride the Serpent," Jeff said, referring to the not-quite-kids coaster that Jeff had almost talked even Lisa on to.

Eve smiled. "You make the decision, the courage will come." She felt A.J.'s glance go over her, and she leaned closer to Blaine. "Besides, we've been here five hours, and I've only spent ten minutes with my date." Truthfully she didn't want to spend much more than another minute with him, but the fact that Melody and A.J. were practically inseparable hadn't escaped her notice.

"Cool," Gabe said happily. "No more odd-man-out."

As they stood in line under the tower, A.J. watched her even though that was the last place he wanted to be looking. Her and *Blaine*. Well-built, tan, good-looking Blaine. He was a jerk. That much, A.J. could tell from halfway across the park. What he couldn't figure out was why she couldn't figure that out. Finally out of sheer desperation, he decided that focusing on her, fantasizing about what could've been or should've been was stupid. It was over, and it was clearly time to move on.

"You know, this thing only holds four at a time," A.J. said to no one in particular. "What are we going to draw straws for who goes it alone?"

"Oh, no you don't," Melody said, clutching A.J.'s elbow. "I've got me a partner."

"Me, too," Eve said, grabbing onto Blaine.

A.J. looked at Gabe with a smirk. "Sorry, big guy. You just drew the short straw."

"You would do that to me?" Gabe asked incredulously. "You would leave me to drop out of the sky all by myself?"

"Yes, we would," A.J. said, and the others laughed as the cage returned to a standing position. The other occupants stepped out, whoosy from the ride but laughing hysterically. He turned to Blaine and Eve and smiled as he swept a hand in front of him. "You guys first." And he followed Melody onto the ride.

Eve chose a middle seat and strapped herself in.

"I wanted outside," Melody said petulantly when it became clear that her seat was next to Eve.

"It's yours," A.J. said instantly relinquishing his seat to her. However, when he realized who he would be sitting by, he hesitated for a moment. Then resolution slipped over his face. "Is this seat taken?"

"It's all yours," Eve said with a tight smile. When he sat down next to her, Eve had to remember to breathe. That tanned, solid arm brushed across hers, and she lost track of her anger at him and the space she was supposed to be occupying in the universe.

The cage jerked to life, and she squealed in surprise.

"Don't worry," Melody said, leaning over so she could see Eve. "If we crash, it'll happen so fast, you won't even feel it."

"Oh, that's comforting," Eve said back.

"Just trying to help."

"It isn't working very well."

"This is nothing," Melody said as the ground disappeared from beneath Eve's feet. "You should've been on the Serial Thriller. I thought I was going to fly right out of that thing."

"Sounds like of fun," Eve said.

"Hey, look there's Jeff and Lisa," A.J. said, spotting them on the asphalt now far below. He waved, and they waved back.

The air that had escaped from her vanished completely the higher they went. She was up here, but she couldn't remember why anymore.

"Is it too late to say I don't want to do this?" she asked.

"I think you made that choice on the ground," A.J. said, looking at her, and when her gaze caught his, the smile in his eyes was genuine. He winked at her. "You made the decision, courage can't be far away."

"Yeah, as long as I don't pass out before we get there." The cage chose that moment to hit the stop at the top of the tower, and Eve let out another shriek. She squeezed her eyes closed, willing time and space to stop right there. "I can't do this."

"Sure you can," A.J. said softly. The cage hit the other side of the slide and stopped. It was at that moment that she felt his hand gently touch the one of hers closest to his clutching to the bar for dear life. With no other thought she grabbed his hand just as the bottom dropped out from under her life.

She screamed, she was sure, but in reality there was only the feeling of flying with only his hand to hold onto. Together they plunged to earth in one heart-stopping drop, and then she was back down although she couldn't quite be sure they hadn't just fallen into some parallel universe. A moment at the bottom just before the cage sat upright, and then his hand was gone.

"That was fun," Melody said.

"Yeah, fun," Eve said shakily. When the cage came to a stop, she stood and nearly lost her balance getting down. Instantly two sets of hands from either side of her reached out to catch her.

"You okay?" Blaine asked, and when she looked at him, fog was all she saw.

"Yeah, fine." She retrieved her balance and followed the others out.

"How was it?" Gabe yelled at them from his position in the cage going up.

"Awesome!" A.J. yelled back, and Eve couldn't disagree.

"I want to do the Wagon Wheel," Melody said when Gabe joined them to try to decide where to go next. "We missed that one."

"I'm going to do this one again," Gabe said, pointing at the Dungeon Drop. "You want to join me, Eve?"

She backed away from him quickly. "Oh, I don't think so. I'm thinking the Wagon Wheel sounds much safer."

"I'm with Eve." Jeff draped an arm around her shoulders.

Gabe looked at his watch. "Tell you what, why don't we split up for awhile? We can meet back here in an hour or so."

"What about Lisa and Ash?" Jeff asked.

"I'll see if I can find them when I get back down."

"Cool," Jeff said. "Lead the way, Mel."

As they walked through the park, Eve noticed how Melody stuck close to A.J., but she also noticed how he managed to put some distance between them. For her part, she put as much space between her and Blaine as she could. She didn't know if he had seen the circumstances on the Dungeon Drop, but she wasn't taking any chances.

"Oh, A.J., remember the last time when we went on Thunder River?" Melody asked, falling into him laughing as she pointed to the sign pointing to the attached water park.

"Oh, don't…" A.J. said, closing his eyes.

"No, you've got to hear this one," Melody said to the others. "We get on this ride, right? And we get drenched. Like what would you expect on Thunder River, but genius here had worn these white shorts that when they got wet, they became like see-through."

"I didn't know they were going to be that bad," he protested.

"He was like a walking Calvin Klein ad for an hour," Melody said. "You should've seen some of the looks he got."

A.J. nodded and smirked at her. "Thank you so much for telling *that* story."

"Well, you set yourself up so nicely sometimes. Like that kneeboarding incident."

They reached the Wagon Wheel and got in line.

"Now that one wasn't my fault," A.J. said.

"It's never your fault," Melody said, not slowing down. "Okay, we went out to the lake. And A.J.'s going to try this kneeboarding thing because he's crazy or something. So he straps this board to his knees, and they take off, and everything's fine. He's all doing all

273

these tricks and stuff—showing off as usual. Then the guy in the boat decides to see if A.J. can do this jump. They're flying across the water. Then just before they get there, here comes this Jet Ski guy, and he was like yelling, 'Ahhhh!' All out-of-control and everything. They were fixing to clothesline the poor guy with the rope, so A.J. lets go of the rope on the outside of the turn, and poof, he hits the jump ramp, head-on. Laid him out cold."

Jeff cracked up as concern traced just under Eve's own laugh.

"Why didn't you go around it?" Jeff asked.

"Around it? I didn't even see the thing until it was right there." A.J. laid his head back and flung out his hands as he closed his eyes. "Man, I was gone."

"It took like, what? Twenty-five stitches to sew up the side of your head," Melody said. "A.J. doesn't knee-board anymore."

"I can imagine," Jeff said. "Twenty-five stitches? Did you go into the paramedic thing after that?"

"No, actually I went to L.A.," A.J. said without a trace of humor, but the others laughed even harder.

"That makes perfect sense," Jeff said, fighting to sound serious.

"Oh, hey, tell them about your pink hair," Melody said as the line moved forward.

"Ugh!" A.J. said, shaking his head at that thought. "I tried out for this punk band out in L.A., but they wouldn't even consider you if you didn't get all wild and stuff. So I dyed my hair pink, put spikes in it and wore all these dog chains and stuff. It was awful."

"Did you get the job?" Jeff asked as he leaned on the railing.

"No," A.J. said in exasperation, "so then I had to go dye my hair back—only it didn't exactly work like I thought it was going to."

"He looked like a skunk in drag," Melody said. "I have a picture to prove it."

"I thought you burned that thing," A.J. said.

"No, I *told* you I burned it," she said, laughing. "You can never have too much blackmail."

"Oh, great."

"So, Melody," Eve asked, thinking back to the most embarrassing story he'd told her. "Did you ever go skiing with A.J.?"

His gaze jumped to Eve, and his eyes said he knew exactly

where she was going with that question.

"No, I've never had that pleasure," Melody said, and the teasing tone had left her voice.

"Too bad," Eve said, smirking at him. "I hear he's a wild man on the mountain."

"Oh, look," A.J. said quickly. "Our ride's here."

"'Oh, look.' That was smooth, Knight," Jeff said, reaching out and collaring A.J. "You just don't want to tell any more stories."

"You got that right," A.J. said.

The attendant opened the gate, and laughing they crossed into a dim brown-carpeted circle. Eve stood by Blaine, and Jeff, Melody, and A.J. went to the other side. A.J. looked at her and smiled, and she returned it with no thought that she shouldn't. She shook her head at him, and he winked. Then the door closed, and slowly the chamber began rotating. Slowly at first. Then faster and faster they went until she couldn't even see anymore. Her body was plastered to the carpeting at her back. The thing tipped up one way, then the other, then the floor beneath her slid a full six inches away from her feet.

When it slowed and finally stopped, Eve laughed at the dazed look on the three faces across from them. Jeff took a small step away from the wall and stumbled slightly as they met at the exit.

"I'm thinking I should've stayed with Gabe," he said.

"The Texas Tornado," Blaine said, pointing up at the giant structure beyond when they exited. "Let's do that one again." He grabbed Eve's hand, and before she really got her footing back, they were leading the way.

"We should come in April all the time," A.J. said as they climbed the ramp to the entrance. "There's nobody out here today."

"Yeah, but those clouds might have something to do with that," Jeff said, indicating the bank of dark gray clouds that had overtaken the sky.

"Wimps," A.J. said. They moved up in line. "I say we hit Greezed Lightnin' again as soon as we get off here."

Eve's head was already spinning, but she wasn't backing down now. It wasn't long, and they were let onto the ride. Melody and A.J. took the car ahead of Eve and Blaine, and just before it took off, A.J. looked back at Jeff who was behind Eve.

"Hands up!"

"They're as up as they're going to get," Jeff said, and Eve laughed as the ride chugged forward.

She closed her eyes, praying this would actually be fun. "Oh, boy."

By the time they got off of the Texas Tornado, A.J. was having the time of his life. True he wasn't with her, but he was closer to her than he had been in more than a month, and besides the fact that Melody seemed not quite herself, everything was wonderful.

"So, Melody," Eve said when they were standing in line for Greezed Lightnin', "you're the one who works at Galaxy Shoes, right?"

"Yeah," Melody said in surprise. "Two years now."

"Man, I've got to get back out there," Eve said. "I got this dress. It's like periwinkle, and I can't find anything to go with it."

"Have you tried white?" Melody asked as the guys quietly bowed out of the conversation and into their own.

"Yeah, but then all you see is the shoes. I tried black too, but that wasn't right either. I've been looking everywhere, but nothing matches it."

"Periwinkle, hmm. That can be a tough. Either it's too blue or too purple." Melody shook her head slowly. "I can't think of anything we have right off hand. You know I did see one in the buyer's catalog the other day that I thought was really creative. It was tan straps, but the back of it was like solid, and it had all these cool color beads on it."

"Oh, you do the buying then?" Eve asked.

Melody shrugged. "Not yet, but I'm thinking about going back to school to get my degree."

"Really? That's awesome. What are you majoring in?"

"Probably management, but I haven't really decided yet."

"Be sure to take some textile classes if you can. They'll really give you a leg up when you get out."

The line moved forward.

"I just hope I'm not getting into something I can't finish," Melody said, admitting that sheepishly.

"Take the first step," Eve said. "One step at a time, you'll be amazed at what you can do. I thought I was toast when I first started. I wasn't exactly the best student in high school, but I made it. So don't let them psyche you out. If you want to bad enough, you'll do fine."

Gratefully Melody smiled at her, and together they stepped up to the gate. Eve arched her back and looked up at the metal monster looming before her. "Ah, man, I can't believe I'm doing this."

"Thrills aren't your style?"

"Once it's over, it's fun. Until then…" Eve made a face at her.

"Well, then just don't look until it's over."

Eve laughed. "That's easy for you to say."

"What?" A.J. asked from behind Melody, and she looked back and shook her head.

"Girl talk," she said. "You wouldn't understand."

"We were talking about shoes," Eve said teasingly, and A.J.'s face fell.

"Ugh. You're right. I wouldn't understand."

Eve looked at Melody and shook her head. "Men."

"They're hopeless."

"Is my head still attached?" Eve asked Melody when they descended the exit ramp after the 360-loop. With both hands Eve reached up and readjusted her skull on her neck. "I think it fell off on that backward loop thing.

"How could you tell?" A.J. asked teasingly. "Air doesn't weigh enough to notice."

"Oh, funny," Eve said, sneering at him. "Your date is so hilarious, Mel. Wherever did you find him?"

"I wish I knew, I'd send him back."

"Hey," A.J. said, trying to sound hurt.

"Don't hey me, Mister," Melody said. "I really don't think it's too funny when my riding partner is trying to figure out how the bar thing works just before we take off."

"I was just asking," he said.

"Well, next time, keep your curiosity to yourself."

"That's hard for him to do," Eve said. "He is a guy, remember?"

"Oh, yeah, I forgot," Melody said dramatically.

"Okay, that could be taken a couple of ways, and I don't like either of them," A.J. said.

"Poor, baby," Melody said, running her hand over his backward blue cap. "He's so mistreated."

Eve shook her head. "Hardly. He deserves everything he gets."

"Oh, yeah?" A.J. asked, jabbing her in the ribs. "Say that again. I dare you."

She tried to get away from him, but he was persistent as he started tickling her harder. "A.J. deserves…" She beat his hands back, but he wasn't about to quit. "…everything … Mercy! Mercy!" She hit at his hands, pushing him away. "Hey, I said, 'Mercy!'"

He let her go.

"You're supposed to let go when somebody says, 'Mercy,'" she said, reaching over and poking him in the ribs. "Don't you know anything?"

"Oh, sorry. I must've missed that one."

"Yeah, that one and 57 others." She jabbed him twice more for good measure.

"Aren't you going to do something about her?" A.J. asked Melody who shrugged.

"Why? She's telling the truth."

"Ah," A.J. said unhappily.

"You'll learn," Jeff said.

"I'll learn what?" A.J. asked.

"Never take them on more than one at a time, or you're done for."

"You tell me this now."

"Hey, you got yourself into this mess. Good luck." Jeff glanced down the park. "There's Gabe." They strode up, and their party was once again complete.

"Well, you guys don't look too sick," Gabe said, appraising them.

"Sick? Us?" Jeff asked as he swayed forward woozily. "Never."

A clap of thunder sounded above them, and Gabe looked up. "If we're going to get on the Cyclone, we'd better get going."

"Forward!" Jeff said like a knight with his sword leading an army.

Together they made their way through the park. Just before they got to the ride, Melody broke away from them. "I've got to go visit the little girl's room right quick."

"Now?" A.J. asked.

"Trust me, now is a good time," she said. "Go on. I'll catch up."

When she veered off, A.J. stood in confusion for a moment.

"Come on, Aj, we'll just be right over here," Gabe said. He looked over at Lisa and Ashley who were following them. "Y'all can even sit on the bench over there and wait for her."

"Oh, Ash, I see funnel cakes," Lisa said, steering Ashley away from the group.

"I guess it's just us then," Gabe said.

"I think I'm going to sit this one out, too," Blaine said. "That Wagon Wheel messed up my head."

"Chicken," Jeff said teasingly.

"It's called knowing when to take a break," Blaine said as another clap cracked above them. He waved quickly. "Have fun."

And so, Eve found herself with three guys walking up the steps to the Texas Cyclone, wondering how she had gotten here, and why she hadn't had the presence of mind to stay on the ground with Blaine. Truthfully she'd much rather be up here than down there except for the little detail of the wood and metal framed roller coaster twisting above her.

"I've got ten dollars that says you won't let go of the bar on that last big hill," Gabe said to Jeff.

"I raise you ten and bet that I won't either."

"You are a disgrace to firemen everywhere," Gabe said, shaking his head. "Afraid of heights. How did you ever make it through the academy?"

"Willpower," Jeff said. "Lots and lots of willpower."

The attendant unchained the gate and backed up.

"We get the back!" A.J. called, grabbing Eve's hand and pulling her down the walkway.

"We get the front," Gabe said, turning the other direction and pulling Jeff with him.

When they got to the car, A.J. stepped in and slid down into the seat. Carefully Eve slid in beside him as she pushed a stray piece of hair behind her ear. Riders filled the cars between them. She exhaled slowly to pull her scattered nerves back to her as A.J.

rubbed his hands together excitedly. "This is great."

"Yeah," she said barely breathing.

Then the hydraulics let the bar down in front of them, and even if she had wanted to, she couldn't get away.

"Here we go," A.J. said, smiling at her.

"Oh, boy."

Twenty-Three

Eve's knuckles went white before they were barely around the first turn. She was hanging on, not because of the ride but so she wouldn't collide with him as the coaster sent her into his seat. He could tell because not only was she holding on, but she kept fighting to slide back into her own space. The first two head-jerking turns were behind them when it hit him how furiously she was holding on.

He knew why. He knew, and yet suddenly he didn't want her to ever be afraid to trust herself with him again. He didn't want her to hang on to life, trying not to touch him, to not to get into his space every time they happened to be together. No, even if they could only be friends from here on out, he wanted her to be able to trust him. He wanted her to know that she could lean on him no matter what. And so around the third turn, he reached over and pried her hand off the bar.

"Hands up!" he said teasingly.

"No!" she screamed as her body collided with his, and he laughed as he laid one arm around her.

"I won't break!" he yelled to her.

A moment of indecision and slowly her other hand let go just as the ride slung him her way. "Well, I might!" she said although there was a smile just beneath the statement.

"Sorry!" he yelled, fighting his way back to his side.

"No you're not!"

"Yes, I am. Here, let me show you." His arm came around her

shoulders again, and then, finally, she stopped fighting and let herself fold into his arms.

He looked at her, and as they flew around the next corner as one, his heart could lie no longer. "See, no breaking."

When she looked at him, her eyes held questions he finally felt strong enough to answer. In the next second, he felt the first raindrops splatter across his arms. His gaze went to the gray heavens above them where his face met up with a hundred thousand of their comrades dropping from the sky.

"Ah!" Eve screamed, pulling her arms over her head for protection, but the downpour had other intentions. Less than seconds later what restraint the storm had exerted at its commencement vanished into sheets and sheets of bone-chilling water.

The coaster rounded the last turn and began its slow climb up the last hill as the riders onboard screamed not because of the ride but because they were getting drenched.

"Oh, it's cold," Eve said, shrinking toward A.J. to get away from it.

There was no real decision as both arms dropped around her in protection from the chilly water. His body huddled over hers in a vain attempt to shield her until they could get back down under cover. At the top of the hill, however, the coaster, which was barely moving at all, angled across the top crest, dropped the first car off, and then jerked to a heart-wrenching stop. Instantly A.J. looked around in confusion. They should be at the bottom by now. Instead, he and Eve were lying nearly backward, looking up at a sky that was dropping buckets of cold, crystal droplets on them.

"What happened?" Eve asked, unburying herself from his embrace long enough to glance around. "Why'd we stop?"

"I don't know." A.J. moved only enough to try to see the cause, but he could see nothing other than gray rain.

"Why aren't we going?"

"I don't know," he said again as confused as she was but struggling to find a rational explanation. "The rain, I guess. They must be afraid the brakes won't work."

She glanced over the edge. "But we can't stay up here."

He followed her glance and sheepishly smiled. "Well, unless you're going to climb down, I don't see how you have much of a choice."

Her gaze went to the sky as the rain slid off her face. "You mean we're stuck up here?"

"I'd say that's a pretty good deduction." Despite the circumstances, he really couldn't complain when he looked at her. "Good thing you wore your swimsuit."

She looked at him incredulously. "Yeah, good thing you didn't wear those white shorts."

Laughter broke through his concern. "No kidding."

Slowly she spun forward in her seat, pushed her feet up higher on the car footboard, and leaned her head back into the deluge. "This is just my luck."

His gaze traced over her, and all the rationalizations that he had worked so hard to come up with disappeared into the streams flowing down her face. "Why?"

Barely perceptively she shook her head. "Look at me. I'm stuck on a roller coaster in the rain with somebody who'd rather jump off a bridge than talk to me."

Confusion traced over him. "I want to talk to you."

For a moment she said nothing. Then she let her head lean to the side to look at him. "It's okay," she said softly. "You don't have to lie about it anymore. I mean, I said I didn't want the whole commitment thing, and then I did a one-eighty on you without warning."

Concern slid through his heart. "That wasn't you. That was me. I should've been honest with you from the beginning. I should've told you about Dustin, about that night ..."

Her eyes were laced with liquid that didn't come from the sky when her gaze slipped over him. "You know, it's not that I don't believe you did everything you could because I know you did. I know you would've moved heaven and earth to bring him back— even if you didn't know him or me at the time. I know that because that's how you are, but I just keep thinking about how much time you had to tell me, how many chances you had, but you never said anything..."

"I didn't know how," he said as guilt slipped into his voice. He wanted to reach out to her, take her in his arms, and somehow go back and start over, but he was here, and here was all he had. "I knew I should tell you, but I just kept thinking about all the things I could've done that night that I didn't do, and all the things I did that I shouldn't have. I felt responsible, Eve—like I was the reason you were in so much pain. I mean I know Dustin meant everything to you, that he was the only guy you could ever love like that. And I understand that—I really do." His gaze found the shadows at their feet. "I just kept thinking if he was still here, if Dustin was still alive, you would never have even looked at me." His hand went up to his hat and ran itself over it. "Then I'd think how completely horrible that sounded, and it was like if I just didn't tell you, if you just didn't know... Somehow I wouldn't have to feel so guilty for loving you."

Her gaze jumped to his face, and he tried to look at her even as he fought not to let the tears burning in his head fall.

"I never meant to hurt you," he said. "That's lousy now, I know, but you've got to believe it. I loved everything about being with you—the popcorn and the painting and just the way I felt when I was around you. I didn't want to lose that. I didn't want to lose you." He shrugged slightly. "I guess that worked, huh?" Quickly he ran a hand over his face. His gaze dropped to his hands. "I just thought you should know that."

The splattering of the raindrops was the only sound between them for several long moments as guilt, love, and heartbreak tore through him. He couldn't look at her, so he gazed down through the wood and metal bars beneath them. Jumping through that jumble looked far less painful than life at that moment.

"You know, there were things that I thought I understood," she said slowly. "Things I thought I had figured out, like if love was strong enough, it could last forever, and that forever actually meant forever. But sometimes it doesn't. Sometimes forever means right now, and if you squander right now, all the rest of forever means nothing. I think about all those moments that I could've had with Dustin, the ones that we would've had if he had lived, but those don't compare to the ones when I had a chance to be with him and I didn't because I thought we had a tomorrow. Sometimes tomorrow isn't real. Sometimes if you don't grab on and hold on to today, all you have is memories of memories that never happened because you were too busy living for tomorrow.

"I won't lie to you. Dustin was a big part of my life, and he'll be part of me forever, but that doesn't give me the right to use him to push my life away now. If I sit here and let my past keep me from my present, then I've made the same stupid mistake I made with Dustin."

It was then that he felt her hand on his shoulder as the splatters slowed. His gaze went to hers.

"I can't promise you forever," she said, fighting through the tears. "I can't even promise you tomorrow, but I can promise right now… if you're interested."

"If I'm…?"

"Because the truth is I love you, A.J. Knight. Right here, and right now I love you."

With a crack his heart burst open. His gaze buried deep into hers. "I'm so sorry."

As the raindrops ebbed from between them, she shook her head. "No, that's the past. Let it go. I have. Besides, I just said, 'I love you,' and I want to know what you have to say about that right now?"

He smiled. "You have to ask?" Then his smile fell as gently he laid his hands on her shoulders. His gaze slipped through her eyes into her soul. "I love you, Eve, and I want to spend every right now I have left with you."

Love, hope, and joy flooded over him as he slowly leaned toward her. When his lips found hers, he knew there had never been anything more perfect in all of his life. As his hold on her tightened, suddenly the coaster chugged upward, jerking so unexpectedly that their noses crashed together.

"Ow!" she said, backing away from him and laughing as she put her hand to her nose. One rung at a time they approached the crest.

He laughed with an apology twined in it. "I kiss you and you say 'ow'?"

"Yeah, talk about 'hands up,'" she said, wickedness lacing her words. Slowly her arm dropped around his shoulders as her other hand wound over his hand that rested on the bar. He caught her intent just before she made it to his lips, and just as they crested the top, she removed the last link of the chain between them. Their lips met again in perfect time with the screams of their fellow riders.

Dropping out of the sky had never been so thrilling, and by the time the coaster braked and slowed into the station, his head was whirling like it never had before. When she backed up to look at him, there was a smirk of satisfaction on her face.

"So how was that?" she asked as though there wasn't a single other person for miles.

"Awesome," he breathed, falling through her eyes. The coaster jerked to a stop, and the bar went up, but neither of them moved. "I love you," he said barely getting the words through the feelings jamming his chest.

"I love you, too," she said, and he could see no hesitation anywhere in her.

"Hey, you two!" Gabe called from the platform. "Haven't you spent enough time in that car?"

Eve winked at A.J. with a look that his heart knew said, "Not nearly long enough." Then quickly she rejoined reality and turned to get out onto the platform. Gabe offered her a hand up, and she climbed out. A.J. wanted all of reality to just go away and leave them alone; however, that not being a logical option, he swung himself up and out of the car only to find her waiting for him.

There was no hesitation as she wrapped an arm under his, and everything in him wished they never had to let go. However, he saw the skeptical look that Jeff shot at him as they headed for the exit, and he knew that they're "right now" on top hadn't followed them to the bottom.

"Okay, Mister." Gabe punched Jeff in the chest which caught Jeff totally off-guard as he was busy watching A.J. and Eve. "You owe me money. Pay up."

"Money? How do you figure?" Jeff asked, never quite making the leap from A.J. and Eve to Gabe's statement as they descended the exit ramp.

"Yep, twenty bucks. You said you weren't going to let go at the top, and you did."

"No, I said I *wouldn't* let go… oh."

"Yeah, oh. You owe me twenty bucks. Now, pay up."

Even as he laughed, A.J. saw Lisa and Ashley standing under an awning across the walkway although the deluge had all-but dissipated. Like it or not, being together with Eve would have to wait. He pulled his arm from her shoulders reluctantly and stuck his hand in his pocket. He wanted to hold her, to tell the world that he loved her, but what he simply couldn't do was to hurt Melody. And he was sure coming off a ride like a love-struck teenager with a woman Melody despised wasn't the best way to accomplish that. Especially when she had been waiting for him at the bottom for more than twenty minutes. However, Eve's fingers never untangled themselves from his belt loop, and his heart loved that feeling too much to explain why she should let him go.

"That's not fair," Jeff said. "You changed the rules."

"I didn't change the rules. It was an act of God," Gabe said seriously. "I guess He wanted me to have that money more than He wanted you to."

"Nice try," Jeff said as they walked up to the other two women.

"Lisa, tell your husband he should honor his debts," Gabe said.

Jeff put an arm around Lisa, and she squirmed away from him because he was soaked. "Don't you know by now he doesn't listen to a word I say? We're married, remember?"

"Ah, jeez," Gabe said, snapping his finger. "I keep forgetting that."

A.J. folded his arms at his chest uncomfortably, knowing how this looked, and knowing that any second Melody was going to walk up furious. Or worse, Blaine would walk up and knock him through the fun house mirror next to the awning.

"Oh, bad news, A.J.," Ashley said, shaking her head.

"What's that?"

"Melody got sick."

"Sick?" A.J. asked with instant concern, and he felt Eve's hand fall from his waist. "What happened? Where is she?"

"Blaine took her home," Lisa said, looking right at Eve. "She was in pretty bad shape."

"Blaine... but...?"

"We told them we could take Eve home," Lisa continued. "Blaine said to tell you he was sorry, Eve."

"Oh," Eve said obviously trying to sound thankful and properly crushed by the news, but no one standing there believed either. She looked at A.J. uncertainly. "Maybe we should call them. Make sure they got home all right."

Gabe looked at his watch. "It'll be at least another hour before they get home. What do you say we head back and grab something to eat between here and there?"

"Now?" Ashley said in surprise. "The park's not even closed yet."

"Yeah, but my shoes are all squishy. That's annoying," Gabe said, lifting one and then the other up to demonstrate.

"Oh, heavens, he has squishy shoes," Ashley said to the others dramatically. "We can't have that."

"Well, if someone would pay me what he owes me, I might be able to afford new shoes," Gabe said as they turned for the gate.

Jeff shook his head. "Then I guess you're just going to have to squish forever."

The other two couples strode in front of them as Eve walked carefully at A.J.'s side, her arms crossed so as not to touch him. "I hope Melody's okay," she finally said so that the others couldn't hear her.

He smiled at the note of genuine concern in her voice. "I'm sure she is. Mel always does more stuff than she should." They walked in lock step for a minute. "I'm sorry Blaine left."

Then Eve looked at A.J. and smiled. "I'm not."

The tissue thin barrier between them ripped in half as he reached over and collared her around the neck. "If I didn't know better, I'd think you planned this."

"I'm thinking Somebody did," she said, gazing at him peacefully as she wrapped her arms around his waist. "But it wasn't me."

His heart carried his lips to her head, and she giggled.

"Got any ideas who I should be thanking then?" he asked.

She arched her neck over his arm and looked up into the now light gray sky above them. "Somebody who understands a whole lot more about life than I ever will." And her clutch on him tightened.

"I hear you there." He breathed softly as he kissed her hair again. "I hear you there."

"They said you should come," A.J. said to Melody five days before the July 4th holiday. "Water-skiing, fireworks, and your very best friend in the whole world all in one place. What more could you ask for?"

"My very best friend, huh? This wouldn't be the same friend who asked me out on a date, then got engaged to someone else while we were there? Would it?"

"Okay, technically you were gone before we got back together, and secondly, we didn't get engaged."

"Close enough. I mean it's not like I've seen you since."

"Okay, so there's another good reason to come—so you can see me."

"Oh, yeah, that's a real incentive. Besides, I don't even know these people. They're your friends—not mine. Remember? Not to even mention the fact that I'd be there by myself. So basically, I'm thinking no."

"But if you come, you'll get to know them, and then they can be your friends, and we can all be friends together."

"Well, as Brady Bunch as that sounds, I think you're going to have to do this one without me. Besides, you'll have little Miss Perfect there to keep you company anyway. I'm sure you won't even miss me."

"You know, Mel, Eve really is a nice person, and I'd really like it if you could at least try to be civil to her."

"I am civil... from way over here."

A.J. sighed. "Okay, look, it's highly possible that I'm going to want you in my wedding..."

"I thought you weren't engaged."

"But for that to happen, I think it would be nice if you at least knew the person I'd be marrying."

Melody went quiet for the first time since "Hello," and A.J. scratched his head waiting for her answer and trying to think of another argument if she said, "No."

"Can I bring a date?" she finally asked, and he stumbled on the question.

"A... date? Well, sure. I guess. If you want to."

"Then I'll be there."

"Wow, Eve, nice suit," Ashley said when Eve and A.J. walked up the steps to the lake house where Gabe, Ashley and Jeff were already lounging.

"Thanks," Eve said, looking down at the all-black mallet that hadn't seen water in two years.

"And what about my ensemble?" A.J. asked, turning to model the oversized knee-length shorts that were six clashing hues of turquoise, blue, green, and orange, topped off with a blindingly white shirt.

"It looks like a garage sale reject," Gabe said.

"Saved me 25 bucks going to that garage sale," A.J. said.

"What'd they cost? Like a dollar?"

"50 cents," A.J. said proudly.

"You paid too much," Jeff said, shaking his head.

"Hey, Aj, is Melody coming?" Ashley asked.

He shrugged. "She said she was."

"And she's bringing a date," Eve said with a lift of her eyebrows.

"Go, Melody," Gabe said.

"So, are we eating first or skiing first?" Jeff asked.

"I vote skiing," A.J. said, and they all looked at him incredulously. "What?"

"Okay, Eve," Ashley said as she narrowed her gaze at him. "Who is this, and what did you do with A.J.?"

Eve just laughed as she huddled into the circle of his arm. He was A.J.—her A.J., the man she had prayed for only in her deepest dreams.

"Ugh, don't mind them," Gabe said with a roll of his eyes. "They're in love."

"Who's in love?" Lisa asked as she walked out of the house with Alex, resplendent in his tiny backward cap.

"Oh, look at you," Eve squealed as she peeled Alex from his mother's arms. "If you aren't the cutest..."

"See, A.J.," Gabe said. "Look how fast you got replaced."

Eve looked back at A.J. and smiled. "You're cute, too." And he bent and kissed her.

"Bleck," Gabe said, standing. "Let's get this boat in the water before I get sick."

"Hey, wait for us! We're here!" someone called from the side of the house, and in the next second Blaine pulled Melody through the bushes, bounced onto the deck, and pulled her up with him. Instantly the whole party went silent.

Gabe was the first to recover. "Blaine, Melody, you guys made it. Cool."

"Let the festivities begin!" Blaine said joyfully.

"I didn't know she was bringing him," Eve whispered to A.J. when the others were getting into the boat.

"Do I look like I knew?" he asked, and she could tell he was as thrilled as she was about the turn of events. Then he sighed and

290

looked at her. "Don't let them ruin this. Okay? I mean you are water skiing today, right?"

She wrinkled her face. "I was hoping you didn't remember that part."

"Here." He held her hand as she stepped in.

"You going to get that?" Gabe asked as he started the boat.

"Got it," A.J. answered even as Eve took the one seat left— right next to Melody in the back. She tried to smile at her seatmate but received only ice in return. What she wouldn't have given at that moment for a bigger boat.

Quickly A.J. untied first one rope, then the next, then the final as Gabe began idling the boat backward into the water. She watched A.J. take hold of the side of the boat even as she tried to figure out how he was planning on getting in. Down the dock, he pushed the boat, and she couldn't help but think she was glad he'd left the white shirt on the dock. That tan, that chest, those muscles. It was all she could do to keep her mind on the fact that it wasn't just the two of them out here together. Lucky for him, she thought, and then buried that thought and its subsequent smile in her shoulder.

At the end of the dock in one fluid motion, A.J. pushed the boat one final time, made a leap into the boat, and landed right in front of her. "Hey, there," he said with a wink when his hands caught the sides of her seat to stop himself.

"Hey," she said, gazing into his soft golden eyes. In a blink he leaned down and kissed her, and once again she wished they were alone.

"Hey, Knight," Gabe called from the front. "Get in your seat or you're going to have to climb up there going 60."

With one more wink, he left her and stepped past the captain's chairs that held Jeff and Gabe up front. The further he went from her, the less she liked this seating arrangement until all the way at the front of the boat, he finally sat on the perch and turned back so he could watch them rather than where they were going.

"Ready?" Gabe asked, revving the engine.

"You know it," A.J. said, and his smile slid across her heart like the rays of warm sunshine streaming down on them.

The lake house had disappeared long before. Out in the lake Gabe slowed to an idle and shut the boat off. "Okay," he said, "who's first?"

For one split second no one volunteered.

"I guess that would be me," Jeff said with a sigh.

"You need help?" A.J. asked.

"No, I've got it."

"Suit yourself." A.J. grabbed the orange flag Gabe handed him. He put it in the air and watched Jeff jump into the water. In quick succession Gabe hooked the ski rope up and swung it like a lasso over his head.

"You ready?" Gabe called to Jeff who waved. The rope sailed out to Jeff who grabbed it. Quickly Gabe pulled the skis out of the back seat and slid them to Jeff. A small fight ensued in the water as Jeff tried to simultaneously keep track of the rope, both skis and his feet.

"You sure you don't need help?" A.J. called, fighting not to laugh.

"Hey, no heckling from the balcony," Jeff yelled back as he finally got all three pieces of equipment in place.

"Just asking," A.J. said with a shrug. Gabe came back to the front and started the motor as Jeff struggled to get into position.

"Get the rope on the other side of your ski," A.J. called, realizing it was twisted.

Jeff wrestled with it and then held up a thumb.

"You ready?" Gabe yelled, looking back over his shoulder.

One more moment, and Jeff went still. "Hit it!"

Like a bronco they were off. A.J. watched his friend as his body went taut with the force. Then slowly he pulled himself up. In seconds he was sliding to one side and then the other across the water. It looked like freedom itself, and A.J. couldn't wait to get out there. When his gaze fell to Eve, she looked at him in barely disguised panic, and he smiled and winked. She was going to love this as much as he did. She just didn't know it yet.

"Who's next?" Gabe asked when Jeff gave up, and Eve's stomach knotted. Gabe looked around at the three on the back seat. "Eve?"

Her chest hurt so badly she couldn't get the no to come out. It was then that she saw A.J. slide from his perch back down into the boat.

"Come on," he said, pulling her to her feet. "I'll help."

Although it should have, that assurance didn't make her feel much better. Nonetheless, she stood and slipped out of her shorts. They stepped to the side of the boat.

"Don't try to be grace here," A.J. said. "Just jump in."

Berating herself for getting this close to the reality of doing this in the first place, Eve dropped her legs over the edge, covered her nose, and then fell into the water. By the time she came up, A.J. was paddling beside her. "I'd give that a ten."

"Shut up." She shook her head, but the smile crossed her face despite wanting to slug him. Together they swam out to where Jeff was.

"Nice moves," A.J. said to Jeff as they transferred a ski.

"I was just happy to stay standing," Jeff said. He handed the other ski to A.J. and looked at Eve. The peace in his eyes transferred into her spirit. "Good luck out there."

"Thanks," she said softly. With that, he swam away.

"Okay," A.J. said, swinging into instructor mode. "Skis first." He wound the skis around so they were pointing toward the boat. "You're going to have to pull one of your feet up here."

Fighting not to float away from him, Eve pulled one foot up, and together they got the first ski on. It flopped out awkwardly to one side as the water lapped up in her face.

"Next one."

She repeated the process, wondering why she had ever so much as mentioned doing this. However, before she had a chance to tell him that, he turned back to the boat.

"We need the rope!"

Gabe started the boat, and slowly it circled them until A.J. reached out like stabbing a fish and grabbed the line. When he turned back to her, Eve's I-don't-want-to-do-this-anymore mechanism kicked into gear.

"I think this was a bad idea," she said, shaking her head.

He smiled. "Mount Everest, here we come." He handed her the rope. "Okay, you have to sit in the water. Pull your skis up in front of you."

"They are in front of me."

"No, up. Out of the water like this." He set his hand at an incline to the water.

She tried to do what he was telling her. "They're heavy," she said, thinking that her feet looked like a giant T in the water ahead of her. Fighting the water splashing up and over her face, not to mention the pull of the skis, she yanked one up and almost got it in place just as it fell the opposite direction and splashed back into the water. Frustration took over. "Ahh."

"It's not easy," A.J. said, "but you can do it. You just have to get both of them up at the same time."

"Oh, yeah. No problem." Pulling until her body felt like it might crack down the middle, she fought the thought that she was going to drown before she got everything into position. The water seemed to be coming from all directions at once. "This isn't working."

"You've almost got it. Think pointing your feet to the sky."

Finally with one massive effort, she managed to get both skis in the air. The water around her pushed her up on its energy and then let her fall, which could've put her to sleep had she been in any other situation.

"And the rope goes between them," A.J. said, tossing it over the top of one ski. He waved to Gabe, and the boat roared to life. Even the rocking of the waves slipped from her mind as fear took over.

"Good," A.J. coached. "Now, when you say, 'Go,' they're going to go, and you've got to hold on tight." Slowly he backed away from her and smiled. "Whenever you're ready."

She exhaled slowly, looked at the boat, and yanked courage to her. "Go!"

The boat ahead jumped forward, and the rope in her hands yanked taut. Her hands, which she had thought were ready jerked forward, releasing the rope, and once again she was in the water— only this time face down. She fought the skis, and the current to get turned back over. Spluttering water, she resurfaced.

"Not bad," A.J. said, swimming up to her. She would've hated to see 'bad.' "Okay, this time when it pulls, use your whole body to hold on—not just your arms, and pull with your leg muscles when it feels like you can stand."

Stand? How about not crash? But Eve just nodded, wishing she could quit but knowing he wouldn't let her do that after only one miserable attempt. The boat circled, and A.J. grabbed the rope. The fight with her skis hadn't gotten any easier, but after two attempts that made her look like an unruly windmill, she got them in place.

"Ready?" A.J. asked, and she nodded. He waved to Gabe and swam away from her.

She forced herself to concentrate as she looked at the boat. "Go!"

The yank of the boat jerked the rope, but she held on with determination. It wasn't called skiing exactly as for a few seconds she didn't even leave the water. Then miraculously the water let go of her.

"Stand! Stand!" A.J. yelled from somewhere far away from her, and she fought to get herself upright. However, at the apex of the stand, her skis decided to split her legs in two, and the rope escaped from her consciousness. Two seconds later, she was once again face down in the water. When she found the surface, she hit the waves with one hand angrily.

"Better," A.J. said as he swam up to her side. He looked like part of the waves just bobbing up and down with them as he retrieved the ski she hadn't realized had come off. Carefully he positioned it next to her. "This time when you get up, don't lean so far forward."

"I think my face is going to have water burns," she said.

He laughed. "I've never seen a water burn. What would you treat something like that with?"

"Well, boyfriend strangulation is the preferred method."

His smile never left. "Oh. Good thing we brought Blaine then."

"Blaine wasn't who I had in mind," she said as her hand worked to get the ski back on.

"Oh? He wasn't?" A.J. asked innocently. "Hmm, then who did you have in mind?"

"I think you know him." The ski slipped onto her foot, and she smirked at him. "He's the guy who's going to kiss me for good luck."

The boat was circling as gently he reached out to her, and his lips met hers. Then he pulled back and gazed at her. "Then I guess I'm the lucky one. Huh?"

Her soul sparkled right through her eyes. "I guess so."

A moment, and then he snapped back to his job, barely grabbing the ski rope before it slid past them. When he swam back to her with it in his grasp, he was all business.

"When you get up, think about leaning backward, not forward. Forward, and you'll crash. Oh, and keep your skis together. Don't let them separate."

She nodded at his instructions as she got herself set back in the water.

"Don't fight it, just let your body do it," he said as he handed her the rope and surveyed her positioning. Everything was set, and he leaned in to her. One quick kiss and he backed away with a wave to Gabe. "Good luck."

When he was gone, Eve sighed the smile away from her heart and refocused on her preparations. The moment that everything felt set, she looked up at the boat. "Hit it!"

The boat slid forward, the rope slid forward, and suddenly she too was going forward. A moment, and another, and her feet came underneath her as she pulled up out of the water.

"Stand! Stand!" A.J. called, and her body slipped into a semi-standing position. "Yeah!"

His instructions ran through her. "Don't lean forward. Keep your skis together. Let your body do the work." Slowly in a wide arc she slid across the waves behind the boat. However, there was too much thinking involved to call it fun or free.

Three-quarters of the way around, she felt one leg losing the battle to keep the skis in line, and with little other thought, she let go of the rope and toppled into the water. When she came up, all she could really feel was tired. She paddled until A.J. made it back to her.

"Yeah!" he said, clapping his hands above his head. "You did it! Good job!"

"I did?" she asked not totally sure this wasn't a dream.

"You did! Good job," he said as the boat came back around. "Ready to go again?"

Slowly she shook her head. "I think I need a break."

"Okay." He waved Gabe closer. "She's getting out!"

Gabe nodded, and A.J. set to work getting her out of the skis.

"You next?" Gabe yelled to A.J.

"Guess so!" he yelled back.

"You need some help?" Eve asked, and just before he said no, he caught sight of her teasing smile.

"Well, a kiss wouldn't hurt," he said, returning the smile.

As the waves bounced her up, her lips found his, and she laughed when she backed away. "Don't hit anything."

He laughed. "I'll try not to."

She turned and swam back to the boat where Jeff bent to help her in. "Looking good," he said as she half-stepped, half-fell into the boat.

"Ugh. That's harder than it looks."

"Tell me about it," he said as she started for her previous seat. "Oh, here, why don't you take this one? It's more comfortable."

Grateful that she wouldn't have to sit in the back with Blaine and Melody, Eve slipped into the captain's chair next to Gabe. "Amazing. I'm still in one piece."

Gabe looked at her and laughed. "Of course, you were in good hands."

The best, she thought as she spun in her seat to watch A.J. get ready for his run.

A.J. watched her swim back to the boat. Half of his attention was on her and making sure she got in all right, and half of it was on getting the skis secured on his own feet. Seeing her ski had done nothing but make him more excited about the prospect of riding the waves himself. Once the skis were on his feet, he waved to Gabe who started the boat and circled it around.

With a lunge, A.J. snagged the rope. He repositioned himself in the water. Then checking each aspect of himself to make sure all systems were go, he got his skis into position. When he was ready, he glanced forward and all he saw was her beautiful face. This would surely be a day to remember. "Hit it!"

Moments later his heart wasn't all that was flying. His skis slipped easily over the glass of water in the wake of the boat. It had been years, and yet it felt like only minutes since he'd done this. With little trouble he pulled the rope in to his stomach and leaned back on the skis as the day slid around him in a perfect arc.

When the boat began its first turn, he took full advantage of it and bounced over the wave until he was right next to the boat. He waved at Eve, and joy was written all over her face when she waved back. Yes, this was perfect—more perfect than he could have asked for. Then as he slid back behind the boat, his gaze snagged on Blaine and Melody. Okay, perfect with them around didn't shine quite as brightly, but he pushed that thought away as he leaped up over the wave on the opposite side of the boat.

He wasn't going to think about them or anything other than the things that he wanted so much to remember about this day. Like Eve, and her kiss, and her hands... When he came back around, mischief caught his heart. Carefully he began working one foot out of his ski. Thankfully there were no ramps to run into around here, but it had been awhile since he'd tried this trick. His foot was nearly out when he picked that ski out of the water and kicked it off.

The effect worked like magic as simultaneously he watched the members of the little expedition jump in surprise. Easily he slipped his foot into the foothold at the back of the other ski and waved to them. Jeff shook his head with reluctant admiration, and even Eve eventually smiled. As he ramped over the next wave and then back over it, forcing the air under his ski, flying wasn't that far away.

He pulled up behind the boat, got his balance and then leaped out of the water, spinning and catching the rope so that he was skiing not forward but backward. It was interesting seeing not where they were going but where they had been. That understanding slid through him as his heart retraced their steps to this point. After another minute, the decision to leave the past in the past traced through him. It was time to look forward, and with that, he made one final leap and found himself looking into the only future he ever wanted to see.

Happiness flooded his soul as her smile found his consciousness. "Make the decision," something in him said, "and the courage will follow." The decision had been made, and he could feel the courage with no question. She was his future, and he was hers. They were together, and that was the only way he ever wanted to face any future he had.

"Are you all going out again later?" Ashley asked as they sat in the various lawn chairs scattered across the deck devouring the hamburgers Ashley and Lisa had made while they were gone.

"I'm not. I'll get more lobsterized than I already am," Melody said, arching her gaze so she could look at her shoulder that had already taken on a bright red hue. "Besides I don't know how much more of that up and down wave stuff I can take."

"Oh, no," Blaine said seriously from the lawn chair he occupied next to her. "Then you're definitely not going out again. We really don't want a repeat of my car after Astroworld."

A.J.'s gaze went to the cocky face hidden behind a dark pair of sunglasses across from him. Why Melody had asked Blaine, A.J. didn't even want to think about. She was too good for that jerk, and it didn't take getting to know him to know that. The designer swim trunks, the expensive sunglasses, the jet-black hair—all choreographed to tell the world, "Look how wonderful I am." Melody didn't need the boat to make her sick, her date should've done a good enough job of that.

However, when Melody glanced at Blaine like he'd just fallen there from heaven, A.J. wanted to do nothing more than dump him and the lawn chair into the shimmering water beyond.

"What're you complaining about?" Melody said with a shrug. "You got your car cleaned. Besides you wouldn't be here today if I hadn't gotten sick that day."

"This is true," Blaine said, bobbing his head with a smirk, and A.J. wished he could knock that head right off those shoulders. Then Blaine looked back at the group, clearly enjoying the attention. "So, Melody's in. Who else is going?"

"I am not!" she said, smacking his shoulder. "Jeez. If the water didn't make me sick, all that hot dogging out there sure did." She pinned A.J. with a skewering gaze before he had a chance to disengage his gaze from them.

"What hot dogging?" he asked innocently. With a rip he focused on the true reason he was here. "I was just trying to keep up with Eve."

The grape soda Eve was drinking spewed from her mouth, and she quickly wiped it away. "Oh, yeah. I'm so sure you were worried about keeping up with me."

"I was. You're such a natural."

"You skied?" Lisa asked her.

"I tried," Eve said in annoyance. "But I don't think I'd exactly call it skiing."

"Oh, this I've got to see," Lisa said. "Count me in."

Ashley laid her hand on Gabe's thigh. "So, did you get to go out?"

Gabe pointed to himself. "Driver."

"I can drive if you want," A.J. said with a shrug. "That way you could catch some waves."

"Oh, boy, that sounds scary," Gabe said.

"I promise I won't run you into anything."

"Yeah, but the question is will you run the *boat* into anything?"

A.J. shook his head. "If the hospital trusts me with the ambulance, I think you can trust me with one little boat."

Gabe didn't say anything for a moment, and then he looked at his wife. "Ash?" She looked at A.J. and smiled. "Have fun."

"You need help?" A.J. asked as Eve prepared to take over the skier's position from Jeff.

Her eyebrows arched. "A kiss wouldn't hurt."

"No problem there," he said, pulling her, life jacket and all, to him. There was something about holding her while the boat pitched and settled. It felt like rocking on life itself, and the last thing he wanted to do was let her go.

"Hey, you two! Cut it out! I'm drowning out here!" Jeff yelled.

A.J. laughed as he pulled back from her and winked. "Good luck."

"Try to keep up."

Jeff stayed to help Eve as she got her equipment on. In the boat Lisa put her hands over her head and clapped. "Go, Eve!"

Go, Eve, she thought with a shiver of pressure. This would be quite a spectacle.

"Got it?" Jeff asked, putting a hand on her back to steady her in the waves.

"Think so," she said, nodding. When he didn't move, she looked at him.

"I think so, too," he said softly. "Have fun."

She wanted to say, I will, but he was gone before she got those words out. Once he was in the boat and had taken his place beside Lisa, she smiled at the symmetry of life. Yeah, she had it, and this time she was going to appreciate it. "Hit it!"

When Gabe took over for Eve on the waves later, A.J. did his best to steer the boat sanely even though he was constantly looking back at his friend's antics. Gabe was anything but smooth;

however, A.J. wondered as he watched the seemingly out-of-control performance how much of it was just that—a performance. As inept as Gabe looked out on the water, no one could be that bad and stay in control.

He laughed with his friends when Gabe nearly lost the rope in the middle of an attempted hand change. When Gabe ran his free hand across his forehead in relief, A.J. looked at Eve and shook his head. "What a ham."

"How did you ever guess?" she asked, and with a smile, he laid one hand over hers as they skimmed across the lake, pulling Lou Costello's younger model behind them.

Although Eve could tell he was trying, Blaine couldn't come close to A.J.'s sheer natural ability. In a way she felt sorry for Blaine, and she felt somewhat responsible for that. He really was a nice guy. He'd just gotten thrown into a bad situation. She waved back at him as he crossed to the side of the boat.

"Don't encourage him," A.J. said in her ear.

She looked back at him. "Blaine's okay if you give him a chance."

But A.J. looked less than convinced, so she arched her neck up to be able to catch his lips. "Besides, don't let him ruin this." As his arms wrapped around her, Eve knew she would never remember Blaine's presence this day, only A.J.'s. He was all she ever wanted to remember again.

The boat rocked in the shallow waves long after they had come back out to it. The stars dotted the sky above them. Blaine and Melody had gone home shortly after they had re-docked—something about Blaine having a headache. Having one or being one? A.J. had wondered, but as the evening wore on without them, even they had slid from his consciousness. He didn't want to think about them or about anything else. He was here with Eve, and his one and only goal was to make the rest of the evening one she would never forget.

As they sat in the back of the boat, his arm steadied her, and she snuggled closer to him.

"Oh, wow, a blue one," Eve breathed, watching the sky beyond as it was lit with multi-colored sparkles of crackling fire.

An explosion blasted above them, and the sky lit into ivory. "Oh, wow. Beautiful."

A.J. couldn't disagree. She was. Inside and out. "Have you ever seen them like this?"

"Never," she said, and his heart tripped over the peacefulness in her voice. Her body relaxed as her fingers curled around his. The fireworks continued above them as she watched. "I had fun today."

He hugged her tighter. "So did I."

"Yeah." She smiled up at him. "I could tell."

"I love water skiing."

Serenity dropped through her eyes when she gazed up at him. "I love you."

Gently he leaned to the side and planted a kiss on her head. "Yeah, seems like I remember that part."

"And don't you ever forget it," she said, arching her face so that she could connect with his lips.

"You never know," he said when they parted. "I just might forget. You'd better remind me again."

She laughed. "We wouldn't want that."

The feel of holding her as the waves lapped up, rocking the boat gently beneath them, lulled him away from reality. Seriousness seeped through him when she pulled away. "You shouldn't do this to me."

"What?" she asked.

"This," he said as the fireworks finale punctuated the rhythm of the rocking of his love when he pulled her back to him.

Jeff and Lisa had taken Alex home. Not long after, Gabe and Ashley had called it a night, but before they left, they had told them they could have the deck to themselves for as long as they wanted it. Snuggling with A.J. on the same lawn chair, Eve thought that they had no idea how long that could actually be.

The white shirt had found its way back onto his body, but that was even all right because he hadn't bothered to button it so instead of hiding anything, it did an extraordinary job of teasing her just to the point of insanity. Softly she ran a hand under it and across the smooth skin of his chest. If anything could feel more perfect, she didn't know how.

"Hmm," he moaned quietly. "You feel so good."

She closed her eyes and huddled closer to him, swinging one sheer-covered leg over his. "Not half as good as you feel."

For a moment they simply sat like that, holding each other and letting forever take care of itself. His hands sliding up and down her bare arms sent shivers of excitement across the same paths that they had just put to sleep. Peace had never felt so incredibly exhilarating. Then his hands slowed to a near halt. A moment, and then two.

"Dance with me," he breathed, and she looked up at him in confusion.

"Dance? But there isn't any music."

His eyes smiled. "Sure there is." Carefully he slid from under her and stood. His hand came down for hers, and when she stood, happiness flooded through her. The sheer black two-piece swimsuit cover-up gracing her body from shoulders to ankles blew gently in the breeze coming from the lake, and she brushed the tendrils of hair out of her face.

Slowly he led her out to the edge of the dock—where the small light on the lake house had ceded its hold on the darkness lit only by the shimmering lights surrounding the water. And then there was only the two of them and the gently rocking waves below. He moved to her and slid his hands around her waist as she wrapped her wrists at his neck.

"What no jitterbug?" she asked with a grin.

"Maybe later," he said, and the seriousness of his soft face pulled her heart to him.

Her temple found his shoulder as her arms wrapped down his back. The world itself floated away as their bodies moved in time to the soft lap of the waves. Water skiing would never eclipse dancing with him on these waves, she thought, releasing everything in life other than him. A.J. Knight, the man of her dreams, her own personal white knight. She would cling to him with her very last breath if need be, and even then he would be with her forever.

"You know, I've heard about people being in love ever since I was a little kid," he said softly even as the pressure of his hand continued to move her side to side. "And I wanted to believe it— to believe in it, but love was never anything but an illusion to me until I met you."

She was listening, and not just with her ears. His body was

telling her as much as his words were.

"I know in this life there are no guarantees," he said, "but I think you should know I've decided to make an exception to that rule."

"Oh, yeah? What's that?" she asked with the softest hint of a laugh.

"This," he said, and his movement stopped. When she pulled back from him, the tiny heart stone shone at her from its perch between his finger and thumb, and all teasing in her vanished.

"Oh, A.J., it's beautiful." She looked into his eyes trying to surmise if it meant what she hoped it did.

He smiled slightly as his gaze dropped. Carefully he took her hand. "I, A.J. Knight, guarantee from this moment on that I'll be there for every single right now God grants me with you on this earth." He slid the ring onto her shaking finger as her tears blurred even his face. "I guarantee that I'll protect you, and that I'll love you every single moment of every single day." He gazed into her eyes with no hesitation whatsoever. "And I guarantee that I'll be honest with you and faithful to you until God Himself calls me home."

Nowhere in her body, heart, or soul was there even a shred of doubt of those words. So much so, that it seemed only right that she make her own pledge—although she hadn't even thought about what she would say until that very moment.

"When you came into my life, I thought that I'd lost love forever, that I would never have it in my life again. What I didn't know is that not only would I find it with you, but that with you, I'd find life again, too. When I wanted to quit, you wouldn't let me, and when I wanted to cry, you let me, and then you showed me how to laugh again. I don't know how I got so lucky or why God decided to bless me with you, but I'll tell you right now, I'm sure glad He did."

His eyes were shining when her words wound to a stop.

"So does that mean the answer's yes?" he asked.

"Well, I guess that depends on what the question is, doesn't it?"

"The question," he said slowly as he bent to one knee, "is: Eve, I love you. Will you marry me?"

She gazed into his eyes, and suddenly her happiness turned to mischief as she looked down at the sparkling heart now on her hand. "Yes or no. Yes or no," she said, turning her hand back and forth. Then she stopped, looked him in the eye, and nodded solemnly. "Yes, A.J. Yes. Of course, I'll marry you."

For one instant he knelt there. Then slowly he stood. His arms slipped around her, and when he pulled her close, she closed her eyes clutching that moment into her soul as together they danced on the water perfectly in time with the rhythm of God's plan.

Epilogue

"You know, a party's just not a party without you," A.J. said, sliding up behind Eve as she stood on Jeff and Lisa's back porch listening to the New Years revelers celebrate inside. He looked down at the drink in her hand that she hadn't so much as sipped. "See, I told you we should've brought something decent."

She looked down at the drink and then turned slightly to look at him. "Have you ever been so happy that you're afraid it can't last?"

"What kind of a question is that?" he asked, lowering his eyebrows with concern.

"It's just… Lisa just told me they're expecting again."

"Again?" A.J. backed up in astonishment. "Wow. They don't waste any time, do they?"

"And Gabe and Ashley seem so happy, and you and I are great."

"Thank you so much," he said smugly.

She reached up and hit him softly. "No, it's just that… I look around and wonder how much longer it can all last. I mean how long before everything changes again?"

The laughter fell from his face as he wrapped his arms around her. "You know change isn't always bad. If it was, I wouldn't have stood up there and took those vows." But she didn't laugh at his joke. Gently he turned her around and took her in his arms. "You know, sometimes when life turns a page, it can actually be for the better."

Liking the warmth of him, she snuggled closer. "Like you and me?"

"Yeah, like you and me." He held her there for a moment. "Think about it: to get to this page, we had to read all the other ones, but that doesn't mean the next one won't be just as good... or better." His lips brushed across her hair. "Just think, what if you'd have been afraid of getting here last year?"

"I was," she said softly.

"And look how great it turned out," he said. "Man, I wouldn't have missed this for the world."

The thoughts ran through her, and then she looked up at him. "It might be better?"

He smiled. "You never know." With that he pulled her to him, and her soul wrapped around that idea. After another beat, he kissed the top of her head. "Now, what do you say we go back in there, throw some confetti in the air, and then go home?"

"Home? But it's early," she said with some doubt about his sanity. "You never leave a party early."

"Well, maybe we can go make our own little party and give Lisa and Jeff a run for their money."

She laughed softly at that. "They're already one ahead of us."

"Well, then we'd better get cracking, woman."

She shook her head and laughed again. "If I didn't know better, I'd think you were trying to seduce me."

He kissed her gently as she swayed in his arms. "If I didn't know better, I'd think I already had."

"You've got a point there." Despite the smile, she kissed him back.

Nodding and smiling for all the stars to see A.J. lowered his lips to hers. "Just trying to keep up."

"Is that a challenge?" she asked, looking into the soul of the man she wanted by her side now and always as he backed up enough to gaze at her.

"It's whatever you want it to be."

"Okay, then let's go throw some confetti already." She grabbed her drink from the railing and tossed it out onto the lawn. Then arm-in-arm they stepped back into the light of the house as fate lifted and then turned the page.

For Real

Two months, eight days, nineteen hours, and a handful of minutes—that's how long it had been since Melody Todd's heart had forever given up hope of being anyone's someone. It wasn't that she wanted to give up hope, but she hadn't exactly had a choice. When Miss Perfection walks in the door, how could anyone else have any kind of chance?

Annoyed with life in general, she flipped her long, course blonde hair over her shoulder as she bent next to the rack of shoelaces that had been dismantled piece-by-piece throughout the day. With an audible sigh, she picked up three plastic holders and replaced them on the rack. Midnight Madness sales were bad enough, but holding one on Leap Year Day somehow seemed unconscionable. True if she was at home, she would only be studying, but even that seemed like a step up from Galaxy Shoes on a sale day.

The test in biology she had yet to study for crossed her mind as the last set of shoelaces found its home. As she stepped away from the rack, her gaze chanced across her watch. Once again she sighed. Eight o'clock already and not only had she not studied like she'd promised herself she would, she hadn't even eaten since before noon. Why she agreed to work these ridiculous hours she couldn't quite remember at the moment. It had something to do with making enough to afford tuition because the scholarship she'd needed hadn't come through. Yeah, it was something like that, she thought as she straightened the rack of backpacks.

"Melody," Nathan, the night manager, said in the whiny voice that raked across her brain like a jagged fingernail.

"What?" she asked, drawing the syllable out into two.

"Look, I admire your forward thinking in getting this picked up, but not at the expense of letting a customer walk out the door." He pointed across three rows of shelves to an expanse of light green stretched across two nicely rounded shoulders. "Unless you want *me* to make this commission."

Melody shot him a shut-up look and turned to stride down the aisle. "I've got it." With purposeful steps she rounded her way into the aisle where the customer was even as she made sure that Farin was safely up front ringing up another customer. Yes, she had this one all to herself. Now if only she could make the sale. "May I help you?"

It wasn't until he turned around that she realized he wasn't examining his own shoes but those of the small boy at his feet. "We're fine," the man said quickly. "We're just looking."

"Oh," Melody said, wishing she was better at high-pressured sales tactics. "I was just..." At that moment her brain caught up with her gaze and throttled her to a head-jerking stop. "Blaine?"

With a start the young man, dressed in smart charcoal pants and a light green dress shirt set off with a green and blue necktie, stopped his assessment of the little boy's shoes and turned to her. "Melody?"

High-pressured sales tactics flew right out of her head. "Hey," she said brightly, and without thinking, she reached over to give him a hug. "It's been awhile."

"Yeah, it has." He accepted the sideways hug with a smile. "What've you been up to?"

"Oh, you know, selling shoes—or trying to." She shrugged and smiled at him as her thoughts turned to her own disheveled appearance. Coolly her hand went up and flipped a shock of hair back over her shoulder.

He glanced down to assess the child's progress. "I didn't know you worked here."

"About three years now." Her brain snapped back into sales mode. "So if there's anything I can help you with..."

With a slightly embarrassed gaze, he glanced down again at the child standing at his feet. "We were just looking for a good deal on some school shoes."

"School shoes," Melody said with a nod and a smile to the small brown-toned face staring up at her. She carefully bent down to the little boy. "You got anything special in mind?"

The boy cowered into Blaine's pant leg.

"We were thinking about these," Blaine said as he picked up the box, "but they're a little steep."

Melody glanced at the box in his hand, trying not to notice the chocolate brown of his eyes. "Hmm. Yeah, those are good—all leather uppers, but if you just want some good, basic tennis shoes, we've got these over here." She stood, looked over the selection to her right, reached out for one, and stopped. "What size does he wear?"

"Umm, well, he was in a four last we checked, but…"

"So we need to figure out a size, then we'll worry about a style." With the precision of a hundred thousand times of practice, she whipped the size plate off the top of the shelves. "Here we go." She bent back down and then decided even that was too uncomfortable so she twisted her feet under her and sat down. "Can you put your foot right here?"

The little boy stared at her skeptically. Putting a strong hand on his shoulder, Blaine led him around his leg. "Come on, Dylan. It's okay." With just more than a little coaxing, Blaine got the boy's foot onto the apparatus.

Quickly Melody measured the small foot. "I think a four-and-a-half would work." She turned back for the shoe shelves. Two swipes and she had three boxes in her hands. "Let's start with these." As she bent to the floor, she swung her hair over her shoulder. "So, Dylan, how's school?"

"Fine," the little voice answered as Blaine helped him slide up on the bench seat.

"What grade are you in—first?"

"Second," he answered softly.

In no time Melody had the shoe laced. Her hands worked to put a shoe on the little foot even as her mind worked through a million questions that had nothing to do with school. One date and one… well, she had never been real sure what that was, but it was definitely something you wouldn't have gone on if you had a wife and child at home. Furtively she checked Blaine's ring finger, left hand. No ring, but then that didn't always mean anything. "Second grade. Are you getting really smart in second grade?"

"I know how to spell knuckle," the little boy offered.

"Oh, yeah? How?" she challenged.

"K-N-U-C-K-L-E," he said slowly as she worked a shoe onto his other foot.

"Wow. That's really good. I couldn't spell that until at least third grade." She caught the smile he beamed up at Blaine and didn't miss the sweet, kind, brown eyes that beamed one right back. Carefully she leaned back. "These are four-and-a-halves, but they might not have enough growing room in them. See what you think."

Smoothly Blaine dropped to one knee and felt the toe of the shoe. "How do they feel?"

"Good," the little boy answered with a hesitant nod.

"How about you walk around in them a little?" Melody suggested.

Slowly the little frame slid off the bench and took three uncertain steps away and then came back. Blaine watched him closely as Melody fought to keep her concentration on the little boy and away from the young man observing him. Dylan slid in between Blaine's knees as Blaine put a hand under his arm. "What do you think?"

The two little shoulders reached for the ceiling.

"We could try a half size bigger," Melody said when Blaine's silence dragged on a little too long.

"We probably ought to."

She swung back into professional mode, and in no time Dylan was walking in the larger shoes.

"What do you think?" Blaine asked to no one in particular. Concentrating on his feet, Dylan nodded. When he made it back to them, Melody reached down and tested the toe.

"You'll probably want the bigger ones," she said. "Otherwise you'll have to be in here again in a month when he grows." As soon as she said it, she wished she had given the opposite advice. However, it was too late to take it back because Blaine nodded.

"Then we'll take them," he said decisively but wavered in the next second. "Oh, how much are they?"

"$30, but tonight it's half off," Melody said as she stowed the unwanted shoes back in the other box.

"Can't beat a deal like that," Blaine said. He started to take the shoes off but stopped. "Can he wear them out?"

She shrugged. "Sure." Quickly she replaced the other shoes as well, but she noticed the rag-tag pair of shoes Blaine picked up from the floor. It didn't take much to see how fast he threw them into the new box and closed it. When he glanced at her, she saw the embarrassment scrawl across his face, but she smiled it away. "You need anything else? A backpack? Shoelaces?"

His smile stretched tighter than the grimace had. "Nope, I think this will get it."

Nathan would probably give her a demerit for not getting them to buy something else, but at the moment she didn't care about anything other than the two people walking with her to the checkout. She wanted to say something to fill the silence between them, but she could think of nothing. She was glad to see that Farin was nowhere in sight.

"I saw Eve the other day," Blaine finally said as they reached the front.

Melody's heart collapsed around the name, but she willed her voice not to register that fact. "Oh, yeah?"

"Yeah, she and A.J. are getting a house out in Rolling Hills."

"Oh, really?" Hurt, unseen to that moment, flooded through Melody's chest. "I hadn't heard that. Cool." Fighting to take her mind off of the conversation's track, she busied herself with the register. "That'll be $16.85."

He handed her a twenty and waited for the change. She didn't want to look at him. There were too many things she didn't want him to see. Quickly she exchanged the money, handed it to him, and slid the receipt into the bag. She folded the plastic handles and handed the bag over the counter. "Your receipt's in the bag."

For one solid second after the bag was in his hands, Blaine didn't move. He had such a nice face, conventional and yet striking. "I guess I'll see you later then?"

"Yeah, later," she said with a quick nod as she pushed her hair over her ear.

One more awkward pause and Blaine reached down for Dylan's hand. "Well, 'bye."

She mumbled something—presumably good-bye but for all she could tell it could've been 'how could you do this to me?' Granted, he hadn't really done anything more egregious than innocently end up on the semi-same date with her, but still. Just the thought of his poor car, the stench of vomit and the sound of her moans filling it, threatened to make her sick all over again. That hadn't been her fault of course. The name A.J. streaked through her mind as the memory rewound a bit more, and she threw a box that had fallen on the floor under the counter a little harder than she really had to.

A.J.

A.J. and little Miss Perfection. Heat rose in her at the very thought of them. Now they were buying a house together. Thrilling. She was absolutely thrilled for them. She kicked another box under the counter. Of all the bad dates she had ever been on, and there had been many, that day at AstroWorld had been the very worst. There had been a time when she had kept up with A.J. feat for feat, but apparently that time had passed.

It was Greased Lightnin's 360-loop that ultimately got her, and in that second she had lost every shred of dignity she had managed to muster in the past 25 years. Of course Blaine, or more precisely, Blaine's car had been the unfortunate recipient of the fall-out from that bad decision. And while Blaine was making an emergency trip to get her home, Miss Perfect had made her move on A.J. Things had never been the same since.

Even as the thoughts continued, Melody yanked two boxes up from the floor next to the women's shelves. Her heart dove for the floor at the mere thought of A.J., her best friend in the whole world. Now he was gone, making a life for himself with her. Her. Eve What's Her Name. So, now they had a house. So, what? They were married. Right? A.J. and Miss Perfect Wonderful, Fantastic Eve were married. And now they were living happily ever after just like the storybook said they would.

Swiping her cheek with one hand and slamming another box onto the shelf with the other, Melody tried to stow the lump in her throat as easily. There had been a time in what seemed a different lifetime that she would've been the first one A.J. would've called with news like this. But now... Now she had to hear it from some semi-acquaintance who only knew her because she'd used him to make A.J. jealous. She snorted softly. "Well, that worked."

With a swift kick she corralled two more boxes to the shelves. "It's over, Mel. It's over. Get over it, and move on already. Just get that through your thick skull, and we'll all be better off." Unfortunately her head wasn't the only part of her not getting the message.

Blaine checked the plate glass window once more from the safety of the darkened parking lot. She was busy—working. She wasn't watching him. That was a good thing, he told himself as he hustled Dylan into the beat up, green Toyota. At least that way she wouldn't notice his current mode of transportation. Not that it made any difference to him if she wondered, he reasoned as he yanked twice to get the door opened and then jumped into the driver's side, grabbed his glasses off the dashboard, and prayed that

Lillian would start just one more time. "Just get me out of here, Baby," he pleaded as he pumped the accelerator before cranking the starter. If only she would get him safely into the middle of an intersection before she decided to die for good, at least he could handle that.

Still pumping the gas, he prodded the little car out of the lot as his gaze found the rearview mirror, and he just had to smile with the sigh. Melody. She was still as nice as he remembered. Sweet and unassuming. Fun even—as long as she wasn't throwing up in your best friend's car. A genuine laugh escaped at that thought, and he squeezed his eyes closed at the memory.

It had cost almost a hundred bucks that he didn't have to get that car back to good enough so that Peyton hadn't noticed. Not that Peyton noticed much of anything when it came to stuff he owned—especially cars. Blaine had lost count of the number of cars Peyton had wrecked since their senior year in high school. First it was a Mazda, cute little metallic number that probably set Peyton's dad back more than ten grand or three. Then there was the red Firebird. That one only lasted a month or so. Then only six months before E-Day as Blaine had affectionately begun remembering it, Peyton got the gold Porsche Carrera GT. Cool. It was the coolest car Blaine had ever seen with the leather seats and the computerized everything.

Blaine still remembered pulling up to Eve's apartment in that car. He had felt like a million and one bucks in it. And walking her out to get in that car… Man, it was the greatest moment of his life. What happened next he still wasn't real clear about—except that by the time he left the amusement park, he was coming to the rescue of a very sick Melody who couldn't walk two steps without him holding her up, and Eve was permanently in the arms of someone he'd never even heard of prior to that day.

The ride home was when the little Carrera had been baptized. He shook his head at the memory. Melody had apologized until she could hardly keep her head up. He still remembered her leaning against the bucket seat nearly lying in the trunk for how far back he had laid it. Without a doubt at that moment she was the sickest human being he had ever seen.

How much of that ride she remembered he had no idea. Most of it she spent moaning and barely holding the green in her face from coming up again. Thankfully when he dropped her off, no one had been at her house because explaining her state and why she was coming home with a guy she didn't even know might not have been pleasant. He had spent the next four hours trying to make the car semi-presentable again, and it was well after midnight when he had dropped it off at Peyton's, grabbed Lillian and headed back across town to the little dump he called home.

A rock descended to his chest when he thought about the place he still reluctantly called home. His gaze traveled from the traffic outside the window to the child in the seat next to him. Asleep already. Poor little guy. Blaine checked his watched with a short sigh. 9:34. Dylan should've been in bed an hour ago. He didn't need to be out shopping. He needed to be at home in his bed getting a good night's sleep for school tomorrow.

Blaine shook his head without shaking it and refocused on the road. It couldn't be helped. He didn't get out of class until 8:00, and there was simply no time between work and class. He shoved his cramped schedule away from his consciousness. It was depressing, but only if he thought about it.

Allowing whatever less depressing thought that wanted to take over in, he drifted back to Melody and the panic that had set in the night she had called him a few weeks later. Had it been him who had thrown up in her car, he would never have made that call. No way. No how. They should've given her a courage award for that one. It still surprised him that they had ended up with A.J., Eve and the gang on that date too. No matter how hard he tried, he couldn't quite get all of the pieces of that puzzle to line up in his head.

Eve was as nice as she had always been to him, and the others were pleasant enough although he really didn't know them well enough to know if that's how they always were or if there was something else going on. It was only A.J. who hadn't seemed all that happy about Blaine's presence. Okay, at the amusement park, Blaine could understand the animosity now. Eve had apologized about it the next Monday. But how long could a guy hold a grudge against an innocent bystander? Apparently, with A.J., a long time.

No, it was plenty clear that A.J. Knight had a chip on his shoulder, and Blaine had dealt with enough chips in his time to know you can either knock them off or steer clear. He was sincerely glad that steering clear was the easiest fork in that road. As he turned into the little driveway, he prayed that the light blue flashes of light through the open front window meant his mother had already passed out on the couch.

The blinding light of the refrigerator stung Melody's overtired eyes. Biology was going to kill her. She rummaged past the mayonnaise and milk and grabbed a yogurt from the back. What she really wanted was chips, but she had sworn on Monday that she was going to start sticking to her diet. Never on the slim side, her freshman 15 had turned into the sophomore 40. That fact wasn't lost on her consciousness. However, as she filled her glass with stale-tasting water, sympathy for her situation invaded her body, and she grabbed the chips anyway.

She needed something. Something to make it through this night—if not this whole crummy semester. First there was Biology that she hated. She had thought the principles of marketing class would be fun until she figured out on the third class that all the teacher did was talk about guns and deer. And then there was math. How they had talked her into taking math and biology at the same time, she would never know.

In her room, she threw the bag of chips onto the bed with a crunch, grabbed her book off the desk and replaced it with the yogurt. With a flop she fell onto the bed and reached for a chip. "The five parts of the circulatory system are…"

He was missing something, Blaine thought as he scanned back across the textbook page. His fingers rested on his head, his thumb holding up the edge of his glasses that he only wore for reading and close-up work. Drafting 202. He should've known this stuff forward and backward by now, and yet somehow this point was eluding him. It just couldn't be this hard. Slowly word-by-word he reread the section that he should've already had memorized. Still what it said was exactly what he was doing, and it wasn't working. In frustration he stood from the little kitchen table and strode over to the refrigerator. One hand slid down to keep his tie in place as he opened the door and scanned the contents. He pulled out a Coke and then looked down at his attire and sighed. Nearly three o'clock in the morning and he was still in the same clothes he'd put on at seven the morning before.

Somehow, some way he was going to have to get a little sleep. He couldn't keep up with this schedule much longer. He popped the Coke open and took a sip. But what were his options? Cut down on work? They'd all starve. Not go to school? No, that wasn't an option he would even consider. He had worked too hard to this point. He wasn't going to back out now.

Straddling the chair, he sat back down, sighed, scratched his head, and stared at the book lying open on the table. Only then did his gaze slide from the printed words up to the four-color illustration at the top and then to the one small angle in the corner. With a clank the Coke can hit the table, and he grabbed his pencil. "Oh, please, please, please, let this work," he breathed, knowing if it didn't he might very well show up for work in five hours in those exact same clothes.

For Real
How long can he outrun the secrets?
Coming...
November 2012

About the Author

A stay-at-home mom with a husband, three kids and a writing addiction on the side, Staci Stallings has numerous titles for readers to choose from. Not content to stay in one genre and write it to death, Staci's stories run the gamut from young adult to adult, from motivational and inspirational to full-
out Christian and back again. Every title is a new adventure! That's what keeps Staci writing and you reading. Although she lives in Amarillo, Texas and her main career is her family, Staci touches the lives of people across the globe with her various Internet endeavors including:

Romance Novels:
http://ebookromancestories.com

Books in Print, Kindle, & on Spirit Light Works:
http://stacistallings.wordpress.com/

Spirit Light Books Blog
http://spiritlightbooks.wordpress.com/

And…

Staci's website
http://www.stacistallings.com

Come on over for a visit…

You'll feel better for the experience!

Also Available from Staci Stallings

In Print

The Long Way Home

Eternity

Cowboy

Lucky

Deep in the Heart

To Protect & Serve

Dreams by Starlight

Reunion

Reflections on Life I

Reflections on Life II

Ebook Editions

Cowboy

Lucky

Coming Undone

Deep in the Heart

A Work in Progress

A Little Piece of Heaven

A Light in the Darkness

Princess

Dreams by Starlight

Reunion

To Protect & Serve

Made in the USA
Las Vegas, NV
16 September 2021

30439498R00194